"Hanse!"

That was Mignureal, and Hanse made a reassuring noise. The intruder was not fighting with a ghost, unless he was a hunchback who was not bent; that unsightly hump on the dimly-seen prowler's back had to be a beer-drinking, attack-trained watch-cat.

Hanse dropped both knives. Naked, he hurried to the staggering male figure. It had both hands up over its shoulders, striving to tear off the big red cat trying to eat holes in his back. Hanse stepped on flat, cold steel, and shuddered. He knew what that was. Putting out a hand, he found a face. With balled fist he struck it as hard as he could. A wave of pain hit his hand and whipped up his arm . . .

Don't miss these other exciting tales of Sanctuary: the meanest, seediest, most dangerous town in all the worlds of fantasy. . . .

THIEVES' WORLD
(Stories by Asprin, Abbey, Anderson, Bradley, Brunner, DeWees, Haldeman, and Offutt)

TALES FROM THE VULGAR UNICORN
(Stories by Asprin, Abbey, Drake, Farmer, Morris, Offutt, and van Vogt)

SHADOWS OF SANCTUARY
(Stories by Asprin, Abbey, Cherryh, McIntyre, Morris, Offutt, and Paxson)

STORM SEASON
(Stories by Asprin, Abbey, Cherryh, Morris, Offutt, and Paxson)

THE FACE OF CHAOS
(Stories by Asprin, Abbey, Cherryh, Drake, Morris, and Paxson)

WINGS OF OMEN
(Stories by Asprin, Abbey, Bailey, Cherryh, Duane, Chris and Janet Morris, Offutt, and Paxson)

THE DEAD OF WINTER
(Stories by Asprin, Abbey, Bailey, Cherryh, Duane, Morris, Offutt, and Paxson)

SOUL OF THE CITY
(Stories by Abbey, Cherryh, and Morris)

BLOOD TIES
(Stories by Asprin, Abbey, Bailey, Cherryh, Duane, Chris and Janet Morris, Andrew and Jodie Offutt, and Paxson)

SHADOWSPAWN

ANDREW J. OFFUTT

ACE BOOKS, NEW YORK

This book is an Ace
original edition, and has
never been previously
published.

SHADOWSPAWN

An Ace Book/published by arrangement with
the author

PRINTING HISTORY
Ace edition/September 1987

ISBN: 0-441-76039-2

To
Robert Lynn Asprin and Lynn Abbey
who started it all
and who
keep on keepin' on

GUIDE TO PRONUNCIATION

While this novel contains a lot of names and a few new words, most lend themselves readily to pronunciation. The author is a reader who despises fiction containing obviously unpronounceable words, along with cute little pips and double dots above letters and three or four unlikely vowels strung together.

Still, a few names in *Shadowspawn* could use some amplification:

Hanse
: rhymes with "dance." That simple; it really is not Honss or Honz or Honssa or Honza.

Mignureal
: The *g* is silent, as in chignon, Mignon. Syllables are about equally accented, with a slight stress on first and final: MIN-you-ree-AL. She's sensitive about it.

Mignue
: her nickname: min-you-wee, equally accented.

Firaqa
: rhymes with "purr-AH-kuh," with the accent on the ah.

Anorislas
: an-oh-RISS-liss

Khulna
: COOL-nuh

Sinajhal
: Each syllable is pronounced: SIN-nudge-HAL.

Tejana
: tuh-JOHN-uh

Vaspa
: Rhymes with "Lass puh"

S'danzo
: These people are the creations of Lynn Abbey, but I *think* it's "sh-DON-zoe."

Shadowspawn
: really isn't "shadow's pawn," but "shadow spawn," as in offspring of the shadow(s).

—A.J.O.

1st October 1985

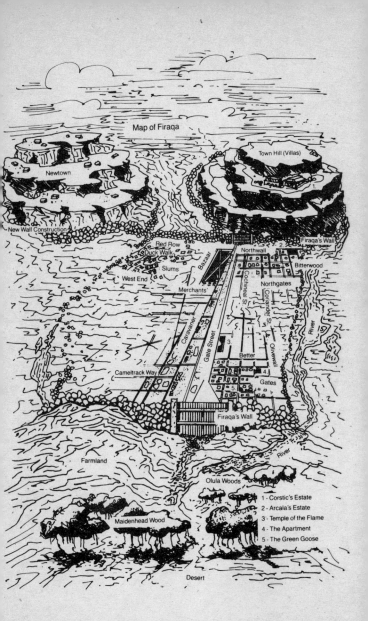

Map of Firaqa

Town Hill (Villas)

Newtown

New Wall Construction

Firaqa's Wall

Red Row
Duck Walk
Bazaar
Northwall
Bitterwood

Slums
West End
Cochineal St.
Northgates

Merchants'
Coriander St.

Caravaner
Gate Street
Better
Olivewall

Cameltrack Way
Gates

Firaqa's Wall

Farmland
River

Olula Woods

1 - Corstic's Estate
2 - Arcala's Estate
3 - Temple of the Flame
4 - The Apartment
5 - The Green Goose

Maidenhead Wood

Desert

STATEMENT OF FURTWAN
COINPINCH, MERCHANT

THE FIRST THING I noticed about him, just that first impression you understand, was that he couldn't be a poor man. Or boy, or youth, or whatever he is. Not with all those weapons on him. From the shagreen belt he was wearing over a scarlet sash—a violently scarlet sash!—swung a curved dagger on his left hip and on the right one of those Ilbarsi "knives" long as your arm. Not a proper sword, no. Not a military man, then. That isn't all, though. Some few of us know that his left buskin is equipped with a sheath; the slim thing and knife-hilt appear to be only a decoration. Gift from a woman, I heard him tell old Thumpfoot one afternoon in the bazaar. I doubt it.

(I've been told he has another sticker strapped less than comfortably to his inner thigh, probably the right. Maybe that's part of the reason he walks the way he does. Cat-supple and yet sort of stiff of leg all at once. A tumbler's gait—or a punk's swagger.

(Don't tell him I said!)

Anyhow, about the weapons and my first impression that he couldn't be poor. There's a throwing knife in that leather and copper armlet on his right upper arm, and another in the long bracer of black leather on that same arm. Both are short. The stickers I mean, not the bracers or the arms either.

All that armament would be enough to scare anybody on a dark night, or even a moonbright one. Imagine being in the

1

Maze or someplace like that and out of the shadows comes this young bravo, swaggering, wearing all that sharp metal! Right at you out of the shadows that spawned him. Enough to chill even one of those Hell Hounds.

That was my impression. Shadowspawn. About as pleasant as gout or dropsy.

THE DESERT

AMONG THE PEOPLE of the desert north of Sanctuary, the sun was called Vaspa. It was also their word for demon. Now Hanse knew why.

He had never ridden on the desert before and hoped never to do so again and as a matter of fact wished he were not doing so now. Today the sun was a demon straight from the Hot Hell. Yesterday it had been a demon from the same place, and presumably the same would be true tomorrow. It was enough to make him think almost wistfully of the Cold Hell; almost enough to make him yearn for a taste of the Cold Hell. Almost.

Besides, they had a taste of the Cold Hell every night. How was it possible that such heat could become worse than chilly so soon after these blood-hued desert sunsets?

The horses and the onager plodded, sweating. Their riders rode loosely, sweating.

The very ground would be sweating, Hanse thought, if it contained a tenth of a thirteenth of a tenth of a droplet of moisture to yield up to blazing, baking, sucking Vaspa. He was reasonably sure that even this perdurable yellowish-buff sand was writhing in pain from the relentless heat. Now and again he was sure he witnessed that writhing, in a sort of wriggly wavering movement just above the ground (if anyone could call this yellowish-tan stuff "ground"). Particularly way over there, where that long snaky razor-backed mountain of sand

5

called a dune stretched like an ugly wall across leagues and
leagues of horizon.

Maybe it's just my eyes, he thought. *We're probably both
going blind, anyhow, from the sun bouncing off this garbage-
heap "landscape" and attacking our eyes. All five of us—not
just Mignue and me, but the horses and that dumb donkey too!*

That dumb donkey, which was an onager and which his
companion Mignureal persisted in calling "Cutie" and which
Hanse called only "Dumb-ass," chose that moment to let go
with its absolutely asinine ear-assaulting Noise. A series of
squeaky, sucked in ee sounds, each followed by an aspirated
aw. The worst and dumbest sounds Hanse had ever heard or
thought about hearing. Dumb onager/ass!

"Shut up, Dumb-ass."

"What's the matter, Cutie, you thirsty?"

Hanse shot Mignureal a dark look. Just then she glanced at
him, all sweet-faced under the muffling hood, and he tried to
make his expression more pleasant; indulgent. He really hardly
knew her, although she loved him and he had decided that he
loved her. He had never realized just how determinedly
pleasant and unremittingly *nice* Mignue was.

I'm getting tired of it, he thought, and then went all nervous
and frowny and thought hurriedly, *No I'm not!*

One of the horses was of that reddish walnut color called
sorrel. The other was black, with the bottommost area of one
leg resembling a short white buskin. A silver-gray stripe
decorated the front of his long face.

"His name?" The man Hanse had bought him from back in
Sanctuary had shrugged. "Blackie," he'd said, and Hanse had
thought *Oh how appropriate. I should have known,* or words to
that effect, and called the animal Blackie.

Oh, how dull and unimaginative, Mignureal thought, and
occupied her mind with working at more interesting names for
the handsome animal. Already she called her mount—a gift
from Tempus, along with their hooded white robes—by the
ancient S'danzo word *inja.* The word meant swift-running
hare, and never mind the redundance. It was a good name,
Mignureal thought, although she had no idea whether Inja
could run swiftly or not. She didn't really want to find out,
either, but would have bet that she would. All sorts of things

just seemed to happen when Hanse called Shadowspawn was about. Some of them were violent and exertive. One of those was the necessity of running.

Though plodding on sweaty horses, they were running right now, in fact. They were running away from Sanctuary, which was—which had been home.

That reminded Mignureal of her parents, her wounded father and murdered mother, and her eyes went all misty again. She kept her gaze fixed straight ahead so that Hanse might not see. Her tears were the twitching twisting of a needle in his belly, she knew. She strove to keep them back. When she couldn't, she tried to conceal them from him; from Her Man.

She knew her man, too, had leaked tears over her mother, Moonflower—and then had gone wild against the killers. That soon led to his feeling the necessity of departing the forlorn town where they had both been born and had lived all their lives. Moonflower had been the nearest thing to a mother he had ever had, although he was not the sort to admit it and had actually pretended to flirt with that mightily overweight woman and mother of several.

Moonflower was—had been—of the S'danzo and gifted with the Sight, the power of Seeing. Only lately had the trait begun to manifest itself in Mignureal. Even then it came on her only with regard to some danger in the immediate future of Hanse, who was forever doing dangerous things and whom Mignureal had seen as a romantic and glamorous man of the world since she was twelve and had started to bud and he was—what? Sixteen? Mignureal didn't know.

She loved him. Despite her mother's warnings and the care the big woman had taken to prevent them from being alone together, Mignureal loved him. Of course Moonflower had known, and known that her daughterr couldn't help it. She had loved him since she was twelve. Thirteen, at least. Now she was sure that he loved her, too. It was strange, having both the agony of grief and the joy of requited love wrestling for space in one's heart. She loved him and he loved her, but they were not lovers.

Not yet, Mignureal thought, feeling joy even while tears of grief slid down her cheeks. The sun stole them in evaporation before they reached her chin, leaving little itchy places on her face.

"Mignue?" It was his name for her, and only his: Min-you-ee.

"Hmm?" She kept her face directed ahead, to hide her tears.

"How old are you?"

"Eighteen."

"Really! I thought you were seventeen. I thought I remembered Moonflower's saying you were seventeen, just a few months ago."

"Well . . . I'll be eighteen in three months. A little less than three months. That's the same as being eighteen," she added, thinking that maybe he was thinking about making love to her tonight.

She didn't know what that was like, didn't know how, and she was nervous about it. She knew that Hanse knew how. She knew he had done it before. That both helped—*he can teach me what I don't know*—and added to her nervousness: *he's an experienced man of the world and what if I'm an incompetent dummy when it comes to—to carding wool?*

At least her mother had never committed the cruelty of trying to frighten her about It. She knew that her parents had liked It a lot, this thing between men and women that was called, among other things, by the euphemism "carding wool." Mignureal assumed that she would like It a lot too, and she was sure that Hanse already did. Besides, she wanted to. With Hanse.

"How old are you, Hanse?"

"What?" he said, to buy a little time. He didn't like admitting what he had to admit in response to such a question, because it told too much about him.

She said, "How old are you?"

Staring ahead at nothing in particular because that was what there was to stare at, she squeezed her eyes shut, real hard, to force out what she thought were the last of her tears. For now.

"I don't know."

"Oh Hanse," she said, for she knew he was from the wrong part of town, that area called Downwind, and that he had hardly known his mother, who had apparently been only casually acquainted with his father. "You have to have some idea. Are you older than twenty?"

"About that," he said, fidgeting in sudden discomfort. "Maybe a little older. Damn. The only thing worse than riding a horse is when you have to get down and try to walk!"

Hanse's age was a subject on which Mignureal had long been as silent as the *g* in her name. Now, for some reason, she could not avoid persisting. After all, they had cloven to one another. Here they were alone, riding north alone, just the two of them. She and her man. She wanted to know everything about him. Wasn't that right? Wasn't that the way it should be?

She said, "Maybe a little younger?"

"Maybe. A little. I've counted off seventeen years, see. I can account for those, but I don't know how old I was when I stole the fig."

Abruptly he twisted around in his saddle, a sort of cradle of leather over wood, high of front and back—pommel and cantle. When he put his hand up to his brow as if to shade those nearly black eyes of his to see better in the glare of sun off sand, Mignureal sighed. He was just avoiding her question, she was sure—but naturally she had to look back. She didn't see anything. She glanced nervously over at Hanse.

"Hanse?"

He shrugged. "Thought I saw something a little while ago. Thought I'd just not say anything but suddenly wheel around this way to take it by surprise, if there was something."

"You mean—people? Those desert raiders Tempus's drover told us about?"

He shook his head. "No, not that. Something small. Just a little dark blob, moving. I mean I thought I saw that, before. Like a little animal, you know. As if it was maybe following us. I don't see anything now, though. Really."

A shiver went through her and Mignureal squinted, lifting her own hand to shade her eyes. She too stared back along their wake.

She saw sand, and sand. Nothing else. No animal, small or otherwise. No vegetation, not even any of the junky-looking desert version of grass or imitation "grass" they had noticed from time to time. Even the onager was only mildly interested in that stuff. She saw not even big stones or rocky outcrops;

those were just smooth mounds, almost eerie lumps of varying size under the yellow-tan sand, which was ripply all around them, like the train of a dull gown. Beyond, the sky was the same old molten copper shot through with silver and traces of orange. It should have been pretty. It wasn't. It just looked hot. A faraway speck of blue "real" sky made her sigh. She glanced at Hanse again.

"Do you see anything now?"

"No, nothing," he said, swinging back around and adjusting the forefront of his robe's hood. It was folded back on top, like hers, but could be lowered so as to cover the face completely. It was called a sand-hood, they'd been told, and in case of a sandstorm the best thing to do was just stop dead still and keep that hood all the way down. None of that had made them happy, although they were grateful for the gifts of the robes in addition to the horse, Inja. Sandstorm? A storm—of *sand*? Hanse and Mignureal devoutly hoped that was something of which they could remain pleasantly ignorant.

"Probably didn't see anything before, either," Hanse said, rubbing his thigh and making a *chk-chk* noise to his horse. "I'm sorry I had to let you know about it. We just saw a long way back. Obviously there's nothing. Just . . . sand." His voice turned sour on the last word.

"Don't be sorry, Hanse. Don't try to be heroic or something and keep things from me, 'for my own good' or some such. All right? I'm not that kind of woman. If something's bothering you, you just let me know too, all right? I don't have to be protected from knowing things."

He nodded without saying anything. She couldn't help another apprehensive backward glance. Nothing. "First you saw something and now we can see a long way back, and there's nothing. I don't like that!"

Hanse didn't like it either but would not tell her so: "I said I *thought* I saw something. We were told that the sun and the desert can play tricks on your eyes, remember?"

"Yes. I've also been told that some things can be visible and then invisible and then—"

"Stop!" He threw up his head. "Ah god, O Father Ils! Not that; not sorcery. Gods, how I hate sorcery!"

They rode in silence for a few minutes, with Mignureal

trying to think of something altogether different to talk about. Oh, of course; she remembered where they'd been, in their conversation.

She said, "Did you say 'when you stole a pig'?"

He jerked his head to stare at her with those dark, dark eyes. "*What?* Why would I accuse you of stealing a pig?" He cocked his head. "Still, it might taste good; did you?"

"No no, not me. You. I mean, uh, back there. Before we stopped. You know, when we were talking. You said you could account for seventeen years, but then . . . something about stealing a pig?"

"Oh!" A smile flashed over his dark face, brief as a glimpse of sun on a cloudy day in winter. "No—fig. Fffig," he emphasized, and then looked away from her, and his voice went low and sort of dreamy again, with memory. "He made me drop it, too."

Sure that her eyes and face were clear of tears, she looked over at him. "Who made you—I don't understand. What's that have to do with how old you are?"

He gave her a look, but when he saw her face turned his way that expression of exasperation became a little smile, almost apologetic. Definitely not like Hanse called Shadowspawn.

"It's my first memory, see. I was five or three or four or whatever I was, and I've spent a lot of time thinking, tallying up the years since then. There've been seventeen. I was young. Real young, I mean; just a boy, just a child. And I was hungry. I'd been hungry for quite a while. It seemed forever. . . . What's forever, to a child? My stomach wasn't a hole in me; it was a knot, so tight it was sore. I was in the market, and everyone looked about eleven feet tall."

Hanse gestured loosely, as if in pain at remembering. "Just me down there, with the stalls and the counters and all the people towering over me, and all of them moving a lot. What seemed to me millions of legs, a whole forest of legs. Just legs, not eyes to see me. No one seemed to see me. And when they did, they didn't pay any attention. Just some homely little ragtag brat wandering around. Probably thought I was looking for my mother. Hmp! I was looking for anyone! Anyone who'd give me something to eat. A word or two and maybe a touch would have been nice," he said, his voice changing, softening and growing wistful and boyish, and he looked away from her.

Mignureal bit her lip until it hurt.

"Anyhow, I got used to no one's even noticing me, so I got close to this one stall and spent a long time easing my hand up there. All quivery and holding my breath. And I touched a fig, and snatched it. It looked huge, and good, and it felt huge in my hand and pulpy and—real good. But then I had to run from the monster."

Swallowing hard, blinking hard, she got out, "The . . . monster . . ."

"Oh, it was a man, of course. I know that now. Not then! Then he was a monster, about nineteen feet tall, and he was chasing me and I thought he'd eat me because I had taken a fig to eat, off his counter. Except that I think it wasn't even his stall or his counter."

Mignureal swallowed hard and felt her eyes blur again.

He was staring ahead at nothing, but this was different: she felt that even had there been something up there to stare at, Hanse wouldn't have seen it. Not right now.

"I remember it all exactly. Want to know what he was wearing?"

"Hanse. . . ." He voice was tiny. She heard its tremor, but apparently Hanse did not. Hanse wasn't even here anymore, not here and now.

"He had a big black beard under a big reddish nose and huge feet in sort of yellow sandals—it was late spring or early summer, I'm sure, because I didn't have much on but I wasn't cold and besides there were fruits in the market. He had big hairy calfy legs coming down out of a tunic the color of cooked squash. And his hands were the size of hams. Huge hairy ham-sized hands, after me, reaching for me with fingers like cucumbers. I ran, and I banged into people's legs and bounced off and just ran on in whatever direction that faced me. He kept coming, and shouting. A fig! Just a fig, that was all.

"Anyhow I ran into the corner of someone else's counter, another vendor's, and that knocked the fig out of my hand. I never even got it, and he didn't even want it! He probably didn't even want me! The big bully just enjoyed scaring the little lost boy."

Or maybe catch him and s-sell him, Mignureal thought, swallowing and wishing this weren't happening. Even his voice had changed. He was almost that little boy again, running from the monster and scared enough to wet himself.

"Either that or hoping to catch me and sell me!" Hanse said, echoing her thoughts so that she jerked her head to look over at him in surprise. "I've thought of that since! Anyhow I ducked around that stall, and around back it was just a tent. Faded old green and brown stripes, going up and down. I dived under it into the dark and didn't move for about three days."

"Hanse—"

"Oh I know it only seemed three days," he said, misunderstanding her reason for saying his name in that low but rushing voice. "It might have been an hour. I was scared. Real scared. I could feel my heart and hear it, along with my blood pounding and rushing. I guess probably about an hour passed with me too scared to move. I knew that at any minute any moment any second he was going to rip up the tent and there I'd be, all in the bright light lying there helpless as a lizard without legs, and he'd Get me.

"He didn't. That bully probably forgot all about me two minutes after I ran around the corner of that stall-tent and he didn't see me anymore. So after a long time I noticed what I'd been smelling. I didn't smell it for a long time. All I did was try to listen but hearing only my heart and my blood gushing through my head. Then I noticed the smell, the odor; and then I saw it."

Silently weeping and wishing she could be holding him in her arms, Mignureal was trying to steer her horse closer to his so that at least their legs would rub, when he surprised her still again.

"Then I saw it," he said again, and he actually chuckled. "It was a little yellow bowl, a ruined one with a crooked lip. Had a dark stripe running around it, wavery, but it was dark there so I couldn't make out the color. The bowl had food in it! A feast had been waiting right there for me, all that time! A few inches from my nose, and me too scared to see it or smell it!"

Mignureal watched him shake his head, the white cloth rumpling and creasing with the movement. The hood concealed his face, except for part of his nose.

"I feasted," he said. "I *feasted!* Took at least two seconds to gobble it all. Maybe three. Then I wiggled out from under the tent and went . . . went away. Back to the market, back into that forest of legs. About a minute later a short really skinny woman with a face like a dried date called me.

"'Hey, boy,' she said. 'Hey.'

"I thought how ugly she was and I knew she was going to grab me for stealing a fig and then eating someone else's feast, and I started to run but banged right into a fat woman in long long skirts. Skirts in about sixteen colors—a S'danzo, of course. I bounced off right into the other woman's hand. She was leaning over her counter, out of her stall. Her hand had a wonderful little currant cakey in it. That's why she was calling me; she was offering the waif a sweety! I gulped it and then I remembered how I'd thought she was a monster or a witch, after me, but how nice she was. That made me feel bad, and I started to cry. I ran. I never even thanked her. I think I learned what embarrassment is, that day. Among other things."

They rode in silence for a long minute or more. The sun was low in a sky going ever redder but still no less hot. The horses plodded, with Hanse far away in his thoughts. Mignureal was unable to speak and working hard to keep her sobbing from his ears.

"That's my first memory, Mignue. Being hungry and alone, real hungry, and just taking a fig, one little fig. Then getting chased that way. I've never been so terrified. Absolutely terrified. Then finding food, and then that woman. Ugly and mean-looking because of the lines in her face—probably old smile-lines—but the kindest person I had ever met. Up until then." He shook his head at the memory, at the irony.

"And my feast, Mignue; you know what that feast was, in that little mis-made yellow bowl with the dark stripe?"

He snorted a laugh that was not real. "That bowl was scraps! You know, table scraps. Some peelings, the end off a cucumber, some crumbs and actually a little piece of bread. A real little piece, with the smell of meat on it. I devoured part of a dog's dinner out of a dog's bowl, that was my feast!"

Quivering, Mignureal pretended to reach down to her foot on the side opposite Hanse, so that she could brush away tears. She straightened slowly, now pretending to be rubbing Inja's neck in the extremely warm place under its mane.

After another while of silent plodding Hanse said, "The other kindest person I ever met was just the opposite. Head like a melon, face like a moon, belly like a barrel and—just big all over. And with a *nice* expression all over her face, all the time, all her life."

"My . . . my mother."

He nodded. "Now you know how much I care about how someone looks, Mignüe. I learned early about how important a person's looks are! Cudget was . . . .Cudget was ugly, and I've got a nose on me like a hungry hawk. That's what somebody said once; I'd been thinking it looked like a buzzard beak. What in several hells am I doing riding across the desert alone with a girl who's absolutely beautiful—that's a mystery and a miracle."

He looked at her then, and smiled, and despite all her intentions and her fighting against it, Mignureal performed that ancient cliché of bursting into tears.

"Oh no!" Hanse said in horror. *She knows her tears are like a needle in my gut—but it's not her fault. Why'd I have to go and mention Moonflower?*

Strange, how rapidly sunset came on the desert, especially to two who had lived their lives in a town on the seacoast. The sky went more and more orange, and then the sun, usually a white glare, became an enormous red ball squatting on the edge of the desert. Swiftly it died there, all bloody on the horizon. As swiftly the brilliantly starlit darkness unfurled across the plain of sand, purpling it.

Hanse might have been an old man on dismounting, from the way he groaned and grunted and complained.

"Ah!" he began anew, when he took his first step away from Blackie. "Ahr! Gods of my fathers, the *thighs!* What straddling a horse does to my thighs!"

Mignureal smiled. "I know, mine too. But that's not what you're rubbing, darling!"

"And you're not! Hmp. The gods better equipped you females for sitting a saddle," he grumbled. "You're practically designed for it! Your thighs are farther apart to begin with. Besides, you women have more padding—I mean, you're different from us in the rear, too."

Her smile widened. "Haven't I just noticed that!"

Hanse was forced to chuckle and go to hug her—hobbling, walking bandy-legged. They embraced until he was swallowing, wanting her out of all these clothes, wanting his hands all over her, wanting to throw her down And. He broke the embrace and, working his shoulders and still wincing when he moved his legs, got out of the long hooded robe.

"Arrgh! If the gods had intended men to ride horses, they'd have . . . I don't know. They just didn't intend for us to, that's all!"

"Try to think how much sorer you'd be if we had walked all this way."

He scowled at her. "Oh stop being so damned cheerful and practical! When I want to complain, I want to complain. It's a sacred right."

"Aye, milord priest," she smiled, also shucking her robe.

Both of them were happy to get out of the voluminous garments, white because they gathered no sun (and indeed reflected it, according to the drover, who certainly qualified as expert as to the desert).

Hanse's faded old russet tunic had three-quarter sleeves and thong laces at the V of the neck, over leather leggings of dark tan, and a pair of good soft boots. He wore his knives, of course, though the big Ilbarsi "knife," long as Mignureal's arm, he had slung from his saddle. He looked neither scungy nor wealthy, which was the way he wanted to look. Mignureal also appeared neither, but she was hardly to be overlooked. She was of the S'danzo, and she was Moonflower's daughter. The bulk of her clothing made her look as if she might weigh two hundred pounds. She did not.

Three of her mother's inordinate number of rings she wore now, if not quite as many colors and patterns of clothing. Perhaps only eleven, including paisley and stripes and the blue and green scarf that tied back her hair, which was deep, true blue-black and had been cut once, at twelve, as part of her puberty rites. She wore singlet and blouse and vest, three skirts and two aprons. Strangely, one of the skirts matched the headband. Hanse had noted that. He had thought of a clever remark about her going conservative but was saving it for a more propitious time. A better one, anyhow.

"How can you stand all those clothes?"

Mignureal shrugged, and her color deepened a bit.

They had stopped for the night at a spot of green. A small well, stone-protected and bearing a sign, managed to support a few yards of scrubby grass and two and a half imitation trees. Mignureal read the sign aloud: it advised them not to drop anything into the water but to be sure to leave for others the droppings of their animals, well away from the well.

"Ickh," Mignureal said, making a face. "Whatever for? And why the sign? It isn't as if we'd be taking our horse droppings with us!"

Hanse chuckled. "You've never been poor," he said.

She wheeled on him, showing that unaccountable offense so many people took at any intimation that they lived comfortably.

"You think we were rich? There were nine of us!"

"No, I mean you weren't poor enough. Not really poor, not dirt poor; not goat-chip poor. I learned about that, early enough. Goat turds are best and I hear camel drops are better. But any manure is a good fuel, once it's been allowed to age and dry a bit. It burns, and it burns slowly. Downwind is full of people who can't afford so much as a stick of wood even for their cookstoves, Mignue."

She put her hands together, not quite clapping them. "Oh. I guess you know a lot of things I don't."

"About being poor, yes," he said, moving about the tiny excuse for an oasis, looking for a trove of droppings from previous stoppers here.

"I love you, Hanse," she murmured, and luxuriated in just watching him. Watching him move. It was coming on for night, and night was Hanse's time. He moved best by night. *The streets are my home,* he had once told another, wiser woman of some sophistication, who as it turned out was sophisticated enough to be using him. *They birthed me and gave me suck.* He was less cocky with Mignureal, because he needn't be: he was more comfortable with her, and could almost be himself. That was not easy for Hanse called Shadowspawn, the thief of Sanctuary called Thieves' World.

Very still beside the well, Mignureal watched him walk, watched him move. She had done so, as unobtrusively as possible, for years. She loved watching him move. So wiry and lithe, so smooth in the way he seemed just to glide, hardly touching foot to ground.

"Hanse walks like a hungry cat," some said back in Sanctuary, and might even shiver a bit. Actually he didn't; Hanse *glided*. His buskins' soft soles lifted only a finger's breadth with each step. They came down on the balls of the feet, not the heels. Some made fun of that (though only when Shadowspawn was elsewhere), because it made for a sinuous glide that was strange in appearance. The better-born watched him with an æsthetic fascination—and some horripilation. Among females highborn or otherwise and including Mignureal, the fascination was often layered with interest, however unwilling. She had never thought or said what others said, predictably: a distasteful, rather sexy animal that Hanse; that Shadowspawn.

Mignureal was watching him now, and so raptly that she jerked when he spoke.

"Hmm. Well, it's this way, m'dear," he said, *gliding* back her way. "Either someone ignored the sign or others have been here recently and used all the fuel supply. We'll not be having a fire. Better break out the dates and hardcrust and that awful saltwater-dried fish. I'll get some beer off Dumb-ass. Oh wait; let's give him the first drink out of that well, Mignue."

Drawing up a sloshy bucket, wood banded in rope, she looked at him. "Why?"

He paused to meet her gaze. "Just in çase. He's the least important of the five of us."

"Oh!" She shivered. She looked into the bucket with new skepticism, then back at Hanse. "But he's carrying all our supplies!"

He nodded. "A lot of which could go on our horses. And I'd hate to have to ride that dumb donkey. Guiding him by his ears, I guess. That leaves you and me." He showed her a sweet look and spread his hands. "But if you drank first and something's wrong with that water, who'd I snuggle up to when it gets chilly?"

"Oh—you!" she said, smiling. And she broke out the copper pan the ass wore. The leathern bag beside it jingled just beautifully. She gave their pack animal his drink. "It's already chilly, by the way. I'll bet *Cutie* here would be just lovely and warm to snuggle up to, too!"

"Eeeee-Awwwww!" Hanse called, unshipping the carefully balanced and pleasantly sloshy goatskin bags from the onager even while he imitated him. The animal's big pearl-tipped ears shifted back, but he didn't deign to look around.

She was right. The world had already become positively chilly, and they both knew without being able to understand the phenomenon that soon it would be worse than chilly.

Hanse hadn't yet noticed. First giving the jingly sack a fond pat, he opened the sloshy one to decant some beer. The wet cloth wrapped around the bag had long since dried completely, and its cooling effect had long since left the beer. Hanse didn't mind.

"Ahhhhh."

"How is it, Hanse?"

"Warm."

"Is that good or bad?"

With a little smile at her lack of knowledge due to inexperience, he shrugged and drank again. "Ahhh. It could be less *hot*. Today I was afraid of using the water just to cool the beer. Tomorrow we'll do that, and remember to re-wet the cloth from time to time. We can use the same cloth to wipe our faces."

"That will be nice, Hanse," she said thoughtfully, "suppose you made sure the sack was tightly stoppered, and we tied it real tight and lowered it into the well. That should bring the temperature down some, shouldn't it?"

Above the beer-sack, Hanse's eyes went large and round. Slowly he lowered the bag, and slowly he turned his head to look, all large-eyed, at Mignureal. "Remind me sometime to tell you why I wouldn't dream of putting any kind of bag down a well."

She looked at him for a moment before her laugh bubbled out.

"Oh! You have, you have!" With a little pouncing movement that swished her skirts, she patted the bag that jingled rather than sloshed. Its leather was seamed with cracks. "How long did you tell me all this silver coin was down that well up at Eaglenest?"

"*Years,*" Hanse sighed, and drank.

• • •

"Shadowspawn schemes to steal from the very Prince-Governor," a certain lowlife had some years before told the night proprietor of the Golden Lizard, who had told Gelicia, proprietor of a popular house-not-home in Sanctuary. "And to make a quick large profit in the doing."

Gelicia had transmitted that information to one Cusharlain, who had been conducting a secret investigation of Hanse called Shadowspawn on behalf of a Certain Party High In The Government. (One of the Prince-Governor's concubines, actually, who also happened to be playing around with one of the Prince-Governor's personal bodyguard, the Hell-Hounds, and had schemes of her own.)

Cusharlain had shown his incredulity. "This young game-cock means to try to rob the very palace?"

"Don't scoff, Cusher," Gelicia said, waving a doughy hand well leavened with rings. "If it can be done, Shadowspawn'll do it. Did you hear about the ring he roached from under the pillow of Corlas the camel dealer—while Corlas's head was on it, sleeping? Ever hear tell of how our boy Hanse clumb up and stole the eagle off the roof of Barracks Three for a lark? Had a prodigal offer from some richie up in Twand, he did; and do you know Hanse wouldn't take it? Said he liked having the thing. Pisses on it every morning on rising, he says."

Cusharlain smiled. "And if it can't be done? Roaching the palace, I mean."

"Why then Sanctuary will be minus one more cockroach/thief, and no one'll miss him." Gelicia's shrug invested her vast bosom with a quake of seismic proportions.

Cusharlain had gone his carefully questioning way, then, and by and by Shadowspawn had indeed broken into the royal palace of Sanctuary, and stolen away the Rankan Empire overlord's Savankh, his very wand of power. For a time he had even become a sort of intimé of that same youthful Prince-Governor from Imperial Ranke. Hanse had gone from being a tool of the concubine and her teacherous Hell-Hound to aiding the Prince-Governor in stopping them, their plot, and their lives.

Half the Savankh's ransom, in silver coin, jingled just beautifully in the good-sized saddlebag Hanse removed from a grateful Cutie/Dumb-ass. The other half he had left behind in Sanctuary, to aid the rebels against the *new* overlords. That was the same night he broke into the palace for the third time, and came away again with the wand of power of the new overlord—or overlady, or over-thing; the Beysa. It was also the same evening on which he had wisely deemed it expedient to betake himself from the city of his birth.

With him on a moment's decision had come the bereaved Mignureal: S'danzo, burgeoning Seer, carefully preserved and sheltered virgin recently robbed of her mother, and sometime tool of gods; benign gods.

She watched him now, watched the rise of his tunic onto the tiny cheeks of his tight backside, as he stretched to quaff just a bit more beer. And she, alone among all others including himself for all his airs and pretenses, loved him. She and a certain goddess.

She noted with pleasure the little breeze that wafted up from the south, the direction of their coming. She did not notice that all three of their animals lifted their heads in response to some scent freighting that lazy current of air, tipped forward their ears and stared in that direction, into darkness. Hanse noticed. He frowned and tightened his lips, and set aside the beer in manner decisive. Without at all alarming Mignureal because he was well practiced at being secretive, he set about checking the several knives he wore.

When nature called, he merely wandered over on the other side of the horses, opened his leggings, let go, and watered the sand. He had no thought at all of Mignureal's convenience problem until her fidgeting elicited a comment from him. She looked away. He spoke her name, in a questioning voice. Then she told him her problem.

"Damn! I'm sorry; I'm not used to thinking about women! Just go over there past the horses, just a little way. There's a great big convenience out there."

"Oh," she said, looking ridiculously embarrassed and adding to it by trying not to look so. She started to move past him, skirts rustling.

"Mignue—don't get out of sight, now."

She spun about. "What!"

"Uh, sorry. I'm sorry. I mean, uh, don't go too far, all right?"

"Of course. I'm not a child, Hanse. You don't have to tell me that. This is Mignue, remember? Your *woman*."

"Of course. Right. Yes. I'm sorry, Mignue."

"And don't you dare look!"

Hanse turned away so she wouldn't see him rolling his eyes toward the abode of the gods.

They ate dates and bread and dried, salty fish, sitting cross-legged on the ground and talking the while, and they kissed several times, while Hanse with great difficulty and admirable resolve curbed himself from fondling. He also drank no beer and, with care not to alarm Mignureal, sat in such a wise that he faced the south and could also see the onager and both horses.

He was not interested in more of the beer. He was on watch. Besides, Hanse and alcohol were only nodding acquaintances. Except for that night when he had slain a Beysib Stare-eye on his way to meet Zip at Sly's Place; he had put away several mugs that night, and fast. Even his elation and the beer, however, had not enabled Zip to convince him to join the Cause to liberate Sanctuary from the Stare-eyes. It had taken Moonflower's death at Beysib hands to do that, and to change Hanse and his life forever. Never mind the time when he had rescued Tempus from the vivisecting monster Kurd; after that night of ghastliness Hanse had stayed drunk for a week or more. And after *that* he hadn't touched a drop for a long, long time.

An hour and more passed and neither he nor the animals heard anything untoward.

More significantly, the animals smelled nothing that alarmed or even interested them, and were at repose. With all three standing over there asleep, a relaxing Hanse responded to Mignureal's request that he tell her once again how it came about that they had the sack of silver coins, and were wealthy.

He told her, pleasantly at rest with his back against one of the unreasonable facsimiles of a tree, and with three of his knives removed. His lean legs were straight out on the ground, ankles crossed. His arm was around her and her hand lay on his tunic–clad chest, where her head was. He had been careful to get her on his right, so that his left hand was free.

Naturally he embellished a bit and omitted a few thises and thats. He was truthful about having had help getting into the palace, that first time.*

More simply put than Hanse told it, he had found and taken the Savankh, escaped, and negotiated the ransom: a few coins of gold and lots of silver. The exchange was to take place near a well in the ruins of Eaglenest, an abandoned manse on a hill outside Sanctuary. It did, but with complications. The two heavy saddlebags full of shining chiming coin were borne by a Hell–Hound named Bourne, who had ideas of his own concerning the ultimate owner of the ransom and the immediate and long–term future of the thief. Fortunately he failed to carry out that plan, which involved his sword and Hanse's head:

"I threw the saddlebags down the old well and sort of dived in after them," Hanse told Mignureal, pausing to direct a stare at one of his own legs. As if it weren't even part of him, the fool thing twitched as a saddle–strained muscle let go with something approaching a bowstring twang. He re–crossed his ankles.

He had also just lied, though surely understandably.

He had in fact fallen into the well, totally by accident. He'd spent considerable comfortless time down there in the wet dark too, before being "rescued" by the governor himself, Prince Kadakithis. A wet and sorrily bedraggled Hanse emerged, leaving his treasure behind, and shortly gained firsthand knowledge of the meaning or the word "torture." At that he fared better than Bourne, who paid the supreme penalty.

"It's really true then," Mignureal said, snuggling. "You *have* met Prince Kitty Cat."

Hanse nodded against the top of her head. "Aye. More than met. He and I've talked, three times. Privately. We—"

"Oh, *Hanse!*"

"Ouch. Be still, will you? The hard part was learning that I couldn't hate him anymore. I think enough of Prince Kadakithis not to call him 'Kitty Cat,' and you won't either."

"I'll try to remember, Hanse," she said, her voice still full

*Detailed in "Shadowspawn," the first of the Hanse novelets, in *Thieves' World*: Ace Books, 1979; and available in reissue from the same publisher.

of excitement. "It's just that I can just hardly *believe* it! You and Kit—*him*! *Talk*ing! Whatever *about*, darling?"

"As a matter of fact the second time we talked it was because he summoned me. He needed my help."

"*What*?!"

He squeezed her far shoulder, hard. "Every time I say something and you make an excited noise you jerk so that you jar me all over, did you know that? This tree behind me's not as wide as my back, and I swear, it bites!"

At that she kissed his chest or rather his tunic, and he paused to kiss the top of her head, or rather her hair.

"Anyhow, that time I sneaked into the palace, because I didn't want anyone to see me being let in; who in Downwind or the Maze would've trusted me after that? Helping him that time got me into a lot of trouble, too—again. But that's another story altogether. The first time—once I was out of the dungeon and the hands of that horse-sized smith acting as torturemaster—he signed a full pardon for everything I'd done up till then. Kadakithis, I mean, not the torturing blacksmith or that big swine Zalbar. You know that; you've seen the pardon with his name and seal on it! I took it straight to your mother—"

"Oh, I remember. That was *years* ago; I was just a girl, then. You brought it to m-mother-r . . . because she could read and you wanted to be sure it really was a pardon." Her voice had quavered, but she managed to fight back the sobs that wanted to begin anew.

"Uhmm," Hanse said, suddenly wondering whether Moonflower had taught her daughter to read. He certainly hoped so. If they were going to be a family, it would be helpful—indeed, wonderful—if one of them knew letters and could read.

He said, "Kadakithis also agreed to forget about the saddlebags, although getting 'em was up to me. He didn't care; he's rich Rankan royalty and it was only money. Besides, he was just *so* pleased and proud of having killed that night. A man, I mean. His first. That was the time I told him my business was thievin', and that killin's the business of soldiers and princes and the like."

"Oh Hanse! That didn't make him angry?"

"No. He laughed! I've told you—I'm not going to pretend that he and I are friends, Mignue, but we couldn't help sort of liking each other. We're about the same age, I think, and he was really aware of that. I remember thinking that he was clever enough to be a thief!"

"Hanse! You didn't say that!"

He chuckled. "Right. That, I didn't say to him."

"It's all just so exciting, darling!" she said, and sort of crawled up him to kiss him.

After awhile, she asked, all low-voiced, if he had killed.

"Yes," he said just as quietly, and felt her tighten while his stomach did. "I never intended to. Killing was never what I wanted to do. I wanted people to *think* I could, and would. Cudget told me, 'Wear weapons openly and try to look mean, boy. People see the weapons and believe the look and you don't have to use them.'"

"Oh, that was good advice," she said, understanding him a little more; why he wore all those knives, for instance, and always wore black at night, or had back in Sanctuary. And why he went about scowling so much.

"It was, and I took it. I didn't want to kill anybody. I didn't know whether I could or not, and really wasn't interested in finding out. All I wanted was to be Shadowspawn, climbing and lurking, sneaking in and out of places no one else can, enjoying the thrill of roaching: taking things and never being caught or even seen. And never having to use these weapons."

Her interruption was a sort of blurted question that surprised them both: "Hanse? Why's it called roaching? Why Shadow-spawn the roach?"

"Hmp! What comes out at night and moves better in the dark than in the light?"

"Oh! I—don't like that much."

His response was instantaneous and fervent: "I don't either."

"Do you like being known as Shadowspawn?"

"I don't mind," he said, but his voice told her that it was more than that; the name pleased him.

She smiled against his chest. She was beginning to feel older. It was part of being a woman. Men had more boy in them than women had girl; Mignureal had heard her mother say that a dozen times.

"It does get silly when someone thinks it's part of my name—name and calls me both: 'Hanse Shadowspawn.' That's silly."

After a while of snuggling to him in silence she said, "And, but—oh. I remember; you said you killed the very first Beysib you saw right after . . . right after mother. . . ." She broke off for almost a minute, getting her voice back together while he squeezed her and nuzzled her hair with his chin.

"And that you thought it was the one who had k—I hope it was, too. Well, um, Hanse . . . before that?"

Hanse stared ahead, thinking. He decided not to tell her about the other Beysib. That had been senseless. The arrogant creature had simply confronted him, and demanded, and Hanse had tried to go on his way, and the Stare-eye refused to allow that, and Hanse blurted a marvelous insult. The Beysib, rather than flying into a rage, seemed to show delight that it had an excuse to kill him. It started pulling out the long sword sheathed on its back, staring at him with unblinking eyes and clear intent. And the throwing knife from Hanse's right upper arm was in its eye and brain in an instant.

He had retrieved it, too, before he went on to his meeting in Sly's Place. It hadn't occurred to him that Zip and the dive's proprietor, Ahdio, would treat him as a hero for having done death on one of the occupying force of invaders.

He told her instead about the first time, a matter of years ago, now.

"I was . . . on the roofs one night, and heard things. I went to look. I had just met Tempus, and didn't know whether I liked him or not. Still don't. Anyhow, he was being attacked, and by several. That was before I knew that he's—he's unnatural, Mignue. I guess he can't be killed. His wounds heal and leave no scars, and Kurd actually cut off . . . parts of him." He swallowed, hard, and Mignureal squeezed and pressed close. "They grew back."

"Oh!" A shudder rippled through her. Believing in no gods, the S'danzo were short on exclamations and swearbys and even such simple ejaculations as "Gods!"

"Anyhow, that night, I didn't think or anything. I saw Tempus under attack and I moved. I had to. I think I killed two of them; I wasn't even sure, afterward. It was all a flurry and a blur, just moving fast and doing what had to be done to help

him. We were pretty much friends after that, and he still vows
that he owes me. I can't see why. I saved him from Kurd all
right, and I *wanted* to kill Kurd! But that night in the
alley . . . could those assassins have killed Tempus? I don't
know. Maybe they'd have left him dead, in pieces, and next
day he'd be up and off to hide someplace, to let things grow
back? I don't know. I still can't get over that business at Kurd's
though, and after. When Tempus grew back fingers and toes
and t . . . tongue." He shook his head. "Ils's Eyes, how I
hate sorcery!"

Another shudder went through her, and she squeezed him
hard enough to hurt. Then she was moving up his chest again,
to his mouth.

"Whether he'd have come back or not is beside the point,"
she murmured, with her lips close to his. "What you did was
noble, and that was *reason* for killing."

Then her lips were all over his and pressing hard. Her mouth
was very warm and soon so was Hanse.

The kiss lengthened and matters commenced to become
involved. Many who knew or had known him would not have
believed it, but it was Hanse who stopped it. True, that was
neither to his nor Mignureal's delight. He was, however,
determined not to let pleasant dallying progress to lovemaking,
and he was only so strong when the juices started flowing and
biology started making demands.

"If we keep this up, I'll just have to have you and—"

"Me too!"

"But it is not going to be out here in the open, Mignue, not
on the desert. It just is not. There's a proper bed up ahead
somewhere for you, and then I want you naked and—"

She stopped his mouth with her hand, nodding, and
mentioned that they really should be curling up to sleep
anyhow. Better get the white robes to use as coverlets, too.

"I mean it's safe to snuggle in our clothes, isn't it, Noble
Hanse?"

She hadn't seen him look nervous or chuckle nervously
before, and it was nice.

He had lied again. The excuse for an explanation he had
given her was not just no explanation: it was not quite the truth.

There were other reasons. The main one was that he was still nervous about the possibility of someone's or something's being out there, following, and he was not about to be helpless in embrace. That, he did not want to tell her: he was on watch. Yet there was more.

To begin with, he was no longer the Shadowspawn or even the Hanse his friends and acquaintances—of which there were rather more than the former—knew or thought they had known. He had changed greatly once, during a time not long ago. Nonetheless it was a time he could not now remember. Both gods and his own wish were involved in that forgetting; he had *wished* to forget it, to gods' disappointment.

It was the gods of his people who had granted him the power of *wish*, for excellent service rendered. Hanse had indulged himself mightily for ten days. All he had to do was *wish*, and it was so. It was incredible and it was wonderful. For a while.

Naturally his wishes, most of them made on whim or the jerk of a knee in an instant, involved females, and beds. Wondering what they remembered, he decided to make a test.

He *wished* that when he reached home, his room above a tavern, Mignureal would be there waiting for him, in his bed.

His intent was an experiment: to enjoy her, then use the *wish* to make her forget, and next day see what she and her mother knew or thought they knew about her activities. Where would they think she had been? He had hurried home, and there she was, in his bed, both visibly and vocally anxious to make love. Because he had *wished* it.

And that was the problem. She was there because he had wished it, not because she had. Or so he thought.

That led him to discovery of a level to which he could not stoop, and Hanse was shocked: he had not known there were any. He simply could not go through with it, not that way. Mignureal was not those other women and girls. Mignureal was . . . different. Moonflower's daughter should not be behaving as she had been that night. He had *wished* Mignureal back in her own home, in her own bed, and for her to remember her visit to his room only as a dream.

Later he had *wished* to remember it the same way, so that the two of them shared only a dream, not memories of what had been reality, however doubly incredible. Had someone told him that he had made a moral decision, he would have protested angrily, feigning even more anger.

After that the power of the *wish* had not been fun anymore, and he had parted with it willingly.

He had been changed forever by that experience, that realization and decision. He also had no memory that he *had* lain with Mignureal, but only in a way: it was in her form that Eshi, goddess of beauty and love, had visited Hanse and lain with him. For Eshi daughter of Ils the All-Seeing liked Hanse more than somewhat.

The senseless killing of Moonflower had affected him as much or more, and changed him even more.

He was still Hanse, that Downwinder bastard (both by birth and by nature, it had been said of him); still the former ward and apprentice of the thief Cudget Swearoath, who became a father-substitute and whom Hanse had seen caught and hanged; still full of needs and inclined to exaggerate and to swagger and to strive to appear to be as mean and dangerous and free of moral restraint as he could.

And now there was more.

Previously he had barely assumed responsibility for himself, and given thought to little beyond tomorrow's breakfast and perhaps a companion for tonight. Now he had embraced responsibility for both himself and Mignureal. Furthermore his own makeup and needs were such that he would not shirk it. It all meant that Hanse had become a man, ready or not and whether he wanted to or not. True, he was a youthful one, sort of a nascent bud of a man, still in the flux of development.

He was, however, no longer the duped tool who had stolen the Savankh for ransom and fallen down a well, and certainly not the younger youth who had roached the military standard to use as pissoir.

Therefore he checked the animals and saw to it that he and Mignureal bedded down near their supplies. Secretly, he kept his weapons to hand. She wanted to be on his left because her habit was to go to sleep on her right side. He was determined to have his left hand free but did not want to say so. He thought of an excuse, and made it sound nice. It worked. She went to sleep that way, fully clothed as he was, partly curled and backed up to his right side.

Hanse lay alert, forbidding himself to sleep.

Not a sound disturbed him—well, the dumb donkey snorted a little, now and again, but where they lay it was so quiet that Hanse could even hear the little whistling sound Mignureal made through the nostril she had pressed against her upper arm.

I hope she doesn't do that all the time, he thought.

That was his last thought before he went unwillingly into sleep, for the follower was very quiet indeed in tracking them, and in coming into their camp. But not for long.

Hanse was shocked into wakefulness by a loud and eerie noise, seemingly close to his ear, and a pressure against his side that was more than just pressure. Since that was not the side turned toward Mignureal, he lurched, rolled, and with a jacking flex of his legs came onto his feet. His left hand was up and back past his head, slim throwing knife poised; the right held the Ilbarsi knife ready for defense or worse.

He was still staring, openmouthed, at the source of that ghastly noise when Mignureal came up to a sitting position.

"Oh Hanse! Look! A kitty cat, way out here on the desert!"

Hanse nodded. "I see him. By the Shadow Himself, Notable, what in all the hells are you doing here?"

The cat, which was very large and very red, immediately took a couple of steps and banged the rearward portion of its body into Hanse's leg. It paced on, purring loudly. Even its tail rubbed him, curling muscularly half around his leg and gliding lingeringly along it. The cat moved on a couple of paces, dragging its body along his ankle, and turned to repeat the process on the way back. Along with its purring, it made an assortment of other sounds, low-voiced but somehow insistent.

"I can't believe it! He followed us! That's what I thought I saw behind us, Mignureal. I did see it! Him, I mean! Notable!"

"This is Notable? But that isn't possible! All the way from Sanc—this is Notable, Hanse, that cat you told me about?"

"Aye. Oh." Hanse thrust the long knife into the ground and made the other one vanish into its sheath even while he squatted. He put a hand on Notable's back, rather tentatively— Notable immediately arched and rubbed in that direction, too, purring loudly enough to rattle glass—and the other hand on Mignureal. "Notable. Look, Notable. Fr—Notable, damn it, *look! Friend,* Notable. My dear—my dearest friend, Min-you-ree-al. Mignureal, Notable. Friend." Out of the side of his mouth he said, low, "He's ferocious, Mignue, and I'm serious. Don't try to pet him."

"Mrarr?"

"What a weird voice he has, Hanse! And he doesn't say what he's supposed to say at all! He hasn't said 'meow' one time! Hello, Notable, you big pretty boy. I'm Mignureal."

Notable cocked his head, ears wagging. Assuming a sweet expression he uttered a sickeningly sweet "mew?" And resumed purring loudly.

"Ohh, what a *lovely* kitty! What a nice little—well, what a nice kitty. Hanse! Let go my wrist, I wasn't going to—Oh, Hanse! He must be half-*starved*!"

"Uh. Notable . . . why in all the hells did you have to follow me? Ahdio must be sick. Or mad enough to punch holes in walls!"

"Miawr!"

"All right, all right." Suddenly smiling, Hanse extended a hand.

Notable backed two paces and stared, tail lashing. "MAOW!"

"All right, all right, Mignue: why don't you get him something to eat, so he'll, uh, like you. This isn't just a cat, believe me. Notable's a watch-cat, and attack-trained. He's also mean as a snake, but only if he doesn't like someone. Or if someone attacks or threatens Ahdio. Well, me, now. He belonged to Ahdio, and—"

"I remember," she said, already rummaging in one of the packs. "He's a one-person cat who hated everyone but Ahdio, you told me, and you hated cats, but Notable right away taught you respect and next thing he was your lifelong friend. And I—I—"

"Yes. You Saw for me. You told me to take him along, that night I went up the wall and into the palace to steal the Beysa's sceptre for the PFLS rebels. Except that you didn't even know I was going to do that, and you had never seen or heard of Notable. You just told me to 'take the red cat.' I did. And he

saved my life. Notable saved my life! I took him back to Ahdio
though, and never dreamed—damn! What in the Hot Hell are
you *doing* here, Notable? We left Sanctuary three nights ago!''

Notable's only acknowledgement was a movement of his tail
at sound of his name. He was avidly watching Mignureal, his
nostrils twitching.

"It's mystical, Hanse, and that's all there is to it. Here you
are, Notable, some nice—oh! He *was* hungry!''

"All right, give him some more. Damn, Notable! I'll be
lucky if ole Ahdiovizun doesn't come after me with a—with
nothing; Adhio's so big he doesn't need to carry weapons!
What are we going to *do* with you!''

Notable's tail moved. He looked only at Mignureal. At
Mignureal's hands, specifically, and his purring was loud
enough to frighten babies. He snaffled up his second helping,
too, while Mignureal stared blinking. Only then did he look
again at Hanse. Notable made a remark.

"Oh no. Notable—at this time of night? We have to get back
to sleep!''

Notable tried the same sound again, with more volume. One
of the horses whickered nervously and stamped a big foot.

"Oh," Mignureal said. "Poor fellow. I'll bet he wishes he
had some nice milk.''

Hanse gave her a look. He sighed and picked up the
earthenware bowl. He rose, grunted at the saddle-born stiffness
in his legs, and paced resignedly to one of the leathern sacks.
Not the one that jingled: the one that sloshed. He set the
reddish bowl on the sandy ground. Notable hurried to it,
peered within, looked at Hanse, looked at the bowl. Notable
said MRAOW! in a voice so loud that Mignureal raised a hand
to her cheek in astonishment.

"Hanse! You're not going to give that cat b—''

The cat was assiduously and noisily lapping up the beer
before Hanse finished pouring.

"A watch cat," Hanse said. "An attack-trained watch cat. A
very large, red, attack-trained watch cat who actually likes *me*.
He also lived in a tavern, remember—Ahdio's. Notable loves
beer.''

Mignureal clapped her hands and fell back laughing amid a

flurry of multicolored skirts. That showed Hanse that she was wearing the dark red color of mourning, after all.

Damn, I thought I'd talked her out of that. She merely slipped that skirt and blouse on over everything else. Notable lapped noisily, meanwhile making a dreadful sound, purring with his mouth open. Hanse peeled his gaze off Mignureal's legs and stared down at the big red cat, shaking his head—and yawning.

"EEEE-AWWW!"

"Oh shut up, you damned dumb donkey, before I sic this demon-cat on you!"

Notable burped.

Hanse and Mignureal watched the strangeness next morning: one by one, pacing with that deliberate and almost regal gait cats sometimes used, the big red cat visited each of the other three animals. One by one, all three calmed. Obviously, one feline and three equines had reached an accommodation.

"I think—I think that just can't be a natural cat," Mignureal said thoughtfully, gazing at him.

"Ils's Eyes, don't say that!" Hanse said, on a rising note, and returned to his careful balancing of their packs on the onager. "Oh, good boy, Dumb-ass! You left plenty of fuel for future travelers. You too, Blackie. All right Inja, what's your problem?"

After awhile he told Mignureal they were ready to travel. He stood waiting to help her onto her sorrel. Once she'd set a foot into his cupped hands and was in the saddle, he fondly clapped her calf a couple of times with a cupped hand. She jerked her leg away, not quite kicking at him.

"You stop that!"

Hanse cocked his head with its extremely black hair and stared at her, brows up a little in silent question.

"Oh! Oh I'm sorry, darling! Old habit! I'm sorry!" And she offered him her leg for another fondle.

Hanse, of course, elected to ignore that. *Tight as a drawn bowstring, he mused sourly. Moonflower over-raised her, damn it.* He knew renewed nervousness about the future. Turning his back on Mignureal while she drooped in the guilt he had chosen to give her, he squirmed himself into the saddle he hated—because it was on a horse.

Meanwhile he grumbled that these beasts should be equipped with steps. "And some way to ride without just having your legs dangle so you have to clamp this beast's big round gut with 'em."

"You don't like horses, do you, darling?"

"I like horses all right, Mignue. I just hate riding 'em." Suddenly he added, "Mention the alternative and I'll break your neck!"

She glanced around to hide her smile. "Oh no! Hanse! We forgot about Notable—what do we do with him?"

"Uh. Hadn't thought about it. But after all, he did walk all the way from Sanctuary, following us . . . why'd you do that, you silly cat?"

Notable paced almost majestically over and alongside Hanse's horse, not pausing as he looked up with cold, very green eyes. Seemingly without effort and without thinking about it, he took care of himself: he pounced cat-light atop the ass's load. Mignureal giggled. Hanse held his breath and the onager's lead-rope. The animal quivered. Then he glanced around, jerked his head a couple of times, and was at rest. Obviously he accepted the unusual rider and its extra weight.

"Oh," Hanse said, meeting the seemingly cool, smirky gaze of the cat. "So you two have already made your travel arrangements, have you? All right, let's go cook in the sun some more."

"Well," Mignureal said, "we're three now." And they were.

Hanse clucked to his mount and flicked the reins. They left the tiny excuse for an oasis and paced once again out onto seemingly endless sand baking under the bright sunlight.

As they rode, he recounted his meeting with Notable, and Mignureal's subsequent blank-eyed "When you go up the silken rope for Sanctuary, take the red cat."

"I had no idea I'd even seen you until you told me that," she said in a drifting voice. "I have no memory of that at all. I certainly didn't know you were going into the palace that night, much less up the wall."

"I know. You have it, Mignureal. You're like your mother:
one of the real S'danzo: you have the Sight. You've Seen for
me three times now. And always what you told me to do or take
was necessary; you've saved my life three times, Mignue!"
And he steered his horse her way, so that they could stretch
their arms to touch hands and exchange a look.

She nodded. "I wish I could remember. But that's the way of
it. The Sight is easier and better—more, uh, acute, mother
said—when it's for someone you love. There are some draw-
backs, too. It—look! a snake!"

They watched the snake, four or so feet long, yellowish and
tan, as it moved in weird wise across the sand.

"Now we know what leaves those weird marks," Mignureal
said. "He seems more nervous about us than I am about him.
Easy now, Inja. He's gone. Probably not even poisonous, like
those nasty little snakes of the Beysibs. Hanse? You said
Notable saved you from one; a beynit?"

"Aye. Taking Notable up the palace wall wasn't easy! I had
him in a leather pouch strapped to my chest, because on my
back he'd have added weight and pulled me off balance when I
walked up the wall."

"Walked?"

"You know; holding a rope in both hands, like this, and
just . . . walking up the wall. It's a lot easier than climbing,
and after all it's not as if I could do it without a rope!"

She nodded, but didn't smile. "I hope I never have to see
you doing that!"

"I can't think why you should," Hanse said. "Not with all
that good Rankan coin we're carrying! Anyhow, once I was
inside the royal apartment I let Notable out of his case. Next
thing I knew I was eye to eye with a beynit, and knew I was
dead. Then Notable scared him into that same bag, and I can
tell you I fastened it tight tight and wrapped it in pillow casing
and wrapped and tied that, too! Then I got the crown, and left
the wand that ugly urchin gave me, except that she was Eshi,
and she said something really strange. So then—"

"It's just impossible to believe that the goddess Eshi
appeared to you, Hanse. I mean, gods and goddesses! We
S'danzo don't even *believe* in such!"

"Well, we Ilsigi do and I do. So you'd better just not talk

about that to me and above all don't make fun. I *know,* Mignureal. I saw that ugly warty skinny girl suddenly go all aglow and become unbelievably beautiful, and I knew! That was Eshi, She Who Is Beauty Itself, and patron of love. And she said, uh . . ." He tried a little lie: "I don't remember, now."

"I know," Mignureal said, wearing a prim expression. "You just don't want to say it to me again. *'Lover,'* hmp! You told me she said, 'Take it! Have you really forgot so soon, godson . . . l-lover.' "

"Actually," Hanse said, staring straight ahead with eyes slitted against the glare, "she didn't stammer."

"Oh shut up."

"Um."

After about forty seconds of that, Mignureal said, "And then she vanished. And when you threw the rod onto the Beysa's bed, it became a snake and crawled under the covers."

Hanse felt the tickly creep of gooseflesh up his back, despite the heat. "That's exactly what happened. I hope it bit her. Maybe she's dead by now."

"Hmp! If it did bite her it probably died of *her* poison! How you doing over there, Notable?"

Notable's tail moved in acknowledgment of his name; Notable didn't even glance her way. He had wriggled into a comfortable reclining position atop the onager's load, and seemed to be staring ahead. Except that he was a cat lying in the sun, coat like flame, and his eyes were closed.

"Handsome boy! Nice Notable," she said, in that unnaturally high voice people reserved for animals and infants. "Just a sweet, uh, *large*—kitty."

"Sure. Mignue?"

"What?"

"Listen, I'd never even seen that scrawny urchin before, and I certainly hadn't been her lover! It's not likely that I'm Eshi's godson either, now is it! She must have meant something else. You know, a parable or something. We all know gods like to be cryptic. Why not? Why should gods say things just straight out, like people?"

"Gods," Mignureal muttered, not looking at him.

"Now listen, I told you not to make fun of gods to a man

who's seen one. How'd you like to get dragged off that horse
and have your tail whopped?"

She swung her white-hooded head to stare at him from large
and deeply brown eyes. "I'd just like to see you try!"

"Would you! Hmm . . . it's pretty hot right now; could
you maybe wait until sundown?"

Mignureal stared into his nigh-black eyes that could be so
sinister, and her mouth worked. Suddenly she couldn't help it;
she was laughing and so was Hanse. It was something at which
he had had precious little practice, but he did a quite creditable
job.

The horses and the onager plodded, sweating. Their riders
rode loosely, sweating. The sun was a demon straight from the
Hot Hell. Yesterday it had been the same, and presumably the
same would be true tomorrow. That was this terrain and this
journey: sameness. Desert and sun, sky and sun. They hadn't
even known it would be here! Heading northwest out of
Sanctuary, they rode across stepped grassland. The grass grew
scrubbier, then sparse. And then there was desert. This
monotonous, seemingly unending expanse of sand.

Mapmakers just don't know everything, Hanse had thought,
but that didn't make anything any better.

They saw no signs of life save for another of those strange
zigzag sets of tracks which they now knew came from a serpent
whose way of moving was strictly its own. They saw, by
looking close, very small tracks; just lines in the yellow-tan
ground that may have been left by some sort of sand-dwelling
insect. No footprints, animal or otherwise. Once Notable
hopped down, landing with a sort of "brrbllr" sound, and
hurried importantly to inspect what appeared to be a thumb-
sized hole. Forty or so horse-paces later he was back with
them, trotting. He looked up at Hanse.

"Mrar?"

"Here, no! Don't even think of jumping up here," Hanse
said, so Notable did, landing with a little burbling noise: he
had pounced easily and unerringly onto the damp blanket
beside Hanse's saddle. "Damn!" Hanse muttered, but Blackie
only twitched, glanced partway around with a little jingle of
harness, and plodded on.

"If he tries that on me and Inja, I'll scream!"

"He won't," Hanse assured her. "Don't worry about it. He's a one-man cat."

"Odd, though," she said, regarding Notable speculatively. "A little fickle, don't you think? He was Ahdio's one-man cat, and valuable to him, I'd think. Then he made up to you and next thing he walks two-plus days and nights, across the desert, to be with you! *That* is un-catlike, Hanse. Now he's Hanse's one-man cat, hmm?"

Hanse shrugged. Without looking he reached back to touch the big red cat. "You riding all right, Notable?"

Touched, Notable began purring.

"You know I never liked cats? At all!"

"Yes Hanse, I know."

"Any animal that can stare down a human ought to be illegal, I used to say."

"I remember."

Hanse sighed and gave his head a single jerky shake. "Notable's different."

He gave thought to the fact that obviously the cat had sense or consideration enough to curb his natural feline habit of landing with claws out, or Blackie might still have been galloping. Now Blackie plodded, heedless that he bore a cat who could have sunk large needly claws into him in less than the blink of an eye or the twitch of an ear.

Notable purred.

They plodded past a yellowish upthrust of prickly-looking, sickly-looking plant, and a moment later the onager strained at his towline. "Rein up a moment," Hanse said. "Dumb-ass wants a snack."

Not true; the onager nosed the pitiful excuse for vegetation and decided he didn't want any. He emitted one of his over-loud squeaks and trotted a few paces to come up between the horses.

A moment later Mignureal said, "You're not going to believe this, but Notable and Cutie-boy there just touched noses."

"Notable? You losing your taste?"

Notable didn't reply. After a time the dumb donkey dropped back, content to follow for a while. He and the horses plodded, sweating. Their riders rode loosely, slumped and sweating. Notable snoozed behind Hanse's saddle.

Mignureal's spotting a blue-tinged patch of sky was an occasion. She and Hanse talked about it for five minutes. For another ten minutes she talked fondly of the changing skies above Sanctuary and out over the sea.

When they drew their horses together to pass the water-sack back and forth and use the damp cloth on their faces, Notable roused. He stretched, sat, licked down one leg, and made one of the most frightening faces on the planet as he yawned. Then he made the easy little hop over onto the rolled blanket and skirts behind Mignureal's saddle. Inja jerked, but merely gave the equine version of a shrug. He resumed being grateful to be standing still.

"Frightened the heart out of me!"

Hanse wiped the frown off his face. "Just likes to visit around, doesn't he. Your turn next, Dumb-ass."

"Hanse, let's give the onager a name."

Hanse shrugged. Having secured the water bottle, he clucked to his horse. "All right. Think of one. 'Cutie' will *not* do."

A few minutes later: "How about . . . Molin?"

Hanse laughed aloud. Molin Torchholder was the Rankan high priest, back in Sanctuary. Why not? Then he frowned. Or was she just using a sneaky way to make fun of the gods? He put his mind to it, and within a league or so he thought of a counterproposal.

"How about 'Enas', after dear old Enas Yorl the mage, or whatever-he-is?"

Mignureal laughed.

Another night, and another day on the desert. The horses and the onager plodded, sweating. Their riders rode loosely, sweating. The sun was a demon straight from the Hot Hell.

The only interesting aspect was Hanse's lesson. Each day, several times daily when they stopped to stretch legs and bend a few times, he practiced. The sand, Mignureal had pointed out that day they agreed to begin the lessons, made a wonderful slate. One merely drew or wrote on it and obliterated that to write or draw again, or moved away for a clean slate. And so

Hanse learned to print his name. Any of his knives served as stylus; the desert was the slate. He had gotten better and better at it. One only made a straight line and another, and bridged them with a line between, and then did the same thing again except that this time one connected the two vertical lines at the top before bridge-connecting them in exactly the same way. H A NsE . . .

He could hardly wait until someone asked him for a signature on something! No longer would that be a source of stress and embarrassment! How glorious, after all these years, to prove himself learned; to be able to recognize and sign his name!

Notable continued his wanderings. He would ride the pack on the onager—Enas, but still a dumb ass—for a time, eventually pouncing lightly down with a bubbly throaty sound on impact, to explore this or that or relieve himself or merely to walk for a while; eventually springing up behind Hanse with another of those burbly sounds on alighting. Once he wandered off on a self-appointed mission of exploration. While dull, the terrain was not flat or totally featureless, so that after a time they could not see him. Mignureal expressed worry. Hanse shrugged.

"He'll be back."

True; flaming red under the white glare of the sun, the cat came back. He returned proudly, bearing a present. The little sand-burrowing chipmunk-thing was not quite dead. Mignureal was horrified and revolted.

"It's something cats do, looking for praise," Hanse said. "G-oood boy, Notable! Let him play with it, Mignue; it's just what cats do."

"It's disgusting! It's awful! I can't stand to hear the poor little thing's cries and hear it suffer that way. Oh Hanse—*do* something!"

Exasperated and showing it, Hanse reined in and slid down to pace over to Notable and his prize. Lying comfortably on the sand, Notable was playing roll-the-squeaky-toy-when-it-thinks-it's-about-to-get-away. Swish-*thuck,* and Hanse had ended the wounded little creature's noise and its suffering by beheading it. He strode stiff-legged back to his horse, dragged himself aboard, and clucked to the beast.

Mignureal's offense didn't merit it but the heat was horrible and Hanse was disgusted with everything in general: he would not speak a word for the next two hours.

Notable wasn't very friendly, either. Toys were a lot more fun when they could move and make amusing noises.

Another night led to another day of sameness. They rode, trying not to gripe about sore thighs and backsides.

Grown irritable, Hanse had become worse then displeased that Mignureal wore so many skirts and blouses and the vest, making her a shapeless, hyper-colorful mass under the white robe that was hardly as white as it had been. Now it was worse. She was bedraggled and sore rumpled by the heat and sweat of day and from sleeping in those same clothes at night. Besides, her hair was all stringy and straggly and sticking together as well as plastered to her head, cheeks, and neck by her sweat. Hanse rode loosely, sweating, and wondered what had happened to lovely, sweet, desirable Mignureal.

Hanse did not have access to a mirror.

As the day dragged on, an awful itch developed between his rearward cheeks. Scratching did not help and was almost impossible besides, in the saddle. He could only grit his teeth. Silently he made vow to drink only beer tonight, so that he'd feel justified in using water to get rid of the itchy salt of sweat. It had become the worst aspect of desert travel, and he wondered why he'd never heard anyone mention it.

The sun was far over in the sky when Notable returned from another of his independent peregrinations. Once again he bore a present. This time a small serpent trailed from either side of his mouth like long copper-and-black moustachioes. At least the snake was deceased. Although more patches of vegetation had begun to appear and even intensify, and they were sure they could see trees 'way up ahead, Hanse and Mignureal had had to halt and dismount. Determinedly he looked the other way while on the far side of the horses she relieved herself. Notable chose to take the gift to her, approaching her from behind. Her shriek must have carried for miles.

It brought Hanse at the run, knife in one hand and sword-like Ilbarsi blade in the other. Notable passed him headed the other way, running as if in quest of a new feline speed record. Hanse found her asprawl and weeping in semi-hysteria, partially in a patch of dark-colored sand, and he saw the menace. He chopped the snake twice before realizing that it was already dead.

Hanse helped Mignureal up and held her while she got her sobbing and then her gulping under control. Then she had to apologize and of course he had to make that's all right noises. That led to her adding more about her startlement and reaction, which moved him to mouthe further soothing encouragement, telling her he'd probably have done the same. They clung together awhile longer, exchanged a kiss made wet by tears and sweat. Each with an arm about the other, they turned—and stared.

Having been affrighted to speedy departure by her unaccountable scream rather than coos of gratitude for his gift, Notable was thoughtfully watching from a comfortable perch atop Enas's pack. He squeezed his eyes shut.

"You damned cat," Hanse snarled. "It's going to be a hot day in the Cold Hell when you get any more beer from me!"

Notable worked very hard to look as small as possible and said "mew" in the voice of a kitten.

Mignureal couldn't help it and needed the release besides: she laughed. Hanse looked disgustedly from her to the cat and back. His expression intensified when she went over to pet Notable. The cat immediately actuated his purring center at full volume. He also forgot himself and tried to belly up to entice her to scratch him there. That was when Hanse laughed; it did him a lot of good to see the smart cat fall off the dumb donkey.

Notable landed in the usual way, blinked a couple of times, and sat down casually to bite a bit of sand out of one paw.

For no particular reason, that was when the thought hit Hanse.

"You know—we're being stupid! Remember the fishermen's adage about not keeping all your catch in one bucket? Look at us! The place for a tidy little fortune in silver coinage is *not* in one single and mighty conspicuous saddlebag!"

"Hm! Well, we can spread it around when we get over to those trees. It will be something to do, and fun handling the coins besides!"

"Those trees may be two leagues and they may be fifty
and—they may not be trees at all," he pointed out. "We need
the break anyhow: let's have the fun now."

"In the sun? Here on the desert?"

"We'll do it on the shady side of the horses," Hanse said,
already pulling the bag off the ass.

Soon she was wide-eyed and making ejaculatory sounds
while he poured the jingling, gleaming contents of the old
saddlebag out onto a piece of tenting. They honored it by
calling it a blanket.

"Ill-gotten gains," Hanse said, joining her in thrusting his
hands into the shining pile and making it jingle. "I broke into
the palace and stole Prince K's imperial staff of office, and this
is half the ransom paid for it. On the other hand, we also
discovered and broke up that plot against him, so I consider
this my reward."

"Hanse . . . uh . . . I don't have any problem with how
you got this. It came from Ranke. We never asked to be part of
their empire, with the prince showing us how rich he and his
concubines were!"

He gave her a thoughtful look and his mouth looked almost
ready to smile. He nodded. Reaching out on impulse, he
squeezed her hand. Coins tinkled.

"Good! Now let's hide coins all over ourselves in our
clothing, and anywhere else we can think of. The big thing is
to keep them from clinking. We can separate some of course,
but we can also tie some in a kerchief or rag, so tightly together
that they don't make any sound."

She looked around. "Hanse? Are you . . . worried?"

"No, but we are out here alone and soon-I-hope we'll be in
some town, and this seems sensible, that's all. Do you think
you could do without your apron and tie up about ten of these
in one end, real tight?"

Doing that, she asked, "Why silver, Hanse? If you'd gotten
this in gold or had it converted it sure would be a lot less to
carry."

"Also a lot more noticeable, harder to change, and very
likely flaunting myself as a target. Think about me, Mignue, in
Sanctuary. What business did Hanse the roach have with gold?
It just attracts attention. To anyone, anywhere."

The look she gave him told him she respected and admired

his thinking. Then she began dragging a tight knot in her apron.

"There. Look, I can push it right down—here, too, and nobody will ever know." In depositing the packet of coins, she thrust her whole hand into her bosom.

"Gulp," Hanse said, enunciating clearly, and then: "Why didn't you tell me you wanted it there? I'd have been happy to help."

She looked at him for a moment, her face infinitely serious while she gave his half-jest considerable thought. Then she leaned toward him. "Here. Yours."

He swallowed. He gave her a kiss on the nose. "If I put my hand in there we never will get away from here, Mignue." Putting on more swagger and a fake voice, he added, "Later, wench." And he rose to tuck coins into the roll behind his saddle. "Easy, Blackie. What's the matter? You smell grass or water up ahead, boy? Is that it?"

In the questionable shade of their horses, they were over half finished with the enjoyable task when the activity and their chatter was interrupted worse than rudely by the rumbling pound of hooves. Hanse was on his feet in an instant, thrusting into the front of his tunic the stocking he had just tied around eight coins. His other hand already had a sliver of steel in it. Then he saw that there were three horses, well separated, bearing four men in robes of dirty white or pale, faded green. They brought their mounts' gallop to a halt in a spray of dust and sand.

Hanse was gazing at three crossbows, cocked and leveled.

"Here, thats look like a lot of trouble 'n' work for you two youngshters," the one with the perfectly pointed beard said, in an accent Hanse had never heard. "Let us helping with those pretty shilver."

"Eashy now, boy." That from the man three feet to the left of the first. "Jusht be letting go throw-knife and use other hand dip it right back into your tunic for what you jusht did buffle there. If it coming out with anything but a packet of green cloth, you gets to wear shteel arrow in your knee. Or maybe crock."

"Crotch," one of his comrades corrected.

Hanse's first thought was as Shadowspawn: anger at himself.

Enjoying being with Mignureal and playing with the money, he had for once forgotten his habitual caution. His next thought was worse, and scary: *Mignureal!*

"Oh Hanse!"

"Worrying not, shweetface," the first man said, swinging off his horse amid a flapping of his long robe of almost white homespun. The other three remained mounted, crossbow shafts leveled at Hanse. "We wanting a few things, but you isn't one of thems. We Tejana isn't the short to being mean to little fat mares, espezh'ly pregnant ones!"

"Preg—" she began, and broke off. She did look that way, she realized, except in the face: fat and/or pregnant.

A bit relieved, Hanse thought to turn and look at Enas. Notable was half-lying, half-crouching atop the pack, staring at the newcomers from eyes in which the pupils were far too huge for the sunlight. His tail was snapping back and forth as if on a taut spring.

"No, Notable," Hanse said, hoping that meant something to the cat and/or that Notable had sense enough not to try taking on three cocked crossbows with leveled arrows of steel.

Turning back to face the thieves again, Hanse said, "I had heard the Tejana were too proud to be thieves."

He had never heard anything of the kind. All he had heard about these nomads was that they were good fighters, good with horses and bad with women, thoroughly independent, and thought they were better than anyone else in the world. Oh, and that they knew how to be mean.

One of them laughed at his words.

"That is nots the only lie people telling about us, boy. Be tosshing your little package in with the resht of those shilver, now, and be backing away from him."

Hanse did, and painfully watched the man begin folding the piece of tenting. The clink-jingle noises as he poured the silver into the saddlebag were not so pleasant, now. It was about to depart Hanse's company. He didn't have to glance at the others or rely on peripheral vision, either. Common sense told him that strings were taut and no one was looking at anything but him.

"You sure were letting this leather get in bad shape," the first man said. "Looks like you were ushe it to dip water out of well for about a months!'' He dropped the tenting. "How much shilvers you got shtuffed down there betwixt your gourds, girl?"

Still seated on the ground, swathed in layers of clothing stuffed with silver coins, Mignureal said, "I am a person with a name. It's Mignureal." She lifted a hand to her bosom. "And this is all me."

Hanse was pleased to discover that Mignureal knew how to lie. Thank all gods her breast didn't clink when she patted it!

"Ugh," a voice said from six or so feet at Hanse's right. "Her giving milk maybe, Quesh?"

Hanse turned to stare at the speaker, who was round of face and wore a brown leather bracer. He stared back for a moment, then glanced at their presumed leader, who was presumably named Quesh.

"Nashemashmachis hemoovlishezh, Quesh," he said, or something like, and followed with more garble.

"Shink shaying you having mean eyes, youngshter," Quesh said, passing the saddlebag up to one of his companions. "Ashking if to being wise if we were leave you to shtaying alive and walking-able."

Hanse continued gazing at Shink. "That's my woman and Shink has a nasty mouth, Quesh. I'm not stupid enough to charge a cocked bow, though."

"Good," Quesh said. "Here, Aksar, what is you doing shtill shitting there behind Shink anyways? We were got two new horshes. You riding one and leading other."

"Her look to me like her were give milk," Shink said, staring at Hanse with a hopeful expression and ready crossbow.

"Shut up, Shink. We were take shomebody's things we need not shay nashty to his woman. Here, Aksar, szhimwan."

Aksar put his crossbow into Quesh's extended hand, swung down, and paced to the horses. The flowing of his watery green robe showed good boots of red leather. Clenching his hands uselessly, Hanse transferred his gaze from Shink to Quesh and took some of the meanness out of his eyes.

"You can buy horses with that money, Quesh. Taking our horses is the same as killing us."

Quesh shook his head. "Twel needing horshe *now*." He pointed to a rangy dune not far east. "That zhluff were being

very closhe. Very nice choom right pasht him. You walking
there, reshting, comforting woman. Besht time for you were
walking to treeline is after shundown. Closhest over there."
He pointed northeast. "We not were trying, uh desiring kill
you twos—we were be leaving bray-horshe and pack." Lifting
his chin proudly he added, "Tejana never taking any shome-
one's shupplies!"

Hanse bit off a sarcastic observation. He was surprised to
hear Mignureal speak, in a perfectly natural voice.

"I am called Mignureal, Quesh, and appreciate your
courtesy. What is a choom?"

He gave her a nice smile, then cocked his head, looking
upward. "Uh—"

"Oashiz," Twel said, from Inja's saddle. "Dam' good
horshe!"

"Right," Quesh said, nodding. "Our choom being your
Oashiz. We go shomeplace elshe; I promishe!"

He turned away and strode to his horse. Gritting his teeth
and hating his powerlessness, Hanse watched him bound into
the saddle. Seeing him able to do that so effortlessly didn't help
the mental state of Shadowspawn.

Shink let loose a string of soft syllables. Quesh shook his
head.

"Shink wanting shearch pack and woman. No. We were
have enough! Treema shmile on you, travelelers! Oh, here."
He slipped a copper circlet off the horn of his tall saddle and
tossed it to Hanse. Hanse stood still, letting the thing drop at
his feet. "Keeping that. You running onto other Tejana, szhow
them it. They taking nothing from you!"

"That's your code, hm?"

Quesh nodded. "Code. Aye. Shlamzhamalnipah!"

At that noise, whether word or words Hanse had no idea,
Quesh's three companions wheeled their mounts—and Inja—
and clapped heels to flanks. The horses bolted, Blackie
hurrying after Inja on a lead-rein. Dust rolled back, and Hanse
kept his mouth compressed. Quesh had remained, his cocked
bow still leveled at Hanse, though rather more casually, now.

"Mip," he said, or something like, and his wiry gray horse
began backing. Quesh smiled. "Good horshe!"

"I hope this too is in your code, Tejana," Hanse said: "Keep Shink with you or he'll come back and kill us both."

"One Tejanit, two Tejana," Quesh said, several yards farther away. "And Shink will not. Haiya!"

His horse whirled and Hanse dropped into a squat while Quesh's horse dug in its haunches to begin its gallop while Hanse straightened, knife already going back over his shoulder. His gaze was fastened on the Tejanit's broad back. An easy throw, with extra force and a bit of loft to compensate for the man's moving away from him—

Slowly and reluctantly Hanse lowered his arm. He slipped the knife up into its sheath on his right arm.

"If I put this in his back his horse will keep right on going, after the others. Then they'll come back, and we'll be dead. No. But we cannot let them get away with—uh!"

Mignureal had just thrown herself against him. He was staggered, since he'd been staring after the galloping Quesh. She was quivering. So was Hanse, in anger. His arms went around her, but he kept staring past her.

"Oh, Hanse!"

"We're all right," he said quietly, "we're all right. Just a minute, now, I'm watching. Um-hmm. They went straight toward that big, uh, lump, leftish, but he's galloping straight north. I'd say they're heading for their camp or whatever it is, and Quesh knows I'd be watching him, so—he's thinking to lead me astray. He'll turn their way, I think; left. I want to see him do it."

"Hanse," she said, against his chest.

He squeezed her. "A minute now, Mignue. Just let me watch . . . that . . . rotten . . . dogson. . . ."

"Hanse . . ."

"Uh. Please, Mignue—I've got to run!"

Abruptly he released her and did run, racing toward the mounded "sluff" Quesh had indicated. While Mignureal turned puzzled, to watch, looking lost, he ran as if a whole horde of demons was after him. And abruptly a flash of red streaked into her line of vision and remained in it, loping after Hanse. Tail high, Notable was following.

"Hanse," she murmured, and sniffed.

The dune *was* close, she saw; in less than a minute Hanse

was bounding up it, slipping, lurching, learning on the run to head up at an angle. Notable maintained his beeline and they reached the summit at the same time. Hanse halted there, to stare northward. Under other circumstances, she might have thought it comical or charming that Notable did the same, his tail straight up. The half minute that followed seemed fifty times that to Mignureal, feeling violated, bereft of silver and dignity and her man.

Then she saw Hanse clap his hands as if in delight. Immediately he turned back toward her, and gestured for her to come.

Oasis, she thought, and glanced around. There was only churned up sand, and the ass. She did pick up the copper bracelet Quesh had tossed to Hanse. A little bulky-heavy with forty or fifty silver coins secreted here and there among her clothes, she went to the onager. She picked up his lead-line.

"Come on, Enas," she said. "Let's go get a nice drink of water and maybe even a little grass, hmm?"

It was Enas's day—or minute—to be amenable; he followed her willingly. Hanse, she saw, had turned away to look northwestward again. Sighing, plodding, wishing he had the decency to be with her, she seemed to spend a day or so just getting to the base of the dune, then struggling up toward him. Once atop the great mound of sand (over rock? She had no idea), however, she forgot everything except what she saw below: a regular grove of trees partly surrounding but mostly at the north end of a grassy plot. It looked almost starkly green against the sand all around it. It was even closer than the Tejanit had indicated! And amid the grass, in the approximate center of the oval oasis—a veritable pool of water!

Staring, Mignureal heard none of Hanse's words, and forgot Enas. Fortunately her hand had gone loose on his lead, or she might have been dragged; the onager brayed happily and lurched down the slope toward the—the *oashiz*; the *choom*.

"—so that I was exactly right," Hanse was saying excitedly, having turned again to stare northwestward again. "They've all headed straight toward—Mignue?" He swung around. "*Mignureal!*"

"Mraowr?"

He sounds just like father, she thought, racing after the

dumb donkey. Ten paces down the slope she had the white robe off and let it flutter away behind her. Then she started opening her vest. She fell, rolled, got up laughing, let go the vest. On the run she began unlacing the blouse of green and blue and yellow and brown paisley.

Hanse cupped his hands to his mouth. "Sna-a-akes!" He yelled after her, thinking: *lunatic*!

"Who cares? Let them look!" Mignureal said, giggling. Another blouse fluttered behind her.

By the time Hanse reached the pool's edge and bent that last time, he was carrying a great bundle consisting of every article of her clothing including singlet and shift and a sort of anti-bounce holster for her breasts. In violet. He had grown a bit fat between top of dune and the pool's bank, having dropped each discarded, cloth-wrapped bundle of coins down into his tunic.

And he saw only the back of Mignureal's very wet head.

"It's that deep?"

She turned to look at him, hair wet and disheveled; she'd been washing it. She smiled and splashed water girlishly. "Oh Hanse it's wonderful! Who ever would have thought a dinky little waterhole could be so wonderful! The emperor's palace pool couldn't be a bit better!"

His glance told him that the pool was perhaps twenty feet across and perhaps thirty long. Maybe a little more. "Dinky, yes, but—damn it, Mignue, that's dangerous! You're in all the way to your chin."

"Oh. No, I'm squatting. I mean you're right there, and . . ." She broke off. She stared at him. She swallowed. The movement of her nostrils showed him that she took a deep breath. She considered, she reflected, she decided. Slowly, gazing at him, she stood.

The water was knee-deep. Hanse quit looking at her head. Swallowing hard, he dropped her clothing.

"Oh, Mignue," he said, and started dragging off his clothes.

"So *that's* what it's like! And it *did* hurt, but that *was* just for a little while! mmm!" She kissed his chest.

"Not exactly what it's like," he said. "Pretending a pile of clothes is a bed isn't exactly what I—"

"A pile of clothes with big hard lumps of silver coins in

'em!'' she said, and laughed, and kissed his shoulder. "Anyhow, I'm glad that's done!"

His voice was a yelp: *"What?!"*

"Oh! I mean I'm glad that's d—I mean, I'm glad we finally . . . uh, what I mean is now I don't have to wonder and worry about it anymore, darling. And I love it! I love youuu," she said, nuzzling.

Hanse sighed and rubbed her back, which was nearly as wet as it had been. So was he, now. He kissed her thoroughly wet hair. "I love you, Mignue. And I think I get your meaning. I hope so. Anyhow, that still isn't quite 'what it's like.' Usually."

She came up onto an elbow again and looked down into his eyes. "Oh? Tell me."

"Well, usually it's, uh, it lasts longer. See, I was just so excited that—"

"Really?" she interrupted delightedly, eyes dancing. "Longer?"

"Uh-huh. Next time."

She kissed his nose and her eyes were still all shiny. "Now?"

"Uhh . . ."

"Hanse—do I really look fat and pregnant in my clothes?"

"Sure."

"Ohh . . . you could at least be gallant!"

He chuckled. "What? Me? Shadowspawn?"

She hit him. He seized her wrist and kissed her hand.

"Hmp. We-ll . . . I—I guess I . . . I mean, it doesn't seem right for me to put m-mourning clothes back on, now, does it—after, after . . ."

"You could probably do without them." He was already dressing. "We aren't taking their advice. We napped, you know. We won't stay here tonight—we're going on over to those trees. I'll say this, though. If you'd looked anywhere near the way you look right now, those dogsons would've taken more than silver and horses! They'd have taken something a lot more valuable."

"Oh darling," she said, knowing what he meant and feeling just as loving and sentimental as he; surely more, since she was a woman. Since he was pulling on his tights, her impetuous kiss nearly knocked him down.

"All right then," she said, after a few moments of consideration. "I won't wear the reds."

"But everything else," he said. Suddenly he chuckled. "Including the money!"

They were both dressed when she realized: "We'll have to walk." It was a statement; he heard no sound of complaint in her voice, and he loved her.

"Right. One on each side of Enas, all right?"

"All—all right. You're sure you wouldn't really rather stay here tonight and walk over there tomorrow?"

"It's really what we need to do, Mignue."

"Well, if you say—need? Why do we *need* to?"

"Let's get movin', darling. I'll tell you as we walk."

"That's the first time you called me that!" And, since he was leaning out to grasp the halter of the grazing Enas, her impetuous embrace nearly knocked him down. Again.

A half hour or so later, as they paced with the onager toward the line of trees that were starting to look as if they might be green, Hanse told her what he was going to do. He did not put it that way; he called it what he had to do.

She pleaded and reasoned, wept and pleaded, railed at him and wept, pleaded some more. Then she went silent and sullen, un-understanding and unable to understand. Until she thought of a new tack and tried reasoning again. Nothing worked, and she was frightened. She could not understand. Hanse was a man, and his manhood was in question. Not to her, no. That was not the point. The point was more important than that: his still developing manhood was compromised in his own mind.

He had dared, and exerted, and narrowly missed death for that money. He had even been tortured. And he had waited for years to fetch it up out of the well. Now those dogsons who couldn't even speak straight sentences or properly pronounce s's had it, simply because they had crossbows.

Worse, they had taken horses from people on the desert. Shadowspawn was a thief, with professional pride. No decent thief would do such a thing; no professional.

"But we still have over half of it, Hanse! It's still more wealth than either of us has ever had!"

"That's not the point. They stole horses. I've got to try."

"Hanse, they may *killll* you!" she wailed, and went off into sobbing again.

They paced on, one on either side of Enas, talking over him. They walked not toward the area indicated by Quesh or in the direction he had ridden. No. They were headed in the direction Hanse was sure all four Tejana had ultimately taken. Toward the treeline, toward what he was sure had to be their nice comfortable encampment among the trees.

"No, they won't. They won't kill me, Mignue, and none of them will need to die, either. I'll wait until dark. And past dark, Mignue. They'll never see me or hear me—until I'm ready."

"Then they'll killll you!"

"Would you stop saying that? Besides, Notable will go with me. Notable, you going with me?"

Notable was snoozing atop the onager's pack. Notable's tail twitched and one eye almost moved.

"See? See? Even that cat knows you're crazy, Hanse! *Don't Do It!*"

"Don't . . . call . . . me . . . crazy, wo-mannn."

"I didn't mean it. This is a crazy thing to do-o!" And she was sobbing again, or still.

"Oh Mignue, Mignue—please stop. I have to. You have to let a man do what he has to do, and I have to do this."

Her voice came back as a declamation, with heat: "S'danzo women don't let their men go and get killed for no good reason!"

"Whoa!" Hanse told the onager, twitching its halter.

Enas was happy to stop. He glanced back, as if wishing he had taken just another bite or two of that nice grass back in the oasis. Hanse stepped in front of him, his hands on the animal's head and halter, so that he could face Mignureal.

"Listen," he said in a quiet voice that made her listen, and from a face set so that she was reminded why so many feared him: Shadowspawn. "Listen. I am sorry that I have to say this now, of all times, after . . ."

He stopped and took breath for a new start. "First, my chosen S'danzo woman, I am no S'danzo man. I am of the Ilsigi, the people of Ils of the Thousand Eyes. I do what I do—

what I must do. No one else can decide for Hanse what Hanse must do. When I decide, Mignureal, don't tell me it's for no good reason. It's good reason to me, and that's enough. I love you, and I want you with me. You just have to stop making fun of me and my gods."

Her eyes, the color of mahogany, were huge and piteous, and the dark that rimmed them now was not all from kohl. "Hanse—oh Hanse, I'm not making fun of you. I would never make fun of you. I love you."

His eyes and his face changed until he looked as much in pain as she. "I don't intend to 'go and get killed,' as you said. I intend to go and get back my money and my horses and my self-respect. If none of that is *good reason* to you, I'm really sorry. I'm really sorry, and O gods of my fathers this is the wrong time, but—but you made a mistake in coming with me and I apologize for pulling you along."

She looked down for a long minute. When she met his eyes again, hers were clear. She spoke very clearly and slowly, in a language he could not understand. The tone of it, the cadence made him think that it was not only in the words of her people, but that what she was saying was some ritual that came from their long history. Others had spoken these words, he felt. Declaimed these words, perhaps.

He waited, gazing at her. As he had expected, she spoke now in his tongue, that which her parents had made hers. He was sure she was repeating what she had just said in that other language, the tongue none knew save the S'danzo.

"I am S'danzo. Thou art my man. I am thy woman. A woman must do what a woman does. A—a man m-must do what a-a man must do."

Hanse nodded, and swallowed. "That's what you just said, in the language of your fathers?"

She nodded. "And mothers," she added.

He reached out to squeeze her hand. "I hear you. I love you, woman."

He held her hand tightly, to prevent her moving forward, to him. She understood. They looked long at each other, and then he let go her hand and moved around to make a clucking noise to the onager.

THE FOREST

GRADUALLY THE DESERT was supplanted by ground less and less sandy, and then with scrubby junkgrass that was not too slow about becoming the real thing. Farther in, northward, they could see bushes with an occasional tree. Beyond that a forest rose, visible even in brightly moonlit darkness. They had no idea of its depth, but had already seen that it ran long, forming a northern border for the desert. Enas became a little difficult and needed a sterner hand on the halter: he wanted to taste some of this nice grass.

"Soon, Enas, damn it," Hanse said. "Now stop trying to jerk your head away or we'll put Notable in charge of guiding you."

For a time they saw no sign of human life. Then they came upon the road Hanse had been sure was there.

"Now that we're sure where it is, let's move away from the road. We'd be better off over nearer the trees." He continued the sentence mentally: *Just in case.*

She regarded the dark forest with apprehension. "Think there may be animals in there—wild animals, I mean?"

"I doubt it. I'm thinking about people on the road, not animals in the woods. This is the very edge of the forest. Meat-eaters follow grazing animals, and this thin strip of grass isn't exactly a savannah to attract them! Notice that Enas isn't the least bit nervous. Doesn't seem to smell a thing he doesn't like, either."

"That sounds good," Mignureal said doubtfully. "Uh . . . aren't elephants grass-eaters?"

Hanse snorted. "Aye. But we won't find any of *those* here! They need a lot more grazing space than there is at the very edge of a desert. We could boost you up into a tree, if that would make you feel better."

"I'm nervous about Enas, Hanse, not me! If something got him, we'd be without animals, and we can't carry all he's carrying. Not and make any sort of time, anyhow."

"We'll have animals," Hanse said darkly.

Resigned to his intended excursion, she said nothing.

"Here look, Mignue—these bushes shield the forest from the road. Why not stay right here, and not go into the woods. It is mighty dark in there, isn't it."

They stopped, attached a long line to one of Enas's hind ankles, and let him start cropping his sweetgrass dinner while they unburdened him. Hanse began opening one of the packs while Mignureal moved among the bushes, into an open area not quite surrounded by them.

"Hanse! Berries! Real berries! Oh Hanse—real *berries!* We really *are* out of the desert!"

Still stuck in the father role that was totally unfamiliar and ill suited him besides, he warned her about eating strange berries. At about the same time she said "Ow!" and Hanse felt that sudden emptiness of stomach that heralded what he called concern and some called fear.

She put it to rest: "It's all right—they're blackberries! I've never seen them except in baskets in the marketplace—I never knew blackberry bushes had thorns."

"Thorns," he said, occupied with what he was doing.

"Well . . . stickers. Ow! Oh it doesn't matter—they're so *good!*" Her voice came closer. "Here, Hanse, have some b—oh!"

She had not known he was stripping and re-dressing. The thief called Shadowspawn had donned his working clothes.

A rangy-lean, youthful man of average height, he seemed taller in his working blacks. Tunic and leggings of unrelieved black joined his dark complexion in abetting his speed and skill at melting into shadows and seeming to vanish. Some naturally thought sorcery might well be involved. Shadowspawn knew better; he was that good. He had not given himself that sobriquet. Someone years back had mentioned that he disappeared as easily into the shadows and emerged as if they had spawned him, and a companion sneer-snarled "Shadowspawn!" and the name was born.

"Thanks, Mignue. Umm. Good!"

She sighed, chewed her lip, and re-accepted what he had convinced her was the inevitable. "Will you want some of my kohl, maybe, to darken your face?"

"I was born dark. No one sees me in the dark unless I smile. I won't be smiling."

She nodded, looking at him in not quite but nearly total darkness, with the moon back over there somewhere above the forest. He was dark-skinned, and the desert had darkened his face and hands still more. His mop of hair was blacker than black itself. Tending to an indecisive curl, it covered his ears without being so long as to touch his shoulders. Deep-set eyes like black onyxes were ambushed under glossy black brows, which just missed meeting above the strong thrust of a nose that was almost but not quite falcate.

Mignureal could see four knives and knew he wore more. Curved dagger on left hip and the long Ilbarsi slicer on his right; the slim flat throwing knives sheathed on his right upper arm and wrist. She knew she had another in a sheath built into one of his buskins, its non-business end imitating a decoration. He carried a few of those nasty six-pointed stars, too, for throwing.

"Am I going with you or do I have to follow?"

"Mignue—damn it, stay here! I'm at home in the dark, you know that. I also know how to be silent, and these boots are made for that. Look at you, in all those skirts! What kind of real running can you do—*or* sneaking?"

Without comment Mignureal began peeling skirts.

Hanse took a step and took both her shoulders in his hands. "Mignue: think, will you. I will be much safer without you."

She looked stricken, but not at any supposed insult; like it or not, she had just heard undeniable truth and knew it.

"It—it's just that I'll be so worried, darling; so scared for you!"

"Can't think of anything to suggest I take along, hmmm?"

She shook her head. "No, I . . . oh, you're thinking about the Sight, aren't you; about my Seeing for you. No, nothing. Maybe that meant there's no danger aft—*Hanse: ride Enas and follow Notable. You will need Enas, Hanse.*"

He peered at her in the dimness that was almost total darkness here at the edge of the trees.

"What? Follow Notable? What makes you think Notable— Mignue?"

"Hmmm?"

"What makes you think Notable knows where to go?"

She put her head on one side. "What makes me think Notable knows—what? What are you talking about?"

"Mignue, stop! You just said—oh. It's Happened."

An all too familiar chill flowed up Hanse's back and he felt the movement of the hairs on his arms. Yet this time he welcomed the feeling, as he welcomed her words. It had just happened again. Had he been able to see her eyes, he'd have known at once. He had witnessed that eerie unfocused blankness suddenly enter them before, for she had just Seen for him. He told her, and of course Mignureal was surprised.

Both of them supposed that a watch-cat might possess more than one doggish trait, and could possibly be a tracker as well. Any cat of any size was born to track and pull down prey, of course; they all had the muscle, the agility, the claws and teeth for it. Too, Notable showed an odd affinity for the bigger animals. On the other hand, neither Mignureal nor her man could imagine how the onager could be of value, other than getting Hanse there faster and without effort. Wherever "there" was. It wasn't as if Enas was about to play war-horse and charge and trample!—or back up to a Tejanit or two and deliver one of those prodigious kicks for which onagers were justifiably infamous.

While they discussed it they were turning Enas's lead-line into a rein. They added a blanket and the padding that had been under the packs, which smelled foul. Shadowspawn wanted both on anyhow, blanket on top. He set a foot against the onager's side while he tightened the strap.

Enas was not happy about being bestridden. He even had a try at bucking, briefly, but responded to Hanse's firm hand and little tug on the rein. Hanse looked at Notable. Notable sat watching Hanse. Notable yawned. With an exasperated frown, Hanse glanced at Mignureal. She shrugged. She had no knowledge of having said a thing about the cat, much less an explanation for her words.

"So much for a tracking cat," he said. Then he added, "Later." They had said more than enough already about his mission—too much.

He made a clicking sound in his mouth while moving his heels against the animal's sides. Enas set off, west along the edge of the trees. Hanse was careful not to look back. He could feel Mignureal's gaze on his back.

A few minutes later he glanced down to see the big red cat pacing along beside the ass.

"Notable? You want to ride?" Hanse patted his black-clad thigh.

A moment later he set his teeth against an outcry while he groaned; yes, Notable wanted to ride, but nearly missed his mark on the moving onager and had to put his claws into Hanse's leg when he landed there. It was all Hanse could do not to hit him.

"Ow. Damn! Those scratches will be itching for hours! Here—wouldn't you rather ride behind me?"

No; Notable got himself situated there in front of him and snuggled up to the warmth of Hanse's loins for a snooze.

"Dam' cat. Remember how we took an instant dislike to each other, back in the keg-room of Sly's Place?"

Notable's tail twitched in acknowledgment. His eyes remained closed. Shadowspawn sighed, and tried urging the onager to a slightly more speedy pace. And scratched at his thigh.

A little over an hour later, a very *dull* hour later, Notable aroused. Rising to balance precariously while he arched his back high, he looked around. Hanse gave him a caressive pat; the cat arched to his hand. Then he pounced to the ground. Hanse reined in, watching Notable keep his tail busy while he looked this way and that. He looked up, made one of his un-meow sounds, and paced into the trees.

"Big help," Hanse muttered. "All he can think about is having a stretch and taking a leak in the woods."

He was about to move on when Notable reappeared to stare at him. Blinking, Hanse stared back. He watched the cat's tail shoot straight up behind him, watched Notable turn, glance back, and reenter the woods.

"I feel like a real dumb-ass, Enas, but—let's follow him."

Branches took their toll on the man whose mount hadn't enough sense not to pass under low ones—or was malicious enough to do so purposefully—and soon Shadowspawn dismounted. Both he and Enas were inexpressibly happier for that. Now Hanse had to deal only with bushes and those trees against which Enas seemed bent on nudging him. They followed Notable.

Hanse heard voices and then the whicker of a horse well before they were there: Notable had led him unerringly to the Tejana encampment.

The only sounds in the woods were those of insects and the occasional faint rustle of a serpent on the hunt. Now and then the insects of a particular area stilled their noise while a silent shadow passed, and soon resumed their discussions of territory and sexuality. The silently prowling shadow in the dark of the woods paused to squat and peer again into the Tejana camp, which was nicely lit by their cookfire. Since the last time the silent shadow had looked from among the trees, Twel had gone limp. He still sat-lay there near the fire where he had been, but now his chin was on his chest. He was no longer interested in his cup.

Good, the shadow and spawn of the shadows thought. *Drank himself to sleep. And from the way he was slurring before, he won't wake before dawn. Lucky Twel—and lucky me! Too bad the other three aren't also complaining of headaches and drinkin' themselves into sleep!*

He heard the faintest sound and froze, fist tight around the dagger hilt, until he felt the barely perceptible bump and knew it was Notable. Another shadow, silently moving in the forest. He wasn't at all red in the dark.

After tethering Enas loosely to the sapling so the dumb donkey would believe himself unable to go anywhere, man and cat had crept almost halfway around the clearing that was the Tejana camp. A single one of those quiet huh-huh-huh sounds called whickers had told him where the horses were, and he knew he was close, now. These wife-deserting, nomadic thieves had the silver with them, naturally. He had heard it clink, heard them talk and laugh about it—and him, while he seethed, listening. He'd seen its flash, too, while Shink gloatingly told off coins, practically drooling. The saddlebag was nowhere visible. Perhaps they had discarded it; it was sadly cracked from years in the well followed by the thorough dryness of the desert.

He had had time to think and think sensibly while he spent many minutes ghosting through the forest. His experience at fighting alone against four men simultaneously was inexistent. His confidence in the outcome of such an encounter was far from high. Accordingly he had made a major decision: barring an unforeseen fabulous opportunity, he would hit the horses and let these swine keep the money. As Mignue had said, he and she still had plenty. And horses were money, too, anywhere.

He wanted the horses. He wanted *saddled* horses. As for the others, he wanted them running. Let the Tejana walk. At least they weren't stuck out on the sun-roasted sand!

Eyes narrowed, the noiseless shadow remained absolutely still while his night-black eyes searched the camp for the others. Ah—yes, Twel must be asleep, all right: there were Aksar and Quesh, over there in the shadows well away from the fire, very close together indeed. And murmuring.

So that's the way of it, he thought, but stopped even the impulse to give his head a shake.

When he was on the hunt, on the steal, Shadowspawn had learned to turn impulses into something else. He controlled them, rather than the normal reverse. Cudget had taught him that, calling them out-pulses. It had cost his student plenty of bruises—even after the student was better at it than the master.

So that's the way of it! That's why Tejana can remain away from their women so long and seem to love it—they do. They love each other.

Well, that should keep those two busy for a while, too. Good!

The trouble was that he no longer saw Shink. He had heard Quesh bid Shink go and check the horses after the little sound one of them made; heard Shink's objection and the subsequent argument. *One of the horses probably got a whiff of Enas,* Shadowspawn had thought, moving a little more swiftly around the camp's perimeter while they noisily argued.

So was Shink with the horses now?

Quesh and Aksar have their substitute in each other and Twel in his cups. Shink?—maybe Shink's substitute is the horses!

He repressed the impulse to smile at the thought: Poor horses!

Silent, a moving shadow among darkness and shadows, Shadowspawn moved to the horses.

When he came to the trimmed sapling that formed a horizontal pole well above the ground, he realized that this was a camp the Tejana used often; consistently, if not constantly. They had troubled to construct a nice enclosure for their mounts. He heard one move then, and saw the equine bulk a few feet away, on the other side of the pole. Shadowspawn moved along the pole to the upright he knew would be there. He nodded and moved on along, hopes high.

That thought was rewarded: he found the saddles and reins. With a tight smile, he went under the pole into the enclosure. Straightening, he took down a rein and made a quiet *chk-chk* noise in his cheek.

It was a good thought and brazen, and yet he was amazed when a horse ambled over.

Hanse rubbed him, received his nuzzling, and petted him. The horse wore a halter. Soon he also wore a rein, and then a saddle. Smiling, the moving shadow bridled and saddled another. And a third. The horses moved about, not at all alarmed. Notable had not entered the enclosure, bless him. Yet surely these animals would not be afraid of a mere cat, anyhow, despite his unusual size.

Let's just keep this nice and quiet, Hanse thought. *I have no proof that ten or twenty more Tejana aren't camped a mile away or on their way here to join these swine!*

Hanse bridled a fourth horse, recognized Blackie by his blaze, and murmured sweet nothings in a big hairy ear. Blackie seemed just delighted to be led over to the saddles; why should Hanse carry them to their destinations when the animals were so amenable? This was proving as easy as picking blackberries. And without the stickers, too! He reached for another heavy cradle of leather over wood.

The down-rushing sword missed his fingers by an inch. With a noise several times too loud in silent darkness, the blade chopped two-thirds of the way through the saddle. Teeth flashed behind the chop, in the mouth of a delighted Tejanit. Hanse's hand raced while Blackie's rein made a whispery sound as it dropped to the ground.

"That you, Shink?" Hanse whispered. His left arm was completely across the front of his body, thumb against his right upper arm.

"Aye," Shink said, still showing teeth in a grin as he waggled his sword free and yanked it back and up for another blow. "And I knowing you too, boy! Once you were being dog meat, gueshing who goes to sholace yer pregnant sow of a wife!"

"Not you, Shink," Shadowspawn said through clenched teeth, and whipped his left arm back to the left with all his strength and speed.

At just the right point in that arc he opened his fingers. The slender leaf-shape of the blade drove several inches into Shink's upper chest. Since the sword was already rushing down, Hanse also hit the ground and rolled, incidentally but expertly kicking the side of Shink's knee, hard enough to hurt the kicker through his soft boots. The knee buckled on the instant.

Unfortunately it was terribly dark and Hanse was almost an inch low of his intended target. The knife half-vanished into the hollow between Shink's collarbones but did not prevent his letting go a distressingly loud cry. Mignureal probably heard that one, even from a league or more away.

At the same time, however, Notable shrieked an absolutely hideous yowl that surely must have been what some called a caterwaul; and from the far side of the clearing and camp, Enas set in braying. He kept it up, too, at the very top of his volume. That corpse–raising monster Ischade back in Sanctuary would have loved it; the dumb donkey's braying was loud enough to waken the dead for miles around.

That was more than Shink did. Shink yelled only once. Then he fell down and kicked while he died.

Enas kept right on eee-awwwing. A sudden thought brought a grim grin to Hanse's lips even while he retrieved his throwing knife and wiped it on Shink's tunic.

"Sorry, Notable," he murmured, and deliberately pricked his feline ally.

Notable at once obliged by screeching out another of his astonishingly throatily deep-voiced, astoundingly loud wails. Hanse whirled and commenced bridling and saddling nervous horses, the while murmuring soothing words in a quiet monotone.

"You were right, Mignue," he mused aloud. "Enas did his part. Wherever those two are running—or three, if Twel woke up, headache worse than ever now—it can't be in this direction! They must think they're surrounded by demons, and surely one already got Shink! Poo-oor Shink!"

When he tried to saddle another horse, he found no saddle available for the meek animal.

Oh, Packhorse, he thought, and ran across the enclosure to kick down a pole. Now all he had to do was herd or lead all seven horses out of here!

He was charging back to get himself into a saddle, any saddle, when he saw the two men. Damned if the damned fools hadn't gone and run in the direction opposite the onager's noise! Straight toward Shink's death-scream and Notable's caterwauling!

They weren't supposed to do that, Hanse thought, if he thought at all, and slammed a knife at Quesh, and missed, and lost the knife into the dark woods beyond the oncoming Tejanit with the great big sword.

For some reason, Hanse yanked out the Ilbarsi knife, almost sword-long, rather than another knife or throwing star.

What am I do-ing, he thought, insofar as he thought at all, and half crouched to parry Quesh's streaking cut at him with a loud skirling clash of steel blades. As if instinctively he sort of danced to one side, at the same time half swinging as if he'd been doing this all his life. He surprised himself still more by chopping into the other man's upper leg.

At the same instant another horripilatingly dreadful noise

tore the air wide open. Poor Aksar's scream came soon after, as a few too many pounds of ferocious cat hurtled through the air to impact his chest with all four paws and about eighty claws. From there it climbed swiftly and, even while twitching one hind leg impatiently against the fabric that entrapped one claw, began hungrily chewing away at Aksar's chin. A howling Aksar let go his sword to flail at the cat. He also turned and started running. Notable remained where he was, chewing and disproving every savant who said that "domestic" cats could not growl. He did not let go until Aksar ran into one of the horizontal poles and doubled almost all the way over it with a great outgushing of breath.

Notable dropped free, regathered himself, and pounced onto the man's back. Relentlessly he gave the breathless Tejanit something else to think about.

"Sorry Quesh," Shadowspawn said to the man writhing on the ground. "Believe it or not, I never meant to hurt you. When you buy a wooden leg and new horse with my silver, you can decide whether stealing from Shadowspawn was worth it.

"Notable! Come on, let's get somewhere else, fast. We have no guarantee that four is all the Tejana there are!"

Still nervous about all the noise, the horses were milling aimlessly. Hanse made sure that the one he mounted was Quesh's gray. Quesh was the Tejana leader, and the other horses might be inclined to follow his. Horses tended to do that, anyhow. Like aimlessly milling and thought-free electorates, they were always anxious to find someone who would tell them just what to do while pretending he knew where he was taking them.

He jiggled, kicked his heels, clicked, and whistled. The gray showed no particular inclination to head for the hole his rider had made in the enclosure. Then Hanse remembered the last word he had heard from Quesh, out on the desert.

"*Haiya!*" he called.

Only the saddle's high cantle saved him from going right off the horse backward when the wiry animal dug in its haunches and bolted ahead. It charged toward the opening Hanse had made in the enclosure as if launched from a ballista or stung simultaneously on the hindquarters by a dozen hornets. Hanse hung on.

The horse bucketed out of the enclosure and onto a trail there. It wound, but Hanse was too busy hanging on just then to give thought to the cleverness of Tejana planning; from its other end, a trail that wound among the trees would not reveal anything about its destination. Hanse was sure that he could hear hooves pounding along behind him but dared not look around. He was completely occupied with the business of hanging on. He hoped with sincerity that Notable wasn't aground, or at least not in proximity to those twenty-four stomping hooves.

Moving fast, the gray emerged from the trees onto the grassy area that lay between the junkgrass strip and the desert. Strong exertion on the part of Shadowspawn persuaded the animal to turn left, eastward.

"You could slow down now, horse, damn it!"

The gray didn't know those words and apparently had an iron mouth and will to match. It kept right on challenging the wind. Making sure he had a good grip on reins and the saddle's pommel, Hanse turned partway around. He smiled. The other horses were following! Saddled, bridled, manes and tails streaming in their own wind, they galumphed along as if in chase.

He didn't see the man over at the treeline to his left, but certainly heard the fellow bawl out something in the Tejana tongue. It must have been another command, because instantly the gray swerved that way, bearing Hanse at speed toward the kneeling man just at the edge of the trees. Twel was leveling his crossbow and sighting along the bolt as if he had all the time in the world. Apparently the shock of all the noise had not only awakened the fourth Tejanit, but sobered him as well.

Hanse dragged at the reins while trying to make himself small atop the horse bearing him speedily toward disaster. "Right, damn it, turn right! Come on, horse! He can't miss!"

That was true. Twel could not miss. Hanse was dead. Except that it was then he discovered the true reason why Enas was necessary to this mission and its survival, and the survival of Shadowspawn. The onager broke from the trees and bushes in a blind charge that took him right over the top of Twel. Enas seemed not to notice and certainly didn't curb his braying. Twel's cry was lost amid that far louder noise.

The crossbow discharged. Hanse heard the keening *whissssh* of the quarrel and gritted his teeth. He neither saw the bolt nor felt it; it had gone wild as Twel was pounded down. At that moment the gray horse under Hanse elected to pay attention to his rider's sawing on the rightward rein. He turned away from the forest again and streaked eastward.

"Enas! Good old Enas! Attaboy Dumb-ass! This way!" Hanse glanced back. "Be careful you don't get run over by my herd of horses!"

Enas came on the run, ears back and tail flowing. So came the other six horses. So did Notable. The cat's speed was incredible. Near Enas well to Hanse's left, he bounded in long crouch-and-launch leaps that resembled nothing more than a jungle cat of prey. He essayed a long leap onto the back of a grass-eater, too, but not as predator.

Enas sucked in a loud indrawn whistle and blasted that breath out in a louder *hawwww*, when Notable landed on his back.

Notable didn't make a sound; he was too busy crouching to hang on. Hanse could only hope that what he was hanging onto were the blanket and the pad on the onager's back, not Enas himself.

It occurred to Shadowspawn that he could probably stroll right into the Tejana camp and collect his stolen property and who knew what else, now. Of course that might not be wise; Twel might be capable of winding up for another shot, and Aksar might already have done so. Too, all the silver might well be on the person of Quesh. Chances were excellent that he would not fancy handing it over, and Hanse could not see himself killing the wounded man for it.

Of course right now all of this thinking was pissin' against the wind, as the saying had it back in the Maze that had been his home.

The triumphant Shadowspawn had succeeded in gaining some control of the direction of his mount's movement, but not of its velocity. Nor did dear old Iron-mouth seem to have any intention of stopping this side of the edge of the world. Several minutes passed, and the Tejana horse continued to ignore strong tugs on the reins.

"I wish I'd heard the Tejana word for stop or slow down," Hanse muttered, worse than exasperated. "If this idiot just gallops until he tires, Mignue may be a hundred miles back! I guess I don't dare say 'mip,' and surely it's nothing so simple as 'whoa!'"

The gray dug in all four hooves. That arrested his momentum very effectively and almost instantly; the horse literally skidded to a stop. Nothing arrested his rider's momentum until he hit the ground six or so feet in front of the skidding animal.

"Hanse? Hanse? Is that you, darling? *Hanse!*"

Hanse writhed, turned partway over, and looked up at a big equine chest, gray. "Nice stop," he muttered. "Now mip, damn it. Mignue? I—I'm all right, I think. I, ah, did some horse-trading." He sat up, groaned as a vertebra or two reluctantly went back where vertebrae belonged, and blew out his breath. Then: "Mignue? What're you doing way down here? Blast it woman—did you follow me after all?"

She came hurrying toward him, out into the wan moonlight from the clump of blackberry bushes. "I did not! This is exactly where you left me, just hours ago! I've been worried just sick, too. I *wanted* to follow, believe me! You—oh! *Look* at all the *hor*ses!"

The other animals were just arriving. Six horses and an onager. Wearing a cat on his back.

Hanse thought about that, and what Mignureal had just said.

"Mignue, we have just traded our silver for several horses, and that includes one faster than a streetgirl's pick-up back in the Maze!"

Enas the onager was a hero. Enas would merely accompany them now, bearing no weight. Hanse arranged their packs on the broader back of a Tejana horse. Meanwhile, as Mignureal delightedly supervised the giving of a bowl of beer to the heroic Notable, Hanse did some thinking.

He was at once proud of what he had accomplished and nervous about what he had done. He was even more nervous about the possibility of the discovery of those deeds by other Tejana. The main group or tribe or whatever it was, for instance.

Suppose they found the raided camp, found one Tejanit dead

and three damaged, and all the horses gone; stolen by a
foreigner or unbeliever or whatever they might term anyone
un-Tejanish. A body of them might be hearing out a painfully
gasping Quesh right now, ready to track the horses east, swords
ready in strong sun-darkened hands. . . .

Still quivery with adrenaline and full of the elation of
triumph besides, Hanse felt no weariness. If Mignureal did,
she did not mention it when he told her they had better move,
right now.

"Where?"

Along the road that led through the forest, he told her, busy
linking horses with long lead-lines formed by straightening
their bridles. To hell with Blackie. Hanse would ride the faster
than fast gray. He knew how to make him go; the horse
responded to rein-signals for directional guidance; and now
Hanse had proven he could make the beast stop, too.

Mignureal found their saddlebag. It was hanging from one
of the beaded Tejana saddles. In the dark and his haste, Hanse
had not even noticed.

"Hanse! It moved!"

"Get away from it!" he snapped, hurrying to her with the
Ilbarsi blade in his hand. Then he saw that it was securely
closed. He took up a ready stance. "All right—take it off the
saddle and throw it on the ground. Then stand away, Mignue.
I'm going to put this blade through it!"

She detached the cracked old bag from the saddle of a wiry
brown horse. She also hung onto it until she persuaded Hanse
to let her open it, with great care, while he stood ready.
Reluctantly and with misgivings, he gave in. Then he saw it
move.

"Sorcery," he muttered, as forlornly as darkly. Hopefully he
added, "Or maybe only a deadly serpent." He stood ready,
long blade poised. "Mignue! Be careful. Stand a little to the
left. There. All right. Slowly, now . . ."

As Mignureal opened the bag it distinctly said "mew," in a
tiny voice. Then the flap was back and Mignureal was
laughing.

"Oh Hanse look! No sorcery—just a darling 'draggled little
kitty." As she spoke she drew it forth: a truly bedraggled,
homely, scrawny she-cat whose coat contained no fewer than

six colors and hues. "A S'danzo kitty!" Mignureal laughed in true merriment, holding the little cat up in both hands and nuzzling it with her cheek.

An embarrassed black-clad hero sheathed his weapon. He raised his eyebrows when he noticed Notable. The red cat stood at Mignureal's feet, gazing fascinatedly up at her find. His tail wasn't lashing; it was drawing lazy pictures in the air.

Shaking his head in incomprehension, Hanse bent to pick up the bag and sling it into the blackberry bushes. He arrested the movement when he heard the clink of silver against silver. Eagerly he peered within.

"Hmp. Hardly a fair trade! The Tejana made off with fifty or eighty pieces of silver and left us that pitiful excuse for a cat and eleven coins."

"It's better than none at all—and we have our horses and theirs too, my hero! But oh Hanse, don't talk bad about her; you know kitties are sensitive!"

"Cats?" He stared at her. "Sensitive?"

"Mraowrr."

"Oh. Right. True, Notable old friend, but you're different. That's just a mangy-looking little beastie with a rumply coat."

"Hanse!" Mignureal said in an accusing tone. "They just haven't fed her decently! You'll see how she fills out when we've fed her and—"

"Oh, Ils's beard, no! You mean to adopt that mangy beast? Mignue . . . we're starting to resemble a troupe of traveling performers!"

She looked at him, her eyes all wide and innocent. "Well, I don't agree, but even if it's true, what's wrong with that? We can't just *leave* her, Hanse. She'll—she'll *die*! All alone, with that forest full of who knows what beasts and monsters!"

Hanse looked into the darkness of the woods. "Will you stop that? We're about to ride into that forest! Come to think, we'd better be about it, too. Mignue: onto your horse. All right all right, I'll hold it. Just get into that saddle!"

"Her." She set the cat on the ground and stepped into Hanse's hands. "Her, darling. Not it."

"Stop calling me darling when you're correcting me and talking me into something I don't want to do. There. Now what do we do with it—her, her! Put 'er back in the saddlebag?"

"I can carry her while I ride . . ."

"No."

Mignureal caught the tone of that. Besides, she had already realized that her proposal was not a good idea. "Yes. Back into that nasty old bag, then, and hand it here. I'll keep it right here in front of me."

Hanse transferred four coins from the saddlebag into his own belt-pouch. He handed Mignureal four others: "Here, slip these into your bosom."

Her voice was plaintive: "I'm full of coins there already, Hanse!"

Staring darkly, he continued to proffer the four silver pieces. Mignureal sighed and stowed them away in her treasure chest. Hanse turned to the packhorse and slipped the remaining three into the first of their packs that came to hand. Battening it, he pushed the sorry excuse for a calico cat into the leathern bag. It emitted a tiny-voiced kitten-sound as he handed it up to Mignureal.

There's something odd about those eleven coins, Hanse was thinking even as he dragged himself up into the saddle of the big gray.

"All right, horse, let's go." He loosened and jiggled the reins at the same time as he twitched his heels into the beast's lean sides.

Old Iron-mouth did not move.

Oh, damn it. If I say 'Haiya' we go off like an arrow from a bow. How do I persuade this motherless son to go at a walk?

Tail high, Notable paced around to face the gray horse. Looking quite small now in contrast, the red cat stared. The horse looked down. He tugged at the rein. Swallowing nervously, Hanse eased his grip. The gray lowered its head. He and Notable stared at each other, then touched noses. The horse lifted its head. Notable paced leisurely around, looked up at Hanse, and crouched.

Oh, no. "Notable, no, don't do th—"

The moment Notable had pounced up behind Hanse, *their* mount moved forward at a sedate walk, heading for the road leading into the forest.

There's something odd about that cat, Hanse thought, even as he glanced back to be sure that Mignureal and the longish coffle of horses were following. They were following. The cavalcade paced into the woods.

As they rode among the trees Shadowspawn strove to remain alert and wary and succeeded only in being weary. Sunset was hours in the past. Midnight had come and gone. He'd had a full day and a fuller night. It had caught up to him now, even while he wanted to be on the alert for more Tejana or whatever animals the inky forest might harbor. Excitement and adrenaline had worn off, to leave him drooping.

At the same time, it was hard to set his mind to anything besides the genuine strangeness of the old saddlebag and its new contents. A diminutive, pitiful looking cat and eleven coins! A small calico cat and eleven pieces of silver.

How?

Why?

Was there something strange about the coins, stamped with the head of the Emperor of Ranke?

For the matter of that, even in his haste how could he have overlooked the bag swinging from the saddle he had picked up, carried, thrown over a horse, and cinched in place?

Obviously it was inexplicable and so not worth thinking about. And so of course both he and Mignureal thought about little else. They rode in silence along a wide path of a "road" that barely accommodated two horses abreast, with any comfort. They other animals strung out behind them.

More hours passed and they heard nothing untoward. Nor did they see anything at all except trees and bushes and shadows, all gray or black. It was not in Hanse's nature, but at last he was compelled to say it:

"Mignue . . . I can't ride anymore. I've heard of sleeping in the saddle, and it sounds good. But I keep jerking awake just as I'm starting to fall off this horse! We'd better stop for some rest and assume the horses will wake us if—if we need to wake."

"We just passed that clear area on the right," she said, thinking that he must have been drowsing and had missed it. "Just a few paces back. Let's call that home for the rest of the night." *And day,* she added mentally.

They did. Somehow Hanse dragged himself around the semicircular clearing, staying awake to do what had to be done. They removed their packs from that horse and made sure he and the others were tethered but had some freedom of movement. When that was done, Mignureal asked him if he wanted something to eat. Receiving no answer, she turned to see what was the matter. She did not have to examine him at any length to discover that he was asleep.

She smiled down at him, putting her head on one side as she gazed at the sprawled Shadowspawn, still in his working clothes. She wanted to do something for him, but knew he needed no cover. At last she lay down beside him in her clothing, on the grass.

With a hand touching him, she lay staring up at a sky growing less dark. She fell asleep that way.

Mignureal awoke before he did. For a few moments she lay appreciating the way the sun pierced the foilage in ways that formed interesting patterns, while the latticework of branches created more nice shapes against the sky. She sat up with care for quiet, thinking that the heroic Shadowspawn needed his sleep after last night's accomplishments. She was in time to see Notable come pacing out of the forest. He stopped to stare at the small calico cat. She was nosing about, exploring only the immediate area, while Notable must have been roaming the woods. Stalking birds, most likely, and likely without success.

Abruptly she went motionless, one paw still upraised, and turned her head to return the bigger cat's stare.

Fearing trouble and noise to disturb Hanse, Mignureal rose as silently as she could and went to them. She noted that the horses had been breakfasting for quite a while; the grass around them was well cropped and a number of branches were missing a number of leaves. Inja whickered. Mignureal petted a soft equine nose in passing, and picked up the colorful cat. Stroking the little animal, she entered the woods until she had a large tree between her and the makeshift camp. There she transacted the important business of nature. She left the calico cat still scratching industriously at the soft mossy earth it was delighted to find.

Mignureal returned to find Hanse yawning and just starting to sit up. She hurried to kneel beside him for a hug.

"One of us is famished," he said, yawning again.

"Two of us are," she chuckled, and added, "likely more than that, too. We have a whole herd of animals, remember."

"A zoo," he groaned. He looked around. "Where's the S'danzo kitty?"

That brought another chuckle from her. "In the woods scratching, after a certain morning business."

"Good idea," Hanse said, and rose, stretching lithely as he entered the forest on the same errand.

He returned to no feast; more bread and dates and cold dried fish, too salty from its curing. Well, it was food. Quality and quantity of food had never been a great need or interest of his, so long as he ate. Merely that had been a problem for too many years—and several times since. Nevertheless he was looking forward to juicy greasy meat and some warm bread, some onions and garlic and something sweet, once they reached . . . somewhere.

He was studying the new cat. What a tiny, delicate head she had! He watched her gnaw and tear off another morsel of the saltwater-cured fish, shake her head at the saltiness, but go right ahead and eat anyhow. Hanse understood. Real hunger was not a partner of fastidiousness; an empty belly was not choosy.

Hearing the clink of coins, he turned to see what Mignue was doing. He met the gaze of a Mignureal whose eyes were very large. She held the saddlebag.

"I don't believe it! How did you do this, Hanse? I thought you were so tired—and despite all the tales I heard I really never knew Shadowspawn was *this* good."

He cocked his head. "What? Do what?"

"Oh stop." She shook the bag. It jingle-clinked. "Are these eleven other coins or did you really get the ones I put in my—" She broke off to dip a hand into her bosom. "You did! They're gone!"

Hanse stared at her. "Now you stop. I have done nothing but sleep and when I woke you were already up. When I put my hands there you'll know it, believe me!" It was his turn to check. "Damn! You took the four I had hidden in here— Mignue! You may be a thief yet!"

His smile faded into smoke when he saw how she was staring. Call it glaring.

Both of them insisted, and their denials and insistences progressed or regressed to border on argumentation. Each remained adamant; neither Hanse nor Mignureal had jokingly "robbed" the other, and neither had put the eleven coins into the leathern bag. Bordering on outright accusation and anger, they stopped abruptly.

Hanse sullenly changed out of what he called his working clothes, still feeling that she had somehow tricked him. The blacks he neatly folded and stored away in a pack. She watched him transfer sheaths, and realized that he had lost a knife last night. Back in russet tunic and leathers, he dragged a red sash out of the clothing pack. She watched him spread it on the ground and line up five coins in the exact center of the long strip of scarlet. He held up four, extending them to her on an open palm.

"No. I'm carrying enough silver, Hanse. You wear those. Put them all in the sash."

She saw him consider thrusting the coins into the warm nook between her breasts, saw him decide against it. Without a word, still feeling tricked and put upon, he added those four pieces of silver to the other five. They were flashy-bright against the red of the sash. Producing some twenty more from here and there, he added them to the others. Each silver Imperial was about the size of a thumbprint. Each bore the head of the Rankan ruler on the obverse, with a stylized lightning bolt and some letters abbreviating something or other that was doubtless important in Ranke. The reverse was a small figure of that nation's chief god and his consort, sun-crowned and looking austerely majestic.

Carefully Hanse folded and rolled the sash, and as carefully tied it around his waist. He knotted. Just as carefully, he was not looking at her.

She watched that, feeling tricked and put upon and thinking that he was carrying this joke too far, that it was no longer a joke, this pretending that she had somehow taken the quartet of coins he had slipped into his clothing last night. Almost in silence, they packed up and rode along the narrow road through the forest. Once again the fun had gone out of life.

* * *

Despite their mutual sullenness and envelopment in thought, they rode warily. More Tejana might well be about, their reputation as desert-roamers notwithstanding. The woods might be tenanted with menace, whether on two feet or four. They might meet someone coming from the other direction, and that someone or someones might or might not be friendly. Thieves might lurk, waiting to strip travelers of everything including life. When they remembered, Hanse and Mignureal scanned the tall trees and broader branches that extended over the road.

They saw and heard nothing but birds. No one complained.

The calico cat was not at all comfortable riding the onager's pack as Notable had done, even after Mignureal planted her there and made a sort of nest for her. With some mews and even a seemingly healthy meow and a lot of large-eyed looking around combined with much hesitation about jumping down, the cat did. She alit with the usual human-shaming feline grace and ease. After that she was happy to walk along, near Mignureal's mount. Today it pleased Notable, too, to walk.

The cool and shade of the forest made a great difference for them all, and spirits should have been much higher. Unfortunately the two humans were busy being sulky and deep in dark brown thoughts.

After about two hours Hanse finally got it out in a blurt: "You really didn't put those coins back in the bag, did you."

She was soft-voiced but firm: "I already told you I didn't."

"I know you told me you didn't, but I told you I didn't too, remember? It just wasn't possible to believe each other." He sighed, thinning his lips. "Who wants even to think about any other possibility? You know I hate sorcery, but . . ."

"Hanse: are you really telling me that you really didn't, that you weren't joking and then got embarrassed and, uh, tried to . . ." She trailed off.

"Oh, shit," Hanse said, showing his hurt, and faced front again.

Another hour or so of silence followed that doomed attempt. At least the birds sounded happy.

After a time they heard water, over on the left somewhere, and before long they came to the skimpy and yet definite path leading off the road on the left, into the trees. The horses acted very interested. Naturally so were Mignureal and Hanse. Neither said anything. He merely turned his Tejana horse that way, and let the gray do the rest. Mignureal and the "herd" followed. Notable decided to creep/hurry on ahead. After a short hesitation, the calico followed him.

"Drop back a little," Hanse said, "in case I duck one of these branches and it gets you." At the same time he was guiding one aside and easing it back in passing, so that it wouldn't spring back at Mignureal.

Mignureal didn't say anything. The sound of water grew louder. Now they could hear it tumbling and gurgling over stones, and knew they were going to find a nice stream. The path wound. Trees and branches were close. First they seemed to thicken, so that it grew both dimmer and cooler. Soon they could see brighter sunlight ahead, and then they emerged onto a short grassy stretch that led to the stream.

The clear water was not deep here, running over stones it had been smoothing for many years. The opposite bank was only a dozen or so feet away and steeper than on this side. With the trees thus held back from the banks, a great deal of sun came through to dapple the grass and gleam like silver on the water. Near the water's edge a number of roots were naked and interestingly gnarly-looking.

The standard cliché-phrases of storytellers had come true for the two city-dwellers: they were in an idyllic glade on the banks of a genuine gurgling brook running right through the forest. It cooled the air, even in the sunlight.

Just as he swung down, Hanse saw the hand-sized fish move past, wriggling along in the water above its own flowing shadow. A lovely thought jumped into his mind. Immediately he tightened his grip on the rein, fighting to hold old Iron-mouth from the water despite its bobbing head. He glanced upstream, where he saw a deeper pool. His lips moved in the hint of a smile, which was more than most had ever seen from him called Shadowspawn, before this setting out with Mignureal.

"How lovely!" her voice came, and he turned to look at her.

She was smiling brightly in an expression of girlish wonderment. Hanse thought she looked just beautiful. He released the gray's rein and went to hold up his hands to her.

That gesture and the loveliness of their surroundings ended hostilities; Mignureal happily allowed herself to be helped down and, amid a swishing and rustling of skirts, pressed close.

"I saw a fish," he said. "Some juicy crayfish are probably lurking around among all those rocks in the water, too. If we're lucky maybe we can have a fresh meal for a change."

"Oh!" She looked in delight on the water. Then, clouding a little: "Hanse? Do you know about catching fish and crawl-fish?"

Hanse shrugged. "I guess I'm quick enough to catch crayfish. As to the others—if I just squat and be real still, I should be able to stick one with a knife as he goes by."

"Wait; I've heard more about using a spear. Maybe a sharpened stick?"

"Hmm. Maybe a stick with a knife tied to it. Ver-ry tight! Good idea."

They let the horses and onager drink, watched the cats appear and nose around, and kept the horses from moving upstream, toward the pool. Hanse found the kind of long straight branch he wanted, about two fingers thick, and hacked it off. While he laboriously bound a flat throwing knife to one end, Mignureal was making delighted noises, wading barefoot with her skirts hiked up. The cats gave her looks from time to time, as if she were quite, quite loony.

Hanse didn't. The looks he shot her were directed at her bare legs.

Then Mignureal caught the crayfish.

It was simple. It caught her. The diminutive version of a lobster saw her bare toe either as a menace or a snack, and clamped on with an outsized pincer. She squealed and whipped her foot splashily out of the water, and the crawlfish let go at the wrong time. It impacted Hanse's leg and dropped wetly, pulpily to the ground. It was swiftly made prisoner.

"That's wonderful, Mignue!" he called. "Catch some more!"

After an instant's worth of dark look, she laughed. The trouble moved out from between them, and was behind them.

• • •

Two hours later Mignureal had gathered three tiny wild onions and a nice supply of firewood, which she arranged in the place where others had obviously made fires in past. She had also washed several articles of clothing and hung them here and there to dry. The horses meanwhile were standing about snoozing; Notable lay snoozing; and the calico cat lay regarding Notable. Hanse had collected a crayfish pinch on the side of his hand and another on one finger, bloodied a toe on a stone, and managed to scoop-toss another crawlfish up onto the grass. He had also stubbed his left big toe, been mildly finned on one hand, and had missed three fish with his spear.

Mignureal really didn't mind: she loved watching him bare-legged in the water, wearing only his breechclout. Wiry and lithe in his clothes, he was surprisingly muscled without them. His biceps and calves were nicely stuffed with those rock-looking bulges that all males wished they had.

Then he speared a fish. Having learned how difficult it was, he was inordinately proud. Unfortunately this white-bellied, orange-backed representative of fishdom was hand-size only to Mignureal.

Hanse's expression of pride had turned to one of dolorous-ness when a whitish shape wriggled right over his foot. Hanse cried out excitedly. In a movement so rapid that Mignureal was hardly aware of seeing it, he bent, snatched the fish splashily out of the water, and hurled it ashore. All in one movement.

Mignureal was still blinking at the blinding speed of her man.

Since this fish was large enough to be the other's sire, as she put it, her man was even more proud than before.

"Maybe I should just stand around here and wait for another one to brush past," he said, trying not to grin. He liked her a lot better this way, looking almost lissome in fewer clothes.

Mignureal avoided making vocal the words that jumped into her mind: *You might starve too, just standing there waiting*. She said, "Shadowspawn! Faster than a speeding fish!"

"That's me!"

They laughed aloud, truly happy here and with each other.

"Uh—you know how to clean fish, Mignue?"

"As a matter of fact, I do. Get away from that, Calico!"

"Aye," the triumphant Hanse said, wading to the bank. "Catch your own dinner, cat!"

Notable bleerily opened one eye to regard Hanse as if he understood the meaning of the word "dinner."

"I do not, though," Mignureal said, "know what to do with live ones!"

"Oh. Simple. Off with their heads. Come here, fish—Ow!"

"Oh," Mignureal said, wrinkling her nose and twisting her mouth. "Ewww! Ugh!"

Moments later the fish were headless. The cats had dinner, or a nice snack, anyhow. Mighty fisherman presented the beheaded corpses to his woman with a newly fin-bloodied hand. He also stepped on one of the crayfish, which grabbed. Mignureal couldn't help laughing when Hanse lurched into an unseemly dance. The crawlfish refused to let go. Hanse sat down abruptly and tried to tug the thing off.

"Owwwww!" He took pause to give the matter a moment of thought then, and pricked the little crustacean with his knife. It let go his toe. Curbing the impulse to stomp it, Hanse hurried to thrust his foot in the water, where he wriggled it with enthusiasm. He also gave Mignureal a dark look. She managed to curb her laughter and look properly concerned.

"I'm sorry, darling. Just the sight of you dancing that way—is it bleeding?"

Hanse looked. No it wasn't, and that was embarrassing, so he kicked water on Mignureal. She squealed and picked up one of the stones they'd placed in the sun to dry. She threw it into the water a foot from Hanse, splashing him nicely. He yelled, tried to kick water at her in retaliation, and slipped. The splash was mighty.

Mignureal cleaned the fish. Hanse steadfastly sought others while he kept the cats away. He was successful only in the latter, and in convincing Mignureal that a little beer in the pan would improve aroma, flavor, and texture. Neither he nor she was quite sure what to do with the crayfish, except that Hanse was certain that one cooked them alive. That elicited another "Ewwww" from Mignureal, so he waited until the fish were frying over the fire amid a marvelous aroma.

"Look!" he called, while pointing across the stream.

Mignureal looked—at nothing—and Hanse popped both crawlfish into the fry-pan. Both scuttled, then stopped crawling. Mignureal looked back from nothing and into the pan. First she made a face, then she gave Hanse a look that mingled disgust and accusation. He put his head on one side and spread his hands.

"I will say this: I'll have a lot more respect for fishermen hereafter," he said a few moments later, examining the bruise on the back of one thigh; he had sustained it when he fell in the water. Meanwhile, the places where he had been finned itched, and his rock-stubbed big toe was purplish. "What labor! What dangerous work! Look at me—covered with bruises, cuts, and pinch-marks!"

"We can always stay here a few days while I nurse you back to health," she said without looking up, and Hanse reached over to pinch her calf. That very nearly succeeded in dumping dinner into the fire. First making sure it was stable, she stood and came at him as if to strangle.

"Oh, oh, Helllp!" Hanse squealed in a ridiculously high voice, falling back on the grass.

Mignureal came to an abrupt and jerky stop, staring down at the large red cat that had seemingly materialized between her and the sprawled Hanse. Notable's loud yowl still rode the air and every hair on the animal seemed to be standing straight out. All three horses were staring. So was Hanse.

"Well I'll be—Notable! Easy, Notable. *Friend*, Notable. Joke, damn it! It's a *game*, Notable; joke! No no Mignue, don't try to pet him just yet!"

Then he was staring anew, this time at the tiny multicolored cat that stood beside Mignureal's foot, back up, ears back and teeth bared as she stared at Notable. The calico hissed.

"I do not believe this!" Hanse wailed. He fell back again and pounded the ground.

"I—I don't either," she said. "It's the first time I've seen him—this way. Frightening! I'm sure that if I'd come another step he'd have . . . attacked. Me!"

"I'm sorry," Hanse said. "But I was talking about that scroungy li'l calico. Look at her! She's putting on a good show of being ready to protect you against him!" He shook his head. "By the Nameless One—I wonder if she likes beer, too!"

"Surely not," Mignureal said, squatting to rub the smaller cat—which jerked at the touch—while staring into Notable's huge-pupiled eyes. "She's a lady."

"A lady," Hanse said, "willing to fight for her lady! She's adopted you, Mignue. You specifically, I mean, the way Notable has me. So! So she's going to be watch-cat, too. I guess it's time we named her."

"Of course it is," she said, remembering to check the fry-pan. Once again she turned the fish, using the knife he had handed her.

"Mignue . . . do you think we might call her Moon-flower?"

She shot him a look and her tears came at once. "How could y—my mother . . . oh how could you?"

Hanse showed surprise and swiftly apologized, but this time he did not dissolve or back down in the face of one of the world's premiere guilt producers: a woman's tears.

"How could I?" he echoed. "In respect, and memory of M—" and his voice broke. He ceased trying to talk at once, and looked away.

"Oh, Hanse," she said, understanding, blinking and giving him a tender look through her tear-misted eyes.

"Of course we will not, though, since you don't like it," he said. He looked at the little animal. "I'd like to call you Moonflower, little 'draggled kitty, and I'll bet you'd love it, too. But . . . I think you name is Rainbow."

"That's nice, Hanse! Rainbow! We love you, Rainbow."

Then all was forgotten but Rainbow, and the eeriness that stole into the glade. The change in the cat was visible in the same way that "watching a baby grow" was possible; it *happened*, and swiftly, and yet Hanse and Mignue did not quite see movement.

Rainbow *changed*. The scrawny cat filled out before their eyes; its rumply, apparently undernourished coat took on sheen and became positively sleek. Within a minute the animal appeared to have gained a pound or two—all it could stand without being fat—and to have eaten just the right things to give it sleekly shining fur.

Rainbow also paced over to Notable, and touched noses. Notable sat down.

"Oh gods," Hanse said in a quavery voice. *"Sorcery!"*

"Please don't say 'I hate sorcery' again, Hanse. Look at her! *Our* cat Rainbow obviously likes the name, and her two humans. And Notable."

A half minute of staring later Hanse jerked out, "Hoy! She probably won't like that fish though, and neither will we if we don't get the pan off the fire!"

"Oh!" Mignureal cried, and jerked the pan away from the flames. That resulted in spilling one of the savory, smoking strips onto the grass. Only the fact that it was very hot indeed prevented her from losing part of their already exiguous dinner to the extremely interested Notable.

"It's done," she said, biting her lip a little while Hanse stared at the fish smoking on the grass. "And that grass certainly won't hurt it."

He shook his head. "No," he said, in a distant voice. "I'm thinking about something else. And staring at dinner keeps me from looking at Rainbow."

Looking at Notable looking at the spilled fish, Rainbow purred.

Mignureal plucked that part of their meal up, from under the big red cat's nose. "Come on, you. You ate every bit of a fish's head, eyes and all. Ooh. I wish I hadn't mentioned that!"

"The thought doesn't spoil my appetite," Hanse said, inhaling a big aromatic breath. "My lady, let us dine!"

She laughed. They sat cross-legged on the grass, facing each other and brushing at the occasional intrusion of fly or cat. The fish was good and the better for the long absence of fresh-cooked food from their diet. The fried crawlfish were impossible. Conversation wasn't much. They exchanged various ideas about the mystery of Rainbow and the eleven coins, but Hanse liked none of them.

"Ver-ry good," he said, giving his middle a fond pat, and Mignureal bowed. That was impressive, from her sitting position.

They finished off the slim repast with a few dried dates they had carried all the way from Sanctuary, and when Hanse gave Notable beer in a bowl, he decided to have some too. He tested Rainbow. Rainbow was not at all interested in beer. That was refreshing. Mignureal succumbed to persuasion, blandishment and dares, and tried some.

"Ewwwww." It was bitter, she pronounced, and that was that. Notable kept right on lapping, while both females played Lady.

"Now it's time we counted our silver, Mignue, and I'm almost afraid to look in my sash."

She nodded, hesitated a moment, and commenced producing coins from here and there on her person. Soon Hanse was gusting out a sigh of relief; his unfolded sash housed twenty-nine pieces of silver, the number he had placed there a few hours before. His lack of lettering did not extend to numbers and counting. It had been simple to learn, with the incentive that numbering what one possessed, spent, and received was far more important than reading and writing.

He numbered their coins by arranging them in neat stacks of ten, which he disarranged with a sweep of his hand when he had done. That signaled Mignureal's turn. She arrived at the same number: their fortune was eighty-nine silver Imperials. Twenty of the coins he counted off into the cracked old saddlebag. Even then he had not done; together they recounted the remainder. Three sets of ten and two of five Mignureal re-secreted on her person. Hanse secreted nine in his underclothing and meticulously refolded his sash around the remaining thirty.

They were well off. In Sanctuary, at least, a good horse might bring six to seven Imperials of silver. Five horses and the worth of twenty or so more, Hanse pointed out, were wealth.

"Anywhere we go, we can live for a long time on what we have," he told her, "even if we do nothing to bring in more."

She snuggled. "I am in good hands," she said, and smiled when one of those good hands slid into her bodice. "But I would not be able not to do anything to bring in more money, Hanse."

Hanse spent a moment chewing out the meaning of her words, and decided not to argue. "Sundown is not too far away," he said. "Unless you prefer more riding in the dark, we may as well call this our camp for the night. I can even write 'HANSE' a few times in the mud there beside the water."

"Good!" she said, and hugged him. "This is the perfect opportunity! Let's take off the rest of our clothes and let me wash them. They'll be dry by morning."

Hanse rolled his eyes. "You sure are changing," he muttered at last.

She smiled happily. "Ohh . . . don't embarrass me, darling. We were going to take them off anyhow, weren't we?"

They awoke hungry and rose with the sun. Mignureal, he saw, was visibly self-conscious until she had put on some clothing. All was unmolested, though it wasn't all dry. Hanse established that his sash felt the same, and was relieved to discover lots of coins in the saddlebag. Good. Here was an end to his fears of sorcery in the matter of the coinage.

He soon learned that he was wrong, which was worse than dismaying. Something possessed him to count the silver pieces in the bag. Naturally he felt compelled to count them again, gritting his teeth and scowling.

He had been right the first time. Twenty had become twenty-two.

They could not leave until he had laboriously unfolded the scarlet sash and stood by while Mignureal counted its contents. Twice. She had been right the first time. During the night, thirty had become twenty-nine. She began examining the packets hidden among her clothing. The second bundle she produced and checked was also short one Imperial.

Hanse sat down listlessly, resignedly, with a long sigh and a morose face. He spoke in a dull voice, looking at the ground.

"During the night *something* transferred one coin from that bundle in your stomacher to the saddlebag, and one from my sash. It isn't possible, but it happened."

"There is another possibility," she said quietly, and he looked up with an expression of hopeful expectancy.

"Let's hear it!"

"The two coins . . . transferred . . . themselves."

Hanse threw up his hands and made a pained face. "Arrrghhh!"

"I'm sorry," Mignureal said. "I can't think of anything else, and I don't like either one either."

"A weird cat to begin with, and now an obviously even more unnatural one," he said, glancing from Notable to Rainbow, "and even unnatural coins! Gods of my fathers, why can we not be free of things sorcerous! I hate s—" He broke off and sat staring at the ground between his feet for a long while.

Eventually he rose. "Hate it or not, damn it, I am stuck with it," he said with a gesture of acceptance, and they began packing the Tejana horse that now served as supply-animal.

"Hanse," Mignureal said, "sorcery is a fact of life, after all. Think: isn't my Sight a form of sorcery, of . . . magic?"

"In a way, but it isn't the same. It's a *natural* unnatural ability, common to one sex of one people: S'danzo women. It isn't as if a spell is on you. Some sort of spell must be on these cats—certainly Rainbow—and on the coins I welcomed so long ago as ransom!"

"Some of the coins," Mignureal said significantly. "Consider this, darling. First the bag was full of coins, and the Tejana stole it. Suppose they took out every coin; they would have done, wouldn't they? Doesn't that make sense? What doesn't make sense is for them to have left eleven Imperials of silver in the bag. But when you regained the bag, there were eleven coins in it."

Chewing his lip, considering, Hanse nodded. "True."

"Then we took them all out. All of them. And next morning there were eleven coins in the bag."

Hanse left off checking the lashings of their packs and paused, leaning with one arm on the horse, to stare thoughtfully at her. Again he nodded. "True!"

"So last night that was still the case. We combined all the coins and counted them. You chose to put twenty into the bag." She paused, looking expectantly at him until he had to nod to get her to continue. "But this morning that had grown to two and twenty."

"It . . . happens at night," Hanse murmured, staring at nothing with narrowed eyes.

She responded with a series of rapid nods. "I was about to say that I'd predict that in one hour or ten hours, those same two-and-twenty coins will still be in that bag."

She kicked it, which did both her and Hanse a great deal of good. The cheery jungle of twenty-two pieces of silver did not.

"But . . . eleven seems to be the . . ." He swallowed before uttering the abhorrent phrase: ". . . the magic number. Oh! Twenty-two is two elevens, isn't it!"

"Yes, but I don't think that's significant."

First Hanse seemed to sag a little. Then he crossed his ankles and leaned on the packhorse to stare at her in an attitude of expectant challenge. "Oh you don't. Why not?"

"Oh now wait, darling, don't be that way. I'm talking from logic and reason, not the Sight, and I could be totally wrong. Probably am."

"Uh. You want to give me your logical reasoning theory?"

She nodded, and extended her left hand. "First, if we take out all the coins right now, I think the bag will still be empty tonight." With her other hand she folded down one finger. "Second," she said, tapping the next finger. "I think there will be eleven coins in the bag tomorrow morning." She folded that finger down.

"Umm. Is that it?"

"That's it, Hanse."

"And what if we leave everything alone?"

"I *think*—and bear in mind that's all it is, now—I think that if we leave everything alone that bag will contain two-and-twenty coins tomorrow and the next day too, and . . . next week."

Suddenly he clapped a hand to his head, then lurched away from the horse and slapped that hand into the other. "Ah, slow, Hanse, slow! I see! You think that we have eighty-nine coins and eleven of them are—something. Ensorceled," he said, pronouncing the word as if in pain. "And that nine of the coins we put in the bag happened to be in that group. But we put the other two unnatural pieces on ourselves, in our clothing, and during the night they . . . *traveled* to the bag."

Mignureal nodded. "*If* I'm right, those eleven coins have to be in the bag every morning. It doesn't matter how many others are, just so these eleven are."

"Thank the gods Rainbow doesn't have to be in the bag, too!"

She glanced at the calico cat. "I don't have any ideas about Rainbow at all."

"Let's get out of here and on our way, Mignue. We'll check the bag tonight, and empty it. We could even try burying those twenty-two, or putting them up a tree or something." He glanced at the stream. "I'm tempted to throw the whole bag in that deeper pool, right now!"

"That would probably be that," she said, but then she frowned. "Unless . . . unless those silver pieces have something to do with *us* especially."

I think they have, Hanse mused, but he would not say it. *I think that bag was not on that saddle when I put it on the horse! Oh gods, what am I even thinking! No, oh damn it no—gods, O Ils how I hate sorcery!*

That day Mignureal urged Hanse for the severalth time to put on the Tejana wristlet. Hanse agreed, mostly in order to shut her up about the thing. Since he habitually wore a black leather bracer on his left wrist, he slipped the bracelet onto his right and squeezed it until it was reasonably snug. Nothing happened. Nothing changed. He merely wore the dumb copper circlet, for her.

The sun was at approximate zenith but not demonic on the forest floor beneath tall, tall trees and the forest seeming pushed a bit to remain reasonably cool, when they met the other traveler. While he was still sufficiently distant not to be able to hear quiet voices, Hanse warned Mignureal against using names. It was too bad, but they had to be wary of anyone they met.

The big fellow bestrode a good big dun-colored horse and led another, which was pack-laden. He was no youngster, Hanse noticed; the lines in his face and around his eyes put him in his thirties or maybe forty. His odd flapped cap, leather left its natural color, showed no hair. No less wary and guarded than Hanse, he offered no name. Shadowspawn did not ask.

He did tell them he was heading for Sanctuary.

"Oh," Hanse said coolly. "I've been there. Not a bad town."

"Not a really good one either, from what I hear," the other man said, in a quiet and unusually matter-of-fact voice. He was a big ruddy fellow who wore a big ruddy moustache; a rather bushy one of an unusual bronze-brown color. His tunic was plain homespun, undyed, with an unusually large neck and sleeves short enough to show powerful arms.

"You plan to cross that desert alone?" Mignureal asked in a voice full of incredulity.

He shrugged. "I'll make it."

"Beware the Tejana," Hanse said.

"Heard of them." The big man shrugged and slapped the handle of a big saddle-sword. He had one sheathed at his hip, too, Hanse noticed. And a shield was slung from his worn old saddle, as well. Round, wooden, bossed with iron. It was of no particular color and bore no insignia. "I can take care of myself."

Hanse showed him a grim look. "So can I. A man's helpless, though, against four leveled crossbow bolts."

"Oh. A smart man is, aye. Yet you're leading horses."

"They robbed us, just the same. Left us the onager and our packs. I followed them. One's dead and one's in need of a leg and one's wounded here and there. Can't say about the fourth. The onager trampled him." Hanse jerked a thumb. "Those are—were their horses. This is their leader's." He patted the gray's neck.

The other pilgrim gazed at him from strangely blue eyes. "You are a dangerous man."

Hanse didn't say anything.

"See anything in the woods?"

Hanse shook his head. "Birds. Cats scared up a snake and played with it awhile, this morning. It didn't look poisonous to me. You'll hear the water in a few hours, and see the path. We recommend the place. Camped there last night."

The other man nodded. "Four of them, hmmm?"

Hanse blinked at the transition. "Four men, four crossbows, three horses. And a camp that's at least semi-permanent; they had rigged an enclosure for their horses. Very bad men, but I never planned to kill anyone."

The other man nodded. "Killing's not your business?"

"No," Hanse said, and did not ask the next question. "We're headed for—what's the name of that town?"

"Firaqa's about two days on north."

"That's it," Hanse said, nodding as if in recognition of the name and looking as if he were considering a smile. He didn't want to smile in delight that he had obtained information by the little trick. He'd never heard of Firaqa.

"You'll be out of the forest before sunset," the other man said, glancing up. "Just follow the road beyond. Oh—I met some mighty nice farm folk yesterday. Hospitable people. Red and yellow house—was yellow, I mean. Yellow dog and several cats. They're nice people, with a good well. He's Imrys."

Mignureal sensed a lessening of wary terseness and at least a tendency toward friendly exchange. "You sure you have enough water for the desert?"

The other pilgrim glanced at her and looked again at Hanse. "You mentioned water ahead."

"Good clear stream. Even has some fish in it."

The other man nodded. "I'll have plenty of water," he told Mignureal, and looked back at Hanse. "You throw, don't you?"

"What?"

'Wearing throwing knives. Left-handed and good with throwing knives."

It was not a question, but it did tread on the border of personal business, into which they had avoided crossing. Hanse said nothing.

"Sorry," the big man said. "An observation. Not trying to pry. Wishing you were going my way."

"Too bad you aren't going ours."

"Well." The big man raised a hand. "Fare you well." He twitched his horse's rein. "Let's go find that stream, Jaunt."

As he started past, Hanse said, "Wait," and the other man's hand was on his sword before his head moved and his gaze met Hanse's.

"Sorry," Hanse said. "I didn't mean to startle you. The leader of those Tejana threw me this before he galloped off with our horses." He shrugged, getting the wristlet off. "We didn't have anything else worth taking. Told me to wear this thing. Said if any other Tejana accosted us, they would just go their way if I showed them this."

Starting to proffer the copper bracelet, he frowned. "It looks unmarked, and I *think* they all wore one. It couldn't be important to me now, and it might be to you. Could save you some trouble; you could pretend that you'd had more horses or money or something, and others already took it and gave you this. On the other hand, I did kill one of them, and left two hurting at least, and chopped the leader in the thigh. You might be careful, in case there's something recognizable about it." He extended the almost-circle of copper. Right-handed.

The other man sat his saddle loosely, blue eyes gazing into almost-black ones. At last he nodded, and reached for the wristlet. Left-handed.

"Thanks. You sure about this? It's decent copper."

Hanse shrugged. "I don't wear copper and I don't plan to cross that desert again. Don't recommend it, either."

The man slipped the bracelet over the turtle-head shape that was the pommel of his saddle, and mashed it to fit. He did that one-handed, with obvious ease. He touched fingers to forehead. "I thank you, pilgrim."

"Uh, H—" Mignureal broke off short of saying Hanse's name. "We've no need now of a desert robe . . ."

The traveler's moustache moved in a slight smile. "Don't believe it would fit me, little girl. I have a light robe, though, on the packhorse." Suddenly he nodded, as if having reached a decision. "Good people," he said in that quiet, quiet voice. "I suppose I might stop at that stream after all."

Hanse cocked his head, then realized. "Don't quite dare trust each other, do we?"

Big shoulders shrugged. "You've gifted me. Now you must accept a gift."

"Don't even think about it," Mignureal said. "You've given us good information."

"You might tell me if there's a marketer or horse-pedlar in Firaqa we can trust," Hanse said.

The big man had long since taken his hand away from his sword; now he held it up, symbolically, while he reached into his big-necked tunic. Hanse understood the gesture. Therefore he tried not to show that he tensed, ready to draw and throw.

"You might try stopping at the Green Goose," the other man said. "And ask—discreetly—for Anorislas. Tell him a man said to call him Bunny. You'll find him unable to be other than honest." He transferred his blue-eyed gaze to Mignureal. "And show him this."

"I—I cannot accept that!" Mignureal said, with her gaze on the proffered medallion or amulet. Triangular, it was composed of pieces of tortoise shell, in various colors. Its border appeared to be gold. It was strung on a piece of rawhide.

"You must," he said, continuing to hold it out. "If you don't take it how can you show it to Anorislas? Besides, if you accept no gift of me in return for one from you freely given, I am shamed. That is my people's belief. You see? You must." After a moment he added, "I assure you that it contains nothing and does not open. And I am no dark sorcerer."

"But—"

"Please. Would you shame me, having been so kind?"

Mignureal accepted the medallion. The big man nodded, glanced at Hanse and nodded again, and paced on his way. Hanse looked after him for a time; the other traveler never looked back.

Hanse called, "Yo!"

The other man reined in and twisted to look back, brows up in a question.

"If you happen to meet a certain Ahdio in Sanctary—Ahh-dee-oh . . ."

"Ahdio. Yes?"

"Uh—tell him you saw the big red cat, and the couple it was with swore they didn't take it. It followed them. Across the desert, aye."

"Tell Ahdio you swore that big red cat followed you, and you definitely did not take it."

Hanse nodded. "Right. With thanks."

The other traveler nodded, turned to ride on along the forest road, and so did Hanse. Then:

"Yo!"

Hanse twisted around to look back, brows up in a question.

The other man was looking back at him, half smiling. "Name's Strick."

"Strick?"

"Right," the other traveler said, and threw up a hand in a loose gesture, and turned away to ride on along the forest road.

"I believe we met a good man," Mignureal said quietly. "What should I do with this, Hanse?"

"Wear it," he said, as they rode on their way. "I believe we met a good man." He added, "Since we didn't cross him."

"He is big, isn't he!"

"More than that," Hanse said. "That Strick's a weapon-man. A soldier, maybe. Or ex-soldier, surely."

They rode on through the woods, talking about the big man and the bland aspect of his attire, even his horse. And about those blue eyes under brows darker than his big droopy old-bronze moustache.

A couple of hours later they emerged from the forest. Ahead lay obvious farmland. A broad road headed north and east. It was unpaved, which Hanse thought was a good sign. Military roads were paved.

Imrys and his wife Tenny were indeed nice and hospitable folk. Even their cats were not overly disturbed about the advent of two more, which Mignue at least knew was unusual. Long accustomed to living with felines, the yellow dog paid little attention to Notable and Rainbow but dutifully barked at the new humans until his master bade him stop. His duty done, the dog pranced about in hopes of a little petting.

Hanse and Mignureal wanted only water and a loft for sleeping. Imrys insisted on providing a bit of oats for the horses and the onager. He also led his own big-hoofed workhorse and the yearling heifer out of the enclosure and into the tired old barn so that the pilgrims' animals might have the enclosure to themselves. That was only intelligence; despite the fact that all the horses were gelding males, no god had guaranteed that all horses would get along.

Tenny insisted that the "guests" share some of the hot dinner she was already preparing. That was not merely a ritual offer, the visitors discovered when they made ritual rejections. Soon Mignureal was aiding the bony, stenchy woman while Hanse helped her bony, stenchy husband in and around the barn. Neither traveler mentioned needing a bath. Obviously Tenny and Imrys had what they considered better uses for their water.

When Imrys agreed, Hanse also played with nine-year-old Little Imrys for a while. They used the side of the barn as knife-throwing target. A knot that was almost a hole was the actual target, but Little Imrys—Rys—never got too close. As a matter of fact his sister Rose, who was a year older, threw closer to the mark.

The beef stew was marvelous and Tenny's bread, hard of crust and medium soft inside, was worth talking about. So were the peaches. All four of the host family kept asking questions, wanting to know about far and romantic lands. Rys wanted to know about Hanse's knives. Rose wanted to know about Mignureal's clothes. Hanse and Mignureal answered everything, one way or another. They claimed to be from Clearfield—which Mignue had made up—while assuring their hosts that they knew no far and romantic lands. They had agreed not to mention the Tejana, or the silver.

When they said they were heading for Firaqa, they were urged to stay out of that stinky city and settle on a farm where air was fresh and animals and neighbors were helpful and trustworthy.

Asked what he did, Hanse said that both their fathers had been shopkeepers, and that was what they knew. It was true of Mignureal, at least. Imrys remarked that with all those horses they might well be able to afford to make payment on a shop in Firaqa and arrange the balance with the owner or a banker, but "You'd sure be far better off to put them good animals to work on good farmland!"

They learned little of Firaqa because their hosts knew almost nothing. Tenny and the children had never been to The City, as they called it; Imrys had once gone there because he must. He had no desire to return. Hanse did discover from something said by Rose and intimated by Rys that the beef stew was special; meat was a sometime fare, here.

They also learned that taxes and their collectors were not too bad. Odd!

After they had eaten, Imrys offered beer. Surprised that neither of his guests wanted any, he and Tenny poured a mug each. They all sat outside for a while just after sundown, pointing toward this or that tree and in this or that direction, talking of farms and mentioning about twenty names of people hereabouts. Good, honest people, Imrys kept saying.

"I need to have a look behind the barn," Hanse said, when twilight was fading toward night.

Imrys allowed that he would amble along. Rys begged to go along and was denied. Hanse mentioned a need also to have a word with Mignureal, and she went off to one side with him.

She agreed instantly to his proposal. The others watched their embrace with delight.

"Always good to drain the holding tank after dinner and a little ale," Imrys said a couple of minutes later, glorifying his homemade barley beer while "draining his holding tank" against the huge oak down past the rear of the barn. "Just not a drinking man, Hanse?"

"Got to liking it too much once, Imrys. Quit for good." His own holding tank drained and his statement at least partially true, Hanse rearranged his leggings and tunic. "Imrys, Mignue wants to make Rose a present of that paisley skirt the girl's so taken with, and I'd like to give Little Imrys my sash. If you don't mind."

"Skirt! Why that's too much, Hanse. And as for that handsome red sash of yours—you must be attached to it. No need to waste it on the boy."

"Imrys, neither of them's new and it's what we want to do. You have any objection?"

Imrys gave his head a single wagging shake. "You just heard 'em. Just sure not necessary, that's all!"

"It's done, then."

"You sure are fine young folks, Hanse. My youngsters will think the moon's done fell and showered 'em with stars! Sure would like to see you change your mind about settling in Firaqa, though."

"Imrys, I've lied to you a little. I—"

"We all have our secrets and folk hereabouts respect privacy, Hanse. No need to say more."

In deep gray darkness now, Hanse ignored him. "I never knew my father. I grew up bad. I was a thief, Imrys. A mighty good one. Then I met Mignureal, and . . . well, I sort of got involved in politics. My last theft was to break into the, uh, ruler's house and take something the rebels needed. Then Mignue and I left, in a hurry. Oh—we didn't steal the horses. Now we're heading to Firaqa to make a new start. Together."

Hanse stopped talking. Most of that was true or nearly, and he felt good about telling it to Imrys. Later, he'd try to decide why.

"A good woman can make a man out of most of us, Hanse," Imrys said, arriving at the obvious conclusions: that Hanse had reformed and that Mignue was responsible. "You sure needn't've told me this, but I appreciate the confidence and I'm glad for you—your plans for a new life, I mean. I never heerd you, though."

Hanse made a chuckling sound. "Well, just know that you've got a friend in Firaqa, or soon will have. One who's awfully good at sneaking around at night."

They had turned away to walk back up to the farmhouse. Imrys's laugh was rather nervous. "Can't think why I'd have need of such a fella, if I knowed of one. I don't, of course. But I'll remember what you said. I'll be wishing you nothing but good luck and, uh, nothing but shopkeeping, too."

Hanse couldn't help his laugh. What a man! With perfect aplomb he accepted all Hanse told him, as well as simultaneously avowing to have heard nothing and vowing to remember.

What a pair of men they had met, the last couple of days! A farmer and a wary traveler reluctant to give his name. Hanse felt good about this land, about heading for Firaqa. *Good people up this way. Let Sanctuary sit down there on the southern coast and rot.*

"Oh," he said suddenly. "I've got a few coppers in this sash. Just let me go into the barn and slip them in our packs."

"I'll just wait and look at a star or two," Imrys said.

Again Hanse marveled: what a thoughtfully thinking man Imrys was! What careful respect for privacy! Inside the dark barn—with a little moon- and starlight slipping in, between the vertical planking—he removed his heavy sash. He took care against jingling as he took out the goodly handful of silver coins, secreted them temporarily, and emerged wearing the sash. He and Imrys walked up to the house.

"I bade the children go to bed, father," Tenny told her husband, "but Mignue said Hanse would want to see them first."

"We both do," Hanse said, untying his violently red sash for the second time in seven minutes.

Immediately Mignureal stood. Her removing the paisley skirt attracted more attention than Hanse with his sash, but of course she wore others under it. Soon Tenny was protesting the gift while her daughter murmured sobbily over it, and Rys was pretending not to be leaking tears while Hanse wrapped the sash around the boy's waist and tied it.

Rose babbled, "But I can't—you shouldn't—nobody ever—" And her weeping intensified.

Mignureal hugged her. And then Tenny. Seeing at a glance that Rys wasn't up for that, she broke off her movement to him. And it was bedtime.

"But I won't be able to sleep for hours!" Rys protested, fondling his finery.

"I'll bet you'd better," his father told him. "You've got some weedin' to do this morrow!"

"Rys," Hanse said sternly, turning back as he and Mignureal headed for the barn with the covered light Tenny had provided. He pointed. "You go to sleep. That way you'll be able to get up all the earlier and admire yourself in the sunlight!"

"Yes sir!"

A minute or so later Hanse was opening the barn door. "Damn," he murmured. "Sir! No one ever called me *that* before!"

Mignureal laughed and hugged him. "I feel so good about what we did!"

"Me too. You'll feel so good about what we're about to do, too!—*after* we empty the saddlebag!"

"Oh faint," she said, remembering an exclamation she was trying to adopt and make automatic.

They did that, and collected the coins from Hanse's scarf too, and ascended to the loft. There they were particularly careful about putting out the wick-light in its perforated iron pot.

It was a lovely night. It was a restful and uneventful night, too, except for the flurry of activity just before sleep. Hanse was right; Mignureal felt good about that. So did her man.

In the morning the saddlebag contained eleven Rankan Imperials. Hanse and Mignureal left them there.

When he mentioned his intention to *lose* another coin here in the loft, tears slid down Mignureal's cheeks. Who in Sanctuary would believe this of Hanse called Shadowspawn! Nevertheless she persuaded him to toss the Imperial into the grass back of the barn. There it would be sure to be discovered, while how sad if it never were found in the loft, since no one ever used all the hay. Worse, it might wind up in the gullet of one of their hosts' three cows, the heifer, or the horse!

She also provided him with a large blue scarf, which Hanse rolled and folded over twenty-eight coins before making a sash of it.

They emerged from the barn to find both children joyously wearing their new finery. Their benefactors said no to breakfast, but were "forced" to accept milk and bread just the same. Thinking of the silver Imperial he had left to be found (and then identified, since Imrys had likely never seen one before), Hanse graciously accepted a small loaf of the good crusty dark bread. After an extended period of embarrassingly familial leave-taking, the travelers set out once again, one coin poorer and yet much richer.

"*Milk*," Hanse muttered as they headed north and eastward through the farm country. "I'll have the runs today, sure!"

"Oh darling, don't even think about that!" Mignureal's voice was as sunny as her smile. In the saddle with no care for her bared calves, she hugged herself. "I feel so good! What wonderful people!"

"Aye," Hanse said, and added wonderingly, "and how strange to realize that they're saying the same about us. Me!"

It was a lovely day and continued so until they took another nice man's advice and took a shortcut through a small greenwood, and were attacked.

He was a nice fellow, and nicely dressed, if decidedly on the flamboyant side. The small hat was an off-yellow, the green-broidered tunic a very bright blue, the leather leggings an almost-yellow natural doeskin. Above a broad, trim black moustache, clear eyes looked charmingly right at Mignureal, and at Hanse when he remembered. He wore a sword with a handsome hilt and handsome garnet pommel in a handsome sheath of black leather-over-wood crisscrossed in X's with bands of yellow-natural leather and set with two—garnets? His horse was a sleekly handsome black with two white stockings. Well wrought, the scrollwork on his blond-leather saddle was stained dark so as to contrast. His name was Sinajhal, he told them, and he was an entertainer on his way from Firaqa to . . . wherever his horse and the Goddess Fortune took him, he told them.

It was hard for Hanse not to like the flamboyant fellow and he knew that Mignureal was charmed by him. Sinajhal told them further, charmingly, of a problem that lay behind him, ahead of them: a particularly difficult tax collector. They would be wiser to take the shortcut through that little wood right over there.

They thanked him. He made a flamboyant bow from the saddle, gave them a charming wave and bade them a charming fare-you-well, and rode charmingly on his way.

Once he'd gone, Hanse and Mignureal laughed about him a little. Impressed with the charm the fellow exuded, Hanse was prepared to dislike him until Mignue called him "that funny man."

They took the shortcut into the nice little wood Sinajhal had indicated, following a winding path that accommodated only one horse at a time.

A good hour later Notable and Rainbow had gone exploring in the surrounding trees and Hanse turned back to Mignureal to say, "I think we're circling," and saw her staring past him with wide eyes.

He looked that way. Once again he was facing a steel arrow set across a cocked crossbow. Holding it was a paunchy fellow of middle age, all in dark brown, including his moustache and beard and his expression.

Not again, Hanse thought miserably.

"Stand and stand away," the paunchy man said. "That means get off them horses and stand well away while I take 'em. Believe me, I want 'em more than you do."

Hanse stared, biting his lip while he considered. "Want," he said, "isn't need."

"Get off the horse, philosopher."

Not, Hanse thought, *again.* And making his voice squeaky he said, "Help! Oh Hellllp!"

"That's not going to help you, boy," the robber said. The crossbow moved. "But you'd better shut up. Now get off that horse! You too, girl. Oh—and keep your hands away from sharp steel, boy."

Hanse heaved a great sigh, thought *Damned cat,* and started dismounting.

That was when Notable proved the robber wrong. The cat came loping out of the woods, said "Yaaaaowrrrr!" or something like, and kicked himself into the air. He landed, all claws out, on the crossbowman's crossbow arm and set in biting. The man screamed. His finger twitched. The quarrel hummed over Hanse's unnamed gray horse, while the robber's upper chest sprouted the flat hilt of a throwing knife. His eyes rolled loosely and he teetered while Notable continued making a fine show of dining on his arm.

If Hanse's foot hadn't slipped he'd have taken the bolt from the other crossbow between the shoulder blades. Since his foot did slip, the steel arrow missed him by six inches and Notable by one. It went straight into the forehead of the paunchy man, whose eyes ceased rolling. Notable let go his hold and yowled the same cry while his quarry fell like a log.

"Shit!" a voice snarled from behind Hanse.

He whirled to see the charming Sinajhal crowding his horse past Mignureal. His glaring gaze was on Hanse. Having decided not to risk taking the time to rewind his long distance weapon, he had discarded it and drawn another. He came rushing at Hanse with his pretty-pommeled sword in his hand.

Hanse tried to rein his horse around on the narrow trail while at the same time drawing the longest blade he had, the knife from over in the Ilbars hills. The first did not quite work; the gray horse was broadside to the charging Sinajhal's when the latter reached them. Hanse's experience in fighting while mounted did not exist. Seeing the sword rushing down and around at him with a lot of force, he ducked desperately. And fell off his horse.

That saved his leg from Sinajhal's mount and his head from Sinajhal's sword. He got out of the way too late for Sinajhal to abort his vicious stroke, however, and his blade chopped into Hanse's saddle.

At about the same time Sinajhal's black mount charged into the gray. His neigh was a squeal. He bucked and kicked. The flying rear hooves rushed past above Hanse, who was in the process of rolling under his own horse. His fist sprouted the long, long knife, which was nevertheless a foot shorter than Sinajhal's sword. Unfortunately the treacherous devil had wrenched his blade out of the saddle by the time Hanse hurled himself under the black horse.

When he pounced to his feet on the far side of the black, it was in time to see Sinajhal looking furiously at him again, and launching another swinging stroke.

Something happened to Hanse's arm. Even while its owner knew that the only thing to do was dive aside, his left arm moved so rapidly that the Ilbarsi blade blurred. It caught the other man's rushing stroke with a horrible impact accompanied by a loud clang. That was followed by an ear-threatening screechy noise as the deflected blade slid down toward Hanse's hand. Despite the fact that his teeth clacked and his arm felt as if he'd been struck by a galloping horse, he twisted his wrist and then his body and banged his blade against Sinajhal's again, this time in offense.

The charming robber grunted and grunted a curse. He also fought for balance atop his horse, since he was leaning well toward Hanse. His peripheral vision saved him from the hurtling red streak that was Notable, airborne and headed for Sinajhal's face with claws extended and fangy mouth wide open. His target swung at Hanse, ducked while the cat whizzed over him, and clamped with both legs to keep from falling.

Hanse availed himself of the opportunity to slash one of those yellow-leathered legs.

Sinajhal cried out, lurched, and fell directly toward Hanse. Unfortunately that resulted in the persistent Notable's flying over the empty saddle again, this time in the other direction. He landed on the gray Tejana horse, which immediately squealed and began bucking and kicking wildly and continuously.

Hanse meanwhile had not been able to shift and pounce backward fast enough to avoid Sinajhal's tumbling against his shins. Hanse fell backward and rolled desperately. He scrambled to his feet in time to see the wounded man glaring at him, propped up on one hand. With the other he was swinging a horizontal cut at Hanse's legs.

"Hanse!" Mignureal screamed, but he was already leaping upward as high as he could, meanwhile doubling up his legs.

The robber's sword hummed through the space recently occupied by his intended victim's ankles. Then he saw those ankles reappear, his intended victim's feet seeming almost to caress the ground in his drop, and a sprawled Sinajhal was staring into the mean dark eyes of a squatting Hanse. It was a vision he saw only briefly. A moment after the intended victim came down, his twenty-inch blade did. It clove through Sinajhal's flamboyant hat and hair and wedged into the skull beneath.

Sinajhal's eyes popped wide and he began jerking all over while his blood spurted. His fingers kept flexing even after he dropped his sword.

Hanse had to use both hands to get the heavy knife out of the other man's head. He didn't think about shaking off the blood and that ugly gray pulp, or about standing back to see whether the murderous robber was dying or might recover. He skewered the Ilbarsi blade into Sinajhal's throat and whipped it out with an attendant twist. That succeeded in ruining the robber's tunic with a great deal of gushing scarlet. The force of its spurting slackened swiftly.

Hanse stepped back from a corpse. He blinked when an airborne cat impacted it with all claws out.

"Never mind, Notable," Shadowspawn said in a voice as grim as his face, and realized that he wasn't even winded.

"Hanse!"

"I'm fine, Mignue. Hang onto those horses!"

"They're busy grazing on leaves. Is Sinajhal—"

"If you were going to say 'recovering,'" he said in a quiet and yet ugly voice, "the answer is no. The treacherous pig has trapped his last pilgrims."

"Oh, *Hanse!*"

"Please don't throw yourself against me this time, Mignue. I'd fall down!"

But she was already mobile, and she did, and Hanse did.

A minute or so later, on the ground, she said, "Oh darling you saved us both! Everyone knows about Shadowspawn and knives, but I had no idea you could fight a *sword* and win! I thought . . . I thought sure he would—oh, Hanse!"

I thought he would, too, Hanse thought, and remembered to let go his weapon at last so he could get both hands on the wriggling woman who was pressing so hard onto him.

Apparently Sinajhal's accomplice had not possessed a horse, unless the poor beast was tied back in the woods somewhere

deeper than Hanse searched. Meanwhile it was not just that
they had lost the gray horse's saddle to the would-be robber's
sword; the gray had fled as well. Shadowspawn was snarling
over the loss of steed, saddle and pack when Mignureal asked
where they would bury the two men.

"Bury!" he echoed, in a voice both plaintive and tinged with
anger. "These two murderous thieves? Let them rot where they
are. The birds'll have their eyes soon enough!"

Mignureal's face and voice showed her shock. "Hanse!"

"I am not going to do sweaty labor for those two men,
Mignue. They tried to kill me and you, and Notable and I
killed them. I am not going to spend the next bunch of hours
digging two holes and dumping them in! As a matter of
fact—" He broke off as he bent to pick up Sinajhal's dropped
sword and heft it. He swung it with an aubible *whup-whup*
before squatting to open the man's belt buckle.

"As a matter of fact hereafter I wear a sword and we both
carry crossbows. Pick up that one's, will you?"

"No."

Still squatting, Hanse turned his head slowly to glare at her.
She was hugging herself, shaking her head. He elected to
swallow whatever he had been about to say. He returned his
attention to Sinajhal's buckle, and stripped off the belt as he
stood. Moments later he had buckled it on.

"Spoils of conquest, is that it?"

"That's exactly it, Mignureal. You liked calling me hero
well enough a few minutes ago. If you don't like this, you'd
better just be quiet about it. And about burying them, too."

She compressed her lips while he collected both crossbows.
She turned away when he twisted his knife out of the paunchy
man's eye and wiped it carefully on the fellow's sleeve. After
examining it closely, he wiped it again before returning it to its
sheath. He had lost one good throwing knife against the
Tejana. Silver Imperials or no, he was not about to waste a
second good blade when he didn't have to. He had paid
premium coinage for that first knife back in Sanctuary, and
never mind where the money came from. Now it was lost,
because he had snap-thrown at a Tejana in the darkness, and
missed.

As to this one; well, this one was a gift from Cudget, poor

hanged Cudget Swearoath who had been mentor and friend and father-substitute. Never mind that the thief called Shadow-spawn pretended to be unsentimental because he thought he should; pretenses and reality were not poured out of the same bottle.

Notable meanwhile was prowling, looking as if true delight for him would be the appearance of more menaces. Rainbow sat watching Notable. The onager and the horses, including the white-stockinged black gelding of the late Sinajhal, were happily munching a bit of grass along with leaves from this or that tree and bush.

"I like his saddle, but I'll bet this nag of his isn't half the horse ole Iron-mouth was," Hanse groused.

"He certainly caught up to us handily. And quietly too," Mignureal said, in the way that bad storytellers referred to as "sniffed."

Hanse didn't even bother to give her a stare. He decided not to check the contents of the bag on the black's saddle or the roll behind it. Not right now. She would just be the more disapproving, and might say something. Sinajhal's belongings, if any, would wait. Hanse felt righteous, just, and justified. Why was it that his chosen woman considered it wonderful that he had killed two men and was like to vomit over the doing and the sight of it, yet had to be superior and disapproving of his taking their horse and weapons?

"Hanse: listen! No, look!"

She had heard the hoofbeats just before the riderless gray horse appeared around a curve in the trail. He was munching on something aside from his bit, and still wearing a ruined saddle. Laughing happily, Hanse went to stroke the animal's head and neck. Meanwhile he murmured caressive words.

"So," he said, but at the last instant changed his mind about saying the rest of it: *We've gained a horse, after all!* No use getting another of those looks from her. Besides, her lip was out a foot already. "So—-you came back to see if we still like you, hmm? Well, I guess I'd run if Notable landed on my back with twenty or thirty daggers, too."

"Meawrg-l-l?"

"Aye, Notable, you. You are one fine cat, Notable. I don't know how I managed without you all these years! Well, just speak up, boy. A man likes company, especially from a weapon-companion who's helped save the wimmenfolk. Talk to me some more."

Chew on that, he thought at Mignureal, and saw that she was, without pleasure. He was inspecting the gray's saddle. If it could be repaired, Hanse didn't see how. He decided to leave it where it was until he could find out, and change horses once again. He would ride Sinajhal's black.

"You're name Blackie?" he asked, and noted that the horse ignored him. On the other hand, so did Blackie. The onager, however, looked up and switched its tail. "No, Dumb-ass, your name's Enas, remember?"

The onager, Ils be thanked, did not reply.

"Hanse . . . ?"

"Umm?" he said, being signally busy at checking cinches and halters and packs while carefully not looking at her.

"If I help you, can we put, uh, sort of drape these two men over horses and take them . . . somewhere?"

He straightened up and turned to look at her with a thumb hooked in his new sword-belt. "Let me tell you what I'm afraid of I mean what bothers me, Mignue. Suppose not everyone knows these two are thieves, or even maybe thinks they're nice upstanding citizens. Then along we come, riding Sinajhal's horse and hauling his body on another. Do you think something unpleasant might happen?"

She considered that, meanwhile returning his gaze levelly. "Hanse, I think that no one is going to say much to the man who, who ended the careers of them both and wears Sinajhal's sword. Besides, what's that in the other one's forehead? Surely it's obvious that Sinajhal killed his partner, no matter that it was an accident. Suppose we just rode out of here on *our* horses, and leave their crossbows? Or even try to put that one back in Sinajhal's hand?"

Hanse started at her and knew she was right. He was impressed, and more. "Mignureal, I love you."

She blinked, gave him a wan smile, and hurried to him for a hug. It was mutual; profoundly and gloriously mutual, that embrace.

"I love you Hanse, oh I love you."

A minute or so later he said, "Uh . . . would you help me get this belt and sheath back around Sinajhal?"

Of course; and she did. He was rebuckling the belt on the dead man when she said, "It is yours, of course, won fairly against a man who tried to shoot you in the back with a crossbow. Hanse . . . I've always lived at home with my family. I thought I was really mature because I took care of my brothers and sisters a lot. But that didn't prepare me for any of this. I'm sorry I went squeamish and silly. My stomach was turning over and over and I thought I was going to throw up."

Hanse's snort was intended as a chuckle. "Me too. Furthermore I'm still not sure that I won't, at any minute."

"I was just so scared! I've never *been* so frightened. For you, darling. I just knew I was going to see you killed, and I kept trying to believe it just wasn't real. Then he—then you— but then you just attacked *him,* as if you had a sword and he wasn't way up there on a horse!"

I can't quite believe that myself, he thought but definitely did not say. *Or understand it either. I didn't realize that all the training and practice with Niko made me so good! Not to mention crazy enough to* attack *instead of ducking or trying to throw a knife or a star! I'm better with weapons and the dodging of 'em than I thought.*

"My desire is threefold," Hanse had said that evening in the ruins that had become, for the night, a scintillant hall of audience. He spoke with some trepidation, for it was to gods he spoke.

To that great glow that was Ils the All-father, Ils of the Thousand Eyes, He who was god of Hanse the Ilsig and his people; and to the darkness that was Shalpa the Unnamed, Shalpa of the Shadows, the Shadow Himself, patron of the night and of thieves, son of Ils and father of Hanse by mortal woman so that he was, indeed and in deed, Shadow's spawn; and to Eshi daughter of Ils, goddess of beauty and love who was very, very fond of this demigod.

And they gave listen, for these were the gods of the Ilsigi and of the town of Sanctuary, and Vashanka was god of imperious Ranke and its empire. Yet as agent of this trio Hanse had done what they could not without his aid: the half-god had destroyed Vashanka, and his power, and had begun thus the fall of Empire.*

He told them, then, what they asked and granted: his desires; his wishes for his life.

"First, that neither I nor anyone close to me, dear to me, ever knows the true moment of my *unavoidable* death."

He had worded it properly, and they understood. They knew of Mignureal, and of her Sight aborning, for they were gods.

"Second, I desire superior ability with weapons, as well as good health and good fortune."

That was a good wish, and cleverly made, and gods were pleased.

They were not pleased with his third stated desire. The youth called Shadowspawn had given it much thought, after ten days of having his every wish granted. He had made his decision, and not without mental agony.

"And third," he told them stoutly, "to forget all that has happened. All that I have done and thought and wished (saving only for a dream that I share with Mignureal, daughter of the S'danzo), since that time when first You did approach me, in the matter of Vashanka."

He who was Shadow Itself was insulted that his son desired no knowledge of their relationship. Furthermore he said so and showed it, for he was a passionate and a jealous god.

Eshi objected too, for she had entertained certain hopes involving the elevation of this demi-mortal and thus demigod into their midst, and what she and he might do then. For Oh, she did like him, this Hanse, this godson.

They argued, Shalpa in anger, until Hanse fell to his knees to cry out in a shaking voice all that he wanted.

"Let me be Hanse!"

Silence came into that unnatural hall of gods' audience then, until Eshi spoke at last. She wore a whimsical smile on her face, which was Beauty, as She was Love Itself.

"It's the damned eternal truth," Eshi said. "Your charming bastard is a damned genius, Shalpa!"

"Yet damned," her brother answered in his rustly voice of

*Detailed in "Godson," in *Storm Season* (Thieves' World # 4); Ace Books, 1982.

audible shadow. "Damned by his own tongue and his own wish. The terminator of a god, the savior of his city and toppler of Empire, the son of a god and lover of a god—and beloved of a god, eh?" He added, with a sidelong glance at his sister. "Damned to mortality, humanity, by his own asinine wish!"

And in anger and disappointment the Shadow of Shadows . . . vanished.

"Tell my father," Hanse said very quietly, "that I have known misery not knowing the identity of my father, and now in knowing it. Tell Him that . . . that his son is strong."

"True," Ils said, "and I'd never have thought it. Done!"

When Hanse awoke he was in the ruins of Eaglenest above Sanctuary, and wondered what in all the Hells he was doing there. He did not know that he had Chosen. He remembered nothing of his birth, of his deeds for the gods, or of his desires and wishes. He had no idea that he was to be unusually proficient with weapons; he must learn that for himself, in the doing.*

He was only Hanse again—or still: orphaned bastard and superb thief.

And still crammed full of needs and self-doubts which he masked with all his might.

And yet; and yet he had changed; and he was changing. Perhaps fighting it and certainly not finding the path easy, the cocky youth was becoming a man.

"Ah ho!" the farmer said once he had accosted the trepidatious Hanse and Mignureal.

"And what have we here? Sinajhal, isn't it?"

"So he said his name was," Hanse said, for he had decided against saying merely that they had found Sinajhal dead.

"Ah ho! So he's come to the end he deserved at last, at last! And you did it, lad?"

Hanse's face cleared a bit, and he swallowed. Yet he painted on a grim expression and used his best shadow-voice when he said, "Aye. He attacked the wrong people, this time. And it is no great happiness for me, being called lad."

*Detailed in "Rebels Aren't Born in Palaces," in *Wings of Omen* (Thieves' World # 6,); Ace Books, 1984.

The extremely lean man made a gesture of apology and respect. "Ah, ah! It means nothing, believe me. Yet it is delight on us all that no old seasoned man of weapons brought down that vampire, but a very young man indeed. And a stranger by your accent—just the sort he loved to prey upon, he did."

"Didn't he just!" So spake the elated Hanse. *And I was worried that we might be accused of murder!*

Meanwhile Mignureal nervously repeated "Vampire?" and the smiling farmer happily assured her that it was only a figure of speech, figure of speech.

"And who might this other be?" The farmer of Firaqa's outskirts drew closer to the other body lying limply over a horse, and crouched to peer up at the face. "Uh! Poor devil— and with Sinajhal's bolt in his face, poor man! Ah, by the Flame—not your father, I'm hoping, young sir?"

"M-mer-m-my uncle," Mignue stammered.

Even as Hanse looked around at her with round eyes, she squeezed forth a tear. Ah, he thought in new elation, *what promise my dear girl shows!*

"Oh my dear, my poor dear, I am so sorry, so sorry I am! And so glad, so very glad that your strong protector here was able to do death on Sinaj—was you who did it, young sir from afar?"

Head up, Hanse said, "Was I."

This time he glanced over at Notable, who sat the onager where he had somehow persuaded Rainbow to join him. The cat's full-furred red tail traced out designs in the air while he blinked long, as cats would. Hanse winked.

"Ha ha and ho ho!" The farmer clapped both hands to the hem of his tunic—beneath which he wore no leggings and no footgear of any kind—and good honest dirt rose as dust. "Some will celebrate this night, they will, for what a bad name that villain gave us all, preying on innocent travelers!" He half turned to point. "Yonder's my home; see the cookfire smoke? And yonder dwells my neighbor Gleenis (owns his own farm, Gleenis does!) and over there is my sister's farm with her husband. Any and all of us would be happy to feed and house you this night, Sinajhal-slayer, happy to! Aye, and your animals too! What say you? Will you stop? What say you?"

"My woman," Hanse said in what he hoped was a desolate voice, "is understandably not minded to celebrate, with her uncle victim of this villain whom I bested at swords even as he attacked. We would see them both buried, and then—"

"We'll do that, we'll do that," the man said, nodding the while and looking unseemly happy in the face of the death of a pretty young woman's uncle.

"How far is Firaqa?" Hanse asked, with another glance at Mignureal, who was still concentrating on putting on bereavement's cloudy face.

"About a half day. Wouldn't want to arrive there after dark, though, would you, now would you? And you will, now, 'nless you gallop all the way starting this instant, right this instant."

While Hanse hesitated over that, Mignureal spoke in a resigned voice:

"Let us tarry here and join them for the burial of our honorable dead and their dishonorable," she said with a little choking sound over "dead," "and then join their celebration. You know Uncle Kadakithis would have wanted it."

"Uncle . . . Kadakithis," Hanse said, looking as if he had swallowed a pin.

"You know how he loved celebrations," Mignureal said. "And how proud he was of you, darling."

And so they stopped, and were well fed and lauded, and celebrated while others labored to bury Sinajhal and the nameless brigand who had been his accomplice but was known to these folk only as Uncle Kadakithis, a foreigner, and both were much flirted with, and in the morning they rode on amid much leave-taking and laden with gifts of food and milk and home-pressed wine and even ale, and they marveled that in killing they had become beloved heroes. They bore crossbows and Hanse wore the late, unlamented Sinajhal's sword while sitting his saddle. And they rejoiced.

That was before Mignureal checked the saddlebag and found that it contained not eleven, but only ten coins. They quieted then, and rode on toward Firaqa under the gray mantle that was the shadow of sorcery.

THE CITY

THEY HAD TO urge their horses, keeping an eye on them the while, through a clamorous, free-form encampment and market of the sort that grew up outside the main gates of most cities. The area was cluttered with tents and people and lots of colors, along with various odors. The cats soon joined the humans above that noisy and often noisome press. Notable tucked himself up against Hanse's crotch and Rainbow against Mignue's, each with a human hand on its body.

Countless people wanted them to buy seemingly countless things, while several others had nothing to sell but wanted largesse just the same. Hanse was tempted to toss one a coin out of the saddlebag just to see what would happen. The thought made him realize instantly that if he passed out a piece of silver here, either as alms or for one of those fat striped melons he'd love to have, the noise level and the press around their horses would increase intensely as well as intolerably. In that case he and Mignue might be hours more in reaching that long wall of yellowish stone. They might well be prevented from reaching it at all. Bad enough having to remain so fixedly on the alert, lest someone decide to slice loose the rearmost horse and have a try at making off with it. Or lest the nervous Notable decide to pounce on someone.

Accordingly he continued pretending to ignore the importuning of pedlars and mendicants alike.

Had that smudge-faced boy really said what Hanse thought—offering his sister for sale or more likely temporary rent?

Had that old woman been eyeing the cats fondly or was that the gleam of hunger in her eye?

The tall iron-bound gates of Firaqa were marked with a carved-and-mounted flame emblem. Both were latched all the way open, leaving an entryway that could have accommodated five riders abreast. Hanse could see the guard in the tower on one side, and the crossbow up there, as well. A yellow pennon bore a white circle containing the red flame insigne.

Other guards, probably members of the city Watch or police detailed to this duty, stood about here below. They were hardly erect and didn't look particularly military or menacing.

Somewhere inside him Shadowspawn growled apprehensively, but Hanse reminded himself that he was a newcomer of some means. He had no past here, and no one knew him. At Mignureal's intelligent suggestion he had removed his sheathed knives, leaving visible only dagger and sword. The Ilbarsi knife they had attached to Mignue's saddle. In Sanctuary Hanse had been at pains to look dangerous. He might wish to do so here, too. But not today, not on entering.

The guards wore shiny helmets like inverted bronze pots divided by wedge shapes of brown lacquer, each topped with a metal crest resembling the fin of a fish. Their hot-looking leather cuirasses were snug over tunics whose color was close to the fulvous hue of the wall's stones. Only one of the three held his lance; the others leaned against the gates' inner edges. Each wore sword and dagger and all were bare-legged to just past the knees, where they wore nice brown boots with laces and short fold-over tops. Boots, pendent crotch-armor and weapon-belts gleamed with a number of smallish square plates of dull metal that looked more like iron than steel or anything else.

A child was clamoring on one side of Hanse and a scrawny, ragged man was pawing his leg on the other side as Sinajhal's black horse bore him up to the open gateway. A sentry watched from where he leaned against the leftward gate. He bumped himself forward with his butt and started forward. Immediately Hanse's stomach tautened and he felt a prickling in his armpits.

"All right, all right, get away from this man now, you two! This is a traveler come to our fair city doubtless to sell some horses, and needn't be bothered by the likes of you!"

The clamorous ones fell back while Hanse tried to look relaxed. The guard smiled at him and at Mignureal, and they continued pacing their horses to and through the gateway. Just inside and to the right, a man in the same uniform with the addition of a darkish blue cloak sat behind a table beside an older man, obviously a clerk. The first man's helmet also rested on the table. Hanse saw an emblem on the front: a stylized flame.

"A greeting and welcome to Firaqa. My job's to ask where you're from."

The truth seemed wisest this time, however much telling it went against Hanse's grain.

"We're both from Sanctuary, here to—"

"That far! And without a caravan, and those good hor— hmm. With saddles and riding bridles as well, eh? Brought those all the way from Sanctuary, young fellow?"

"Only three of them. We were ignorant enough to cross the desert, and got attacked by Tejana. They—you know about Tejana?"

The man, who was apparently chief of guards here, nodded and waved a hand. "Oh yes. I'm afraid we know about the Tejana. Killed others in your party and you two managed to flee?"

Almost Hanse wisely let that pass, but his pride would not allow it. "Not quite. They stole our horses and a few coins we had, four of them with crossbows so that we hadn't a chance. They left us stranded on the desert with only the ass—the onager."

The man and a couple of other guards were giving him their full attention, now. So was the clerk, an oldish man who was not writing, but staring with his mouth drooping as much as his left eye.

"My man followed them," Mignue said proudly. "Just couldn't bear to let them get away with it. I think he was as outraged that men who knew the desert would leave us that way, as he was angry that they had robbed us." She gestured at their menagerie. "These were our horses, *and* theirs."

"Theirs?" The seated sentry let a more attentive stance replace his easy lounging attitude.

Hanse was nervous about this, and not because he thought these people might think kindly of the Tejana. He was not anxious to announce himself as a fighter, or as a thief—even if it was his own horses he had stolen.

"I sure recognize 'jana horses when I see 'em, Sergeant," the burly older sentry said, nodding.

"I tracked them to a camp at the edge of the forest," Hanse said. "They were celebrating with strong drink. Drunk or asleep, with the horses penned a little way from the clearing." He shrugged. "It was late at night and dark in those woods." He made another of the shyly boyish shrugs he knew how to use. "I got our horses back. And took a little interest, while I was at it. Their horses."

The fact that the sergeant and another of the guards were grinning openly emboldened him to add, "They got to keep the coins."

"Quite an accomplishment," the sergeant said. "Tejana actually left their horses saddled and bridled?"

Damn it, Hanse thought, and shook his head. "They were haltered. They make the halters so that the reins attach. Since the raiders were drunk and sleeping or nearly, I took the time to add the reins and saddle all the horses but one." He smiled the boyish smile and made the boyish shrug. "No more saddles."

The old clerk-scribe grinned broadly, showing unexpectedly good teeth, and two guards laughed. The sergeant chuckled. "No trouble?"

"The trouble was in getting the first horse to go!" Hanse told him ruefully. "Those Tejana use voice commands, in their own language. When I said the right one, all they'd do was gallop. All I did was hang on. See, I'd ridden that dumb donkey to within a little distance of their camp, and left him in the woods. And this part you won't believe."

"It's a good enough story," the sergeant said, leaning back in his chair, "and my name is Gaise, sergeant of the City Watch, Gate Division. Try me."

"We were galloping by when I looked over and saw that one of the Tejana had come out of the camp with a crossbow and was kneeling, aiming at me. I'll admit it; I couldn't get the horse to turn that way or any other way. Then the onager heard the horses rushing by. He came hehawing and galumphing out of the woods. He ran right over the man who was going to shoot me.''

When the general loud laughter died down, Hanse added, ''That's why he's not wearing the heavier packs anymore. He earned a light load.''

''I'd say he did. And so did you. No other trouble?''

Hanse shrugged and spread his hands. ''I told you, Sergeant Gaze.''

''Mind if I ask your name?''

''Hanse. This is Mignureal.''

''Honz. And Minyourall.''

Hanse had already noted that these people tended toward broader a's than he was accustomed to. ''Hants,'' he said, pronouncing exaggeratedly.

''Min-you-ree-al,'' she corrected.

The sergeant laughed. ''Gay-sse,'' he re-pronounced, and his men laughed.

''Business aside, Hanse,'' Gaise said, rising languidly and stretching a little, ''I'd love to ask why you came here. That's personal curiosity now, not official inquiry.''

''Wish I could tell you later, Gaise. What we want to do now is find a place to stable these horses until we sell a few, and more importantly a place to stretch our legs and sit on something besides saddles.''

''And get a nice meal for a change,'' Mignureal said, since it wasn't necessary to mention that they had enjoyed nice meals each of the last two nights.

''Anyhow,'' Hanse decided to say, ''have you heard news from down Sanctuary way lately? Anyone come here from there?''

Gaise shook his head.

Good, Hanse thought. He said, ''The town's never been much, and we never liked the Rankans or the governor their emperor sent out. Awhile back we were invaded by people-things called Beysibs.'' He described the unblinking invaders from the sea. ''They—took over. Lording it over everybody. Their leader's a woman, or a female anyhow. Moved herself right into the palace where the governor had always been. They

are arrogant. Just acted as if we were the unhumans, 'stead of
them. Law died, in Sanctuary. A Beysib killed Mignureal's
mother, right on the street, over nothing. That decided us to do
what we should have done already, and we did.'' No need to
mention that he had slain the slayer, not while talking to police
who could decide to tell him to move on!

"We left Sanctuary with two horses and an onager and a few
coins," Hanse went on, "along with the few possessions in
those packs. Oh, and my cat here, Notable. We arrive here
with the onager, another cat, and six horses. The Tejana
actually helped us out! We're here to stay, we hope." He
showed Gaise a sweet youthful smile. "If I'm not too stiff to
get off this horse."

Gaise smiled and opened his mouth, but it was the clerk with
the stringy gray-white hair and bangs who spoke.

"What do you know about Ranke?"

"Never been there." Hanse made his answer deliberately
short. He was tired of hanging about here answering questions.
It was past mid-afternoon and besides another traveler had
already ridden in and right past them, unquestioned.

"No," the scribe said. "I mean the Rankan Empire. We've
heard a rumor or two."

"So have I," Hanse told him. "All I know for sure is that
they didn't do anything about the Stare-eyes' invasion of
Sanctuary, which the Rankans called theirs. Still, for all I know
a whole army arrived a day after we left, and wiped out the
Beysibs. Look, uh, I'd be happy to come back and talk some
more tomorrow, but we really do need to find a place to stay,
and some other things."

Then he remembered. "Oh—Sergeant. Do you and your
men know an inn called the Green Goose?"

Gaise started to answer, but broke off as a troop of five more
guardsmen stamped up. Their leader was cloaked as Gaise
was. He spoke:

"Sergeant Gaise, I relieve you and your men."

With a nod, Gaise looked up at the tower. "Ock! See
anything terrible?"

"No Sergeant!"

"Come on down, then. Sergeant Rimizin, we stand relieved." That ended the formal changing of the guard, and

Gaise pretended to yawn. "Another nice dull day, Rim. Hope you have the same sort of evening. I'm just going to walk this nice couple around to the Green Goose. Came up here all the way from Sanctuary, and had a little Tejana trouble along the way."

"Looks like they came out ahead," Rim said. "Tejana horses, ain't they?"

"Aye. We've also kept them here too long. They're anxious to get out of the saddle and I don't blame them. You can get the story another time."

"Damn!" Rimizin said, looking past Hanse. "Looks like you kept that horse here too long, Gaise!"

Hanse turned in the saddle to see the gray horse with his tail up. He heard the last of the plopping noises behind Gray. *Good,* Hanse thought. *That's what they deserve for keeping us in the saddle, blabbering in the sun! A nice steamy mess they'll have to clean up. Too bad it won't be Gaise and his old clerk!*

Gaise laughed. "My fault. I'm sorry, Rim. My boys and I just went off duty."

"Next time we visit an inn together," Rimizin said dryly, "you pay! Taff—grab the nearest beggar and tell him we've got some fuel here he can peddle. Drag him if you have to." He looked up at Hanse. "Ever meet a man named Ratsiraka, down in Sanctuary?"

"Never did."

"Good for you. Welcome to Firaqa." Rim waved a hand loosely. "Go find the Green Goose, afore another of those animals gets the same urge that gray one did."

"Yes sir, Sergeant. My pleasure, Sergeant. Sergeant Gaise—you want to ride?"

Gaise chuckled, punching the tower man in the arm as he came down and one of the new men started up the ladder. "I don't know Tejana voice commands either, Hanse!".

Mignureal and one of Gaise's men laughed aloud. Hanse shrugged. "Mount the other black. He's never been Tejana property—except for a few hours."

Gaise started toward Blackie; Rim made a motion; the two sergeants stepped aside. The men of Gaise's command, relieved and apparently through for the day, were drifting away. Hanse pretended not to notice Rim muttering to his fellow sergeant, with a glance or two Hanse's way. Shadowspawn's back began prickling. He glanced at Mignureal. Now Gaise was nodding, shrugging, giving Rimizin a slap on the upper arm.

"Later," he said, and went back to detach Blackie from the line of horses. He mounted swiftly and expertly and paced up beside Hanse. "Hanse, MinYOU-reel—this way."

"Min-you-ree-al," Mignureal said.

The ruddy-faced proprietor of the inn under the sign of the Green Goose was impressed to receive guests escorted by a Watch sergeant. Too, he and Gaise were obviously on friendly terms. That impressed Hanse; that he and Mignureal arrived with six horses not to mention an ass impressed the jowly proprietor, Khulna. "Aye," the tall and balding man said with the slightest of nods, he could accommodate those animals. He was afraid that Hanse and Mignue must look out for the smaller ones themselves, however. Yes, he had a nice room, upstairs and in back. "Aye," he said with the slightest of smiles, the door had a good inner lock.

"Let's hear about money," Hanse said, and Khulna asked how long they'd be staying, and about the horses. "Awhile. Days. Maybe a week or longer. We'll be selling several of the animals as soon as we can without hurrying so much that we take just any price."

"Let's talk about the weekly rate, then. Meals?"

"Uh, all right. Never more than two a day, and we don't eat much to begin with, either of us."

"Anh-huh," Khulna said, and looked upward to let them see that he was calculating.

He named a price, in copper coinage. Sparks, he called the coppers. Hanse asked how that compared to the cost of a loaf of good bread, and then a horse. Next he asked about silver and both Khulna and Gaise raised their brows. Khulna gave him an answer in grains and Hanse asked about coins.

"Whose coins?"

"Ranke," Hanse said.

"You talking about Imperials?"

Hanse nodded.

"Every Rankan Imperial I've seen has been good silver,"

Khulna told him straightforwardly. "Not only that, I'll admit I love 'em. You come up with one of those and you have a month's lodgings, assuming you sell some horses."

"I don't want to talk about a month, not just yet."

Khulna shrugged. "Then I owe you some difference. That would give you some Sparks to spend here in Firaqa, too."

Hanse decided he'd done being cautious. He would check elsewhere later. He said, "Please don't be alarmed when I bring a sheathed knife out of my tunic."

"With Gaise standing behind you?" Khulna's face cracked in the slightest of smiles.

Hanse thrust a hand down into the front of his tunic and pulled out the sheathed throwing knife. He offered the blunt, flat end to the innkeeper, who accepted the invitation to draw it. He looked impressed when the blade emerged.

"You throw?"

"I try," Hanse said, and tapped the sheath against his palm until the coin dropped out. He laid it on Khulna's counter.

Khulna picked it up, handed Hanse the knife, examined the coin, squeezed it, squinted at it, walked over to the window and peered at it again. He returned. "I owe you some difference," he said. "Sparks all right?—Firaqi coppers?"

Hanse shrugged and Khulna reached under the counter. He counted out a fair number of square copper coins, each with a round hole in the center. "Look about right to you, Gaise?"

"What do I know about money, Khulna? I work for the city."

The two men laughed in what Hanse took for a ritual. "Does that look satisfactory?" Khulna asked.

Hanse looked straight into the large man's eyes. "I can't say. By this time tomorrow I'll know."

"Anh-huh, I'd say you will. You, uh, have some more of those?"

Hanse stared coolly at him. Khulna spread his hands. "Sorry. What I was thinking about is the danger to you. I could put them in a safe place for you. If you have more, that's better than carrying them around."

Hanse turned to Gaise. "What's Firaqi law about doing physical harm on an assailant or would-be robber, Sergeant? Even unto death, say."

Gaise raised his eyebrows and both hands. "Who knows? If someone accosts you and you defend yourself, that surely couldn't be against any law in the world! Are you good with that sword?"

"Yes." Hanse's voice and his expression matched: flat.

"Better than the man you got it from?"

Hanse's stomach tightened. Hanse didn't even blink. "Aye."

Gaise continued looking relaxed and friendly. "A farm lad came in the gate last night saying that a certain trickster, confidence man, and stand-man had been killed in Olula Woods by his latest intended prey. Was that you?"

"What's a stand-man?"

"A fellow who has a sword or knife in your back or an arrow aimed at you and says 'Stand and stand away.' Means dismount and give me what you've got. We've been looking for one. He eluded us and we think he got out of the city a few days ago. Rimizin thinks you rode in on that fellow's horse."

"His name was Sinajhal," Hanse said, "or so he told us. Flamboyant, just brimming over with charm. Met us on the road and gave us a little lie to get us to 'shortcut' through some woods. Some farmfolk we met were delighted. They treated us as heroes and buried him last night, a few hours from here."

"That's your first service to Firaqa and hereabouts," Gaise said. "Was he alone?"

"No. The farmers didn't recognize his partner. So, just in case, we told them he was Mignureal's uncle. He's planted, too. Wearing one of Sinajhal's crossbow bolts in his forehead."

"*Fore*-head!"

"The partner was in front and Sinajhal was behind. I ducked."

Gaise and Khulna laughed aloud. Once they'd quieted down Hanse urgently requested that they tell no one of either the Sinajhal business or the coin. "I don't want anyone to know we have money, or that I'm dangerous." Sobering and gazing thoughtfully at him, both men promised.

Then Gaise said, "Are you good at throwing knives too, Hanse?"

"Yes."

"Umm. Should I be worried about you in my city, Hanse of Sanctuary?"

"I am not after anyone and I am not looking for trouble. Obviously Mignue and I have wherewithal. If anything, I'll be wary of becoming a victim in your city, Gaise."

"I will be working," Mignureal said. "I tell fortunes."

"What?" That was Gaise, but all three were jarred by her speaking; she had been silent for a long, long while.

"Are there no S'danzo in Firaqa? It is the trade of many of us S'danzo women."

Khulna slapped the counter, which startled Hanse. Khulna was startled to be facing a man in a semi-crouch, wearing a dangerous look. "Sorry! I just remembered. S'danzo—yes! I know of two, and aye, they read the future for a coin."

"I hadn't intended for you to be working, Mignue," Hanse said.

"I will be. A woman of the S'danzo does not not work."

They stared at each other.

"Think I'll have me a cup," Khulna said into air gone suddenly tense. "Gaise?"

"Draw two," Gaise said, uncomfortably watching the young couple.

"Uh, Hanse? Is that right: 'Hanse'?"

"Aye," Hanse said, without looking away from Mignureal. "No I don't want anyth—yes please, draw three. Get ready, Notable."

"You never said anything to me about intending to work the way your mother did," Hanse said awhile later, in an accusing voice.

The horses and ass were stabled and their owners were settled in a comfortable enough room in the Green Goose, upstairs in back. Notable had immediately demanded to be let out, proving that he was housebroken. Hanse and he had also swiftly proven that the little roof just outside the window was perfectly all right with the big red cat. As a matter of fact Notable preferred to remain out there, curled up on the green roof over the Green Goose's storeroom. He had delighted Gaise and Khulna by the way he went after that beer, and now he needed a snooze.

Rainbow had watched everything, and Hanse and Mignureal crossed their fingers in hopes that the calico cat was either housebroken or a fast learner.

"Yes I did," Mignureal said lightly, busily unpacking and placing colorful things here and there. "Back on the desert. You remember. Do you want—"

"No I don't," Hanse said. "I don't remember anything of the kind."

She paused to look at him. "You said that with the coins and the horses we had enough to live for a long time. I told you I would not be able not to do anything to bring in more money. You didn't say a word, then."

Hanse's mouth formed a silent o. He remembered. True, he had not argued. For one thing, he'd been too busy working out the meaning of her oddly worded sentence.

"Do you want to hide your black clothing or just leave it packed?"

Hanse blinked, still thinking about "not be able not to do anything" and having to lurch to follow her leap from a subject she obviously considered closed.

"Ah—I'll lay it out under the mattress. But—"

"I'll do it. Umm, nice mattress too, darling. Stuffed tight with shucks so it's firm but soft all at once."

Bent over the bed with both hands on it, she looked up at him, and Hanse swallowed. Not only did it resemble his own sweet look that she must have borrowed from him, he was looking right down into the front of her undertunic and blousy over-tunic. He wasn't looking at coins, either.

"All that talking and dreaming about a real bed," he murmured. "And now we have one, and what are we doing? I'm griping at you again."

"Oh Hanse, you're not *griping*. You just for—"

"Sh'up, woman," he snarled in an unreal voice, "an' getcher clo'es off. That bed wants testing."

"Yessir."

The mattress proved to be just right.

Khulna's wife Chondey nudged him when the new couple came down to dine in the Green Goose's common room. They were positively glowing. Head on one side, the considerably overweight woman watched them with soft eyes. Whether she was beaming or simpering or looking wistful was open to discussion.

Hanse and Mignue meanwhile had their first view of Khulna's wife and his plump daughter Chiri, who served them. Seven of the other diners and drinkers were male. The two females were plumper than Chiri. Most of the males flirted with her, but kept their hands to themselves. Her father, after all, was there, and he was no small man.

These were less noisy, Hanse noted, than the patrons of places he was familiar with back home. He did not mention that to Mignureal, since nearly all his experience was with low dives.

Though still aglow when they arose, he had insisted that they secrete the "good" coins again on their persons before coming down here to the common room. The saddlebag and the cats should be safe in their room, he said. Let someone just try to sneak in there, with Notable on the premises!

Then he had to wait while Mignureal pinned up her hair, looking into the wall-mounted mirror of metal. He was impatient but soon glad, for he liked her bared ears and the nice circlets that swung from their lobes. He liked the way she looked now, too, across the small table from him.

As for Mignureal, she would have preferred to have his seat on a bench against the wall, rather than her chair. She did not know that Shadowspawn was practically incapable of sitting with his back to a room, and would have been both uncomfortable and unhappy in her seat.

Chondey's food may not have been wonderful, but it seemed so. Her beautiful tan bread, studded with tiny bits of nuts and dates, was definitely wonderful. Hanse ordered ale with his baked chicken and was surprised to discover that it was no better than beer. He had always heard otherwise and besides it sounded better. Mignureal would not try it, but agreed to drink Khulna's weakest wine with her meal. They would ask around about Firaqa's water tomorrow.

He told her of his other plans.

He would buy two purses from one vendor and two others from another. Why? Oh, just caution; any seller would wonder why a person would buy four purses at a time.

"Caution," Mignureal said, and nodded, and she sighed.

They would carry most of their wealth inside their clothing, Hanse went on, but wear outer purses in the normal way, with a piece of silver and a few local coppers. In the event they fell prey to cutpurse or ripsnatcher, they at least would not lose much. He would also inquire around about the value of various metals and monies here, and try to learn if an honest banker or moneychanger was to be found in Firaqa. He would do a far better job of learning the value of their horses by going to two or three dealers, pretending to be a prospective buyer. He'd also inquire about Anorislas.

"Why not ask Khulna, Hanse? If he doesn't know him, he could ask the others here. This is no huge city, after all."

Hanse only looked steadily at her without expression.

"Oh," she said. "Caution."

"Right. Migue, I am wary and cautious. Besides, Strick said to ask *discreetly*. He must have had a reason. Suppose Anorislas is what is known as an unsavory character? You know, like that fellow Shadowspawn we heard of back home. Khulna would wonder why I am interested in contacting such a fellow. And Khulna is a friend of Gaise. Gaise is with the City Watch. That's police—a grabber. Both of them know too much already, because I was tired and not cautious enough."

"I suppose I never am," she said with a sigh.

Hanse looked at her very seriously. "No, Mignue, you aren't. That makes me worry about you."

"I promise to try to be more mistrustful of others." Abruptly she leaned toward him across the small table. "Hist! Look at Chiri. D'you think she might be a Stare-eye in disguise, come up from Sanctuary to Get You?"

Hanse rolled his eyes. "Ah," he said dramatically, "I am doubly accursed! A dumb-ass onager and a smart-ass woman!"

Mignureal laughed. "Well, I really will try. You could probably stand to be less mistrustful, too. I think I'll call you Caution. It can be your—what do they call it? Your war-name. What horses do we intend to sell?"

"Once I get a fair idea of their worth, why not let prospective buyers decide? The one someone chooses first will be the first we sell, and so on. When we are down to two, those will be our horses. As to Enas—him we don't need, but he

could be valuable in some close trading. A throw-in, as in 'All
right, give me a million coppers for Blackie and I'll throw in
that handsome intelligent onager who once saved my life.' "

She smiled but went immediately serious. Her hand touched
his. "I have a special request. Let's keep Inja. I like him, and
he has a name. Besides, he was a gift from Tempus and that's
special. Let's let him be my horse."

The trouble with that, Hanse reflected, was that Tempus and
his band knew horses and had no bad ones, although of course
Tempus hadn't given him a *Trôs*. Too, that horseless Tejanit
had chosen Inja over Blackie. Inja might well be their most
valuable animal! Too valuable not to sell? *But*. No use getting
into a discussion or argument about it now, when all was
speculation. Besides, the animal *had* been a gift. Perhaps they
should keep him because he was a better than good steed.

Hanse nodded without comment.

"I love you, Hanse. You're a good lover, too!"

"With you," he said gallantly even while his chest swelled,
and he hid behind his mug.

Chiri wandered along with her pitcher and tried to fill it, but
he assured her that he had enough. Chiri switched plumply
away to refill the mug of a man who'd had enough but didn't
think so.

"I want to find out about other S'danzo here, too,"
Mignureal said.

He nodded without saying anything. He was not enamored
of the idea of her setting up a table and sign to read futures, but
had decided that he had better just shut up on that matter.

At last he said, "We can do that, too."

"I'm glad to hear you say 'we,' darling. About the purses
and the horses and all you kept saying you would do that, but I
want it to be we. After all, there's nothing for me to do if I just
wait here for you—'Caution'—unless I try to help Chiri and
her mother clean up, or help in the kitchen."

Hanse looked at her with his teeth in a corner of his lower
lip. Hanse the loner had not considered going about with her. It
just hadn't occurred to him. He operated better alone. At least,
he always had, because that was what he knew before Cudget,
and after Cudget's execution. This business of teaming, of
pairing off and taking responsibility for two, was a lot more

than he had thought about. She was right about just staying here, too; she'd have nothing to do. And he did not want her going about a strange city without him, seeking S'danzo or any other thing.

"We should think about other lodgings," he said. "A room or three, I mean. This is an inn, after all, and the very first place we looked. Perhaps a villa, in the aristocratic section?"

"Oh my yes, and with suh-vants as well!" she said with a bright smile, and tried another little sip of the yellow-white wine. "I do like the idea of an apartment of our own, though."

Good, he mused. *Then you'll be occupied with cleaning and cooking and fixing it up for us, and not about going out on busisness matters with me!*

"You will need some clothes, Hanse. And everything we're wearing has got to be cleaned."

"I can't argue with that. Cleaned about three times! I swear I still feel desert sand in my leggings!"

"We do have a lot of silver, Hanse. You might consider a new pair."

Hanse was frowning at that concept when he became aware of Khulna's approach. They looked up at the ruddy-faced Firaqi with the bulging apron. If ever there existed a lean innkeeper, Hanse mused, he could charge extra just to let people see him. Khulna was unimpressive as to breadth of shoulder. Nevertheless he was large with a large paunch, his wife was plain fat, and their jiggly-plump daughter was working on it. Just now Khulna was standing by their table, smiling.

"What do my favorite guests think about Firaqi cooking?" he asked.

"I don't know about Firaqi cooking," Hanse said, "but your wife's is wonderful, Khulna!"

Mignureal was nodding. "This bread is so good that she'll have me fat in no time!"

"That's what happened to the three of us," Khulna beamed, and slapped the bulging front of his apron. "Glad you like it. What can we do to make you happier right now?"

"You could tell me what sort of area of town this is, Khulna, and advise us of the bad areas."

Their host bent down with a reddened hand on their table.

"People tend to refer to this south end section as Gates," he said. "Decent folk live hereabouts, and we keep the streets well lighted. The main temple of the Flame is not far from here. The Reds—that's the police—like to watch over us here, too. Because nothing ever happens!" He laughed and continued after Hanse and Mignureal had dutifully chuckled.

"The villas are mostly to the north, on Town Hill. That's what that section is called: Town Hill. The higher the home, the richer the owner. You," he said to Mignureal, "should never never go west of the street called Caravaner, and you, Hanse, were better not going over there at night. And armed by day. That area is known simply as the West End. Deeper in is an area that's a veritable maze. That, my friends, is *rough*."

"Really?! The *Maze*?!"

"Yes, really, a maze—wait. Why do you ask that way, and exchanging looks as well? Hmm?"

"Careful about treating us as your children, Khulna," Hanse said pleasantly. "Because where we came from the worst area in town is also called that: the Maze!"

"Flame deny it! Really? Maybe there's a maze everywhere," Khulna said. "However, here it's called Red Row. I came into town off the farm over a half-score years ago, and I've never been anywhere else. I'll never understand you world travelers. But I appreciate you!"

Hanse, who was hardly a world traveler, nodded with aplomb.

"Horse dealers?" he asked. "Honest moneyhandlers?"

"'No man recommends his own moneyhandler, lest he be blamed later.' You know—I really don't know much about horses or dealers either. To me, horses are dangerous at both ends and uncomfortable in the middle."

Hanse surprised all three of them then, himself included, by standing and clapping Khulna on the upper arm. "Agreed! Agreed!"

"Hoy, hold it down over there, Khulna," someone called. "Some of us are trying to drink!"

Automatically Hanse started to bristle, but Khulna half-turned to smile at that grinning patron. "Quick, Lallias, name me two men in Firaqa who know horses and are honest!"

"Whew," the heavily brown-bearded man called Lallias

said. "Two! And *honest,* even! There's my brother, of course, and Veldiomer the Sumian . . . uh . . ."

"Don't forget Anorislas," a red-bearded fellow called.

Lallias nodded. "Oh yes, Anorislas. Aye, he knows horses. I can't vouch for his honesty . . ."

"I would!"

Hanse asked for and received fair directions; both those men were in The Quarter, wherever that was. He also ascertained that Khulna knew neither man. Lallias, meanwhile, wondered if Hanse were interested in buying a good horse.

Hanse hurriedly said "Aye, I may be," before Khulna could speak, and gave the innkeeper a finger pressure to warn him to silence.

At once Lallias suggested his brother, Horse, and asked where Hanse might be in the morning. Hanse countered by asking where Horse could be found, and Lallias countered that by saying he'd be here in the morning to "lead you there." Hanse looked a question at Khulna. Khulna shrugged; his expression said that as far as he knew, Lallias was all right.

"Noon," Hanse told Lallias, and gave the fellow his name.

"New in Firaqa, are you?" That from the man who had suggested Anorislas's name.

"Aye, he is, but he is an old friend of mine," Khulna said, and Hanse was both impressed and grateful. He showed Khulna as much, with a look.

"You'll want to see Anorislas," the red-bearded man said.

Hanse asked for and received his name: Bronze. Then someone called for Chiri, and Chondey squealed with a small grease fire, and Khulna hurried to her, and Hanse and Mignureal followed. Once the very minor fire was out and they had gained food for the cats, they went upstairs.

"A good start," he said, after he had closed and carefully locked the door while Mignureal made herself a hero to the cats. "Some names, anyhow."

"I loved it," a glowing Mignureal said. "Do you know I've never been in an inn before, much less a common room! What fun! Everyone a friend!"

"Maybe," Hanse said, and embraced her, and kissed her.

She wagged a finger. "You were going to be less mistrustful, Caution!"

"And you were going to be more," he said, wagging his finger after he had pressed it to an intimate place.

Mignureal's eyes went soft. "Is it time for bed?"

Hanse squeezed her and kissed her again. "Let's do it again—look in the saddlebag, I mean," he added, when he saw her look. "And do you know we put off looking into Sinajhal's pack until we were alone and had time, and still haven't done it?"

"I think I don't want to look into that saddlebag anymore," Mignureal said, suddenly wearing a disconsolate face.

"I don't either," Hanse said, picking up the container in question. He opened it, and upended it over the rumpled bed.

No genius was needed to count not eleven, but ten coins.

"First we had eleven," he said, staring at the gleaming pieces of silver, "and couldn't get rid of them. Suddenly one just—disappeared." Hanse sighed and shook his head. "*Sorcery.* Do you think it had something to do with the coin I left for Imrys and his family? Maybe if I give one away, one of these disappears?"

"We could try that, and see."

"Whew. That's going a bit far."

Mignureal chuckled. "I knew you'd say that! But I suppose it's possible. The coins were somehow sent to us, as a sort of test of whether we're charitable or not."

"Well, I hate to make the test. If we give one away and another one doesn't vanish, we're out a coin. I'm not very charitable, Mignue."

"I'm not either, really. I can't think of anything else. I'd hate to think it had something to do with Sinajhal."

Watching her suddenly hug herself, Hanse put his head on one side. "Sinajhal? What d'you mean?"

"Well . . . I just hate the thought so much I hate to say it! I don't want to think that the only way to get rid of the coins is if you kill ten men!"

Hanse swung away, shaking his head. He turned back to look at her very seriously. "So would I. Let's not think about that one."

She nodded with enthusiasm. "I'm willing! Can we stop talking about it altogether, now?"

"I'll mention one other thing, first. Suppose we spent these coins?"

"From the looks of things, it would just reappear here."

"Uh-huh . . ."

"Oh, *Hanse!* We can't do that! We have plenty. We don't have to cheat people!"

"Well . . . we'll do this—we'll put one of those in our outer purses and then who cares if anyone steals it!"

Both of them liked that idea. While she chuckled, he bent to scrape up the ten Imperials and return them to the old saddlebag. Next he dumped onto the bed the behind-the-saddle roll of the late, charming Sinajhal. He opened it.

The reasonably nice, striped blanket was wrapped around a number of objects. The flattish wine skin Hanse sloshed and pronounced nearly empty. Naturally he picked up the folded red sash next, noting with a smile that it lay atop a green tunic, equally bright.

"Want to unfold this while I just try the tunic?" he said, extending the packet formed by the sash. Mignureal took it, but a moment later she had to laugh at Hanse's suddenly morose face, as well as at the mint-dyed garment he held up against him. The tunic was too large for Sinajhal, too large for Hanse, and might not be tight on Khulna.

"Damn!" he said in real disappointment. "Damned dumb stand-man! Older than I am and definitely not new at thieving, but he never learned to be discriminate in what he stole!"

She laughed. "Oh Hanse, I'm sorry—but what a phrase! The Undiscriminating Thief!"

She ducked her head at his look, and tried to look sober while she unfolded the scarf. She found six Firaqi coins of copper and two of silver, flame-marked. That was nice, and of course she was right in pointing out that the tunic might serve them well as a gift to someone—Khulna? The problem with selling it was that it was undoubtedly stolen and wouldn't it be just lovely to try selling it to a big man and discover that he was its original owner!

Hanse had already laid aside, without excitement, the dagger he found. It appeared to be of fair workmanship, but wanted examination and testing before he could trust it. The "jewels" in the hilt he was sure were glass.

"Not much of a treasure trove," he muttered, examining the trove's final treasure: a hinged, fold-over wooden square. He removed the ribbon and opened out a double beeswax tablet. One surface was blank. Into the other had been scratched a number of words, one under the other. Hanse looked at the list, seeing only letters. Squiggles etched into clay or wax.

"What is it?" Mignureal asked.

"Words," he said, and handed it to her for translation.

She read off the list:

ELTURAS
ESTANE
LALLIAS
PERIAS

THUVARANDIS

When she had finished and looked up questioningly, Hanse was frowning, pursing his lips in thought. "That's all?" he muttered distractedly.

"That's all."

"You said Lallias," he said slowly. "That's written there? Right, then. It must be a list of names. One of them is the man downstairs. The one who's going to take me to his horse-wise brother. Or . . . so he says." He paused to contemplate the strange list some more, seeking its significance, if not its meaning.

"There's a space here," she said. "It's as if another name should have been written between Perias and Thuvarandis. But the wax is smooth there."

Hanse continued silent for a few seconds more. Then: "Let's not wonder why 'Lallias' is one of five names that stand-men thief had listed on a wax tablet behind his saddle, all right?"

Mignureal was frowning, staring at the list, and her "All right" failed to sound convincing. "But, Hanse. The list is in alphabetical order. And—"

"Didn't I hear an L for the first name? I mean, I know some things, Mignureal. I can print my name, and I know an H when I see one, and an L when I hear one."

"No, Hanse; it's an E. E, then L. It sounds the same.

Anyhow, the list is **E, E, L, P**, space, **Th**." She pronounced the theta diphthong that way, as in "th-ink."

"Does that spell something?"

"Not that I can s—no. No, it couldn't. There's no vowel between **P** and **T**. I'll tell you what is between them, though. The letter **S**." She said it significantly, and she looked up significantly.

He looked at her. "Sssss," he said, showing that he knew an **S** sound when he heard it. "All right. That's important?"

"I hope not," Mignureal told him, looking unhappy. "It's the first letter of Sinajhal's name."

He looked stricken for a moment, but then gave his head a jerk and made a gesture of dismissal. "Why would he carry a list that had his own name on it—and in alphabetical order, too! He sure looked the sort to put his name first, to me!"

"Oh faint! You say *'Why'* and don't find a logical answer and act as if that settles that. We can't think that way—we have a *Why* about the coins and a *Why* about Rainbow and a *Why* about this list, and—" She trailed off, shaking her head and spreading her hands. "See? Everything is a big *Why!*"

They gazed at each other for a while in distress; caught up in something beyond their explanation and not at all happy about it. Hanse began moving the trove off the bed with a resigned air. "Think it's about time to go to bed?"

"Definitely."

Firaqa was different from Sanctuary, the newcomers discovered next day when they followed nicely simple directions to the bazaar.

Much could be deduced about climate and rainfall, heat and humidity, by the construction of buildings and their roofs. On the other hand, such logical deductions could be thwarted by something so simple as terrain and thus which building materials were available.

Roofs in Firaqa had plenty of slope, as did those in Sanctuary. That indicated a goodly rainfall. Roofs here differed in that they tended to be painted, in green and blue and yellow. Before long Hanse and Mignureal learned that was in imitation of the colored tiles used by wealthier Firaqi, and on some of the roofs of buildings in this area owned by better-off citizens. Those were tall tenements or apartment buildings, mostly.

The roofs overhung the buildings and run-off ducts ran along their bases. These gutters were intelligently slanted: under the lower ends of most were rain barrels. Other gutters ran into pipes or closed ductways leading into the buildings. That, again, obviously depended upon the wherewithal of the owner, or in some cases of the leasing occupant.

At any rate, here in Gates buildings and homes with running water stood side by side with those that had only barrels.

The newcomers learned that the forest they had passed through was called Maidenhead Wood, for a reason lost in time. It was relatively nearby and once had been a lot nearer, since the farmlands south of Firaqa, at least, had emerged years agone from the clearing and uprooting of trees. Naturally many buildings the couple saw were constructed of wood overlaid by some sort of plaster or stucco. Plenty were of stone, however, since the much-quarried area called Redstone was also close by, to the northeast. Foresting and quarrying, carpentry and woodcutting remained major industries hereabouts.

The stone was no more red than "red" clover. It was pink. So were the stone buildings. Since the stucco tended to be tinted or painted a sort of fulvous yellow, often set with doors of blue or green or red-brown, Firaqa was a pretty town. At least, Hanse reminded himself, this area called Gates was.

They did not bother to take the scenic route Khulna had suggested. Instead they went over to the street running from the gate through which they had entered, and turned north along that laid-stone thoroughfare. It bore a fine impressive name: Gate Street. Khulna had told them to go three streets past the Temple of the Flame, and turn left. That was Cameltrack Way, and led right into the open market. He had mentioned Merchants' Street, as an alternative to the bazaar.

"Things tend to be less dear in the bazaar at home," Hanse said. "Isn't that true here?"

"Aye," Khulna said. "I thought—" But he let it go, not wanting to mention that he had supposed a couple with Rankan silver would want to spend more for whatever it was they intended to purchase.

They walked up Gate, knowing that the broader street called Caravaner lay somewhere to their west, running the length of

the city and continuing through the Newtown area that had
grown up outside the gates, to the northwest. For different
reasons and with different reactions, Hanse and Mignureal very
much noticed that a display of bosom was in among Firaqa's
women this year. Meanwhile, skirts were long enough almost
to hide the feet and, when worn by women of wealth and/or
station, covered the feet utterly and even swept the ground.
Only a few wore their hair loose. Mostly it was done up,
sometimes ornately, and decorated with pins and combs and
ringlets.

Mignue noticed that seven in ten of the women's tunics
showing as blouses above their tightly belted skirts were this or
that shade of yellow, and two of the remaining three in ten were
white or that shade called natural.

They were not shocked at the frequency with which they
noted red hair—only because Chondey had prepared them this
morning. They would see many dyed heads, she had said.
Scarlet tresses had been all the rave the past couple of years,
since the consecration of the newest Hearthkeeper, who
happened to be a redhead. They had nodded and Mignureal had
thanked her. They hoped to find out what a hearth-keeper was
without having to ask.

Many of those they saw on and along Gate Street wore a
string of the square copper coins called sparks on thongs or bits
of wire about their necks, so that numerous people of both
sexes seemed to be wearing the same necklaces. The number
of coins strung thus, however, varied from one wearer to the
next.

They were surprised to see so many men wearing hats,
usually gray or maroon or dark-blue brimmed ones, turned up
in back and on one side. The few they remarked whose hats
sprouted or trailed feathers had to be the wealthy. Those men
tended also to wear brightly colored leggings—often startlingly
brightly colored ones even to Hanse—and heeled boots under
tunics that, cinched with great big belts, tended to blouse out
below and even stand away in a ripply effect. Hanse realized
that he was seeing every color of tunic save red, although some
were striped with lime or scarlet or cinnamon or a sort of
raspberry pink shade he did not like at all. Even most of the
plain white or "natural" tunics were striped at sleeve bottoms

and hems, and sometimes multiply striped. Patterns were unusual.

Some older citizens wore robes. Once Hanse saw two women in yellow-gold robes, hardly flowing and yet somehow modest, pristine. Walking tall, orange-red veils flowing long down their backs, they looked straight ahead and spoke to no one. The singular pair was escorted by three men of the City Watch. Citizens were obviously deferential, and actually inclined their heads on passing or being passed by the two haughty women in their flame-hued robes, escorted by the stiff trio of men who wore uniforms and stony faces.

Hanse assumed that these women were Somebody, but decided against asking. He hoped they were the occasion of all the respectful attitudes; he'd hate to have journeyed to a city where one bowed one's head every time a helmeted, armored grabber passed!

The poorer citizens and lower classes wore what they wore about anywhere: whatever they could find and afford to make.

While a number of men wore arms, he noticed, quite a few did not. It was surprising to see people without so much as an eating dagger in evidence. Walking sticks or staffs did seem to be in vogue in Firaqa; Shadowspawn was well aware that such made felicitous weapons unless someone got in too close too fast. He had naturally chosen to wear a dagger openly, with another one concealed. Well, two, but the one was after all just part of the decoration on his buskin. He had decided against wearing Sinajhal's sword until he saw how things were, in Firaqa.

He heard the word "Flame" quite a bit, in passing snatches of converse. Several men of the Watch were very visible, all uniformed as had been those at the gate. While they saw no chariots, a couple of laden wagons passed, moving slowly in the center of the street. Each was equipped with jingling bells that effectively warned anyone out of the way. A few passersby were on horseback. All held their animals to a sedate walk save one; he moved his mount at a trot. The fact that he also kept scrupulously to the center of the street was notable.

"I'd say we have a law about chariots inside the city," Hanse said, "and about how fast horses can move, even on this wide street. I like that."

"City rulers concerned about the safety of citizens? How wonderful!"

And how strange, Hanse mused.

Twice they observed the passage of covered, pole-mounted conveyances swaying on the shoulders of four knotty-calfed bearers. Servants or slaves, bearing masters or mistresses of wealth or dignity—perhaps even both—to some important destination. In both cases the bearers wore matched tunics— "Like a matched set of horses," Hanse murmured—and the second sedan chair was escorted by an armed man, walking close to the drawn curtain of his employer's lofty seat.

Hanse and Mignureal were looked at, too.

She sighed. "Obviously strangers, aren't we?"

"Um. How d'you feel about putting your gourds on display?"

"Nervous." After a few paces she added, "How do you feel about wearing one of those odd hats?"

"Oh, I don't know," Hanse said with a little smile. "I might like it."

"I'll bet the *S'danzo* here do not put their breasts on display," she said primly, emphasizing the proper word for "gourds."

Hanse said, "Um."

He and Mignureal saw no S'danzo. They knew they were approaching the Temple of the Flame well before they reached it. It soared; it bulked.

The temple was the size of several large dwellings, and with the gold-gleaming onion-like dome it lofted taller than any apartment building. White stone, this main Temple of the Flame, and well kempt. Two sets of nine steps lifted it well above street level, so that all must look up to its porticoed face. The columns were yellow-gold, or orange-yellow, or whatever the term should be; they were carved to resemble the fire whose color they imitated. Mignureal remarked no statue up there, and said so.

Hanse looked again. She was right. "Well, how do you build a statue to a flame?"

"Hmm," she said, and they walked on, glancing back now and again at that lofty and more than imposing structure wherein, presumably, dwelt the protector god of Firaqa.

"Hanse," she said, with that lilt in her voice that said "Guess what" or "Have you ever thought" or "Oh look." She said, "Look back at the temple now—look above it."

He did. He saw smoke. True, only a tenuous vapor was rising, but it was darkish. Hanse nodded. "Um. Smoke. I guess that's what we should expect to see above a place called the Temple of the Flame; smoke. What would be inside but a big fire? No statues, I'll wager. Just a flame, always tended. A Flame that never goes out, I'd wager. If it does, the chances are that so does Firaqa."

"Ewww. That's . . . ewww."

"Careful. We're in a strange town. Another part of the world, with different gods and beliefs. I didn't say I believed it, Mignue. But this isn't the territory of Ils and Shipri and the Nameless Shadowed One. Gods are strong in their own territory, but weaken with distance from it. When you get to a new territory, its gods are supreme and your own are weak."

"Oh. But then how come the Rankan gods are so strong back ho—back in Sanctuary?"

Hanse shrugged as they walked on. "Probably because some people wanted them to be and didn't think much or care about facts everybody knows about gods. Besides, something happened to Vashanka, didn't it!" Hanse, who as gods' ally on another plane had slain that god of imperiously Imperial Ranke in the only way an immortal could be slain and who remembered nothing of it because he had chosen so, smiled. "The All-seeing Allfather sure proved Himself that night!"

Then he added thoughtfully, "We'd better find out a few things, and we'd better be careful about what we say, too, Mignue, in a strange town of strange gods. That includes 'Ewww.'"

"It's strange, all right!"

As Khulna had said, Cameltrack Way led directly into the bazaar. And ended there, or became the bazaar. Perhaps once Cameltrack had connected Gate and Caravaner, and the bazaar had just grown up, naturally enough along the caravan route through Firaqa, and kept growing. The sprawling open market was larger than Sanctuary's, but was the same or nearly. Noisy and full of people hawking and haggling, constantly amove;

bright with many colors of clothing and wares and the striped awnings above merchant stalls; alive with aromas ranging from leather to horse to perfumes to sweat to cinnamon to garlic to oil to the cooking goodies some always sold because others were always ready to eat.

Hanse and Mignureal spent nearly an hour walking through, looking and looking while shaking their heads at eager vendors, trying to maintain a straight line toward the market's far side, opposite Gates. They saw several police as well as private guards, and were not unhappy about it; Shadowspawn was or had been a cat burglar, not a cutpurse or ripsnatcher or mere grab-and-run thief. At last they emerged to realize that a caravan of some sort must have passed only recently. Half a dozen adolescents were clearing the broad street of droppings.

"So there's where we're not supposed to go," Hanse said, looking across the street at the establishments of leatherworkers and others who picked up transient trade by situating themselves here. "Behind those is the dreadsome West End, and the maze called, gasp-gulp, Red Row." He made his voice sinister and yet quavery. "D'you suppose there's a Vulgar Unicorn back there?"

"Surely there can be only one Vulgar Unicorn in all the world, and only one Sly's Place. But I'll bet there are dives just like them, with the same sort of trade. I won't be finding out!"

I will, Hanse thought, and turned back. "Let's find some purses. Stay close, all right?"

They bought two purses at two-for-a-copper, and hid them in their clothing, and well away from that pedlar they bought two more, of thicker leather. Very secretly, they slipped a couple of coppers and one of what Hanse called the "homing Imperials" in the purses they wore openly.

Then Hanse did a bit of wandering and polite questioning, telling a number of people that a man had offered him a Rankan silver coin, an Imperial, and should he accept it? Was it good? Was it as good as Firaqi?

Three men at once said yes, assuring him that the Imperial was worth sixty—an extra ten coppers here; a woman snapped "Ranke!" and spat; two women and another man agreed that an Imperial was worth sixty-two, and pointed to a money-changer. Since he told them he offered a hearther-and-nine for an Imperial, Hanse decided that their coins were indeed worth a hearther-plus-twelve: a Firaqi silver coin and a dozen sparks. It was pleasant to have some idea of the value of money here, and of his.

"I think the fellow feels that what he has is worth sixty-two," Hanse said. "And he wants coppers, not silver."

"Oh. The first might be so, but of course I have to keep food on my table," said the Changer, who looked as if he might be able to squeeze the result of his eating habits into the green tunic from Sinajhal's pack. "Of course if he wants coppers, I might be able to go sixty."

"Suppose it was two Imperials and he wanted twice sixty plus three?"

The fellow regarded Hanse with a whimsical expression indicating that he realized—with surprise—that he was talking to the possessor of two pieces of Rankan silver. "Your accent . . . you and your wife haven't just come up here from Ranke, have you?"

Hanse shook his head. "No no, Mrsevada. You see, we just sold a horse, and—"

"A horse for a hundred and twenty sparks? Oh by the Fire That Ever Burns—I wish you had come to me! That was no fair price, lad. He took advantage of you."

"You deal in horses, do you?"

The Changer smiled and his eyes positively twinkled. "Oh, I deal in about everything, my friend from Mrsevada. About everything. Now a good gelding, with good teeth and plenty of life and work left in him, would have had you and me discussing seven or eight hearthers."

"Actually," Hanse said, continuing his education, "it was an onager."

"Ah. Oh, well then. Depending upon its age and condition, I still might have gone two-fifty; that is, five hearthers. Oh my. I do wish you had come to me first!"

So, Hanse mused. *A good horse is probably worth twelve and Dumb-ass should bring seven or eight, then. Glad I stopped here!* "Listen, the coins are in my sheath, which is inside my tunic. I tell you this so you won't be alarmed when I take it out."

The Changer's eyes rolled and one hand casually left the

counter. Hanse was sure he had just marked the location of a
guard, and laid his dimpled hand on a weapon. Hanse held up a
hand, fingers spread, and smiled.

"Slowly," he said. "See; left-handed, too."

Mignureal turned away to hide her smile. When she turned
back the relieved Changer was gingerly extracting the dagger
from the sheath Hanse proffered. Both of them watched Hanse
upend the sheath and whack it down into his palm. He held out
the two Imperials.

"I'll take a hundred and twenty-three," he said.

The Changer regarded the bits of silver, regarded Hanse.
"May I?" He examined a coin, then the other. And regarded
Hanse. "My feeling is that we are through bargaining, so I'm
going to count a hundred and twenty-two Firaqi coppers into
your hand." Simultaneously bringing up a metal box, he
smiled. He banged the box rather sharply on the counter.
"Sorry I haven't any Mrsevadan."

Hanse knew the fellow was assuming the transaction to be
closed. He decided to go along. He glanced to one side, then
the other, and smiled.

"Good signal. When you fetch out the moneybox you bang
it and that big sword-toter over there came as alert as a cat that
hears a noise in the mouse-hole."

"You are a sharp-eyed and sharp-minded individual. My
name is Tethras. Now mind the counting; keep me honest."

Hanse and Mignureal did just that, never taking their gazes
off the Changer's plump and hairless hand and the steady
chink-chink of square, holed coins of about the same color as
the fingers that handled them. Six stacks of ten became three of
twenty. And again. And he added one.

"There."

"And one, Tethras my friend, and one. My name is Hansis,
and this is Min."

"Min-you-r—" she began, but broke off. Oh. Caution. This
time it was Hansis and Mign, then. She hoped he didn't make
up more names and places they were supposedly from. She'd
have to make a list.

Hanse was saying, "Do you work for someone with an
establishment elsewhere, Changer, or are you in business for
yourself?"

"Sharp-eyed devil," Tethras said with a chuckle and another genuine twinkle of oddly light brown eyes, and added the hundred twenty-second spark. "I have associates, but no formal banking establishment. My home is on Bitterwood."

"Is that on Town Hill?"

Tethras laughed aloud. "Not quite! Northgates. That's just northeast of the main Temple. You've been learning our city."

"I try," Hanse said. "And we really do have some horses."

"I and one of my associates would love to see them, Hansis. And might I suggest you obtain a piece of wire from—oh, here. Take these. My dear, why don't you string some of these around your neck, and you too, Hansis, so that you haven't all your milk in one bucket, as 'twere. Purses are not so safe as one's coins on a wire about one's neck."

"Unless someone grabs it from behind of a dark night," Hanse muttered. "Why, this is copper wire."

"Aye. I'm afraid the two are worth that extra coin, too, but I would love to see those horses. As for the danger on a dark night . . . that might be true, Hansis of Mrsevada, but when a man carries a very good throwing knife concealed inside his tunic, I assume that on dark nights he has it to hand and knows how to use it." He turned his pleasant look on Mignureal. "You, Min, now you do be careful of a dark night, and mind where you go!"

"She carries three throwing stars in her bosom," Hanse said, stringing coins, and was careful not to laugh when Tethras and Mignureal did.

"Any time, Hansis," Tethras was saying a couple of minutes later. "You know where to find me, and I do deal."

Nodding, Hanse and Mignureal left the Changer, holding hands and enjoying the heavy feel of copper coins on their upper chests. Hers made *jing* sounds against the medallion Strick had given her.

He succumbed to her urgings and tried on a ready-made tunic, in white with a vertical blue stripe running up and over each shoulder. It was too long, he said, and was assured that it could be hemmed to his preference before he could sneeze twice. He didn't think he cared for the white, he said, standing there in front of the stall and removing it as he had his own; and the small, bent man with the balding head and great big nose urged on him a green one. It was too narrow in the shoulders.

"Look at my fabrics, look at this! See this! I can habe one to your bery own measure by sunset. You can come back then or in the morning. Wouldn't this nice orange look nice on him, hmm?" He held it up, beaming at Mignureal.

"No, but that russet would."

"Russet, russet oh aye, and a fine piece of cloth this is. Look at this—not a mark in the weabe, not a single flaw, and two horses couldn't pull it apart." Grasping two edges, he whipped his arms apart so that the cloth made sharp popping sounds. "Aye, you'd look handsome in this and see a lot of serbice from it too, young sir!"

"What would you want for a tunic from that," Hanse asked as if idly, holding his new red sash against the cloth and cocking his head as he studied it.

The cloth-and-clothing dealer was studying Hanse's new necklace. "Well now you habe to consider that this is bery good cloth, woben down in Suma by a woman who's been at her loom for thirty years, and now it's come all the way up here, brabing the terrors of the desert and Maidenhead Wood, just so that I could put my master-tailor skill to work on it to make you the handsomest tunic in town, I say in all Firaqa, young sir. Why I'd habe to habe twenty coppers. Unless you are in some sort of trade or a farmer; we do always need meat and milk . . ."

Hanse hadn't the faintest notion whether that was a fair price or not. Surely not, though, since it was the first one stated! He blinked, worked at a well executed look of shock, and stepped back a pace. "I am amazed, sir! I had expected to hear about half that."

"Half that! Ah, arghh! Half, he says! Ten coppers for a fine tunic, made with lobing skill of fine fabric! You would hoard your fortune and pauper me and all those I support! Half! Oh, young sir! Tell me now, were you considering a nice round neck or—"

"No, like mine," Hanse said, touching the tunic he had not yet resumed. Only a female or two paid any attention to the dark young man standing there shirtless and rangily muscular above his stained leather leggings. "With laces."

"Ah, the B-cut and laces as well."

"No no," Hanse said, holding up his tunic. "A V-cut neck."

"That's what I said, a B-cut. More labor for me! No no, I should habe to habe at least—oh Guardians help me! I suppose I could go without meat for a fortnight and make the garment for sixteen coppers."

"Perhaps I was a bit hasty," Hanse said, glancing around. "Mignue: d'you think that woman over there with the fabrics piled behind her; don't you think she looks the sort to charge a sensible price?"

"She might. But then you might consider all the people this nice man supports and go ahead and give him the dozen copper coins he wants."

The vendor, who of course might or might not have been a tailor, was having a hard time keeping up. First he started to tell them about the shoddy workmanship they could expect of the woman Hanse indicated, then heard Mignue's pleasant words about him.

"Yes yes, heed this beautiful creature, young sir and think about—what! A dozen!" He threw up both hands and looked as if he was trying to send his eyes to the heavens with them. "Twelbe!"

After a bit more of that, they agreed on fifteen because the man was obviously not about to come down any more. Hanse left an "intent payment" of five sparks, and told the fellow—Kuse—that he'd be here for it on the morrow. Ten minutes later Hanse bought an absolutely plain natural-colored readymade from the woman nearby, for thirteen coppers. He paced back to Kuse.

"Here," he said, passing over his old tunic. "Make the new one exactly like this. I'll see you in the morning, for both."

"Oh No! You bought that from *her!*"

Hanse lowered his lids a bit to stare into Kuse's eyes, and spoke in a low voice that commanded attention. "Kuse, we've done business and you have my money. Now don't start working on losing the sale and getting your head cracked as well."

• • •

The eardrops Hanse bought Mignureal were unusual and unusually handsome and she tried not to weep.

"No one ever gave me earrings before but my mother, never in my life!"

"Well," Hanse said uncomfortably, embarrassed both by her effusiveness over so little and at being hugged in public, "it isn't as if they're pure gold or anything. Besides—it's the first time I ever bought any jewelry, too."

He did not add that he had stolen a few pieces in his time. Some mighty fine ones. And disposed of them in exchange for money for rent and food, mostly with a man named Shive, a special sort of Changer in Sanctuary who asked few questions and whose sideline was the disassembling of jewelry. Few people recognized their own stones, in different settings, and none recognized their own gold or silver when it was re-formed or melted into essential formlessness.

"I love them! I love you, Hanse! Ummmm!" she said, gripping his arm—the right—with both hands and pressing close.

They roamed the bazaar, Hanse still uncomfortable with her holding onto him, pressing so close and looking lovingly at him. She had to look up, but only because her height was five feet. They saw and remarked on the booth under the awning striped in more colors than any other, but had no reason to hurry to it. Perhaps a half hour later their peregrination led them to it, and Mignureal gasped while her nails gouged Hanse's arm.

The girl on the other side of the counter was about thirteen or fourteen, despite kohl-darkened eyes and rouged lips. She wore great big earrings and a top striped in four colors, under a sort of outer shift or singlet. It was a very bright orange. She was idly laying out cards. Less than two feet behind her, drawn curtains—in a paisley pattern—indicated that most of the stall was a private chamber.

Mignureal's hands slid off Hanse's arm as if she had forgotten it was there. She approached the stall.

"Can the cards reveal the true location of the spirit-stones of our people, cousin?"

The girl looked up in considerable surprise. "I—I don't know you!"

"I am Mignureal, daughter of Thegunsaneal and Moon-flower, True Seer of Sanctuary. We are of the Tribe of Bajandir."

"True Seer?"

"Aye. Is your mother in back with a *suvesh*?"

The girl nodded, smiling at the S'danzo word and very interested, now. "I am Zrena, daughter of Tiquillanshal and Sholopixa who is called Turquoise. We are of the Milbehar. You have just come here? Oh! We are so few, here!" Her eyes lifted and she looked past Mignureal at Hanse. "Oh. Is he—"

"My man, but not of us. He is Hanse."

"Oh."

Still standing back a few paces, Hanse saw a well-dressed woman emerge from a side door of the stall. She was smiling as she hurried away. Heard a good Seeing of her fortune from this Turquoise, he mused.

The curtain drew back then, and a woman emerged. Hanse swallowed. She was not so corpulent as Moonflower had been, but just as round of face, with the same gleaming blue-black hair and vehemently colorful attire. Though it was not in the style of Firaqa, the low line of her bodice was. In that area, Turquoise was as capacious and mobile as Mignue's slain mother had been. She stopped short, gazing at Mignureal. Her expression was one of total friendliness and welcome as she spoke a string of words that Hanse had never heard before. Or if he had, from Moonflower or Mignue or her father, he wouldn't recognize them anyhow.

Mignureal replied in the same old tongue only the S'danzo knew. Hanse did recognize her name and the word "Moon-flower." The woman smiled broadly. A nice feeling flowed warmly through Hanse. Well met, he thought. These, he could be sure, were friends. The S'danzo were like that; all were cousins, everywhere. He had thought more than once that it would be nice to be one; to belong to such an extended family. To any family.

A uniformed man moved past him from behind, hand on his sword, and came to a halt in a daunting stance beside Mignureal.

"Here! You know you are forbidden to speak that foreign tongue in this city! You two want me to take you in?"

Behind the broad back and arrogant voice, Hanse's stare went dark, from slitted eyes, and his fingers twitched.

As the startled Mignureal turned to face the Red, or City Watchman, Turquoise put on a face of embarrassment and sorrow unto desolation, and sweetly relieved herself of a lie: "Ah, I am so sorry, sir. It is my sister's daughter from far away, and I have not seen her for so long! In my excitement I lapsed into the ancient language of our—tribe."

"Far away, huh? Where from, girl?"

The quiet, flat and very male voice came from behind him: "Why don't you ask Sergeant Gaise that, Watchman." The voice held not the hint of a questioning tone.

The Red whirled, his hand leaping back to his hilt. "What did you say?"

Hanse met his eyes directly and repeated each word, a little more slowly and with exaggerated enunciation.

"I heard you, I heard you! What did you mean by that?"

"I mean that our friend Gaise knows where she's from, and could tell you if you asked him and if he felt like it. Come to think, Rim knows, too."

"Rim?"

"Oh, sorry. Guess I know him better than you. Sergeant Rimizin."

"Who are—just what busin—" The guard turned back to the women; their stares weren't so discomfiting and they didn't talk back. "Try to be careful, Turquoise, damn it," he said, his voice much different from before. "I can't overlook it all the time, you know, no matter how nice a fellow I am."

Without looking at Hanse, he moved away.

Three S'danzo stared worshipfully at Hanse. So did the man in the adjacent stall.

Mignureal said, "This is—"

"Hansis," he said, moving forward and wearing his best charming-boy smile. His tunic was perfectly plain but he felt positively elegant because it was new. "A greeting, Turquoise; Zrena. And be assured that I knew Mignureal's mother far better than I do those two members of the Watch who happened to be at the gate when we rode in yesterday afternoon."

For a few moments longer they stared, and then they began laughing, and so did Hanse.

After about an hour of half listening to babbling in which he was hardly a participant—and very aware of Zrena's big dark eyes, always directed at him except when he glanced at her—Hanse turned to the fellow in the adjacent stall. He was selling fruits, including some beautiful peaches.

"I've come a long way and am not sure about the sun here," Hanse said. "Is it as close to noon as I think?"

"Probably. Mighty close. Where are you—never mind! After hearing wha' you said to that fartmouth Red, I woulden dare ask where you're from. Have a peach. It's on Yashuar," he said, slapping his chest. "I do love to see someone stand up to a little Watcher trying to throw some weight around. You really know a Sergeant Gaise and—wha'ever tha' other name was?"

Hanse smiled a tiny smile, mouth closed. "Thanks, Yashuar," he said, and picked up a peach. "Name's Hansis. Tell me something, will you? Firaqa's police wear sort of yellowish-tan tunics, bronze-looking helmets, and leathers—boots, belt, chester, sheaths. Sergeants wear darkish blue cloaks and no crests on their helmets. Not a sign of red on 'em. So why are they called Reds? Not from blood on their hands, I hope."

Yashuar leaned on his stall's counter, a broad plank covered with a striped cloth decorated with stains from various fruits. He popped a fruit fly between his hands, looked at Hanse. He smiled.

"Oh no, Hansis, not from blood on their hands. They're mosely all righ', really. No, up un'il about fifty years ago they wore red cuirasses and orange crests. The Flame, you know. So everyone called 'em the Reds. The uniform got changed, bu' the name stuck."

Hanse shook his head. "Smiling gods, what a wonderful peach this is! Juicy as—but Yashuar . . . you can't be old enough to remember that!"

"M'father told me. Old customs and names die hard and slow, Hansis. Listen though, I'd be'er tell you about a custom of yours you ough' to try to change, in Firaqa. Jus' try to rememmer to swear by the Flame, or the Hearth, or the Eternal

Fire, or even smoke or the Very Brazier, you know? Even by
the Eternal Chasti'y of the Hearthkeeper, that's all right,
although maybe no' in mixed company. Lots of gods where
you come from, Hansis?''

"Lots. Not here, hmm?"

"No' here," Yashuar said, shaking his head very solemnly
indeed. "The Flame and His Children, Bu' They Have No
Names For They Are As Smoke. Yea, Indeed, the Holiest of
Smoke."

"That sounds like something you memorized long ago."

"Righ'. All Firaqi did. And we were taught tha' all other
gods and faiths are false. Some even believe that, and plenty
who don't cer'ainly pretend to, 'specially when it's convenient.
Fartmouths!''

"I'd better thank you twice, Yashuar, and run. Got to meet a
man on the other side of town." Hanse moved a swift few
paces. "Mignue: I have that meeting at noon and that's about
where the sun looks to me. Turquoise, if you promise to keep
her right here, I'll be back later when I've finished my
business."

"Oh darling, how nice of y—" Mignureal began, and stood
gazing at his back as he went through the crowd. Not as he and
she together had, she noticed. He seemed almost to be
sprinting, and yet she never saw him so much as touch anyone.
Supple and swervily sinuous as a cat, she thought, and turned
back to her delightful conversation.

Lallias was waiting at the Green Goose, though Hanse was
hardly late. *He's anxious,* Hanse thought. Likely the man had
already conferred with his brother, Horse. They set out for The
Quarter, Hanse walking with this man with the bushy brown
gray beard etched with a lot of silver.

"Nice warmer," Lallias remarked.

"What?" Hanse glanced around. "What's a warmer?"

"Oh, sorry; forgot you were new here. Your coins necklace.
We call 'em chest-warmers. Usually just plain 'warmers,'
though."

"Oh."

As they walked, Hanse asked a number of the same

questions he had already posed to others. He was impressed to receive essentially the same answers. He remembered to ask about the significance of hearth-keepers.

"The Hearthkeepers," Lallias said respectfully. "The purest maidens in all Firaqa, no matter their ages. Their minds and bodies, lives and souls, are dedicated to the Eternal Flame. Here, get away, there. We haven't any money for such as you!"

"Oh," Hanse said, pretending not to see the beggar. "And does their clothing imitate the Flame?"

"Aye. The most recently consecrated Hearthkeeper is indeed doubly sanctified, since the very color of her hair—its *natural* color—is that of flame itself. She will be a good omen for us all, she will."

"Uh-*huh*. That means I saw two of them, just this morning. And what do the Hearthkeepers do, Lallias?"

Lallias waved a large hairy hand. "They are *much* respected, Hanse. No one says ill of the Hearthkeepers. They are . . . they are the Hearthkeepers."

"Oh," Hanse said. After a few paces he asked, "And what do they do, Lallias?"

"Here, around this corner. They preside over many festivals and public occasions. They preside over the sacred hearth of the Flame, and see that it never goes out. They are sworn to give their lives to prevent that."

That seemed safe enough, Hanse reflected. A strong gust of wind or a few buckets of water could kill a fire but neither was likely to slay a human! Nor did it seem likely, in a city where the Flame was the one revered god-symbol, that someone would pop into the Temple and try to blow it out! He refrained from saying any of that, merely crossing the street at Lallias's side and turning down the next one.

An attractive young woman, décolleté down to here, gave him a charming smile. But that was probably because she was trying to peddle sweets and he wore a warmer full of copper sparks.

"In a way the Hearthkeepers have the most power of anyone in Firaqa," Lallias said. "They are the court of very last resort and appeal in life-and-death cases."

"Um. Lallias . . . you said 'in a way.' The Hearthkeepers

don't rule, and I gather the High Priest doesn't either.
Assuming there is one, I mean. It doesn't much matter to such
fellows as you and I are, but I don't know anything at all about
the power in Firaqa. Who does rule?"

Lallias made a snorting noise. "Aye, there's plenty of
sacerdotes—priests—and a high one, too. There's also a Chief
Magistrate, but he doesn't rule. He judges and Decides. Then
there's the Council, but they don't *rule*, either. They meet and
act important and decide about streetwork and edicts and
zoning and like that. The real power, I say *power*, Hanse, in
Firaqa is divided between sor—what's that racket?"

That rattling racket was a driverless wagon careening up a
side-street behind a runaway horse with huge manic eyes.
Horse and wagon came clop-rattling around the corner. It
nearly tipped over, strewing nice fresh melons along the street,
as the animal swerved. Its new course happened to be directly
at the two men crossing the street.

Hanse moved as fast as ever he had in his life.

Lallias did not, and was trampled.

The horse seemed not to notice. With blood bright and wet
on its legs and hooves, it fled on.

Safely out of the way, Hanse swung back and resisted the
impulse to charge after the wagon. He was not much on being
the hero without reason, and saw no particular reason to try
pouncing onto that runaway cart to grab up the reins. It wasn't
as if it contained a screaming beautiful damsel in distress! He
wasted no more than a glance on the yelling, arm-waving man
who came running, pursued by two Reds. The driver, Hanse
assumed, and squatted beside his guide. Lallias lay twisted in a
miserably ugly posture, with two limbs and his head turned the
wrong way. He was also no longer Hanse's guide, because he
was no longer alive.

A shaken Hanse rose from the dead man. He took a step, and
suddenly was sweaty all over, with a light-headed feeling. An
instant later he was obliged to sit down, very suddenly. He sat
there in shock, beside the corpse of his guide, in the street.
Dimly he heard, without registering or responding, all the
excited people-noises: "Are you all right?" "Are you hurt?"
"Are they hurt? What happened?" "Argh, smoke and embers!
Look at that one's neck!"

Dully Hanse saw some fellow race into the street a block down and pounce onto the wagon, well ahead of the running driver and two Watchmen. The man's bellowed cries of "**WHOA**" came clearly to Hanse's ears.

"How heroic!" "Did you see that?" "Is he hurt? Why's he just sit there?"

Just what the world needs, Hanse thought dully. *More heroes.*

"Are you all right?" "Is he hurt?" "Are you hurt?" "This one must be in shock; t'other fellow's dead; tromped. What happened?" "Ashes and smoke, what *happened* here?"

A few moments later his brain was clearing and his thoughts became more intelligent. The hero had gotten the produce-wagon stopped. Soon he and it and the owner and the two Reds would be coming back up here, and they'd be just bubbling over with silly questions for Hanse. That could lead to all sorts of things, especially for a foreigner.

"His name's Lallias," he told the gabble-babbly assembly at large. "My cousin," he said, rising. "Oh! Oh Holy Flame! My *wife!* I've got to see if my wife's all right!"

The last he yelled in a voice as fearful as he could make it. The ploy helped him burst through the little crowd to race away. In no particular direction; he just *ran* for four blocks, in three directions. Seeing a pair of flame-robed Hearthkeepers, he made a wide curve to avoid them. Hanse wanted neither to bow nor to offend.

Lallias's information about the hearth-maidens was useful, at least, to keep a man alive and safe, he mused; *just don't say anything against 'em! Meanwhile the real power in Firaqa is divided between sore—what?*

That thinking decided Hanse that he was fully recovered from shock, and capable of rational thought. *Guess it's going to be Anorislas after all.* He glanced at the sky. *Plenty of time,* he thought, and went into a wine-shop in quest of directions to that area of Firaqa called The Quarter. Three people insisted on chiming in to give him directions, and two of them twice assured him that he couldn't miss it.

Wondering just how ancient that anile cliché was, Hanse headed for The Quarter, in search of Anorislas.

• • •

"My name is Hanse. I'm up from the south—"

"Down near Sanctuary?"

"Aye," Hanse said guardedly, but long, lean Anorislas only nodded. "I have some horses. In Maidenhead Wood, my companion and I met a big man with a lot of reddish bronze moustache and an odd sort of leather skullcap. Had the look of a military man."

He paused. The other man only stared at him from enigmatic light brown eyes that looked rather puffy because a lot of the lid showed. He showed nothing.

Hanse understood. He smiled just a little. "He was as cautious as you are being now, and so was I. We warmed a bit, slowly, and I asked who I might see here about selling the horses. He bade me see Anorislas."

"Uh-huh. What else did he say? Do you know his name?"

"About the last thing he did after we had parted was call out—'Yo,' he called. When I stopped and turned in the saddle, he said his name was Strick. I took that as a sign of friendship, and told him my name, then. He also said to call you Bunny."

At last Anorislas smiled—showing a broken front tooth, just left of center—and nodded with some enthusiasm. He was a tall man and lanky, though starting to swell just south of his belt. His big hands seemed to hang from big wrists and prominent wristbones. He wore a lot of brown hair, very curly and showing a little gray. The curls sort of straggled down his forehead above one of those little noses with which the gods saddled some men so that they had a boyish, almost unfinished look.

"That's Strick, all right. We c'n relax now, Hanse. Just do *not* call me Bunny! That's that confounded Strick's joke!"

Hanse nodded, and waited.

"How many horses, Hanse? Oh, like a drop of wine?"

"No, thanks. We have four horses and an onager to sell. I left Sanctuary with a horse and the ass. Just north, a friend gave me another horse."

"Now that's a friend!"

"Well, he has plenty and felt he owed me something. Up on the desert, we were attacked by Tejana. Four of them. They took our animals and rode off. I took them back."

"Whaat?!"

Hanse shrugged. "I took my horses back, and theirs. That onager saved my life!" he added, seeing an opportunity to heighten Enas's value.

"The Tejana, ah, surely objected."

"Aye."

Anorislas bobbed his head just a little in time with slight laughing noises through his nose. "All right, I'll stop asking. You left Sanctuary with a horse and an ass and reached Firaqa with six horses, and you want to sell. Pure profit for you, eh?"

"Hardly. We had some silver. *That* I didn't get back from those dogsons."

"Oh. Sorry. I had the impression that you left them all dead." Anorislas was almost smiling, as if at a mild sort of teasing joke.

Looking very steadily into those lid-heavy tan eyes, Hanse said, "Not all of them."

Anorislas gazed at him for a time, not quite pursing his lips and looking very thoughtful indeed. "I'll make note not even to think of being less than fair with such a dangerous man, Hanse ti'Sanctuary." He held up a staying hand. "No no, I wouldn't anyhow. In the first place, I don't do business that way. Can't. I have a fault; a curse, actually. It's honesty. Can't help it. That damned Strick . . . ! Well, anyhow. You have for sale three Tejana horses and another, your pack-animal I suppose, and an onager. I am in that business. Where are they, Hanse ti'Sanctuary?"

"Right now we're staying at the Green Goose, because Strick recommended it. The horses are stabled there."

"Easier to look at them there, then. What time 'morrow?"

Hanse shrugged. "Early."

"I can be there by the second hour, or just a little later."

"All right, Anorislas. Until then."

Anorislas stood looking after the lean, supple fellow until he was out of sight around a corner. It was mighty hard to believe that such a youngster had stolen horses from four Tejana and left some of them dead. On the other hand, he was definitely a cautious, wary young man, and did have the look of danger about him. Still, that starey, almost mean look . . . and that swagger . . .

• • •

The sun was waning, the eastern sides of buildings going dark, when Hanse reached the bazaar. It was much less crowded, now. He found Mignureal inside the stall, in animated conversation with Zrena and her mother. What was her—oh, Amethyst. No no, Turquoise. He found that he did not much mind that he had not been at all missed. . . .

They were invited to dinner. Hanse had spent a lot of years being anything but a social animal, and was understandably nervous. On the other hand, he was ready to sample Turquoise's cookery. As it turned out, it was her rail-thin husband, Tiquillanshal, who did the cooking. They lived in the rear of their stall, which extended enough to form three rooms.

"I never met a slender cook before," Hanse said, and 'Quill liked that.

Displaying a gold tooth in his grin, he said, "That may bode ill for your palate and your belly, Hanse! Mayhap my cookery is so bad that even I can't eat it." He tossed a crisping doughcake high, caught the flattish patty neatly on the wooden spatula, and slapped it back into the fry-pan.

Hanse chuckled. "I'll take my chances, Quill. Your wife and daughter look well enough fed!"

Again, he had said just the right thing. "Ah, yes. I do hope I can put some more meat on Zrena's bones, though. She's barely plump. And I wish you luck as well, my friend; that Mignureal of yours could surely use some feeding."

Caught without comment, Hanse thought of Mignureal's corpulent mother and lean, lean father, and realized that he had learned something new. Some men loved fat women best, just as others loved bosomless ones. He belonged to neither company. He only nodded, smiling weakly, accepted the beer Quill proffered, and a few moments later burned his fingers on one of the marvelous patties.

The food was greasy and good enough, the company warm and signally friendly. The conversation was all right, though Hanse was very aware of being the only non-S'danzo present. He learned that Turquoise's talent at Seeing was slim and fleeting, and apparently she engaged in considerable charlatanry. It was a surprise to him that many S'danzo did. So far Zrena had shown no Seeing ability at all. All three of their hosts were much impressed that Mignureal had the true talent. Hanse was proof. He had to tell his stories of how she had Seen for him, on several occasions. That was a little difficult. He felt it necessary to leave out this and that, and embellish and twist a bit in telling those stories, in order not to reveal his occupation and hitherto violent life.

Mignureal was invited not only to visit as often and long as she wished, but to join them here in their booth in the bazaar; that Hanse definitely caught. She assured them that she would be back, but he also noted that she did not commit herself to the other. The invitation to spend the night, Ils be thanked, was obviously only form.

On their way back to the Green Goose he tried to talk about their offers and her promise. That was when he learned something else he hadn't known about Mignureal: when she did not want to discuss somethting, he might as well drop it or resort to violence. Hanse dropped it. He told her what a warmer was, and about the Hearthkeepers. Having thus warmed her up, he described his adventure.

She was predictably horrified by the death of Lallias, and squeezed his hand tightly as they walked through the long shadows of Firaqa. And she was pleased that he had met and discussed preliminary business with Anorislas.

They saw no one bent on robbing them or worse, but did see three several Reds, which indicated cause and effect. Hanse hailed them all in manner friendly.

The Green Goose was alive and lively with diners and drinkers. Their hosts were surprised that Hanse and Mignureal would not be taking dinner. Hanse assumed that their sadness was affected; Khulna and Chondey had saved the cost of two meals! He did collect a pint of beer and some food suitable for cats. Chondey noticed his new tunic and was complimentary. Lallias was not mentioned.

Notable and Rainbow were tail-snapping sulky at having been left alone in the room all day, but forgot that in their delight at seeing the food. Chondey had not scrimped or sent scraps. Both the outsized red and the diminutive calico purred helplessly as they hoisted tails and fell to. Above, their pet humans happily indulged in the long embrace they had foregone on entering, in order to see to feline needs.

Hanse and Mignureal looked at each other. The expressions of both showed apprehension and worse.

At last Hanse said, "We have to look, Mignue."

"I . . . don't want to. Can't we just go to bed? I'm really tired, and after that hug I'm all . . ."

She broke off, for Hanse was staring. The great sigh she heaved made an interestedly watching Hanse think about bed, too. Unlike Tiquillanshal, Hanse preferred women who were fat in only one place. Two, maybe. Yet he was adamant, and shook his head doggedly.

"We have to look."

With a resigned nod, she picked up the accursed saddlebag, then looked up and was surprised to see that Hanse had taken up and opened the beeswax tablet. He extended it to her. Mignureal swallowed, and looked.

She sat down very suddenly. She stared at Hanse. With coins gleaming on the little oval rug and his new outer purse in one hand, he stared back.

"The silver coin's gone from my new purse," he said in a dull voice. "Evidently they won't even stay in there as bait for thieves! Assuming that yours returned to the bag, too, we're not cursed with ten anymore; we're short another Imperial. The bag contained nine coins."

Noticeably pale, Mignureal turned and flopped face down on the bed. She said nothing, but held that posture. It should have been exciting-enticing to Hanse, but under the circumstances it wasn't. All sexuality had been chased from his mind by the revelation of purse and the triple-damned saddlebag. She just looked pitiful. He went to her and sat on the bed to rub his woman's back. It was quaking. He realized that she was weeping.

After awhile she showed him the tablet and its *revised* listing:

ELTURAS
ESTANE

PERIAS

THUVARANDIS

Lallias's name, she pointed out with a shaky hand, had vanished from the list. But its space neatly remained.

Damp and prickly all over, Hanse tore open her purse. It contained two coppers.

He sighed and stared at the wall, absently patting her back.

This time there was no question. Each of them had put one of *those* coins into the purses they had bought just today, to wear openly. One of those coins—probably both—had returned to the saddlebag, where for some reason they silently "insisted" on being; obviously *had* to be. Meanwhile Lallias's name had been one of those on the fold-over tablet, and he was dead. Now his name had inexplicably disappeared, and so had one of the coins.

One of the coins was for Lallias, Hanse thought. *Or represented Lallias. It's gone, and so is his name from Sinajhal's list. One must have been for Sinajhal, too, then. He died, and one vanished. And she must be right: so did his name.*

That was an explanation, and explanations, like names for things, always felt good. This explanation however, left much unexplained, and did nothing to allay apprehension, nervousness, and genuine fear.

It proved not a good night for lovers. They had too many worries and so said too much and did not do enough. Worse, Mignureal drifted into sleep while Hanse was still worrying and wondering aloud. The tension he had been trying to talk away returned, worse. Now it was tightened by hurt and anger.

He was in no good mood when he awoke, just after sunrise. He rose at once and was sitting on the side of the bed pulling on his buskins when Mignureal made sleep-sweet noises and moved. Her hand touched his back. Hanse went on dressing.

"Oh!" she said, moving swiftly into a sitting position; a sight that, since she was naked, Hanse did not want to see right now. "The man about the horses—Anorislas!" And she hurried bouncily out of bed.

Hanse stood, too. "Take care of the cats, will you?" he said casually. "I'll be back with good news and a pot full of silver, as soon as I can."

"Oh," she said in a small, disappointed voice. "I—but I . . . you mean you're just going to . . ."

She broke off, since Hanse was already letting himself out. And he hadn't even looked at her. It was not the first time he had made her weep, but it was the first time through deliberate cruelty.

Hanse found Chondey and Khulna up, of course, and at least acting unsurprised that he was. He was alternating bites of sausage and peach when Anorislas came in. Hanse pretended to be in a normal mood and a few moments later they went out to Khulna's stable. Dumb-ass greeted them with his usual comment, at top volume. Oddly, it was the big gray that whickered and stretched his muzzle to Hanse.

He said nothing about which horses he wished to keep while Anorislas examined them, and so of course the man who *knew* horses at once singled out Inja. That did not help Hanse's mental state any, or his sour feelings toward Mignureal.

"That one we're keeping," he said, and his tone made Anorislas give him a swift look.

"Too bad for me," he said. "He's the best of the lot, that fellow. Before I go further in my thinking, why don't you tell me which other one you have decided to keep?"

Hanse shrugged. "You're the horse expert. Which one should I keep for myself?"

Anorislas showed him that broken-toothed smile. "The one you're keeping."

Hanse didn't smile. "And after that?"

"You trust me to tell you? I could choose the least of the lot."

"Not likely," Hanse said, in that same flat, unfriendly tone and wearing the same unfriendly face. "Strick's big, and I'm mean when I'm cheated."

Anorislas gazed at him for a time, then nodded and made a couple of clapping motions as if dusting his hands.

"Something's happened since you saw me yesterday, and you're hostile. That makes it hard. You're a proud man, Hanse. You know that some others are, too."

Hanse blinked. "Like you, for instance."

Anorislas nodded, and kept right on looking at him.

On the point of saying that which would end the inspection and their business because his inner needs were busily jerking his knee and trying for his tongue, Hanse grew up another mite.

"You're right," he said, staring with the same face. "Something happened between then and now and I'm sour this morning. But it doesn't have anything to do with you. That good enough, between proud men?"

Anorislas could not help but smile. He knew what had been said, beyond the words. This cocky youngster had admitted that the older man was right, and also let him know that he had just heard the nearest thing to an apology he was going to get. Pushing it further, Anorislas knew, would be closing the door on business dealings between them. Anorislas of Firaqa was a dealer and a horse-trader. He knew that stupid men—and helplessly bellicose ones; perhaps the same thing—demanded specific apologies even when one had been tacitly given. Business was a little more important than pride. A little; provided that a man didn't have to swallow any.

He swallowed none in saying, "It's enough, between proud men. I had to force myself to come over here this morning. Had a little woman trouble last night, damn it."

He saw from the southerner's eyes that he had just forged a bond between them, and Anorislas kept his smile inside. He made a show of checking the horses again, although he had already seen that they were clean, good animals. For one thing, those Tejana devils didn't have any other kind.

"We already know which one's the best animal. Next after him I'd pick this gray. The Tejanit."

"What about that black one?"

"A good enough animal. Clean enough lines. Good legs, I'd say. You asked for the two best, though."

"The gray belonged to the Tejana leader. I'll keep him."

Anorislas nodded. "Your business. You elect to keep the two best money-bringers in the lot."

Hanse said nothing.

"I'll need to try each animal," Anorislas said. "Meanwhile though, unless one of these fellows acts bad under the saddle, I'd say I could part with forty hearthers. Oh, sorry; that's Firaqi silver coinage."

"I know what hearthers are, Anorislas. I even know that's not *too* bad an offer, for four horses and an onager. I'd say they're worth about . . . fifty-six."

Anorislas gave him an open look and leaned against a stall. Enas nuzzled his arm in hopes of a handout. The dealer ignored him.

"Hanse, that may well be about right, if they're all as good as they look and behave under the saddle. You might well be able to sell 'em for that. Not to a dealer, of course. A dealer has to make a profit. I'm a dealer, Hanse. You might sell all four in a day or a month or three months, and so might I." Anorislas shrugged, paused for a few beats to let this truculent southerner consider that, and added, "If they all work well, I might come up to forty-five."

Hanse looked as if he was on the point of smiling. He didn't. "Try my horses, dealer. Then we'll talk. Later this morning, or this afternoon?"

The other man smiled and made as if to move to the stable door. "Like to have that gray for myself. I've got other business this morning. We can go back inside and sign something, with your innkeeper as witness. I'm not unknown. Then I could meet you back here at . . . sunset?"

"I'll meet you here when you say, and *we'll* go do that."

"Good for you. You know, I'm almost astonished that you and Strick exchanged names. He's a cautious man, and I'd say you never trusted anyone in your life."

Hanse only stared. That was good enough cover for his thoughts: *You put it in deep that time, Strick's friend. Twist it and I'll have to tell you to walk away.*

Anorislas was a dealer and a horse-trader. He knew eyes, and postures, and he knew when he had stabbed, inadvertently or no. He also knew enough not to twist it. "I could be back here at noon or a little past, Hanse."

Hanse nodded, and they left the stable.

Hanse walked back into the inn thinking how he'd point out to Mignureal that she had, after all, gone to sleep while he was talking, let her apologize, and say a nice thing or two. Then it would be all right and they would go look around for a more permanent place to live.

Khulna greeted him by delivering a message from her: she had gone to the bazaar to visit with her new friends. Khulna saw emotions flickering like lightning on Hanse's face. The taverner seemed to want to say or ask something, but refrained.

"Oh yes," Hanse said, covering fast. "She had that early meeting with them. I nearly forgot. I'll be meeting Anorislas back here at noon. Better slip me something for the cats, will you?" While he waited, he mused, *She sure had to rush, to get out so fast. She was very sure she didn't want to be here when I came back in! Damn. I guess we've just had trouble.*

The trouble was that now he had no idea what to do with himself. The only definite was a negative: he certainly was not going to the bazaar, new tunic awaiting or no! He visited with the cats for a while.

"Think I'll go for a walk. Damn, Notable, sometimes I wish you were a dog. A dog could walk along with me. Whoever heard of anyone walking around with a cat pacing alongside, or on a leash? Especially a great big red one!"

Sitting and working on his paws as if somehow the area between his toes had become just filthy overnight, Notable paused with one foot up to stare attentively. "mew," he said, in that disgustingly sweet voice he sometimes used.

"Trying to let me know you'd be just ever so sweet, aren't you, you big fake? I love you, Notable, I swear—but I just can't take you out that way!"

Notable put the foot down, stared, and turned to pounce up on the windowsill. He stood staring at it in obvious signal until Hanse opened it to let the cat step out on the roof. *Guess I ought to get a washtub or something with dirt in it for him,* Hanse thought, pretending not to watch.

Then he spent the next twenty minutes trying to get the rotten stubborn beast back into the room.

Only then was Hanse able to go for his walk, since he had nothing else to do. Without even thinking about it, he reverted: automatically he was looking upward. Gauging this roof and that for distance between, climbability and slant; this salient as a possible handhold-footrest for climbing; the availability of this or that window. What was a man to do, when he had spent his adolescence doing just this, and yet no longer had to worry about those matters that of necessity had occupied his thoughts:

tonight's meal, tomorrow's breakfast, and maybe picking up a little nighttime companionship along the way?

At least looking this way, with a consummately practiced eye, was interesting and passed the time.

Somehow it passed, and he spent three hours with Anorislas and a friend of the dealer's. They took the horses over to the main gate, and out, and the two men tried the horses while Hanse mostly watched. Later he learned about Anorislas's honesty.

"These are good animals, Hanse. Even the onager. He'll probably be heading out with the next caravan. You've learned or decided that good horses are worth about a dozen hearthers, haven't you?" The Firaqi paused long enough to see a tiny smile of corroboration. "Right. But see, Tejana horses are prized, and I can get probably fifteen hearthers apiece for them, Hanse. It just wouldn't be right not to tell you that. I tried not to, but it's not possible for me to be other than totally honest."

Hanse was more than impressed, although the last part was surely unnecessary bragging. Few things made him so suspicious as a man who *proclaimed* his absolute honesty.

"Meanwhile, though, I won't take just any offer for good animals, and I am not wealthy. I'd like to hand you fifty hearthers and take the five animals; and I'd like to stop in at the PR office and sign an agreement to pay you more as I sell the animals. I'll guarantee you a dozen each for the horses and seven for the onager. That comes to fifty-five; just the figure you mentioned, remember? And I'll agree to pay you half of anything any of them brings in over fifteen."

Hanse was staring, close onto being dumbfounded. "I can't decide whether to say 'That sounds like you left me nothing to dicker about,' or 'Why should I trust you?' What's a PR?"

"Public Recorder. We both agree to an official document while he witnesses. If I break the bond, I go to prison. See, in a way you're loaning me money at no interest. On the other hand, I'm the one who now has to feed and stable the horses. Your interest will be anything I can get over fifteen. I think I can."

Hanse wished the man had never suggested such a bargain. It was one of the hardest decisions possible, for an orphan street-urchin become thief who had learned long ago never to trust anyone. And yet, and yet . . .

In the office of the Public Recorder he watched the man write out just what Anorislas had said. The smallish fellow had dusted the document with powder and was preparing his seal when abruptly one of the principals turned and walked out. Both Anorislas and the PR stared. In less than a minute Hanse returned, with a well-dressed man who looked unsure whether to be affronted, afraid, or complimented.

"I found the most honest-looking man in Firaqa," Hanse blithely declaimed, having merely approached the first decently attired passerby he saw. "Sir, I beg you: read aloud this document the PR has just prepared."

Still looking mostly confused, the fellow had been complimented too highly not to comply. He read, and Hanse heard the same words Anorislas had spoken, with embellishments obviously added only to protect the seller. He thanked the man profusely, watched him depart, and bowed to the drop-jawed horse-dealer and the PR. Then, slowly but with pride, Hanse printed his name at the bottom of the sheet.

Anorislas was laughing. "That's about as clever an action as ever I saw," he said, bending over the page. "And I appreciate it. Now don't you be insulted, Blomis—you know I can't read, either!"

Hanse had to laugh. Blomis the Public Recorder never did.

Anorislas's moneyhandler was a portly man with extremely thin, cloud-gray hair and a large moustache, completely white. His clothing was black, mauve, and russet and his name was Perias. Hanse watched his fleshy, ring-glittering hand count out fifty pieces of silver to Anorislas, who stepped back and gestured, with a smile directly at Hanse.

Hanse swallowed as he stepped forward to claim the stacks of flame-marked silver. *I'm rich!*

"Who do you bank with?" Perias asked, and one thing led to another.

Hanse learned that Perias was partners with several people, but the name that was obviously supposed to impress was Arcala. Once again his misplaced pride kept him from gaining information; he would find out about this Arcala from someone else. Also about the partner who was a wealthy widow "and not all that old, either!"

He received another document and four pieces of silver, which he stowed away. The other 46 would remain with this moneyhandler, in what Hanse was assured was the safest keeping in Firaqa. He even learned how money made money. Aye, he understood that his 46 coins were worth 2,300 copper sparks. Perias told him that if he did not touch them, they would grow within one year to 2,346, or just short of 47 hearthers. That was thrilling, though despite anticipated income from Anorislas, Hanse couldn't see how he could leave all the money untouched for so long. He asked if it earned even when he had to take some out. Perias managed not to stare or smile at his ignorance. He solemnly advised that the balance would indeed earn. Though Anorislas obviously wished to go, Hanse tarried to ask a few questions about rents, in Firaqa. Ah, Perias knew of some property . . .

Buyer and seller departed Perias's place of business. Hanse had noted how low the sun had slid. Anorislas bade his friend or assistant lead the animals away, and suggested that he and Hanse stop at an alehouse for a cup. Hanse told the dealer that he needed to meet someone in the open market. A couple of blocks later they parted company and Hanse hurried back to the moneyhandler.

His question surprised Perias, who advised that "we" considered a silver Imperial to be worth a Firaqi plus eleven; more in volume.

"What's volume?" Hanse asked.

"Well, if you brought in ten or more, we could talk sixty-two of our coppers to the Imperial."

Hanse thanked the man and left, surprising Perias more. The banker's parting words were "don't forget that nice property on Coriander, now!"

Hanse found his way back to the PR, who advised that the document from Perias said just what the banker had told him. Hanse hurried to the bazaar. He worked out his finances as he walked. Eleven of *those* Imperials from the total of 85 left 74. Now, at 62 coppers each . . . He bogged down. Working it out in his head wasn't possible. It remained thrilling. He had no thought for his presumably waiting new tunic, and it was not Mignureal's presence in the open market that hurried his steps. In his excitement over a newly-learned knowledge of money, Hanse wished to talk again with Tethras, that money-handler in the bazaar.

Tethras was about to leave, but listened long enough to forget about hurrying. He spoke very quietly.

"I had no idea, Hansis. You are not one who flaunts your wealth. Now let me affirm this. You possess fifty Firaqi silvers and *seventy* Imperials, and you have an income as well. Is that what you have told me?"

"Yes. And of course a couple of horses and this—warmer." He flicked his coin-necklace with a finger, watching Tethras make swift notations. "I want to know what you would offer for the Imperials, and what, oh say forty-six hearthers would be worth at the end of a year in your keeping."

Tethras cocked his head. "Forty-six. May I ask why you mention that particular figure?"

"Because I know what Perias would pay me," Hanse said, holding the other man's eyes.

"Ah. Perias. Yes. Umm. You know that *Arcala* is main partner in that establishment?"

"Aye," Hanse said casually, vowing that he *had* to learn who this Arcala was. "But I do not know who backs you, or partners with you."

He received three names, and once again was obviously supposed to be impressed with the first: Corstic.

"Who's Corstic?"

Tethras showed true surprise, but muttered "Oh, I forget how recently you have come here, Hansis. Corstic is Arcala's chief rival! They two are surely the most powerful men in Firaqa!"

"Oh."

"Hansis, I will need to confer. May I expect you here in the morning?"

"Someplace more private than this."

"Of course. Meet me here and we will go elsewhere, all right?"

Hanse nodded. Without another word he turned away, sure that Tethras was gazing at his back. With the glint of silver in his eyes.

Hanse reached the S'danzo stall wearing his new russet tunic, and carrying the day-old one. Turquoise and her daughter were so sorry to tell him that Mignureal had left, just a few minutes ago. Perhaps if he ran . . .

Hanse thanked them, and in the orangy light of a sun squatting on the horizon, he walked back to the Green Goose.

"Hanse! Oh the tunic looks *wonderful* on you! What have you been *do*ing all day?"

He maintained an impassive expression in the face of her smile and delighted greeting. "Selling the horses," he said coolly.

Her smile could not endure the chill. "Good. I—I thought you'd come to the b—oh! The new tunic . . . you did come to the bazaar."

"I got to Turquoise's stall just a few minutes after you left, she said." He was squatting, stroking Notable and Calico while incidentally making himself unembraceable. "Did you eat there too, before you left?" he asked, looking at Notable because he wouldn't look at her.

"No, darling! I left in plenty of time to meet you here for dinner. Hanse?"

He waited, but she left it at that until he looked up.

"Oh Hanse please—what's *wrong*?"

"You know what's the matter." He rose, looking as stern as his tone.

"I don't, oh I don't!"

Notable banged his leg in enthusiastic rubbing, and Hanse looked down. "I don't see how you couldn't know."

"Hanse, darling, I—" She had to pause and take a deep breath to control the quaver in her voice. "I don't, Hanse, I swear I don't know what's wrong. What have I *done*?"

He hissed air through his nostrils. "What do S'danzo swear by?"

"Oh, *Hanse!*"

He looked at her after that piteous wail, and reflected briefly on how difficult it was to remain chill and angry when it was with *her* and he really didn't want to. Still, there was some satisfaction, a sort of pleasure, in feeling hurt and making sure he hurt back. *Oh faint,* he thought, in a sort of mental mockery.

He paced. *What I should be doing is babbling away to a delighted Mignue about the horses and what I've learned about money and my shrewdness! Instead, I have to keep this up; how can I stop?* He paused to look at her stricken face. Even her nice pretty body looked suddenly smaller, saggy. Forlorn.

"I was really shaken about the coins and the names last night, Mignureal. Having to live with something sorcerous this way and not knowing what's happening or what might happen next, or why . . . ! I couldn't sleep and needed to talk. You'd let me know you wanted to make love, but I just couldn't do that right away. I had to, to settle down some, first. And you went to sleep while I was talking. I didn't even know it until I asked you a question. What I wanted to do was kick you right out on the floor. What I did was lie there, tense all over again, and stare at the ceiling. Not that I saw it! If I'd had a whole sack of, of wine, I'd have drunk it all, I swear. Just to relax and be able to sleep."

"Oh Hanse!" She sank down onto the bed, to weep. "Oh Hanse I was just so . . . I didn't even know—oh I'm so sorry! I'm so sorry!"

He gazed at her for a moment, looking so tiny and pitiful and lovable. Then he went to her because he had to. After that one thing led to another, and they were past that one. They were also very late getting downstairs, and their dinner consisted of what Chondey had left.

They slept late next morning, and when they came down a man was waiting. Gaise, Sergeant, City Watch of Firaqa. All friendly, he nevertheless was here on business. Gaise had questions.

Had Hanse been in company with one Lallias, when that poor wight had been run over by a runaway draft-horse? Um-hmm; and why had Hanse run? Ah, well, that might have seemed intelligent at the time and Gaise could understand panic, but foreigners need fear nothing in Firaqa merely because they were foreigners! Fortunately there had been several other witnesses, and Hanse was not in the least implicated. And what business had he had with the deceased? Ah, and had he then succeeded in finding this Horse? Oh, good. Anorislas was known as a man honest almost to fault.

Perias and Tethras? Of course; everyone knew of them and their partnership establishments. Opinion? Well, they were bankers; everyone who had business with bankers had opinions, and most conflicted. "No man recommends his own moneyhandler, lest he be blamed later." No, no further questions; Gaise merely expressed a wish that Hanse had seen his way clear to tarry and tell what he had seen. Of course; he'd be delighted to answer questions, now. Let no one say that Firaqa's police were not helpful to citizens and travelers; newcomers and multigeneration citizens alike!

Yes, Firaqa had laws against chariots in the city, and laws about wagons and horses, and their speed, and where they must remain. The center of the street, aye. Ah, the wagon driver!

Well, the poor fellow had been popped into prison. It wasn't that he had done anything, really, or even been negligent. The man Lallias was dead, and someone had to be responsible. A runaway horse wouldn't do, although it had been executed, just in case. Neither would the unidentifiable child do; the one who had struck the standing, peacefully snoozing animal in the flank with a wire necklace containing a few copper coins.

"Oh, that's *terrible!*" Mignureal blurted.

"I cannot argue, Min—uh . . ."

Gaise smiled and gestured helplessly, while Hanse only muttered to the wall: "Executed . . . the . . . *horse*?!"

Once again, Mignureal pronounced her name. And asked about the poor wagoner. A farmer in town to peddle his melons, she learned. And what would happen to him? Well, Gaise said, a fine had been levied, and the fellow couldn't pay it. The sergeant shrugged, as if that explained everything.

"How much?"

"Three hearth—excuse me. Three silver pieces."

"We know what hearthers are," Hanse said, defensively.

Mignureal glanced at him. That was not what was important! That poor man was in *jail,* because a child had shocked his horse into panicky runaway, and had run over a man. That was what was important: the farmer in prison, for no reason save want of three silvers. Laws that insisted that someone had to be responsible for *everything,* she thought with anger, marked a sick society.

And what of the melons, she thought to ask. Ah, they were a frightful stench already, rotting as they were. But—but if he were not imprisoned, she reasonably pointed out, he could sell his melons, which was why he came to town in the first place. Then he'd have money to pay the fine!

Ah, true, unfortunately true, but the Law was the Law, and all that stood between civilization and the chaos of barbarism. And besides, he no longer had a horse to pull his wagonload of melons, had he?

Mignureal looked at Hanse, and thought of all the silver pieces they had realized this day, from the sale of a few horses. . . .

Hanse asked about power in Firaqa. He'd heard that the Hearthkeepers held most power in Firaqa. Then he had been told that two men named Arcala and Corstic held most of the power in Firaqa. Just before he was killed, Lallias had said that the power in Firaqa was held by sore—something. What?

All were right, Gaise said, but the banker and Lallias had been more right. The Hearthkeepers were public, and were indeed the final court of appeal. Even the Chief Mage had to defer to them. The what? The city ruler, or nearly; the Chief Magistrate, elected official here; sort of a duke of the city, or mayor. Aye, there was a council, too. Firaqa, after all, embraced not just the city but a broad area all around it. But what about this Corstic and Arcala, then?

They were the two most powerful men on the Council, Gaise explained. That made them the most powerful men in Firaqa. People said ill of both or swore by both. If both opposed another candidate for council or Chief Mage, that man could forget being elected. If one opposed but the other favored—too frequently the case, naturally enough since they were rivals, Gaise said with a helpless gesture—then things got exciting indeed. Such a situation added spice to the dullish dish of life, in a well-policed and mostly law-abiding city. Firaqa had ever been protected by casters of spells, and—

"What? You mean *sorcerers*?" Hanse's eyes were large.

"Aye. It has always been so, here. It is just the way things are, you see. It isn't as if we live under any shadow or anything. All the mages of Firaqa help the citizenry."

'Protected' means 'dominated', Hanse thought. "Ah, gods!

All the time, Gaise? These *protecting* sorcerers are always *helpful?"*

"Well, no, Hanse. I mean, the law is for us, but obviously right now it isn't helping that melon-peddling farmer any. If you and I developed a real feud, I mean really bad blood, then . . . but that's no good as example. We of the Watch are prohibited from personally seeking the services of a mage, and we swear not to. Every civil servant does, including each Council member. Suppose you really did Khulna a wrong, left here still owing money, maybe, and for some reason the law could not help him. If Khulna obtained the services of a mage and paid his price, obviously the result would not be to your liking. It couldn't be said to help *you,* then. You might of course go to another mage for a counter-spell, or something severe enough that Khulna would agree to have his advocate's spell lifted."

"Advocate?" Mignureal asked.

"When you are a mage's client, he is your advocate."

"Ah gods," Hanse muttered. "What I hear is chaos, all designed to keep the mages employed and probably wealthy!"

"Oh, wait now, nothing of the sort! A civilized society of law *needs* its spellmasters!" Gaise said, showing affront. "They generally do well, true. But it's *without* them that we'd have chaos!"

"Suppose Hanse went to Khulna's 'advocate' and offered him more to take off the spell, or do something to Khulna? Or both?"

"Oh, never!" Gaise assured her. "That would be unethical! The mages have their ethical code, after all, and they too are bound by the law. Khulna's advocate simply would not do that. Furthermore, he's bound by the mages' own code to report your attempt to subvert him. They have their own organization or guild. All practicing mages in Firaqa are members."

Probably call it the Parasite Guild, Hanse thought darkly. *The sorcerers are feeding on this society and Gaise is too dumb to realize it. I guess everyone is. They just accept it.*

"When the mages bring up a member before the Ethics Committee of their own FSA, we stand aside. If he is found guilty of ethical misconduct unto criminal act, then the law acts. If he is merely reprimanded for a lapse in ethics or a *questionable* act, we do nothing. If it happens again, of course, he's in a lot of trouble."

"FSA," Hanse repeated. "Firaqi Sorcerers' Association?"

"Spellmasters' Alliance," Gaise corrected.

"Uh-*huh*. Well, in essence this FSA tells the law what to do, then!"

"That is not the case," Gaise said, with emphasis. "In the matter of the runaway horse and wagon that killed that fellow Lallias, for instance, no one considered consulting the FSA." He chuckled at the concept.

"Suppose the farmer was ensorceled," Mignureal said. "Or his horse was."

"Ah, but that was not the case. A child was seen to strike the horse. And no mage has come forward, anyhow. They do, in such situations. If there's any suspicion of ensorcelment and no mage has come forward, the magistrate defers judgment until the FSA can be contacted. That's one of the purposes of the Council and the Chief Mage."

"Uh, does Chief Mage mean *that*, Gaise, or Chief Magistrate?"

Gaise said, "Yes. That is—"

"Is he always a mage?" Mignureal asked, frowning and fingering her medallion.

"No. Sometimes he is, sometimes not. In olden times, he was. Over the years, the mages have backed away a bit. Not that they are not supreme in the city, but the Chief Mage no longer has to be an FSA member. That was so even before I was born. You see, long ago the mages here drove off the foreign Wizards. They were the Nisi—something. That's only memory, now. But before the mages and the FSA, Firaqa was a wizard-dominated hell."

"And now it's a mage-dominated . . . heaven?" Hanse said.

"Our present Chief Mage is not a spellmaster—and I have to go."

"I wish you didn't have to," Mignureal said. "There's an awful lot we don't know!"

"Well, you two nice honest people don't have anything to worry about, surely!" Sergeant Gaise said jovially, and departed.

Hanse and Mignureal sat and stared at the door, and then at each other.

"*Sorcery,*" Hanse muttered.

Since she had seen no real wickedness in this town and did not share his extreme aversion to magic and magicking anyhow, that was not nearly so disturbing to Mignureal as the injustice of a farmer's languishing in prison because he hadn't the price of a fine for something beyond his control. True, she had heard a number of anomalies unto contradictions, along with unexplained details. But wasn't that always the way of it with government and the law, anyhow?

"It may not be a heaven, but all we've seen here is a peaceful city full of nice people, darling," she said. "The system must work, and the law does. All I've heard that is bad is that poor farmer. But that's the civil law, nothing to do with the mages. Consider the awful situation we left behind, in Sanctuary!"

Hanse just looked at her. After a time he said, "What's strange is that no one we've talked to has even mentioned sorcery or sorcerers. Or mages or 'spellmasters,' either."

"Because they just accept it, Hanse. It's the way life is, and the government is, in Firaqa," she said, with a little shrug.

Hanse did not share her insouciance; indeed, he didn't share anyone's mere acceptance of much of anything. He had thought of something that might affect hers, however, and he hit her with it:

"Aye, well you might consider why in a town *protected* by mages, there are so few S'danzo and the ones we have met are forbidden to use the old language!"

On legs with the bulgily overdeveloped calves his weight made necessary, Tethras walked Hanse out of the bazaar and into a nice inn, where he doffed his handsome feathered hat and ordered a custard cup for each of them. It was a new dish to Hanse, and he liked it. Too bad Mignureal had elected to remain at the Green Goose. He had wondered why she hadn't wanted even to come along to visit with the S'danzo in the bazaar, but she had said she intended to later, and he hadn't cared to question her much.

Quietly, at their corner table, Tethras advised that Corstic,

Tethras and Associates would pay a total of 86 Firaqi silver hearthers for Hanse's 70 Imperials. That was over eleven coppers difference or "bounty" for each silver piece of Rankan coinage. Further, Tethras pointed out that Hanse was receiving something called "interest" of two percent from Perias. Corstic, Tethras and Associates would pay him two and a quarter. That translated into an additional six coppers a year, on the 46 hearthers Hanse had specified.

"I paid five for this hat you've been admiring," Tethras said, translating the offer into terms even more real.

Hanse held his chin down so that the Changer could not see him swallow. Happy day, several years agone, when he had stolen the governor's wand and ransomed it back! How lovely it was to be treated as a man of property whose business was sought after!

Tethras was not finished. If Hanse would agree to leave at least one-half of his payment for the Imperials with Tethras's establishment for a full year, all figures changed. That brought Hanse's head up.

"We would like to have the Imperials, which contain more silver than ours," the Changer explained. "If we do not have to part with the full amount at once, however, we will pay you for the privilege. We should not care to buy the Imperials from you and see you leave us to deposit the money with Perias and Associates! You have to bank with someone, after all. Therefore, we would offer a full hearther-plus-twelve for each of your coins, and pay you interest at the rate of two and one half percent for the year. Name a total amount and I shall show you what that will gain you, within a year."

Hanse named one, and then another, and the profits were just beautiful.

The man of property made agreement with Tethras, who was not averse to Hanse's request that they go and see Blomis the Public Recorder. Tethras took up his dark-blue hat turned up behind and on one side, and they did that. Blomis was very impressed indeed. Tethras also agreed to walk with Hanse to Perias's establishment, but of course would wait several doors away. Perias was understandably reluctant and then affronted, or acted so. Hanse remained adamant, and left with his Firaqi silver. Tethras was indeed waiting, standing comfortably on those huge-calved legs of his and looking almost romantic, Hanse thought, under that handsome hat.

"Tethras," the man of property said thoughtfully, "you are going to pay me two and a half percent. What if I were borrowing money from you?"

"The interest rate per year would be fifteen percent," Tethras said matter-of-factly.

"Ah," Hanse said. He did not admit that for the first time in his life he understood how bankers made money. It did seem to him that they could pay a bit more . . .

"And now," Tethras said, "as to the Imperials?" He chuckled. "The sooner they are in my possession, my friend, the sooner you begin earning interest!"

"Hmmm. Let us see if Mignureal is in the bazaar. Where would I buy one of those hats?"

Mignureal was inside, with Turquoise while the latter Saw for a client. Hanse waited impatiently, while a wriggly Zrena admired his new hat. So did Yashuar, in the adjacent stall. Then so did Mignureal and Turquoise, as they emerged from the private chamber reserved for Turquoise's work. Hanse drew Mignue aside and asked whether she was still "wearing" her portion of their fortune.

She looked odd, he thought, but nodded. "Of course! Why do you ask?"

"Yesterday I did business with a Changer, but this one today made me change my mind. We are converting our Imperials to hearthers at a fine profit, Mignue, and they'll be earning more money for us as well! We can look at the details together later; I want to! Meanwhile we can relieve ourselves of this burden and let our money start earning more for us."

"That sounds wonderful, darling! But Hanse . . . *here*, in public?"

He shook his head and moved back to the S'danzo stall to ask a favor of Turquoise. Soon he and Mignureal were in the dwelling behind the stall, divesting themselves of their fortune and amusing themselves at the same time by plucking coins out of each other's underclothing. Hanse did not mention the several Imperials he was retaining, because he was Hanse. He counted seventy handsome clinking likenesses of Ranke's

Emperor into a glazed pottery bowl, carefully set its cerulean lid into place, and bore it out with them. Amazing, how much it meant and yet how un-heavy it was.

"I feel just pounds lighter!" Mignureal said, almost giddily. Hanse's mood of excitement and joy was a communicable state.

"So do I," he said, grinning. "Thank the All-father you don't *look* any lighter in the chest! Oh, Turquoise: we're only borrowing this bowl for a few minutes, that's all. Be right back with it."

This time it was Mignureal who read aloud the newest document, while Tethras and Hanse beamed at each other. Tethras's large and well-armed bodyguard, who had as the Changer put it "minded the store" in his absence, remained impassive. Probably used to the jingle of lots of coins, Hanse supposed. He and Mignureal returned the bowl, told Turquoise and Zrena they had business and must hurry, and departed the open market practically at the run. This time they learned from Blomis that for copying and storing documents the City imposed a charge. Hanse happily paid. Now he had all the originals, each bearing Blomis's PR seal, and Blomis had the copies in his Public Records.

Trying not to skip and at that running a little, Mignureal and Hanse went straight back to the Green Goose and to bed.

Hanse had explained their dealings and their fortune, with figures. They were visiting with the cats and talking of going down to dinner when the notion struck him, for no particular reason: he opened that accursed saddlebag. Once more he upended it over the rumpled bed. Mignureal's stomach knotted when she saw all the color go out of his face as he stared at the bag's shining yield.

"Six! O god O Father Ils, what's *happened! Three* coins have vanished, just today!"

Quite naked in the act of dressing, Mignureal bit her lips as she met his stricken stare. "Hanse, uh . . . I—"

"What! You what? Tell me!" His anguish threatened to become fury.

"I couldn't stand the thought of that poor farmer in prison with the gods know what befalling his family, Hanse. That's why I stayed behind this morning. I—I came back up here and took three of *those* coins. My paying his fine didn't restore his horse, but at least he—"

Hanse was laughing. "Good! Good! Let the city of Firaqa worry about those horrible coins!" He whacked his hands loudly together. "Good, Mignue, good!"

His jubilance relieved her nervousness. She had feared his reaction but had just had to do it. They had so much, and that poor man . . . ! As for why she had taken three of *those* coins, rather than delving into her underwear; well, she had a reason. The man's imprisonment was unjust, and so the city was undeserving of such cruelly gained money. She did not tell Hanse why she had chosen to use three pieces of ensorceled silver . . .

Her surmise had been right, too. In the morning Hanse was more pleased with the fine trick she had played on the city than horrified by the fact that the saddlebag once again contained nine Imperials.

Next day they looked at apartments. Late that afternoon they found the wonderful place near the bazaar. A good-sized room nicely carpeted, adequately furnished and without peeling plaster; a small kitchen area with cabinet and a little stove; a nice enough bedroom with bed, a standing press, and two storage lockers. Best of all, running water! They liked the fact that the place was on the second floor, with one window overlooking Cochineal Street and the other an alley. Both were closed with real glass! Pets were fine here, "so long as there's no mess, mind, and no loud noises, now; everyone else here is older folk!"

Hanse persuaded Mignureal to put off committing themselves until next day. Hours later, despite her expostulations, he went out their window in the Green Goose, in his working clothes. Not long afterward he slipped silently into the apartment on Cochineal by way of the alley window, and lay down on the bed. Since he awoke after sunrise, he assumed that no untoward noises attended this place and the neighbors. Furthermore, absence of bite or itch proved that the only live creature on the bed had been he. Swiftly he changed into the green tunic, rolled up the black garments, and eased out the window.

He entered the Green Goose in the normal way, surprising Khulna and his family. Went out for a walk early, he told them, and soon he and Mignureal were excitedly breakfasting.

That day they took the apartment on Cochineal and paid a month's rent. However unnatural, their two cats *were* cats, and were not happy about moving and having to break in new territory. They stiffly paced their new home for hours, sniffing everywhere, shying at any noise or movement, and in general manifesting their discomfort. After a couple of hours, Mignureal stayed with them while Hanse went back to the Green Goose.

Khulna unhappily tendered a number of copper coins as refund for unused room and uneaten meals. He said he hated to lose such nice kids even more than the money. Hanse shocked him by pushing back most of the sparks.

"You're a good man, Khulna; you're good people. We'll come back now and then to eat and to visit. You be sure to let me know when we've eaten up that money."

Then he had to submit to Chondey's embrace. He returned to the apartment to "relieve" Mignureal in staying with still-nervous cats. Mignureal had been cleaning with compulsive diligence. Now she returned to the inn, to clean up their former room. Chondey and Khulna survived the shock. So did Rainbow and Notable.

They discovered what fun it was to sit in the window and watch passersby on the street just below, and to snooze there in the afternoon sun. The window's sill became theirs. After a few days Hanse and Mignureal contrived to extend it into a broader shelf. The cats felt obliged to go stiff and slinky again, sniffing the addition and playing Oh You Insensitive Humans Have Spoiled Everything. Then Notable decided to try it anyhow, and soon he and the calico were appreciating the additional space at the window.

Hanse was happily surprised by the cooking of both Mignureal and the old couple along the hall, who tried to adopt them. The cats thrived on the cooking of both. A new disagreement stemmed from Mignureal's forgetting the time on their fourth day here; she stayed until sundown with her fellow S'danzo. Worse, this was the same day on which he had bought her a nice tunic, in the yellow so popular in Firaqa. Her coming in so late spoiled the surprise, and his mood. The argument went a bit far and sent Hanse angrily out, on that fourth evening, to walk alone with his anger.

Hours later they made it up as usual and once again rumpled the bed. Hanse was both happy and proud that he had turned down a clear-cut invitation at the western edge of the bazaar. The shapely flirt was part of a caravan, passing through, and had probably only thought it would be an adventure to card a little wool with a town boy, anyhow.

Two days later Mignureal announced, with care and after they had eaten a good meal she had prepared, that she was joining Turquoise; going to work. She produced a copper from her sash and held it up for Hanse's inspection. Yesterday afternoon, she explained, Turquoise had been Seeing for a *suvesh*, faking it as usual, while Mignureal sat silently by as if she were an apprentice. Abruptly she had started to speak, disrupting everything. Except that she was Seeing for the client, clearly. In short order her words proved absolutely true: the client found her lost brooch in exactly the unlikely place Mignureal had said. She returned to add another copper to her payment, and to advise Turquoise that she'd be telling just everybody about her and her wonderful apprentice. It was that coin which Mignureal now held up so proudly before her man.

"My very first earnings, ever! Now that it's happened, I've broken what mother called the 'casual acquaintance barrier' in my mind, in my ability, and I know I can do it again. And again. I am employed, Hanse!—and as a S'danzo should be!"

He made supportive noises and tried very hard to seem to share her excitement and pleasure. He did, and yet he did not.

Part of his problem was that he had no employment and did not know what to do. He had been well trained in a particular profession, and his natural ability had made him superior in that nocturnally-practiced occupation. Now that he had no need of practicing it, he had no notion as to what to try. He had always looked for opportunity and loot rather than for work, or for what others called work, anyhow. Accordingly three nights later, when she had had four more successes with complete strangers, he found an excuse to be angry, and to depart their apartment.

That night Shadowspawn struck, in Firaqa.

Like a sinuous black cat bearing a mouse, he returned proudly with a good bracelet of silver and garnets, and a striped sash of rich silk. Mignureal was shocked. She was not pleased, understanding, or supportive.

Hanse stormed out again. He actually went back up a wall and across two roofs before throwing the bracelet in an almost perfect toss through an open window. It was the same window he had used to enter that second-story room of a nice dwelling, and to emerge again with scarf and necklace. This time the window was open because the owner's husband and brother were waiting inside with crossbows.

A bolt sang evilly through the air a foot or so above the black-clad thief. He was naturally offended at their reaction to his returning the bracelet. While they made a lot of noise and loosed another steel shaft despite being unable to see him, he took his leave. Shadowspawn eased backward off a ridgepole, slid partway down that roof and pounced easily to another, and became one with the shadows of night.

Less than an hour later he gave the sash to a painfully young whore he met in a dive called the Duck's Teat, probably because it was located down on Duck Walk on the wrong side of Caravaner. Not only did her wool prove not worth carding, he scratched for the next three days and nights. At last he immersed most of himself, grinding his teeth against the pain of water hotter than he could stand it, and forced himself to stay there long enough to murder the infesting vermin.

Furthermore, a worse than miffed Mignureal spent two of those days and nights with Turquoise and family and returned to the apartment on Cochineal only when her period started.

At last both of them apologized and both claimed fault, though Hanse could not admit his problem about her working while he did not. There was some weeping, to the considerable interest of the cats, and a lot of embracing and sniffling and protestations of devotion. All was well again, and both Sinajhal's list and the nine coins in the abhorrent old saddlebag had remained unchanged for many days. Along about then he learned about her physical state, and was a long, long time getting to sleep.

Next day the saddlebag contained eight silver Imperials.

• • •

Hanse had something to do. Like most active but jobless men of pride, he threw himself into his self-appointed task the moment Mignureal left for the stall in the bazaar. He stood to prove very little, really, since the names on the list remained as before. Nevertheless, he asked. He asked at the gate, and found Watch headquarters and asked there, and gained Gaise's help. Gaise had no information for him, however. Hanse spent the day at it, and learned nothing. Nervously, he even approached the main Temple and asked a priest. Apparently no one had died yesterday, in all of Firaqa.

He was no good company that night. Cats and Mignureal trod with care around him, so that at least no trouble rose among them.

In the morning he was at it again, asking all over the bazaar and in and out of ale- and eating-houses. No, no one knew of any deaths day before yesterday. No, no funeral processions.

He felt needles along his back when he heard the hail and turned, on Better Street, to see that it was a Red who called him by name. Hanse did not know the man and approached him with apprehension.

"You are the one, aren't you? The sergeant wants to see you. Said he had something for you, about your query yesterday. Sergeant Gaise?"

"Yes! Thank you!"

Today Gaise had gate duty, and Hanse found him there, sitting boredly.

"Oh, Hanse! You seemed so wrought up yesterday that I thought I ought to tell you. Know a taverner named Jumnis?"

"Jumnis? No. What tavern?"

"Uh . . . the Bottomless Cup, on Olivewall."

"Olivewall. Is that a street?"

"Right."

Hanse shook his head. "I never even heard of that street, much less the Bottomless Cup, or Jumnis. Why, Gaise?"

"Jumnis. He was missing yesterday. Never opened the place. No family. Late yesterday afternoon one of our boys helped one of Jumnis's two employees break into the place; he knew the fellow. They found Jumnis, dead on the floor between bar and door. Had his cloak on, as if he was on his way in or

out. The poor employee started in babbling in terror that he
hadn't had a thing to do with it. Our man had only to touch the
body to know the truth of that. Jumnis was stiff and cold. We
couldn't find a mark on him. We think he was just closing up
night before last, and died. Had his day's proceeds right there
on the floor beside him, in a locked box.'' Gaise shrugged.
"We're calling it heart failure. That's what we and the leeches
always say when nobody knows why a man suddenly drops
dead. You know: if you're dead, obviously your heart failed!
So, presumably someone did die day before yesterday, after
all. But it's not who you were wondering about, hmm?''

Hanse shook his head and swiftly made up a half story:
"Who knows? Mignureal's a S'danzo. She has the Sight, you
know, and she—she just had a feeling. I'll ask her. She's with
the S'danzo stall in the bazaar, and maybe he had been in there.
You know, getting a reading. How old a fellow was he?''

"Oh, thirty-five, thirty-six. Native to the city. Did well with
that place, too. Property, fat account with Tethras. Now we
have to find a relative.''

Hanse managed a smile. "Well, let me know if you don't,
and I'll see if I can make you believe I'm his long-lost younger
brother.''

Gaise laughed, and thought of a joke he wanted to tell, and
that was that. Hanse told Mignureal. Nothing was proven. A
man had died and a coin was missing. That was hardly cause
and effect, and neither Hanse nor Mignureal had ever so much
as seen this Jumnis, so far as they knew.

Two days later, however, he learned from Tethras that
Jumnis and Lallias were long-time pals. As far as Hanse was
concerned, he had proof: Jumnis's life, too, was connected to
the outré coins. Like Lallias, Jumnis was gone, and so was his
coin.

"I want to call it proof," Hanse told Mignureal.

They had eaten at the Green Goose, because they had
needed to get out of the apartment. Now he was enjoying an
unusual second mug of beer. She still nursed along the same
wine she had ordered when they arrived—which Chiri had
proudly brought her in a nice goblet of formed blue glass. A
delighted glance from Mignureal had been greeted by a smile
and wink from Chondey.

"We already assumed that the coins are linked to the lives of men, Mignue. Firaqi men. We were afraid they also had something to do with me. Remember your fear that a coin vanished when I killed someone? Well, I had nothing to do with Lallias's death, even though we were together. Still, a case could be made that if he hadn't been taking me to Horse he wouldn't have been there in the first place, and wouldn't have been in the way of that runaway horse. Oh, I know you never mentioned that, Mignue; I thought of it, just the same. But this Jumnis! Neither of us ever heard of him or his alehouse or even that street. But he was connected with Lallias, and he did die, and a coin did disappear."

He sat back, looking almost proud. Almost, because it was really no explanation at all, and they both knew it.

"There is one other part of that I like," she said, looking into her deep blue glass. "It doesn't have to be violent death. You said Jumnis didn't have a mark on him. He died of natural causes." She swallowed and her expression changed into one less pleasant. "Just . . . death. That's the connection. Death."

The shadow of sorcery still hung dark and heavy over them. It affected their thinking and their attitudes and thus their relationship and sleep. It was an oppressive weight on their very lives.

Next day some people up in Newtown complained, and some Reds arrived and did some checking. The neighbors were right about the odor, and the water. The corpse down the well appeared to have been dead about three days, and with his head bashed out of recognition he had certainly died violently.

The coin might have represented him, then, and not Jumnis.

The only aspect that could be interpreted as positive for Hanse and Mignureal was that at least they were sure Hanse had had nothing to do with the man's death—his violent death. The shadow of sorcery seemed to darken, to grow more oppressive. It affected their mental state and ability to think, their sleep and everyday lives, and thus their relationship.

Three days later Mignureal came home badly shaken. She was sure that she had Seen violent death for a client, which was

no pleasant matter. After comforting her for a while with
considerable laying on of hands, Hanse thought to ask her the
man's name.

She knew at once why he asked: "It's not one of those on the
list," she said irritably. "His name's Ganther."

"Ganther," Hanse repeated, and upended the saddlebag.

Eight silver coins jingled out. He lined them up neatly,
comforted Mignureal some more, and suggested a visit to the
Green Goose. Mignureal pepped up, blinking mistily and
showing him the best smile she could muster. After popping
the coins back into the bag, they left the apartment and the
cats, who were pretending to be kittens playing tumble.

Hanse didn't open the bag until after Mignureal had left,
next morning. It contained seven Imperials. That was enough
to make him sit down suddenly. He sat thinking for a long
while before slipping one of those coins into his outer purse.
Then he took up his hat and left.

He was on his way when it occurred to him that he probably
should not go to Gaise again. An imaginary conversation ran
through his mind:

*"A man named Ganther? Aye, he was strangled, poisoned,
hanged and chopped into little pieces last night. What do you
know about it, Hanse?"*

"Nothing."

*"Then how come you popped in here asking whether
someone named Ganther might have died yesterday?"*

*"Uh, well, Mignureal read for him yesterday, and, uh, she
thought she saw violent death in his, uh, future."*

*"Hmm. That's twice this has happened, isn't it. Hanse, I'm
sorry, but I think we'd better go and ask Mignureal some
pointed questions. And maybe the FSA will want to talk with
her, too."*

"Why?"

*"Well, there is reading the future, Hanse, and then there's
cause and effect. I'm sure that nice girl is purely in the first
business, but . . ."*

No. He wouldn't go to Gaise. *The strain on both Mignue
and me is bad enough already, without making him suspicious
and maybe subjecting her to that. No. I'll just think of
something else.*

It was the wrong time of day and not Hanse's sort of behavior, but he entered at the nearest alehouse sign. He ordered the smallest quantity of beer available and didn't finish it before he gave up and left. No one was talking. He entered another, and learned nothing there except that drinking beer in the morning was not likely to become a habit with him. He paused outside the third place to put on his toughest face before he swaggered in, and ordered tea.

No one said a word about that; the four men at the table near the door were talking about that fellow who'd fallen out of the window of his third-floor apartment last night and splattered his brains several feet up the wall. Weird. Probably drunk, one said, wagging his head and sagging low over the table.

"People should have rules about drinking. Never alone and never at night!"

"That's the dumbest flamin' thing I ever heard, Stumpy. What a man shouldn't do is drink in the daytime! I wouldn't, either, if I wasn't such a weak pile of horse biscuits!"

"My rule's never to drink before breakfast," a third member of the party said. "Never!"

Ils's eyeballs, Hanse thought, *I haven't had a thing to eat!*

He was on the point of losing his patience and turning to ask them the name of the dead man, when Stumpy did exactly that.

"Who knows?" one of the others said.

The proprietor looked up from arranging mugs and called, "Ganther. His name was Ganther. And he was pushed, I'd bet my last barrel!"

Hanse swallowed hard, then did it again. He tried burning his mouth with tea and discovered that it wasn't that hot. *Ganther.*

"Why do you say that?" he asked.

"Now here is a smart individual," the proprietor said loudly. "He looks perfectly capable of handling all four of you without thinking about it, and what is he drinking of a fine sunny morning? Tea! Tea, by the Flame!" He turned his gaze on Hanse. "Because people don't just fall out of windows, that's why! Someone pushed him, mark my word."

"I fell out a window once," Stumpy mumbled.

"If we all come in here an' ordered tea, Bim, you'd starve! Can't make no money servin' tea!"

"Starve, my butt," Bim said. "I'd have a heart attack and fall down dead if you was to come in and order tea! Want a refill? Oh, uh, come back sir—didn't offend you, did I?"

But Hanse was already out the door.

He walked, thinking. *Ganther*. He never did get around to eating. He walked. He walked Firaqa, thinking and thinking, and he noticed no one and nothing. He walked for hours, thinking, and when he came to the northward gate he went on through and wandered some more. *Ganther*. He ran into two people, one of whom threatened him even after Hanse's apology. Hanse showed him the cultivated stare and half crouch, and the fellow decided that the apology was sufficient after all. He went his way and Hanse went his. Eventually he realized that he was in the area called Newtown and thought what a shame; he hadn't been paying attention, and then the other thoughts closed in again, and the feeling of helplessness, and he was on his way back toward the gate when it occurred to him that it was mid-afternoon and he still hadn't seen a thing of Newtown. His stomach rumbled, reminding him about something else he hadn't done.

The shouting match the couple was having just ahead made him pay attention; those two were *mad*.

Suddenly the redheaded woman pounced at the skinny man, probably her husband or her man at least, and started in pounding him with both fists. He hit her back, good and hard in the face, and Hanse stopped dead still because he was walking right toward them. The woman let out a yell and flopped backward, raising a little dust and showing a lot of leg, and Hanse saw the flash of steel in the man's hand as he shouted something really nasty and took a step toward her. A guard came from the gate, at the trot. The man took another step, steel in hand, and started bending over her, and the Red shouted. The woman was screaming. The skinny man looked at the guard, at her, and back at the uniformed man just as the guard reached him and reached for him with both hands.

The skinny man stabbed the gate guard in the neck and the woman shrieked as if the blade had just gone into her.

"Stop! Stop where you are and drop that knife!"

That order was bawled from the guard-tower beside the gate. Hanse looked up to see that the Red up there had his crossbow wound up, while a swift glance showed him that the sergeant on the gate was pointing at the skinny man with his sword while another Red was on one knee, aiming his crossbow. It occurred to Hanse that it could be wise to become less of a target. He fell flat. Meanwhile the woman was screaming loud enough to shame Enas and the skinny man stabbed the sagging guard again before turning to her as if he didn't hear a word or have any notion of danger.

When Hanse looked up between the hands he'd used to cover his head, the skinny man was reeling. He had sprouted a crossbow bolt in his thigh and one in the body, just above the belt. At that he held himself on his feet, got himself turned back to the screaming, crawling woman, and raised the dagger again.

Mighty good shooting, an impressed Hanse was thinking, just before someone's aim slipped and a crossbow quarrel appeared in a burst of blood, having slammed completely through the lunatic's cheeks and mouth. Now he was yelling, with blood pouring out of his mouth. The fourth shot was perfect, and he fell right down and kicked like a chicken whose head had just been wrung off.

That took care of it, fellows, Hanse thought urgently. *Stop shooting now, all right? He isn't between you and me anymore—nothing is!*

He was up on one knee, in the act of rising, when the woman snatched up the fallen man's dagger and charged the guards, screaming through her sobs.

She loved him, Hanse thought. *They always do.* And just in case, he went flat again.

When he looked up a few seconds later, the woman was sagging, moaning instead of screaming. The dagger lay at her feet and her hand dangled unprettily from a broken wrist. She was lucky, Hanse realized; the man with the crossbow had used it to whack her knife-wielding arm. In seconds he and the sergeant had rope around her other wrist and were winding the rest of that length of line around her body.

Hanse got to his feet again and moved up to look at the two men on the ground. They lay close together. He squatted between them.

"You don't happen to be a leech, do you?" the sergeant asked a half minute later, trotting up.

Hanse looked up. "No, but it wouldn't matter. They're both dead."

"Dead! Ock's dead—aww, he killed Ock, damn it! That rotten bastitch!"

Hanse nodded, rising. "Had no idea what he was doing. Drunk or just out of his head. If your man had had his sword out, I guess he'd be alive." He didn't mention that Ock had been plain sloppy, running up to a dagger-wielding berserker and reaching for him with both empty hands.

The sergeant was squatting beside the dead guard. He looked up sharply. "I remember you. From down south, with a string of horses, wasn't it?"

"Name's Hanse." Hanse nodded. "Oh—Sergeant Rimizin, isn't that it?"

"What're you doing out here, Hanse? Where're your horses?"

"Sold 'em," Hanse told him. "That's why I was walking. I went out to Newtown . . . hoping to see a man about a job. I was just on my way back when I saw these two yellin' at each other. When she jumped at him, I stopped. I wasn't about to keep right on walking with those two between me and the gate, as wild as they were acting."

"Uh-huh, that was wise. So how come you hit the ground?"

Hanse showed him a tiny smile. "I saw two crossbows and I was in line with them. Hadn't seen your men shoot before, Sergeant. Had no idea they were so good."

Rimizin nodded and looked more pleasant, but couldn't smile with his comrade lying dead beside his foot. "That was probably wise, too. Both those boys are better with a crossbow than I am."

Hanse shook his head and heaved a sigh. "Never used one. Is there anything I can do to help, Sergeant, or are you about to tell me to move along?"

"We'll take care of it, Hanse. Go ahead on your way. We don't need a witness for this; three men of the Watch saw it all."

Hanse nodded and went on his way, hoping that the Reds and some magistrate weren't so angry about Ock's slaying that they took it out on the woman. She had lost her head in an idiotic argument, and lost her man and the use of her wrist and her freedom too; for a while, at least.

He was well through the gateway and walking along Gate Street when the thought struck him, and the bottom dropped out of his stomach. He ran all the way home and loped up the steps two or three at a time. The cats scooted fast, Notable aborting an attack on the invader at the last moment, when he saw that it was his human who burst through the door and grabbed up the saddlebag.

It contained seven silver coins. Hanse's stomach was lurching and he was all prickly, leaking greasy sweat when he remembered that he'd put one in his outer purse. He checked. It was still there.

All seven were still there next morning, too.

"I don't know whether to be glad or sad," Hanse admitted, feeling Mignureal squeeze his hand as they gazed down at the Imperials he had just poured out onto the bed. He worked his hand loose to put an arm around her and press her close to his side. "We know that not *all* violent deaths have anything to do with the coins, and the coins mustn't have anything to do with me, because I was *close* to those two, and here are the coins. On the other hand, we'd be two nearer to the last of 'em. . . ."

The oppressive weight of the silver pieces and the list remained. Two young people were in love and far from home, and yet their relationship was troubled and in trouble. That was the pressure, the knowledge of living with sorcery and being so helpless; waiting for another death and another vanished coin. They discussed approaching a Firaqi mage to see if they could find information or a counter-spell, and only after an argument decided that they were afraid to do that. Notable became impossible and Hanse was surprised and delighted to discover that the cat would accompany him on walks more closely than a dog, day or night, without a leash. Anorislas sold two Tejana horses for thirty-nine hearthers and Hanse, having come very close to striking Mignureal last night in another argument, spent all four pieces of Firaqi silver on a fine silver-backed comb and brush set, two gemmed hair-combs, a dress cloak for himself and a far better one for her, a pair of excellent goose-feather pillows, and the flimsiest mouth-wateringest night "gown" he could find. Mignureal Saw good and bad, and brought home money. She Saw nothing for her or for Hanse. Nor did she have any flashes or even new surmises about the bag, the coins, or the list.

Hanse found a throwing knife worthy of him, at last replacing the one he had lost in the raid on the Tejana. He practiced his throwing in the crossbow practice yard behind Watch headquarters, and before he left he had turned down a job offer from Gaise's superior. He spent two days helping their landlord paint and patch roof leaks. "You're good on roofs, Hanse," he was told, and his smile was real while he nodded and said nothing. He wouldn't accept payment, but he and Mignureal—and the cats—appreciated the food that turned up so mysteriously. Mignureal saw a man die in the bazaar, killed by a hired guard in the act of robbing Yashuar, but no coin disappered. Cause for joy? Hanse worked with Anorislas for three days and decided that he still didn't like horses. One night while he sipped beer alone in a place called The Alekeep he was joined by a pretty woman of twenty-six or so with just about the best figure he had ever seen and after an hour of converse discovered that she was not a professional but did want to take him home with her. He tried to tell himself that he was justified and entitled, since he was here alone because he had stormed out of the apartment after another row. The problem was that he could not convince himself that Mignue was in the wrong, and so guilt sent him away from that astonished and disappointed woman.

On the way home some idiot actually sought to waylay him. An instant later the poor wight was staring, openmouthed, at the throwing knife poised high in his intended victim's left hand and the dagger held low and ready in the right. The waylayer ran away and Hanse was in a much better mood when he reached the apartment. There, more apologies and mutual blame-acceptance led to more rumpled sheets.

Next day he bought a lovely blue-and-cream vase, superbly glazed, and a nice silk wall-hanging painted with a pretty calico cat. Mignureal wept in happiness at such luxury;

needless decor! The very next day the bazaar guard near the S'danzo booth abruptly clutched his chest and dropped dead, and Mignureal came home fearful. She had known the man as Tink and learned his real name only after his death. It was Estane. Yes, that name was missing from Sinajhal's list, leaving a space behind, and of course another coin was gone. For no good reason save fear and pressure Hanse and Mignureal slipped into an argument. Hanse tore the remaining six coins from the accursed bag and threw them away. Then he reverted to natural: he went out black-clad and went up a wall and across a roof and partway down another and in a window, to depart moments later with a jeweled dagger and two gold pieces while the man and woman slept on in their bed beside the window. He arrived home with his ill-gotten gains feeling much, much better—except that Mignureal was in bed with Calico and covered, her back turned, and she would not turn over or speak a word. And next morning the six Imperials were back in the cracked old saddlebag.

That helped him and Mignureal make it up, united as victims of the sorcery they lived with.

"It's the strain, the strain, darling," she said, hugging him.

When she mentioned his theft a half hour later, Hanse was not ready to be reasonable. He muttered "nag" and departed for a wander. Notable and Rainbow insisted on accompanying him and resisted his efforts to send them back. Six blocks away the three of them witnessed a swift and ghastly violent death. Hanse raced all the way home and jerked open the old leathern bag. It contained six coins. With a yell he broke; Hanse slammed the silver pieces at and through the window of the second-floor room. While Mignureal stared in horror, tears starting to seep from her huge eyes, glass tinkled and Hanse jumped up and down on the saddlebag. Only when he became aware of the squeal of urchins and others outside, snatching up that which was surely a Flame-sent gift to the deserving, did he cease stomping. He smiled.

"Why didn't I think of this before! Let others have that damned strangeness and the daily horror and strain! Let *them* have the curse we don't deserve!"

After that they sat on the floor holding each other, quietly trying to discuss the incomprehensible and hardly discussable. At least and at last they were well rid of the accursed coins!

Hanse promised to fix the window right away.

They were dreaming, and should have known better. They were manifestly cursed with the unnatural and the preternatural; the sorcerous and the accursed. The coins were there in the saddlebag in the morning, shiny as if just-minted. Hanse and Mignureal were days recovering from that shock, if they recovered.

Passing the soaring Temple next day, Hanse hatched another idea. This one was truly a plan, considerably more rational than hurling the coins through a closed window and jumping up and down on their former container. He hurried back to the apartment, forgetting to swagger and try to look dangerous. It didn't matter; he was moving too fast for anyone to get in his way.

He emerged cloaked and wearing his Firaqi hat with the new green plume above the russet tunic and handsome new flop-top boots. He cut a fine figure as he paced deliberately up the street. The anomaly was that this dandy bore a cracked old saddlebag that looked as if it had failed to survive a flood and should have been discarded years back.

His goal was more than merely discarding the accursed bag. With that same deliberate pace, cloak fluttering, he ascended the many broad white steps to the Temple of the Flame. Seeing a middle-aged Hearthkeeper in her fiery robe, he not only bowed but swept off the hat so that the plume streamed through the air. She looked fondly after him, charmed by this presumed son of wealthy parents who brought up their boy to revere the Flame and the Keepers of its Sacred Hearth.

Hanse moved deliberately up the wide center aisle, boots clicking echoically on marble. He felt marvelous, jubilant, as he paced toward the lofting far end. There, from its broad brazier atop a stepped dais, rose living flame; the Eternal Flame that was the blessing and the life of Firaqa.

Seeing the staring sacerdote who was the Flamekeeper on the steps above sprawled worshipers, Hanse decided that he'd better emulate them. He sprawled beautifully, counted his heartbeats through a hundred—noting how they were speeding up—and rose slowly. Holding the bag partially extended before him, he ascended the steps toward a thick-walled, iron-banded stone brazier ten feet across. The flames licked high in yellow and white and orange. Hanse felt the heat as he approached.

Robed in yellow, the staring priest held up a staying hand. He was a tall, wispy-haired fellow of about forty who looked as if he ate sparingly about every third day.

"What do you, young sir, that you approach so close to the Flame Itself?"

"I will show you," Hanse said, and opened the bag. "Six silver coins, bearing the likeness of the despised Rankan Emperor, worshiper of false gods he exports unto foreign lands! They and the bag containing them are my gift to the Flame on behalf of all Firaqa. The cleansing Flame shall consume this Rankan bag and melt the idolatrous coins it holds!"

Good speech, he thought; *sounds properly nonsensical to impress a priest!*

Lifting the bag higher, he hurled it into the huge brazier. He heard a gasp from the Keeper of the Flame. Hanse stood watching a moment, hoping to see a new and hotter fire as the bag caught. Abruptly he shuddered, assailed by a sensation of eeriness beyond unpleasant. Shivering despite the heat, he hurried down the steps and out of the Temple.

Hanse felt very, very good. Once again he wandered Firaqa. Automatically his dark-eyes gaze roved, looking at this and that building with a thief's eye for potential burglary. . . .

He even gave a copper to a tongueless beggar.

When at last he returned to the apartment on Cochineal, it was only moments before the arrival of Mignureal. He caught her to him and hugged her hard. They held that embrace for a long while before he eased up. Only partially releasing her, he told her what he had done, and watched the smile flow over her face like morning sunshine racing across a field of flowers.

"Oh Hanse! That's wonderful!" She laughed aloud. "Sacrificed to the god of Firaqa! How clever of you!"

"This time we can be sure we're done with the curse," he said, just as jubilantly. "At last we can be sure we'll never see the accursed things ag—ho, what's that?"

"Hm? Oh." She held up her parcel. "A new pane for the window. It's waxed membrane; you've no idea how dear *glass* is here!"

"Maybe we should have brought in some of that desert sand we had far too much of a month ago! Well, we'll put in a glass pane before we move—you know, when we buy our villa, milady! Meanwhile, I'll get that in right away." He glanced at the window. "But not now! Let's go out and celebrate—and I mean someplace better than the Green Goose, too!"

They spen a jubilant night and most of a piece of silver, and slept well for the first time in at least a week.

When they awoke, the cats were amusing themselves, playing with the five silver Imperials they had found . . . somewhere on the floor.

Mignureal slumped down to weep.

THE SORCERY

ELTURAS

PERIAS

THUVARANDIS

"WELL," HANSE SAID, "at least we're rid of the rotten *bag*!"

No one laughed. Now they knew; now they were sure. They had not been able to remove the coins from the bag for longer than a day. Yet *something* removed them, some force, upon the death of this or that Firaqi; some curse that consumed a coin in concert with a man's life. The had indeed rid themselves of the aged saddlebag, once the property of the governor of Sanctuary. The coins were another matter. Now Mignureal and Hanse knew; now they were sure. They had no power to rid themselves of the coins. They would always return, until five more men died.

A new fear sneaked in, and settled in, and gnawed. Suppose the final piece of silver represented . . . Hanse?

Hanse had heard the news before he met Mignureal in the bazaar. A priest of the Holy Flame had died yesterday. In an accident unparalleled in Firaqa's history, the sacerdote had fallen into the temple fire of which he was custodian.

"That lean and greedy dog tried to get those coins I threw in," Hanse said as they walked homeward. "And furthermore one of them represented him; that's why the number is down to five. He's the only victim who's been *directly involved* with those accursed Imperials! The question is . . . did I cause his death, or did the coins?—or whatever it is that's behind them? Suppose they . . . it . . . wanted him to die? Was I *led* there? Are we free, Mignue? Can those coins somehow be *ruling* us; controlling us?"

"There aren't answers to those questions, Hanse. Let's don't—"

"There are! There is an answer to every one of those questions! We just don't know how to ask, or who. Someone knows the answer; the answers. Some . . . thing, whether it is force or person or demon or—or god."

"But we don't know who or what or how, Hanse. We can't know. Let's—let's don't talk about it."

"By every hell, Mignue—what else is there for us to talk about?"

That plaintive outcry he blurted loudly enough to turn the heads of other pedestrians. Hanse did not notice. He stared ahead with stricken eyes. He could not have felt more burdened had he borne on his back his weight in stone. Mignureal wisely said nothing. She knew how he hated sorcery; for one thing it robbed him of control, a real need in him.

Her boyish man needed solace, recreation, therapy. Mignureal tried, in the apartment that was too frequently more apart\ment than lovenest.

He tried to be secretive about it, and so she only bit her lip, hard, when all in snug black garments he went out the window and vanished into the night.

Sometimes I know what an immature girl I am, she thought, picking up the calico cat. *It hurts to realize that he is such a knowing man of the world, so experienced, while I'm such an ignorant girl. I rile him because I don't know how it is that I should behave, and so I behave as some mixture of my mother and me and—a silly girl. And yet in other ways he is such a boy! Sometimes he makes me feel* old, *more like his mother than his . . . than his . . . his woman.*

Oh Hanse, Hanse, why must you be cursed with such deep needs!

Why can't I be more a woman and you more a man?!

Shadowspawn roamed night-cloaked Firaqa, and no one knew. Shadowspawn entered the very temple, the main Temple of the Flame, and no one knew. He and his girl-woman had no need of money, but that was not why Shadowspawn went forth and stole. It was his solace, his recreation, his therapy. It was his need. His concentration on what he did was absolute, and in that was escape and a taste of heaven; the therapy he needed. The concentration never broke. He never thought of anything else, and in that was the therapy: total escape.

Shadowspawn faded in and out of the shadows of Firaqa, and no one saw. Except the man emptying his bladder in the street behind the Rampant Goat.

When he returned this time, Mignureal was not abed with her back turned. She was awake and seated in the chair facing the window. Expensive oil burned aflicker in the little brass lamp he had bought, in the shape of a woman's cupped hand. Rainbow lay curled on her, snoozing while Mignureal stroked absently, and stroked and stroked that soft multicolored fur. And stared at the window, and waited. She had dug her nails into herself from time to time, when she felt sleep creeping over her.

Shadowspawn came slipping in that window, out of the shadows of night and more silent than a whisper so that Notable stood abristle, and Shadowspawn looked into the hurt, even accusing eyes of Mignureal.

He could cope with her turning her back and refusing to speak. With her staying up for him, with her staring eyes, he could not cope. He was wordless. He felt embarrassment and hated it, as he set down the single golden candleholder from the Temple of the Flame. It was a triumph, and he was proud. The very Temple itself! In and out with his prize, and never seen or heard; never an alarm! And yet he could not be proud, not now. He was embarrassed and he hated that. He felt a boy under stern parental eyes, and he did not like it. Nor could he cope with it.

He could only be Hanse. He had to cover, and he did that by pretending anger. He stalked to the door, where he paused to turn and give her a look before he walked out.

He had been a loner and pride-driven, needs-driven for a long, long time. He also did not drink, and was proud of that control. Still, now and then, in stress, he had done. Tonight he would drink. Tonight he went to a dive, heedless of his attire, and he drank. No one spoke to or approached the silent, dark-clad and sinister young man at the corner table in the Rampant Goat. An underdressed young woman alone gazed at him for a long time with bright eyes, but he never glanced at her and something close to fear kept her from approaching him. Someone approached her, and she left with him, his hand down her dress. At the door, she glanced back.

The sinister yet magnetic dark one stared into his alecup, saying nothing, now and again signaling for more, and no one spoke to him or approached him.

Until four men did.

The one called Malingasa had recently gone out to relieve himself, and had seen this same lean, supple and night-clad youth ghost across a pallidly lit section of night. Hanse had been found out; Shadowspawn had been seen. He was known to these four as a nighter, a youthful man who could vanish as if materially into night's shadows. He was alone and lonely and bereaved, and these four men wanted him; wanted his services.

Nevertheless he denied what he was, and he denied them.

They pressed. They talked quietly but almost openly, for they knew what he was. They wanted a break-in and a theft. It was a job that required more than one person as backup and support, but that absolutely wanted one specialist. A human cat. That component they lacked. They wanted Hanse; no, they wanted Shadowspawn. He refused and they pressed. They cajoled and threatened and filled his cup; they dickered and flattered him. Perhaps most importantly, they told him that it would be difficult and that they knew no one who could accomplish such a feat. Unless . . .

He was Hanse with his needs, deviled by sorcerous coins and troubles with his woman, unemployed and made to feel embarrassed and useless even tonight, after a triumphant practicing of his trade and his expertise. And now, by these four he was wanted and needed. As a professional; as Shadowspawn.

He agreed, and they had of him his name and he theirs: Malingasa and wall-eyed Marll; Thuvarandis—now *there* was a familiar name!—and Clur called Shorty. Yes, Hanse would meet Shorty just up the street tomorrow, at dusk. They were agreed. The four men dribbled away, not leaving together, a newly sharp-witted Shadowspawn noted. He waved off a refill, waited a few moments, paid and went home—to the sheet-covered back of a sleeping Mignureal.

In the morning he awoke after she had risen. Under the sheet, he pretended sleep while she finished preparations to leave. He knew when she went to the door to the other room and paused to look back at him, but he did not move or open his eyes. He heard her leave, and noted with some feeling of guilt how she was so quiet about closing the hall door. Hanse knew he would not have behaved so.

But I am not gentle Mignue, he mused. *If I were like her, she'd probably never have paid any attention to me at all. Then we—oh, this is silly. What-ifs don't count for anything. I'm Hanse and she's Mignureal. What's more, I am Shadowspawn.*

And Shadowspawn's talents were needed.

Hanse lay where he was, under the sheet, thinking amid a mix of emotions. *They even cojoled me,* he reflected with a joyous feeling of pride. And although he didn't know who the target was, or where, he was going to do it. Of course casual mention had been made of the fact that he was a foreigner living respectably in Firaqa, accepted for what he appeared to be, and that word could possibly get out that he was also a professional thief who was probably in their city because he'd been chased out of his own.

He considered and tried to plan, despite limited information. Then Notable decided that he had lain there long enough. Notable mounted the bed. Hanse let the cat walk his body and opened his eyes only when the padded feet were on the sheet covering his chest. Huge green eyes stared down at him.

"Aww, you damned cat. You I can trust, Notable. You love me, don't you!"

"Meraw."

Hanse reached up to stroke the big red cat, which leaned into his hand until it moved him aside. Hanse rose. Gods, but he was practically gurgling with seeming gallons of beer that wanted out! *Consider yourself lucky that you don't have a headache,* he thought. He pulled his cloak about him and hurried down the hall to the privy. Feeling much better, he ambled back. He fed the cats while tearing off morsels of tough-crusted bread with his teeth. He peered out the window above the alley, twisting to look upward.

"Easy," he muttered, nodding.

He made a temporary parcel of working clothes and weapons. Dressed in the off-white tunic and hat, he strapped on a couple of knives and, for the first time, buckled on Sinajhal's sword with its fancy hilt. Then he left the apartment.

The bazaar was already crowded. Well away from the S'danzo booth, he found the couple who sold nearly everything. He surprised them by asking for the largest piece of gut they had.

"You got a window that big?"

Hanse shook his head. "I want to make a waterproof parcel."

"Oh. Pig's gut'd be a little small, then. Dear, don't we still have that horse innard? We've never cut it up, have we?"

"Just taking up space," she said happily, and found it.

Hanse established that no odor attended the large piece of tissue, and bought it. Back in the apartment, it became the container for a carefully rolled set of black clothing, along with two knives, three throwing stars, and the Ilbarsi knife. *If anyone asks,* he thought, *I'm checking our recent work on the roof!* He went out the window, and up. There he secured his parcel, and came back down the wall to his own window. No one had happened along the alley and no one would be going up onto that roof but Hanse. No one had seen and no one but he knew of the location of his working clothes.

Since he had no idea where the proposed theft was to take place, he decided to explore the well-to-do neighborhood called Northgates.

It wasn't as if that area of the city was near any gates at all, but area names had a habit of being born without regard for logic. He found no business establishments, only large houses on large lots. The lots were for the most part well shrubbed and shaded by tall trees. He noted the smaller dwellings of servants, along with stables and hen-houses. Here and there handsome statuary rose, and of course he saw dogs. The tall fences and walls he passed were hardly as high as the one around the governor's palace of Sanctuary. Nor was any of these dwellings so lofty as that mansion.

Shadowspawn, who had broken in and out of Sanctuary's palace three several times, saw nothing here that looked overly difficult.

Of course I'm in a town of mages, he reminded himself, and thought at once of the sorcerous attack that time he had broken into the dwelling of Kurd, to rescue Tempus. That had been the first time Mignureal had Seen for him, bidding him take a forgotten pot. It had happened to contain quicklime. Had he not heeded her, and had it not rained, he'd have been found dead there outside the vivisectionist's grim keep; strangled by attacking vines.

Hanse made a mental note to obtain some quicklime, just in case.

He reached the city's northward wall, which he saw had been well reinforced here. By the well-moneyed citizens in these manses, he supposed, and looked up over the wall. Beyond it rose Town Hill. It occurred to Hanse that he had never wandered up there, and that his target might well be one of the landed villas on that shrubby, tree-studded hill. Well, he'd find out soon enough. Too late now to go fetch his horse and ride up there, playing sightseer or perhaps messenger.

Messenger!

That thought sent him boldly over to the winding street called Bitterwood, and up to two manses. No one came to the door of the first, and Hanse smiled. Avoiding the place with the wall and three dogs, he approached another door. Again there was no response, and he decided to try the smaller house to one side and beyond the big home. He was surprised when it was opened by a plump, attractive and red-tunicked young woman with glossy black bangs and a décolletage that had to be called extreme even in Firaqa. She looked at him from beneath long lashes. Indeed, she looked him up and down.

"Please pardon me," he said, sweeping off his hat to reveal hair as jet black as hers. "I am looking for the dwelling of Tethras the Changer. Can you help me?"

"Why?" She stood gazing at him, one hand on a broad round hip and the other well up on the door's inner edge.

"Wh—oh, I have a message for him. Rather I am to leave it, since he is in the bazaar, surely."

"What is your name?

Hanse cocked his head. "Why?"

"Because mine's Janith and I watched you pass awhile ago and I'm alone and really lonely and you're the cutest thing I've seen in months."

"I do not believe this," Hanse muttered, not quite stammering.

"You believe this, don't you?" she said, bending far forward to afford him an inspiring view down her low, low-cut red tunic. It appeared to contain two large peeled pears separated by a deeply shadowed canyon. She imparted movement to the pears and changed the shape of the canyon by moving her shoulders. After giving him a moment to goggle, she looked up into his eyes from beneath long black lashes.

"Come in and see what else I have that you won't believe."

He was a little late for his appointment with Shorty, and he would never be called Saint Hanse.

Clur called Shorty conducted him to a certain place west of the bazaar, west of Caravaner Street, and Hanse had indeed come into Firaqa's maze, Red Row. At least he didn't have to enter blindfolded, or any such nonsense. The other three waited in this odd place that seemed to have been a stable, then a dwelling, and now to be abandoned. Its single window was boarded. The floor was not; it was earth. An oil lamp shared a tabletop with a squat, fat wine bottle and five unmatching cups. There were four chairs and a stool, on which sat gray-thatched Thuvarandis, with his back against the wall and long, long legs stretched out.

Blond Marll poured wine, and they talked. Hanse instructed them to call him Shadowspawn, and to refer to him only by that name. They accepted that without question or comment, which touched off a spark of suspicion in the back of his mind. They talked.

They did not say so, but Hanse began to gather that he was part of some sort of larger plot. Political, maybe. Integral to their plans was a theft from the palatial Town Hill home of one Corstic. Aye, Corstic the mage; Corstic the banking partner; Corstic who was one of the two primary powers in Firaqa. As a matter of fact, the more powerful of the two, as Hanse had already learned. Corstic possessed in his home a certain figurine, and these men wanted it.

"Gold?" Shadowspawn asked, again shaking his head at the silent offer of wine.

"No. The figure is of a cat, and it is of porcelain the color of pearl."

Hanse nodded. The thing was presumably without direct monetary value then, and so held another sort of worth to these men.

They knew where it was, or at least where it had been three days ago. It rested on a table, right out in the open. It might weigh between one and two pounds.

"You want me to break into the mansion of a powerful and wealthy mage, and all you want me to bring out is a little porcelain statue of a cat. That's all you want, from a wealthy home."

"Right," Thuvarandis said in his deep bass.

Marll with the one off eye said, "We don't even want that. We just want it out of Corstic's possession. So long as he has it, we and you and all of Firaqa are in danger, because we could be in his thrall anytime he chooses."

"Careful not to say too much, Marll."

Hanse thrust out a pointing finger at the speaker, Malingasa. "Listen, I don't want to hear anything else along those lines, you hear? You want me and my services in this, you tell me what you know and what I need to know and then more. Because only I can say what I *might* need to know. If what you're looking for is hired help to be kept ignorant of what's going on, run out and find one while I get on back home."

Silence followed that outburst, if that was the term; Hanse had spoken in no loud voice and without apparent anger. Malingasa stared, eyes larger, while Shorty and Thuvarandis gazed at Malingasa. Thuvarandis was smiling. Marll emptied his mug and wiped wine off his blond moustache.

"You know," Thuvarandis said quietly, "under the circumstances I'd have said the same thing."

Malingasa jerked his head to shoot him a look, but closed his mouth with obvious effort. With a nod, he looked back into the dark, dark eyes of their cat-thief.

"You're right, Shadowspawn. That's the way it will be. And

yes, the porcelain cat is all we want. What we intend to do with it is destroy it. It must be done in a specific way, under specific circumstances. It's in Corstic's private quarters and workshop, which is on the second floor."

Hanse glanced around. "And where do we think Corstic's going to be?"

"In Council meeting. Council meets on Ganeday night."

"That's two nights hence."

"That's right."

Hanse sighed. "I am not interested in Firaqi politics, and I've never cared for cats, and I hate sorcery. Your gain in this is not mine, but I see plenty of risk. The phrase is: What's in it for me?"

Marll smiled. Thuvarandis chuckled. He sat up straight on his stool, brown-legginged knees high.

"Two things, Professional. First—whatever you carry out of there in addition to the porcelain cat! We want nothing else. We won't even ask what you picked up. You might want to carry an empty sack or two in with you. . . ."

Hanse didn't quite smile as he nodded. He glanced at the others. "Are you in agreement with that, Shorty? You, Malingasa? Marll?" It was hard, looking at the man; Hanse was never sure which eye to look at.

They were all in agreement. They wanted nothing else; they would take the cat and ask no questions about whatever else stuck to his hands. They could even recommend at least two fences—er, Changers—who asked few or no questions.

"Why is the figurine important?"

"It is an aid to sorcery; a certain form of magic," Marll said. "That need not worry you. I have touched it, and Thuvarandis has. So has its previous owner, who is Arcala. It is not dangerous of itself, Shadowspawn."

"Which of you is a mage?"

Thuvarandis's bass boomed a good genuine laugh. "Excellent question!"

"I am," Marll said.

"So I thought. What help can you give me?"

"Some. But I haven't the powers to remove whatever wards Corstic has on his home. He is far more powerful and proficient than I."

Hanse sat straight. "You are telling me that I am going against sorcerous protections Corstic has set about his house."

"We assume as much. Wouldn't you, if you were all that he is?"

"That's no answer and proves nothing," Hanse said, "but yes, of course I would. I don't have to like it. Oh—what about dogs?"

Shorty slapped his leg. "We will take care of the dogs! No sorcery about them!"

"Tell me how, Shorty."

"He is to a bow," Marll said, "as you are to . . . night work, Shadowspawn."

Hanse nodded. "Which of you is a worker in porcelain?" *"What?"*

"By Ganeday afternoon I want a figurine," Hanse said. "A cat that resembles Corstic's as much as possible. People see what they expect to see. If he is accustomed to seeing the thing in a particular place, he will, or will think he does. If I leave one that is reasonably similar, days and even weeks or months may pass before he notices that it's missing. I'll take a cat-figurine in with me, and bring one out with me."

They sat gazing at him in silence until Thuvarandis said, "Very good, Professional. My dear friends, this is *one* of the reasons we have found the best man for the job to hand!"

Marll was nodding. "You shall have it, Shadowspawn. Since it is not a heavily detailed figure and I have seen it many times, I will see to it. I can even—well. It will be more than reasonably similar."

Hanse looked at Thuvarandis. "I asked what was in this for me and you said two things, Thuvarandis. What's the other?"

"The fact that several people have tried to break into the home of Corstic the master spellmaker, Professional. Only one man succeeded."

Hanse raised his eyebrows, which were just short of being one. "And why have you approached me, rather than him?"

"I said he succeeded in breaking *in*," Thuvarandis told him. "He did *not* break *out*."

The sense of challenge soared in Shadowspawn, enveloping itself with his pride, just as Thuvarandis had expected.

● ● ●

The maze called Red Row was a place of darkness and shadows when Shorty and Malingasa walked through it with Hanse, and out. Since he did not respond or speak, they too went quiet. They turned time after time, along one twisty or truncated street after another, and were approached by three beggars and four slatterns. They emerged onto Caravaner, just south of the open market. Hanse looked both ways, then turned to look back the way they had come.

"Think you could find your way back?" Shorty asked.

Hanse looked into his eyes. "Yes."

"Thuvarandis will see you tomorrow afternoon, in the bazaar," Malingasa said.

Hanse looked into his eyes. "So he said." And he set off walking northward along Caravaner. They watched.

"Friendly fellow," Malingasa said.

"A real professional, Malin. Lookit that walk!"

"Like a cat," Malingasa said.

Shorty laughed.

First Hanse removed any trace of his grim look from his face, then knocked. Zrena acted a little strained when she opened the door, and he knew he was lucky. Mignureal had stayed with them, and could have no idea that he had not been home, either. While they were affable, both Quill and Turquoise shot looks at Mignureal, which told Hanse that she had told them something, at least. Mignue, obviously, didn't know what to do or how to behave. She sat nervously fondling the medallion she wore; Strick's gift.

"Now that we are all truly uncomfortable," Hanse said, "I'd like you to come home, Mignue."

Whatever she had told her fellow S'danzo, she showed that she wanted no scene here and no loss of face for anyone: she stood up at once.

Turquoise smiled brightly. "Ah, young people and their problems! We had ours, Hanse; Quill and I certainly had ours! Have you eaten?"

"No, but it doesn't matter. Mignue and I need to talk."

Quill stood and pointed a finger, then shook it. "Take this as an order, Hanse! Wait right where you are for six shakes of a snake's tail."

Hanse tried to look as if he was suppressing a smile; what he wanted was out of here. "Yes sir."

Quill nodded and strode out of the room. Gazing after him, Mignureal directed a strange look at Turquoise.

"Six . . . shakes of a . . . *snake's tail?*"

Turquoise laughed, and went off into a story about how Tiquillanshal had begun to say that years back, after such-and-so an experience and and . . . Mercifully, Quill was swiftly back. He carried a covered bowl, which he proffered to Hanse.

"Quill, I don't need to be taking food from you! We—"

"Well then take it as a gift to the cats, blast you for an ungrateful cold-faced loon, and get out of here before it goes cold!"

Hanse swallowed, cradled the bowl to him with one arm, and squeezed Quill's upper arm. "Thanks, Quill."

Quill met those dark eyes, and smiled a crooked smile. "Get out of here."

Ten steps away once the door had closed after them, Hanse said, "I'm sorry, Mignue."

"I'm sorry too, darling. I—I just stay so worried about you, when you're gone. And you don't need to—to s-steal."

They walked for a time in silence, while he gathered words. "Mignue, I do. It's what I do, and I do it well. It's the only occupation I've ever had and I am just about the best there is. When I'm in my blacks and working, I forget all my worries. Trouble between us, the coins; everything. I just concentrate on what I'm doing. I love it. It makes me feel good. *Good!*" He shook his head. "How can I explain? The good feeling you get when you know you've Seen for someone, and accomplished something with it? That soaring feeling when we're making love? I don't know. It's just that I feel so good. I am . . . I am king of the night, contained by the shadows; *part* of the shadows! I'm there and I'm not there, and no one knows."

"Oh faint, I—oh *damn!*"

"*Mign*-ue!"

"What about the *danger,* Hanse?"

"I—" And at that moment he realized the truth of it, and he said it aloud: "I love it. I think I must need it."

"Oh, Hanse! I don't! I worry so! When you go out, when you're not there and I know you're . . . you're . . ." She shook her head with a jerk and made a sound more forlorn than exasperated. "So then I'm angry. As angry at me as I am at you. So next I start thinking morally: He's out there *stealing!* Pretty soon I have a reason for being angry and wanting to make you feel guilty, and bad, and don't have to admit that it's because I'm so worried about you."

He heard that as revelation, as well as honesty that he believed beyond him. He respected it, and yet he said, "Besides, roaching *is* wrong."

She made a snorting sound. "That's true, but you know that never bothered me or mother either. It was thrilling to me. I loved to watch you move and think about how you lived with danger and didn't care, too brave to bother, and how you went through the night, up walls and across roofs, all silent and romantic and—what you said. King of the shadows. And I knew you never stole from anyone poor."

It was his turn to snort. "See? That's my morality; I'm a *moral* thief, Mignue!"

"I just never thought what it would be like not to stand back and look at you, but to be with you; to be a part of you. I never realized how I would worry. I just loved you and wanted you."

He didn't say anything because he couldn't. They remained silent while they approached a Red walking toward them, patrolling the night. They all spoke pleasantly, and moments later she blurted:

"You even saved Tempus's life, twice, and, and you—you ran after the Bey-thing that k-killed mother, and you—you killed it! For mother. For me!"

"I . . . had to. I never wanted to kill anyone. When I was caught—seen, I mean—being Shadowspawn, I ran. I never thought about attacking someone who saw me, uh, roaching. I swear. But Mignue, anyhow; if I hadn't been *me,* if I hadn't been Shadowspawn, I'd never have been able to help Tempus that night he was attacked, or get him out of Kurd's bloody claws, or run after that murdering Stare-eye, either. I wasn't even thinking when I did that. But see, *I knew how.* Because I'm what I am."

She heaved a long sigh. "I know. It's just—oh Hanse, we've passed our door!"

He chuckled and hugged her there on the street, as best they could manage while he hung onto that warm brown bowl. Then they went back in, and up to the apartment. The cats greeted them noisily.

"Forgot to feed them," Hanse muttered. "Tonight, I mean! I fed them this morning."

He uncovered the bowl, releasing a marvelous aroma and revealing a stew that, like most stews, looked far less attractive than it smelled and would taste.

"You'll love that, Hanse. So will they. Oh, and I've already had plenty." She went into the bedroom.

He spooned a dollop into the bowl of each cat and shook his head with a little smile, watching each poke its head toward the marvelous-smelling mass, jerk back and shake it hard, and give him a dirty look. Both kept stalking the bowls, though, checking and re-checking. He had seen it before and decided that they weren't waiting for the food to cool because that concept was beyond their understanding. Maybe they knew that some magic would make this badness edible, and maybe they didn't. But they never walked away from over-warm food and interested themselves in something else. They kept trying.

Maybe cats don't understand that hot things grow warm and then cool, he mused; *maybe cats believe in miracles.*

Maybe I do.

That led to a thought he did not summon and did not want: *Being Shadowspawn and Mignureal's man both at once may not be possible.*

He sighed and tapped the keg, once again grateful that the short but enormous old woman on the first floor was truly a master brewer. With a mug of beer and a spoon, he sat down with the bowl.

He called, "You know, the difference between dogs and cats is that a dog would have shoved his snoot in first, and got it burned. Cats always look and sniff first, don't they. Umm. This is good! Good old Quill!"

Once he heard voices, but realized they were wafting in through the broken pane in the window in the other room. *I've got to fix that damned window,* he mused.

She came back in wearing the long, colorfully embroidered robe that had been a gift from a grateful client. In one flash, she had Seen the bag of gold the woman's son had buried in the back yard before he had been killed, and told her exactly where to dig. Mignureal had no idea how it had happened. That was Seeing into the past, and the only mind that knew where the gold was belonged to a dead man. "Sorceress!" Hanse had said, and pretended to cower in fear from her. That had been a good night. There had not been enough of those.

He devoted himself to cup and bowl, putting off the talking they had to do.

"Can I get you anything else, darling? Oh! I—I haven't—I haven't cooked for you at all today!"

"Not a thing. As a matter of fact I'm stuffed and better stop."

He rose and replaced the bowl's matching lid, since he had not been able to eat all that Tiquillanshal had given them. Leaning against the wall, he faced Mignureal.

"Shadowspawn isn't quite invisible. Not always. Last night a man was taking a leak in an alley I jumped across, and saw me. I didn't see him. When I came in and you were waiting up, staring, I was embarrassed. I didn't know what to do and couldn't think of anything to say. I never had a mother, not really I mean, but you were like a staring mommy and that made me feel like a little boy. So I . . . ran away. No, wait. Let me tell you this. I went to a place called the Rampant Goat, and drank. That's why I went to that dive: to drink, and be alone. That's what you tell yourself when what you really want is to be wanted, isn't it. But that man was there, and recognized me. Four men approached me. Four men who *wanted* me."

"Oh, Hanse!"

He averted his glance because she looked as if she was straining against a chain, wanting to run the few steps to him. He looked back at her when she had finished wiping her eyes. For the first time, he wished the robe didn't have a scooped Firaqi "neck" line.

He told her the rest of it then, standing in the kitchen leaning against the wall, while she stood in the bedroom doorway in the lovely long robe, staring. He told her all the rest of it except the part about Janith. Her eyes were glistening with tears before he had finished:

"So I hadn't been here at all when I came to the bazaar for you. And night after 'morrow, I'm going into Corstic's home."

"You . . . are going."

"Aye. They came to me when I needed. I've given my word. I am going in."

Her great sigh made him squeeze his eyes shut, because of the low-cut robe. She looked away blinking.

"No secrets anymore, either," he told her. "Today I bought a waterproof bag and hid my blacks up on the roof. That way I could climb up and change and you'd never know it. I was afraid you'd try to burn them. That's how far apart I felt we were, Mignue."

Staring distraught at the wall, at nothing, she said "oh" in a tiny voice.

He said, "I guess this is where we—where you decide whether you want to stay here or go to—no. Or whether you want me to go stay somewhere else. Me and Notable."

"Mraowr?"

That was convenient; to have something to do, Hanse drew Notable a little beer. Rainbow stared, one paw up, while Notable crouched right down, hunkering protectively over his bowl. Curling his tail around himself, he guzzled. Hanse faced Mignureal again. She was shaking her head, looking at him with a stricken expression.

"Oh Hanse. It can't be that way. How can I leave you, or let you move out?"

"If all we're going to do is make each other unhappy, we'd be better off."

She took a step and slid down into a chair, as if weak. "We haven't had much time together, Hanse, and we've had to live with those awful coins and that list, too. We haven't had a natural moment together since we left the forest." She made a helpless gesture that was pitiful.

"Strain and pressure, every day and every night," she said, staring at the tabletop. "Thinking about the coins. Dreading those coins, and the list. And not able to do anything about it. Walking over here, I told you how I saw you before, how I thought of you. A little while ago I was thinking about that while I took too long changing clothes in the bedroom. That made me realize: I haven't been fair. What happened to the way I felt about you and what you did? Because I love you I worry, and because I worry I want you to change? But then what would you be? You'd be someone else!"

No, he thought, *because I'm not going to stop being me, and part of being me is being Shadowspawn*. But when she looked up he nodded, and held her eyes.

"I haven't been fair either, Mignue. We're so different. I've always been a loner. All I had to think about was Hanse. So then what I wanted was to be just the same, but have you too. All one way."

"No you haven't! You've been so good to me, so protective and understanding! Don't say that about yourself!"

"Let's argue about that."

That led to a stare and then laughter, which led to a release of tension and an embrace, which lengthened, and led to the other room and bed and a greater release of tension.

"You know," he said later, lying on his back with his hands clasped under his head. "Perias is a Changer we almost did business with, or did, briefly, and his name's on that list. Now I've met the Longfaced Four. I think Shorty's pretty much hired help, and Malingasa's probably more enforcer than brain. I think Marll is probably the leader but Thuvarandis is probably the real thinker who advises Marll. Probably. He's also the nicest and the most understanding—and *his* name is on that list."

"Ahhh . . . all right."

"I think that's all. But I need to talk about something else. I need for you to hear it and think for me. I think those four are part of a plot involving politics and magic. Of course in this town the two are linked. Maybe the Longfaced Four *are* the plot. Maybe they represent someone who's totally in the background. Arcala, for instance. You know, the other master mage."

"I know."

"Well, then—I wish you drank beer!"

"I can take a hint; I'll get you a cup," she said, and squirmed off the bed.

He watched her walk naked into the kitchen. Gods, he loved to watch that sight! Then she came back, and he loved to watch that, too. *Janith,* he thought scornfully. *What a fool you are, Hanse!*

He hitched himself up so he could hold the mug in one hand and get his other arm around her.

"Careful with the fondling now, darling. I'm supposed to be doing some important listening."

"Uh. Well, my 'rules' about what to call me and how to refer to me when I'm not around; I think they accepted that too easily. And my outburst, challenging 'em about treating me as hired help—they accepted that the same way. Not a word from Marll and Shorty. A few quiet accepting ones from Thuvarandis to Malingasa, who was hot. Then cool quiet acceptance from him. You know . . . once back in Sanctuary a couple of people took me into a plot, and what they were really doing was taking me in. I was their *tool.* It was your mother who warned me, although not quite that specifically." He paused for a sip of beer.

"A tool is something you use until you're through with it or it breaks, and then you discard it."

He waited. Mignureal didn't say anything.

"If you're asleep I'm going to strangle you and feed you to the cats."

"I'm not asleep. I'm thinking. You've had so much living, Hanse! So many experiences! You're cautious and wary because you've *learned* to be. I never had to be. That other time you were taken in. This time maybe that's what they're doing and maybe it isn't, but you know enough to suspect. That will make you careful and that's good. I understand and respect your wariness and carefulness a lot more now, darling, than a month ago when we came here."

He squeezed her closer, briefly. "Five weeks ago," he said. She squirmed. "You're right! We're practically natives!" She waited. Hanse didn't say anything.

"If you're asleep," she said, "I'm going to pour beer in your ear and call Notable."

Hanse broke up just as he sipped. Laughing, he choked. Coughing, he fell off the bed.

In the morning the shelf still contained five Imperials; the list was unchanged. Hanse told Mignureal his plans for the day: he would fetch his horse from the Green Goose, and ride up on Town Hill. And around. And around.

She looked at him with a nervous expression. "I wish—" she began, and broke off. "Please be careful, darling. I love you."

He nodded and hugged her. "I love you too, Mignue."

An hour later he was out of the city proper, hatless and cloakless, and pacing the big gray up the road that wound up the beautiful hill; the hill was steep enough to necessitate a winding ascent. The horse was full of ginger, having been stabled for so long, and Hanse had to hold him in strongly. He found the house, a true mansion on spacious grounds. He studied it and its trees and shrubs, its flowerbeds and herb gardens, its salients and windows—and dogs—as well as he could without moving in close. He squinted at two outbuildings, marking windows. Its handsome stone wall needed no study; it was nine feet high and spiked on top. Astride the still nameless horse, he reached out and touched the top of the wall. Simple. Many of the trees were truly towering ones of age, and a score and more of those lined the inside of the wall. Easy. Made to order for swift easy entry. He saw an area where the grass was a different color and marked its location by a tree and an evergreen bush; he would avoid that patch as a possible trap.

I'll stay away from that herb garden, too, just in case. Damn. I really don't know enough about Corstic.

He rode the horse around up there as long as he thought he dared, and rode down. After letting the horse run for a half hour, he hauled him in and headed for the gate. On a whim he turned left to ride into Northgates. He paused for a while before a certain manse and its servant house, thinking. After a time his mouth twitched in a not-quite smile, and he rode on. *I have no need of Janith*. At the Green Goose he handed the horse over to the boy-of-all-work Khulna kept around, and made the boy's eyes shine by giving him a copper. Sure that the big Tejana horse was receiving fine care, Hanse walked through Firaqa to the open market. He caught sight of Thuvarandis almost at once. Hanse approached him.

"Pardon me, sir, but do you know whether there's a decent tailor working here in the bazaar?"

"Ah—over on that side, I think. Here, I'll walk you."

"We need a meeting, tonight," Hanse muttered.

Thuvarandis accepted that. "Three of us can be there. I'm not sure about Malingasa."

"Tell him it's more important than whatever else he's doing. I'll have drawn a map. We have plans to make. Tell me where to find a lot of silk rope. Yes, it's expensive but it's what I need, and I mean a lot of it. I'll meet one of you in the Rampant Goat, at about the thirteenth hour?"

"That's . . . pretty late."

"Last night I gave up dinner with my woman, and tomorrow night I won't be eating. I never eat, before a big one. A meeting is *important*, but the thirteenth is the earliest I can be there."

"All right. And I'll have the rope."

"Good," Hanse said, and swung away to head for Mignureal's stall. Whether Thuvarandis stared after him Hanse never knew; he did not glance back.

He had already told her that he'd meet her at the stall and they'd go home and eat, because he had to go out. He assured her that he wanted her to wait up and repeated that before he left for his meeting with the men he called the Longfaced Four. He had also told her he was going to test them.

Hatless, he was enveloped by the dull black cloak he had just bought. Under it he wore five visible knives and Sinajhal's sword. He walked rapidly but never so fast that his feet came down on his heels. He stared straight ahead, wearing his forbidding look and seeming to glide. The long night-colored cloak made him look a lot taller. A young couple approaching him, walking arm in arm, stepped off the curb into the street while he passed. He did not glance at them.

In the extremely dimly lit Rampant Goat, he had to squint, but saw no one he knew.

"You look like the party a fellow in back's waiting for," the bartender said; he had two thumbs and nine fingers and greasy-looking black ringlets hanging down all around his face. "Yer name Shad?"

"Aye. You know what would be a great name for this place? The Vulgar Goat!"

"Rampant works all right. Through that curtain. Want something?"

"A cup of good beer," Hanse said, looking around. He saw that same extra pretty, beautifully shaped woman, and the moment they made eye contact she started toward him. He took the gray mug, said, "The party in back is paying," and walked that way. She cut around a table, eluded a reaching hand, and intercepted him.

"Headin' for the back room?"

He nodded.

"Should I wait for you?"

He shook his head.

"This's a one-way attraction, huh?"

Hanse almost smiled at that. "No. You know what you look like. It just isn't going to happen." He turned halfway around to call, "The party in back's buying her one, too!" Then he stepped around her and went on back behind the old forest green curtain. They were there, all four of them, sitting around a table with four cups and a candle.

He swept back his cloak. "Anyone recognize this sword-hilt?"

"Ashes and embers!" Shorty swore. "That's Sinajhal's!"

While they noted his knives, Hanse told them about Sinajhal, and his partner.

"Anyone know his name?" He described the man.

Shorty sighed and nodded. "Ravas," he said quietly.

"R-r-ravas?" *That's an* r *sound,* Hanse thought, when Shorty nodded.

"You're that bad, hmm?" That was Marll. "Why tell us? Why the dramatic flashing of a dead stand-man's sword?"

Hanse let the questions lie there. "I scouted Corstic's house for a long time today, on horseback. The wall is simple. Here, I drew a map, later. Look, now, and remember. Shorty, we need some real noise over here, on this side, to pull the dogs and maybe a guard or two. I saw three dogs and a pup. The pup could be the noisiest, bear in mind. Can you handle that?"

Shorty gave him a look, and nodded.

"I go over the wall right here, off a horse. Who else is going in?"

Thuvarandis stood and stretched. "We all are. And two

others. Shadow, I apologize. We failed to tell you two things. We didn't start thinking about this on just yester day or last week. Shorty is assistant cook for Corstic. That's our long-term advance planning. Corstic will be gone, and *no one* is going to be awake. That includes servants and dogs. On the other hand, we won't use the gate, just the same."

"Over the wall," Malingasa said.

"I lose a nice job tomorrow night," Shorty said, with mock despair.

"So you didn't tell me and let me plan and think and work all this out," Shadowspawn snarled. "What else don't I know, damn you?"

"Don't," Malingasa said in a low, dangerous voice, "be damning me, Southerner."

"Oh, sorry," Shadowspawn said, in an even quieter voice. "Would you please just look at the dart target on that wall?"

Automatically they turned to look, and in ten or eleven seconds Hanse put three knives into the target. None quite touched another. Eight eyes turned back his way to stare. Malingasa looked really mean. Hanse walked past them to retrieve his blades and let them watch while he slipped them back into their sheaths.

He said, "Well?"

"Very . . . impressive," Marll said.

"That's what I mean. A man has to do something when he's angered; you expect me to waste these hands hitting a wall? So last night you weren't sure enough of me to tell me about Shorty's job there, even though I asked. So what else don't I know? Wait, answer this one instead. Corstic will positively be at a meeting of the City Council, and both dogs and staff will be asleep. True?"

They nodded; looked at Shorty. He said, "I'll take care of their food. Corstic will never know, see, because I know he's made himself immune to all drugs. He'll come into town for the meeting. A while later, everyone else will drop off." With a smile, Shorty shrugged and spread his hands.

Hanse said, "Huh! Then why do we need a wall-climber when you could let us in the front door?"

"Because he closes off the whole upper floor the moment he

comes down and I know there are wards on the doors. It's got to be from outside."

"Huh!" Hanse swung away, turned back with a dramatic rustling of the black cloak. "Something *else* no one bothered to tell me! I think maybe we should wait until next Ganeday, to see if you don't think of something else still that the poor *southerner* doesn't know."

They looked at each other. Thuvarandis spoke.

"That's our story, Shadowspawn. I will swear it. And you're right. Last night we were not sufficiently sure of you. Now it's obvious that you have worked all day, for us and this project. I willingly apologize again, but you are a cautious man who understands our caution. Would you please proceed?"

"Shorty," Hanse said after giving them all a look, "all I need is an arrow around a sort of gable-thing way up there above a certain window, with a lot of silk line on it. Thuvarandis has the line."

Hanse paused to look at the tall man. Thuvarandis bent, grunted, and came up with yards and yards of coiled rope.

"Beautiful," Hanse said. "Shorty, can you do that? I'm no expert with a bow, but an arrow sure is a great way to get a climbin' rope hitched way up high. I've done it."

"I can do that, Shadowspawn."

"What are these marks on the map, Professional?"

"This big jagged circle is a patch of grass that doesn't look like the rest. That makes me suspicious and I intend to avoid that patch. This **X** is the herb garden."

"Why the herb garden?" Malingasa asked.

Hanse had been going to tell them everything he had seen, and opined, and decided. Now he thought: *To the sixth hell with 'em.* He merely said, "Who knows what interesting spices a master mage might have, hmm?"

Thuvarandis was leaning against the wall, long shins crossed. "You are indeed the cautious type, Professional."

"I'm what you call me, Thuvarandis. Let me tell you a story. I'll shorten it. Once a friend of mine was in the hands of a real monster. A swine who enjoyed tying down living people, then making cuts on them and paring off bits and pieces. You know, a thumb here, a slice there, a strip of skin here, a nose or a few toes there. I went in after my friend. Just when I decided that it was the easiest thing in the world and was slipping through some tendrilly shrubs to get up to a window, those shrubs came alive. The tendrilly branches wrapped around me like so many snakes. Constrictors. Now, Shorty: does Corstic take an interest in his grounds? Do a little gardening?"

"Ye-esss," Shorty said, in a low voice that didn't quite quaver.

Hanse shrugged. "That's not encouraging, is it. If I could fly, I would not set foot on those grounds. Now I have another question. I've been a loner for a lot of years, and never been caught. Our subject will be gone and all his doggies and servants will be asleep. The job is to get up to the second floor, get a little statue out, and get myself off the grounds. As I see it, Shorty and I can handle it all. So why will *five others* be on the grounds? To watch Shorty and me? Or as executioners, to discard the tool once it's been used?"

Malingasa stood up so fast his chair banged over. Hand across his belly and on his swordhilt, he stared into nigh-black eyes. They stared right back.

"*Sit . . . down . . . Malin.*"

That, to Hanse's surprise, came not from Thuvarandis but from Marll. Hanse half bent over the table, beside Shorty and on his left.

"Partner, would you move your hands, please?" he said politely.

When Shorty did, something blurred across his face. Four men stared at Hanse, who held the dull green mug that had been on Shorty's right.

"Fire and ash!" Marll muttered.

Hanse said, "I'm just awful fast, Malingasa."

Marll looked at the balding man. "Malin, I said *sit down*."

That was a kindness. Malingasa resumed his seat. He looked neither happy nor pleasant.

Hanse straightened, looked into Shorty's cup, and set it down before its owner. He took up his own and drank. "Damn. And I asked for good beer! Marll, the figurine?"

"It's been made. It was being glazed again, or I'd have brought it tonight. Whenever and wherever you want it, Shadowspawn."

"All wrapped up and then in a good bag to carry into

Corstic's, and out. Leave it at the fruit-seller's stall, next to the S'danzo booth in the bazaar. Tell him it's for Hansis. Han-sis. I have to tell you that I'm nervous. One of you dislikes me more than somewhat and I don't really know any of you. Let's have one rule from Shadowspawn: I don't want to see any bows or crossbows tomorrow night. And now tell me when.''

"How about no swords either," Malingasa said. "Or do you want us to come with our hands tied, maybe?"

Thuvarandis said, "Damn it, Malin . . ."

Hanse sighed. "Why are you doing this, Malingasa? We have to work together, and I don't like this southerner-equals-enemy business a bit, or your challenges either. What am I to say? Swords don't bother me, Malingasa. Knives don't, either. I have no reason to start throwing knives, you can all see that. But I'd be terribly nervous with long-range weapons around."

"There will be no crossbows or bows aside from Shorty's bow," Thuvarandis said. "Shorty: carry only two arrows, all right? I can understand Shadow's nervousness. For that reason too, Malingasa will not be present."

"What?"

Hanse said, "About the time . . ."

Malingasa said, "Now wait a minute!"

"Fourteenth hour," Marll said. "Corstic will have been gone an hour, and not back for two more, at least."

Hanse nodded. "I think we've said it all. We can go over the wall easily from horseback. I go alone. I won't think about anyone but me and Shorty, and the job. What about when I come out, with the figurine? I gather I'm not to toss it down."

"Definitely not," Marll said.

"All right," Hanse said. "I'll give it to you once we're outside the walls, because when my feet touch ground I'll be movin' fast. Oh, someone will have to be outside the wall, minding the horses, won't he. If anything happens, the statue will be here. What's the bartender's name?"

They told him. Hanse looked around at them, noting Malingasa's hot look of anger. "By 'morrow night at about the fifteenth," he said, "you should have what you want and I certainly hope I have something of value!"

He turned and left.

· · ·

Mignureal looked up as Hanse entered the apartment, carrying a gut-wrapped parcel. She wore a questioning look and the beyond fetching bedtime "garment" he had bought her. Twice as sexy as any woman in any dive, she came to give him a kiss. He could not resist a bit of fondling.

"It's still on," he told her. And he added, "There is danger."

"Oh! What did you tell me *that* for?" She stepped back.

"Hoping you could See for me."

She sighed. "Hanse, I've told you. I can't just *do* it, not for you. Either it comes or it doesn't. Sometimes I fail to See anything at all for paying clients, believe me."

"So then the client becomes a *suvesh* and you make up this and that?"

"Uh-huh."

"Tsk-tsk," he said, reminding her that theft came in many forms. He hefted the parcel. "Guess what?"

"I just wouldn't kno—no! Hanse! You've been up on the *roof*?"

"Right past the window."

"Hanse! I never heard a *thing*!"

"He comes, he goes, and you never know he's been until he's gone and so's your—*nose*!" he said, darting his hand at her face.

She jumped back, giggling and jiggling. "Oh Hanse!" Then, "I'm really glad you haven't shown me your collection of noses, darling."

"That was a great loss," he said, slinging aside the cloak and laying out the parcel to open it. "See, Notable got at my collection. He ate all thirty-nine noses."

"Ewww."

"Mawrr-r," Notable remarked sleepily at sound of his name.

"See? He just said 'I sure did.'"

"Ewww!"

"What? I take off my tunic and you say 'e-ewwww'? I thought you loved my mighty thews. Whatever that means."

"You're certainly in a good mood. Everything went your way? You said you were going to test them . . . oh my, I do like those legs."

"You sit there flashing yours to the hip and comment about my legs?"

"Hmp! I thought you hadn't even noticed. Anyhow, you're flashing yours all the way up to the chin, darling. Oh faint— you're *dressing* again?"

"Aye, and so are you," he said, drawing on the tight black leggings. "Your cloak should do, though. It's time you saw something."

"Listen, Han—Shadowspawn, if you think I'm going up walls and over roofs with you, you can just forget it!"

He chuckled. "No no. I said I want you to see something, Mignue. Y'have to go outside, though. With me."

"Ohh . . . here I go and get all bathed and almost-dressed in this bit of naughtiness you bought me, and *you* want me to cover up with a *cloak* and go out*side*. What *for*?"

He tugged down the black tunic. "To git raped in the alley," he said, and lunged.

Her squeal becoming laughter, she raced into the other room. He stood grinning after her while he strapped on his knives. He loved the way she looked in that bit of net and a wisp of lace, all the color of midnight; what there was of it.

She returned clasping her cloak. "Oh. I do love the way you look, Shadowspawn. You don't intend to use all those knives, do you?"

He shook his head, flexing each sheath-equipped arm. "No. You've seen me throw."

She nodded. "I remember your telling me out on the desert that no one could miss with those throwing stars, and then we spent the next hour looking for the one I threw!"

"Never admit it. Everyone believes no one can miss with one. And I've told just everyone in Firaqa that you carry several in your bosom. I've even put up signs."

"Uh-huh. Print them yourself?"

"Oops. Well, so every now and then I lie a little. Come on, let's go out. Gah! All right, Notable, you too. Did you see that? He sure knows the word 'out'! Come on, Rainbow."

Rainbow didn't really care to be disturbed, and so Mignureal picked her up. Notable bolted through the door the instant Hanse opened it and hit the steps at racehorse speed. He was waiting down by the outer door by the time they set foot on the steps.

A few minutes later, mouth open and Rainbow forgotten in her arms, Mignureal stood in the alley and watched Hanse go up the wall. She saw him reach the roof, looking like a living shadow in the moonlight. She gasped and whirled when he pounced, to shoot right over her head to the roof across the alley. Staring upward, she marveled that she didn't even hear any impact. He had certainly gone across fast enough, but seemed to alight as if he were afloat. She kept staring upward, seeing nothing.

"Hoy little girl," a low voice said. Mignureal jumped. "Want to git raped in the alley?"

She stared, and out of the shadows he *appeared,* walking toward her.

"How did you—you just—oh!"

He had just pounced sideways into a deep shadow, and it swallowed him. Shadowspawn vanished. Gooseflesh ran up her arms and Rainbow stirred, feeling fright.

"Hanse? This is scary. Are—are you still there?"

"Aye."

His voice seemed to come from right down on the ground, now. Was he squatting? Mignureal couldn't see a thing. Just shadow. With a voice. She shivered. "I can't even *see* you."

A step, and he was right there, visible. "That's what I wanted you to see, Migne. Or rather, not see. I wanted you to know. I swear it isn't sorcery, but some people think so."

"It's as if you're Shalpa incarnate!"

"Shh. His name isn't to be spoken aloud—and besides, you don't believe in gods, remember?"

She stuck her tongue out and made an obscene noise.

"Would you take the cats back in, now? I'll be right up."

"Hanse—"

"I mean it. I'll be right there."

She went, having to coax Notable. Thinking about her man's incredible and worse than discomfiting ability to vanish, to become one with the shadows, she mounted the stairs like an old woman. When she entered the apartment he was there, pouring beer from a mug into Notable's bowl.

"Whew," Shadowspawn said. "I've been waiting for-*ever*. See someone you know and stop to talk?"

She sat down, and Rainbow jumped unnoticed from her cloaked arms. "You—the window?"

He nodded, saluted her with the mug, and drank.

"I just wanted you to know, Mignue. I thought of this last night. I mean, it isn't as if you can come along and watch me work."

She sat gazing at him, nodding, on and on. At last she seemed to awake as from a trance, and stood.

"I'm . . . glad to know, darling. It's scary and it's wonderful. I can't believe some sorcery or god isn't involved. I've also been shocked half out of my skin. I'm going to bed."

He grinned. "Better not be planning on going right to sleep!"

It seemed inconsequential and mundane next day, when Anorislas advised that he had sold another horse, and paid Hanse eleven-and-twenty-five. He went away unable to understand why Hanse showed no joy or much gratitude or indeed much in the way of emotion at all.

Hanse was jittery that night, and Mignureal oddly silent. No, he would not eat, not before he—went out. Mignureal found that she was not at all interested in food. He alternated trying to rest on the bed and pouncing up, to exercise.

As Firaqa grew darker, so did Mignureal's mood.

"Are you taking Notable?"

He looked at her, hoping she had something to offer. Maybe there was no danger after all, he thought. He nodded.

"Aye, I think I will." He rolled and stood up from the bed again. "It's about time I went over for the horse."

"You're going in those clothes?"

"I'll change after I get the horse."

"Oh."

He clasped his good cloak about him and turned. She was pasted against him in a moment. Yet she still had nothing to tell him; no Seeing had come upon her. With the delighted Notable, the parcel of clothing and the other one containing the substitute figurine, Hanse went out the door. He had waited

and waited, hoping she would See something; now he would
be a bit late.

Well, they'll wait for the professional!

"Hanse."

With a sensation of spiders running a relay race up his back
in response to that strange voice, Hanse turned back.

"Are you taking gloves, Hanse?"

He nodded, staring at her and her large round eyes.
Mignureal did not even appear to be at home in there, behind
those staring eyes. He had witnessed this before, of course,
and he recognized the phenomenon. That did not mean that he
would ever be accustomed to it, comfortable with the inex-
pressible eeriness of it: The Seeing had come upon her.

Then it occurred to him that seeing and Seeing were not the
same. "Aye," he said.

*"Good. Do not touch the spikes on the wall with bare hands,
or the pearl-white cat, either. Oh—how interesting! Perias the
Changer is taking dinner with Corstic tonight."*

He stood staring, and watched Mignureal come back into her
own eyes. Her voice was perfectly natural:

"Forget something, darling?"

He decided to tell her later. After. He shook his head, and
started to turn away.

"Be careful, darling!"

"I will. I will, Mignue."

Notable stayed close as they walked through nighted Firaqa
to the Green Goose. Hanse could find no significance in
Perias's presence at dinner; after they ate both he and Corstic
would be going to the Council meeting anyhow. Would have
gone already, in fact. The other part was easy: the spikes and
the figurine must be coated with a contact poison. Now he must
hurry, to warn Thuvarandis and the others. He speeded up to a
trot, which was fine with Notable.

Khulna's boy Tip was snoozing in the stable, but roused
himself swiftly to help Hanse bridle and saddle the big gray.
Hanse sent him into the inn for a piece of fruit; any fruit. By
the time the lad was back from a mission that was a ruse,
Hanse had changed clothing in the horse's stall and re-covered
himself with the cloak. Now it concealed his working clothes.

Another copper coin found itself into Tip's eager hand. With Notable clasped to him atop the clothing parcel, Hanse rode away.

The screaming cry came two blocks later, and it was not Tip: *"Hanse!"*

His heart and stomach lurched, not quite in unison and hardly smoothly. He hauled in the horse and waited trembling while Mignureal came running. She carried Rainbow in her arms, he saw. When she reached him he'd have seen it even in less moonlight: the eyes. It had happened again.

Hanse shuddered as those round, glassy eyes stared up at him.

"Hanse: Something has happened! Do Not Go! Stay . . . outside . . . the . . . wall." And then, a moment later: "Hanse? Whatever am I doing out here on the stree—oh! It Happened?"

He nodded, sliding his fingers into her hair. He swallowed. "Aye. You bade me keep Notable with me and wear my gloves. Please go and wait at the Green Goose, will you? It's only two blocks, and you're a long way from the apartment."

"All—all right, darling. I will. Oh!"

Completely out of character, Rainbow had pounced from her arms onto the horse's broad back, behind the saddle. The animal started and Hanse had to cling with both legs while actually putting muscle into dragging on the reins. The horse half reared, then settled and was still. He shook his head, rattling the metal of his harness.

"Rainbow! You bad—"

"Don't scold, Mignue. We both know she's no more a natural cat than Notable. But no, I'm afraid you can't come along, Rainbow." Hanse twisted around and lifted the calico, which did not resist going back into Mignureal's arms.

"Be—be careful, darling."

"I will. See you later."

He sat there on the horse and watched her all the way to the end of the block. Then she made the turn toward the inn, and Hanse released a long breath. With a glance up at the moon, he twitched his heels. Despite her warning, he had to go. He had to try to warn the others. The first part was the hardest: the necessity of obeying the law all the way to the gate, by keeping

to a sedate walk in the center of the street. His mount no more
wanted to do that than Hanse did. It seemed to take forever to
reach the northward gate.

"Going to give this boy a good run," he said as casually as
he could, passing the bored sentinels.

"Do him a lot of good, too! Good-lookin' animal! Bet he
can go like the wind!"

Hanse kicked, bent forward, and said, "Haiya!" The gray
hurtled away like an arrow from a bow, and Hanse's cloak
nearly strangled him. He grabbed it at the neck but made no
effort to slow the animal until he was starting up Town Hill,
and then only long enough to roll up the cloak and secure it to
the saddle. Then he jerked his heels.

"Want to run uphill, big boy? Haiya!"

The horse went up the hill road as if it were a plain.

Along the way four riderless horses came galloping at them
from the opposite direction. They broke around Hanse and his
mount without slowing that which was obviously a headlong
bolting flight. He knew then that Mignureal had Seen true
again, and that he was not going to be in time. He spent several
hundred feet just slowing his mount to a trot.

Shadowspawn saw and heard the crackling, popping, dancing horror before he reached his goal.

A tall torch blazed atop the wall surrounding Corstic's
estate, and another sent flames high from the lawn just outside the mansion. And they were not, Hanse saw, natural
torches. . . .

"oh, oh gods, oh gods," he muttered, and could not have
raised his voice had it been his own body ablaze there atop the
wall, rather than the writhing, fiery form of Marll.

As to the huge torch on the lawn near the big house and so
clearly illuminating it—that was Corstic's *former* assistant
cook. Shorty was a lot taller, as a pillar of yellow and white
flame. It lit the home of Corstic the mage far more brightly
than it should have done, and the mansion seemed all aflicker
in that unnatural light.

Corstic had found out. Corstic was at home, and exacting a
ghastly price of the plotters.

Somewhere on the spacious green grounds someone was
screaming, screaming, enough to make Hanse want to sob. It

was a man he heard, screaming piteously, on and on in the voice of a woman. Corstic was exacting from him the price of conspiracy, of invasion of his grounds. Corstic, all of whose servants and dogs were presumably asleep. Corstic, master-mage of Firaqa. Compared to him and his powers, the invaders were helpless children. To him, they must be as annoying crickets at night were to Shadowspawn.

The heart-wrenching sound of shrill male screaming rose even above the crackle and pop of the human torches and the ceaseless roar of the nearer one.

And gods, gods, O Allfather Ils; now Hanse could smell it even as he heard the bursting of blisters of fat: roasting human flesh.

A ghastly voice from above his head gasped out words, wetly: *"Runn . . . Pro . . . fession'l . . ."*

Shadowspawn glanced up just as a thigh-thick branch cracked loudly amid leafy sounds as of a tree in a high wind. With only a glance up he was somehow able to croak "haiya!" as the branch broke off and came hurtling down at him with a leafy rush. Impaled and swinging hideously from the down-rushing bough was Thuvarandis, transpierced by the largest spear imaginable. And yet Thuvarandis, horribly, monstrously, was not dead. His wound was awful. His eyes were worse.

The big gray horse bolted in instant response to the vocal command. Hanse could only cling to the saddle while a spitting Notable clung to his thigh, but Hanse never felt the imbedded claws.

The human pillars of flame continued to blaze high, illuminating most of the grounds. They crackled constantly, and the odor grew while Hanse's empty stomach lurched. He gagged and retched helplessly.

He got the horse to a stop again. He was still close to the wall, but farther south, now. He soon wished he hadn't stopped the gray here, for hanging limply over the wall a few feet away under more towering old trees, was another man. Ils's breath, could any poison work that fast, to arrest and slay him in the act of climbing over? Not four feet away from Shadowspawn the body seemed to tremble, and then with a *whoomp* and a rush of air that flapped the horse's mane, the dead man burst into flame.

For an instant Hanse saw the corpse swell, saw bubbles rise, and then he was hearing their *pop-pop-pop* amid the crackle of wetted flame. A moment later fire went leaping twenty feet straight up, white and yellow tongues dancing, and Hanse wrestled the horse around to rush back to Thuvarandis. A sideward glance showed him the figure of a man limned in a well-lighted upper window; the window next to the one by which he had meant to enter. The man's hands rose, his arms spread . . .

Branches began cracking loudly as they tore themselves from trees and hurled themselves through the air. They rushed at such speed that he could hear their passage, in a series of middle-range whooshes. Leaves brushed his face, racing past on torn-off boughs.

Hanse forgot Thuvarandis; the poor miserable creature could not be saved anyhow, but Hanse had thought he might slay him to end the unnatural suffering Corstic imposed. He forgot the unknown screamer, forgot the porcelain cat and the loot he had dreamed of. Yanking his mount around, Shadowspawn galloped pell-mell down the winding road and off the hill. Somehow rushing branches missed him. He did not slow the gray horse until he could see the city gates. The torches there made his backbone crawl, but they were the same natural ones he had noted as he rode out. In the open night air they had no odor, and yet he still fancied that he could smell the stench of roasting human flesh.

Somehow he remembered to draw his cloak about him, to hide his blacks. Coiled and quivering against his crotch, Notable did not at all mind being covered up.

The guards jovially commented on the obvious fact that the horse had been well run, and helpfully reminded his rider that he'd better wipe him down in this cool night air, once he removed the saddle. Hanse rode on, nodding, unable to speak although his mouth was loosely open. His stomach was still lurching.

Tip saw to the care of the gray, receiving more coppers than he had previously seen at one time, and somehow Mignureal and the shaking, staring Hanse made it home. The cats stayed very close indeed.

Only after she had helped him get out of his clothing did

they discover the blood all down Hanse's thigh. Yet there was no way he could even think of chastising Notable; had Shadowspawn possessed claws, the gray horse might have been half skinned by the time he succeeded in quitting that hill of horror.

Hanse slept badly, curled and shivering and mumbling from time to time, while Mignureal held him and stained the bedclothes with her tears. His arm dangled over the side of the bed. It touched the red fur of a large cat, also curled tightly and ashiver, even in sleep. Mignureal could not separate hand and cat, not for long. She gave up, and held her man.

Next day a numb Hanse learned that Perias the Changer had taken dinner with Corstic the previous night, and had been stricken and fallen dead on the spot. Corstic had discovered a plot involving an apprentice cook, and others. Now Corstic and Arcala were accusing each other; Perias had been Arcala's business associate. Corstic had not gone to the meeting of the Council, but had heroically remained at home, alone amid unnaturally sleeping servants, to combat the plot and the invading plotters, with great success.

What had they been after? Why, his very life, what else?

False, Hanse thought. *They*—we *sought only to steal a porcelain cat, monster!* And he rushed home to find new horror.

Aye, Perias's name was missing from the list, and another of the silver Rankan coin was gone.

But only Perias's name was missing, and only one coin was gone.

The names that remained on the list were Elturas, and Thuvarandis.

Ah no, O Ils my father no, no! The man had an entire tree-branch all the way through his body and hung there from it; a branch the size of my thigh! He cannot *be alive!*

And yet the tall thin man with the white hair had to be alive—or not dead, at any rate. Not quite. His name remained on the list. Only one coin was gone. It corresponded with the name and the life and the death of Perias. Somehow, sorcerously and horribly, Corstic had to be *keeping Thuvarandis alive.*

And not, Hanse thought, reeling and feeling the urge to vomit, *to nurse the poor wight back to health, for that cannot be done! The monster keeps him alive to torture him . . .*

. . . and doubtless to question him. How long, before a living dead man gasped the word Shadowspawn, and described the man who wore that name? How long, before Corstic translated that into a foreigner; a southern foreigner named Hanse?

How lucky Malingasa was, to have been separated from the incursion only the day before!

That night Hanse broke a thirty-hour fast with bread and chicken, fruit and beer. Knowing he could never rest again, he was thinking about it, pondering a future without sleep, when he fell asleep. He slept, truly slept as if he would never awaken and could never be awakened—until the night and his slumber were split by a high-pitched sound loud enough to bring out Firaqa's volunteer fire fighters blocks away.

Hanse came awake as he always did: fully, and ready to face demons. This time he awoke with Notable's yowl still ringing in his ears. His first action could have been considered strange, for the loner Shadowspawn: he shoved Mignureal violently and tumbled her out of bed. Immediately he flopped the other way, and came up in a second with a knife in each hand.

At the same time someone cried out. Hanse saw him only dimly: the dark outline of a man staggering about the room, flailing as if fighting a ghost.

"Hanse!"

That was Mignureal, and Hanse made a reassuring noise. The intruder was not fighting with a ghost, unless he was a hunchback who was not bent; that unsightly hump on the dimly-seen prowler's back had to be a beer-drinking, attack-trained watch-cat.

Hanse dropped both knives. Naked, he hurried to the staggering male figure. It had both hands up over its shoulders, striving to tear off the big red cat trying to eat holes in his back. Hanse stepped on flat, cold steel, and shuddered. He knew what that was. Putting out a hand, he found a face. With balled fist he struck it as hard as he could. A wave of pain hit his hand and whipped up his arm. He cursed.

The invader, that cliché of a shadowy figure, grunted and fell like a dropped sack of grain.

"Hanse?"

"Get a lamp lit, Mignureal. Notable's just saved our lives from a prowler with a sword."

"Prowler?" Her voice still came from the floor where he had sent her so violently, to save her.

"Assassin, then. Hired murderer. *Light the lamp*, Mignue! Notable? It's done. Good, marvelous boy, Notable. Now let him go while he can still talk to us."

Notable must have relinquished his needle-toothed grip, since he was able to say "Raar-rr-rrr," or something very close. He kept it up, "rr-rr-r-r-r-rr," sitting on the floor close to the fallen intruder. The baleful stare of those big green eyes looked positively hungry. Hanse was moving unerringly in the darkness, fetching several hundred feet of silken line, an unintended gift from Thuvarandis. He made a good job of immobilizing the intruder's wrists, even before Mignureal brought the lamp alive.

Hanse gazed down at Malingasa.

He chewed his lip for a moment, staring at the man, before he took the line around his ankles a few times and knotted it. While he checked the bonds on Malingasa's wrists, Hanse identified him to Mignureal. Having hurriedly donned her robe, she sat on the floor with her legs tucked. Rainbow walked onto her thighs and settled between them. Mignureal began stroking her absently. Only Hanse saw how Rainbow glared at the man on the floor. Then he, Mignureal, and both cats jumped when the knock sounded on the door. Hanse went, taking two knives and pulling a cloak around himself; not the black one.

He edged open the door to face the old cooper who, with his wife, shared the floor with them. Mignureal heard Hanse telling the fellow how lucky they *all* were; they'd had a prowler but Notable had attacked him and frightened the poor devil right back out the window. Their fellow tenant went away saying he felt more secure, knowing of Notable's presence.

About the time Hanse had the door closed he heard footsteps ascending the stairs, but then he heard their neighbor relating the story to the landlord's wife. She came and knocked anyhow. Hanse talked very quietly, telling her that Mignureal had already returned to sleep. Oh yes, they were fine, both he and she and "those darling kitties." And once again he closed and secured the door. He returned to the bedroom to find Malingasa awake and staring up at him. Hanse squatted quickly.

"What's this about, Malingasa? So you and I aren't friends; so all right. But only we two escaped the trap at Corstic's. Why come here to murder me in my bed?"

"You Bas—"

Hanse popped his palm over the bound man's mouth. "Hold your voice down, Malingasa; some people in this building are trying to get back to sleep. Talk quietly and be still or I'll get that cat to sit on your chest. Now go ahead. You're right about my being a bastard, but what's that have to do with it? You some sort of bigot about that as well as about *southerners*?"

"Hanse," Mignureal said in a thoughtful voice, "he thinks you must have set up the trap, since only you survived. Right now he's wondering how I know." Then her voice changed: *"Your name is Malingasa and your mother is Yorna and your father was Malint. He died of an illness your mother calls the Green Disease. That was three years ago, or was it four? You were married to—uh, Isna, is that right?—Yes, Isna, but just a year ago she died in childbirth. Oh, poor man! The baby was all right, but you knew you could not care for it—her—and gave her to a youngish couple, but the beasts vanished from Firaqa with her. Am I now the only person who knows about that, Malingasa?"*

Malingasa lay on the floor shuddering, rolling his eyes. "Ss . . . orcery . . ."

"She's a S'danzo," Hanse told him. "She has the talent, Malingasa. She learned that from your mind, or your liver, or however it works; even she doesn't know. It came on her twice last night. Before I left here she warned me not to touch the spikes on top of Corstic's wall, and told me that Perias was dining with him."

"I did? You didn't tell me I told you that!"

"I was going to, Mignue. You know what kind of shape I was in when I came off that hill."

The man on the floor said, "You . . . were up . . . there?"

"Aye. I was late, because Mignue came after me. Out on the street, Malingasa! That time she told me not to go; to stay outside the wall." That Hanse had told Mignureal, who sat nodding. "I went anyhow. I'll tell you true: I didn't care an ant's eyebrow about you, or any of the others except Thuvarandis. I galloped out of the gate and galloped all the way up the hill, in hopes of stopping him from going over the wall. Four horses met me on their way down at the run, saddled and bridled but riderless. I saw the terror in their eyes and knew I was too late, but I went on anyhow. Want to know what I saw when I got there? Well, do you? Do you want to hear about it, Malingasa?"

Hanse shook him. Rainbow stared at him. So did Notable, tail moving restlessly. Malingasa made a moaning sound.

"Want to go out to the north gate now, and let the sentinels tell you I went out saying I wanted to give my horse a run, and came back an hour or so later at the gallop, on a lathered horse? You and I are the lucky ones, Malingasa, damn you. The whole place was bright as day—because Shorty over by the house and Marll up on the wall were torches, just yellow-white flame licking twenty feet high. Someone else was screaming, in there somewhere, shrieking like a child. I never saw him."

"Stop!" Malingasa was shuddering. "Oh, stop! I believe you."

"Do you? Can you imagine Thuvarandis up in the air with a big thick tree-branch through him, *all the way through him*, Malingasa, and yet him still able to talk, trying to warn me? Then that branch snapped and rushed down at me, like a spear with him hanging on it. My horse bolted. That's how we found another man. Whoever he was, he had too much yellowish hair and a leather tunic over—well, I think his leggings were red, but I'm not sure. I won't lie or pretend; I was terrified. He was hanging over the wall, and just as I got there he burst into flame, too, and Corstic had *three* torches. Your friends, Malingasa, with you not even there and me not able to do a thing."

"Stop!" the violently shivering man said. "No, no more! I believe you, I'm sorry, yes, yes, that's Corstic—ah Flame, oh

mother-r-r . . ." He flailed his head back and forth. "Now
he'll get me, too! He'll have to! Ah no, no, oh . . ."

Malingasa broke off, his face to one side. He was weeping.
Hanse looked down at his own hand, with distaste. The hand
was spattered with the other man's tears and saliva.

Hanse sneered. "I'll tell you one thing more, Malingasa. It
won't be so hard for your delicate mind and courage to handle.
I *fled,* man. I ran! I ran as hard as that horse could take me,
because whole branches were ripping themselves off trees and
rushing through the air, right out onto the road outside the wall.
I think the man I saw in an upstairs window couldn't see me,
but he didn't care; he wanted to wipe out anybody and
everybody! I'm not sure how I escaped. I came all the way
down that hill at the gallop, and every second I expected to feel
a tree slam into my back. I'm alive because I was lucky,
Malingasa; Mignureal and luck. She made me late. You're
alive because you were such a shit to me that they wouldn't let
you go in there with the big boys. Now you're either going to
tell me what it's all about," Hanse said, realizing the probable
efficacy of direly threatening a man shaken as badly as
Malingasa obviously was, "or my cat Notable and I are going
to start playing vivisectionist with you."

His knife flashed before Malingasa's eyes and Mignureal
said, "Hanse!"

He gave her a glare. Then he winked. While she was trying
to work out the meaning of that, her mouth began moving.

"Mal—Malingasa," she murmured, "was one of the ones.
So was Thuvarandis, and Perias, and a—a Ravas, yes, Ravas,
and others."

Hanse stared at her. Her eyes seemed all right, if starey, but
her voice was perfectly normal. She seemed to be Seeing, but
in a different way. "One of the ones that . . . what, Mignue?"

Malingasa was sobbing when Mignureal said, "Did that to
Corstic's wife. Tell us, Malingasa, if you believe you have a
soul and might be able to save it from Corstic. Or would you
rather be—be . . . Nuris! Would you rather be Nuris?"

Malingasa jerked at that, and cried out so that Hanse clapped
his hand over the balding fellow's mouth again. When he
removed it, he wiped drool on Malingasa's tunic.

"I'll . . . I'll tell you," Malingasa said, in a small pitifully choked voice disrupted by sobs. "Oh, oh, m-mother, m . . . I'll tell you . . . no, not Nuris's fate . . ."

"Who's Nuris?" Hanse demanded, and Mignureal said, "Who?" in a natural voice, and he looked sharply at her. Suddenly he realized that more was happening here than Mignureal's Seeing. And he was right.

Malingasa told most of it, mumbling and sobbing. Even after Hanse had cut loose his ankles the man made no movement. And yet now and then he paused, or answered a question with an almost pleading "I don't know!" and Mignureal abruptly Saw and filled in that blank, while she sat on the floor stroking Rainbow.

She and Hanse learned a great deal more than they had expected. It emerged in spurts and out of synchronicity, but they were able to put together the story. First they heard from Malingasa about the mass rape, but Mignureal supplied other aspects, details, and at last the background, so that a narrative formed.

Years ago, a fellow named Nuris was a sorcery trainee, an apprentice mage with innate predictive or Seeing talent. Too soon, Nuris decided that he was better than that. He was led to that premature feeling of worth and competence as mage partly because of his very apprenticeship. He chafed as apprentice to a mean and ever-sneering, never-pleased man: the master mage Corstic. Nuris's abilities grew without praise, and so did his dissatisfaction unto bitterness.

His master's wife chafed just as much, for Corstic was just as cruel and stingy with her. He was master of his art and skills; a great and a mighty man who was growing mightier. The day would come when he would rule Firaqa, and be called lord. The honor of being his wife should be enough for her.

Of course it was not, and in time she and apprentice Nuris commiserated. Two mistreated people solaced each other. That relationship developed, whether they wished it or not, and in time it led them to her bed. If not quite able to forget their troubles, they were at least able to enjoy themselves and each other.

They did, for months. Until Corstic found them out. He

must have known for some time before he acted, for his plan was no simple one.

It was not difficult for him to imprison his affrighted wife in a room of the manse. There he left her, further adding to her anguish by telling her as sinisterly as possible that now he would see to the fate of Nuris. What pitiable attempts to escape that miserable woman made! Shurina broke her nails, bruised her arms and body in hurling herself against the door. Those attempts availed her exactly nothing save pain and despair. While she had learned a few sorcerous tricks and even spells as Corstic's wife, Shurina had no powers to free herself or to affect her husband, who was well protected by his own ward-spells.

She could do nothing for Nuris, and could only wonder at what evil her husband would inflict on the poor fellow.

Corstic was at that business. He had already devised his plan. Some outraged husbands slew one or both of the illicit lovers. Ah, but Corstic was a master sorcerer! How could people suffer for such an insult to his pride, if they were merely dead?

(On hearing this—unaccountably, from Mignureal—Hanse shivered. He had seen Corstic's defenses and retaliation only hours ago. What a chilling mind the man had; what talent for wickedness and horror!)

In his own chamber, the unsuspecting Nuris soon dropped over in sorcerous unconsciousness. Now Corstic isolated and captured the young man's *ka*; that invisible spark some called "a soul." The mage ensorceled that human awareness into the body he had already prepared and caged: an unnaturally large red cat.

After concealing the cage but leaving his apprentice's visibly breathing body as if merely drugged, Corstic went to his wife. He fetched her to Nuris's chamber. Bound, she helplessly watched her husband's carefully slow, bloody slaying of her lover. Shurina had no notion that a part of Nuris, his very essence, had been saved, and trapped in the body of a cat; such knowledge on her part would have lessened Corstic's delight in her horror. The mage even laboriously cleaned up all evidence of the murder, knowing that being forced to remain there and watch was further anguish for his bound wife.

The next part of the master spellmaker's vengeance and retaliation was to reverse the roles of sufferer and helpless observer. Along with the smilingly presiding Corstic, the caged cat must watch while Shurina lay helpless on the same bed whereon she had taken solace with Nuris; "Vilely disported herself," as Corstic put it. Now ten men assaulted and misused the naked and weeping woman.

Each man received a single silver coin on completion of his rape, and departed. At last all were gone, leaving on the bed a bruised and bleeding shambles of a woman.

Mockingly, Corstic tossed onto his wife's quaking form a coin for each of her rapists, and he added one for himself. His next act was to leave her, taking the cat. Though he feared no tale-telling from an animal whose teeth, whose mouth and nose connection were such as to prevent speech despite the efforts of any mage, Corstic's wish was to reduce Nuris further. Nuris would always be aware, but unable to act as a man, even a man in a cat's body. He was a prisoner in that body. He could not direct it. He was a cat.

As for the hired despoilers: those half-score men knew what they were doing and what they had done. The only spell laid on them was on their tongues; they could never tell anyone what they and Corstic had done. Naturally, neither could the cat that had been Nuris—no, that *contained the essence* of Nuris. Fearful or living with remorse or both, some of those men fled Firaqa. Others did not. As time went on some prospered, as some men would; others did not. They led, in other words, what seemed the normal lives of normal men.

Corstic left Shurina to her pain and her anguish for days, accompanied by that silver which he termed the price of her body. Knowing that she suffered thus, both mentally and physically, pleased him. Then Corstic transferred the *ka* of his wife into another cat.

"A . . . calico cat," Mignureal murmured, stroking Rainbow.

No one knew that her body was already mindless when Shurina "fell" from a high window of Corstic's palatial home. Corstic, of course, showed much public grief but all could see how he strove to be stoic. He was called courageous.

He had defeated the plotters he saw as betrayers of his

kindness merely by having housed them, suffered them to become a part of his life and live in the blaze of his greatness. He had buried their awareness in the bodies of the two cats, and he had destroyed their human bodies and buried them in the earth. He killed them, murdered them . . . but saved a *mocking portion of their humanity; their human-ness.* They were not quite cats and yet they were less than people trapped within cat-forms.

Corstic intended to keep them as pets; pets to be tormented both physically and emotionally; to be reminded and to be sneered at.

"They escaped."

Hanse jerked in startlement at Mignureal's murmured words. She sat staring at nothing as she stroked Rainbow.

Hanse glanced at Notable, who sat with his gaze fixed on Malingasa. Notable looked distinctly hungry. Hanse regarded Rainbow, who remained in Mignureal's lap as she had since the beginning of the revelations that tumbled forth from both Malingasa and from Mignureal. Rainbow, too, glared at the man on the floor. Hanse looked again at the five silver Imperials. They lay on the floor as they had throughout the questioning, and Malingasa's broken narrative, and Mignureal's even stranger than usual Seeing.

The cats had escaped, Mignureal said. Unfortunately, he who had been Nuris was discovered as a stray and taken in a caravan to Sanctuary. There he became one of Ahdio's two watch-cats. He was surly, and yet became Ahdio's friend; Ahdio's cat. He existed as a cat that drank beer and acted as a watch-dog and alarm for Sly's Place. He was not Nuris. He was Notable; he was a cat.

And then Hanse came to that back room of Sly's Place, heavy with the aura of the outré because of his birth and his association with gods and with Moonflower and her daughter. Hanse came into Notable's presence, and awoke the magic-sensitive in Nuris/Notable, and awareness of what he had been. And he clove to Hanse.

That was one explanation; another was simply that a cat liked a man, particularly after they teamed to break into the governor's palace of Sanctuary, where they were nearly killed by serpent and by human guard before they emerged and descended the walls again.

The later link with the calico cat on the desert was only partially coincidence. Rainbow, not-quite blindly seeking Notable, was found by the Tejana. She was in need of water. They gave her that, and netted her. Only they knew whether they wanted a pet, a mouser, or food. Hanse and Mignureal, Mignureal murmured dully, had been *led* only to a degree; they had not been mere tools and automatons in all this.

"And so six coins are gone," Hanse said slowly, "and six men are dead—six of the rapists! Eh, Malingasa?"

The sobbing fellow only trembled and moaned.

"*Yes,*" Mignureal said.

Hanse glanced at her. He said, "And the eleventh coin, one of those five—it represents Corstic. And you, Malingasa; one of those who 'employed' me and who has told us so much but not all . . . you are another of the rapists. But something is missing here, villain. How is it that you overcame the spell not to tell, and still live?"

"*Hanse!*"

The sharp urgency in Mignureal's voice brought his head around instantly. She was pointing at the coins. Untouched on the floor, one of them had begun to quiver.

At the same time their captive made a choking noise and commenced jerking in ugly spasms. While the others stared, hair rising, his arms twisted into ugly travesties. Suddenly they heard the cracking of bones, and watched those ruined arms become grotesque, useless shapes. His skin swelled and trembled while he struggled to get to his feet. And then he erupted all over with hideous boils.

"G-aaah," Malingasa said, and something dropped from his mouth onto the floor.

Notable pounced upon it and happily devoured that pink and still-warm tongue. Already pale, Hanse gagged and looked away. That helped little: he saw that one of those accursed coins had turned to copper.

In less than a minute Malingasa had become hideous; sickening. He staggered, got to his feet while the revolting boils stretched his skin until they were shiny and swelled still more. Making horrible tongueless sounds, he staggered again and left by the same route he had entered: he hurled himself out the unpaned window.

Staggering nearly as badly, Hanse hurried to the window to look down. "Could—could he have survived that fall?" He glanced at Mignureal.

Silently she shook her head. Again she indicated the coins. They had become four, of silver.

Hanse spoke low: "One more gone: Malingasa. But only one. Cor—the monster has still not let Thuvarandis die."

He stared at Mignureal for a time, his eyes unnaturally round and bright. He looked at the cats, at the coins, at the floor where Malingasa had lain so long. A great shudder went through Hanse, and he turned to the beer. As he filled a cup he felt the thumping contact with his leg, and looked down at the red cat.

"Right; you too, boy! Uh, Notable; uh, Nur . . ." He trailed off in confusion. Then, "Miggue! How is it that Notable is a cat and Rainbow is, and yet she remembered and headed for Sanctuary? And what about the coins—and Mignue! *How is it that you know all these things you've said?*"

Mignureal sat on the floor, stroking the calico cat between her cloak-covered thighs. Her face was serene as she looked up at him.

"I *know,* Hanse. Shurina was wife of a master mage. She learned some few aspects of his trade; some lesser spells. When he locked her again in her prison room to suffer after the rape, she was not idle. Agony and outrage drove her and would not allow her to take refuge in shock. She bound the coins to her with a spell. And she laid a spell *on herself,* against forgetfulness. Even then she didn't know his plans, or that he was preparing a cat for her *ka.* It wasn't Nuris-Notable who began all this, Hanse. It was Rainbow. I mean Shurina."

"Oh." After a moment, he said, "But how is it that you—" He broke off.

The calico cat Mignureal had held so long now stirred. She rose and turned to climb carefully up Mignue. Rainbow gazed long into her eyes, and then Hanse watched the cat press its small pink nose to Mignureal's. He had accepted a great deal this night, because he must. Now he accepted this too, and understood: Not Rainbow, but Shurina had just told Mignureal that she was right, and had kissed her.

Mignureal hugged the cat to her face. "All the things I've *known* tonight, and said. Hanse; they weren't the S'danzo Seeing. Shurina has somehow . . . told me. I have merely been speaking for her."

After a long while of silence, Hanse said, "I think I'd better have some more beer."

"Uh, Hanse . . . would you pour me some too, please?"

"Notable is my friend," Hanse said. He sat on the stool, mug in hand, staring at nothing in particular. He had the attention of Mignureal, and Rainbow-Shurina, and Notable-Nuris. "He has saved my life at least one and a half times. I can't call Thuvarandis friend, but he's no enemy. He cannot deserve what Corstic is doing to him; no one could deserve this. The man needs to be dead. Surely after all this time he deserves his death."

He looked up, then, and his eyes were black coals and yet seemed to burn. "Corstic needs to be dead, too!" He sighed. "I must break into his lair after all, Mignue."

"Oh, *Hanse!*"

Shurina, however, spoke more eloquently than Mignureal. She hurried to Hanse and paced back and forth, rubbing his legs. Hanse let his hand trail along the calico's back. Suddenly he turned to Notable.

"Notable! Can you understand me? Do you know what I am saying?"

Gazing at him, Notable twisted his head abruptly to bestow some strong licks on his coat. Then he sat down to look at Shurina rubbing Hanse, and at Hanse.

"I think . . . I think Shurina understands," Mignureal said. "Notable *is* a cat, I think; merely a house for Nuris's *ka*. But Shurina is aware in there. She must be, darling. I *know* that she spoke, through me. It was different from the Seeing, Hanse; I heard the words. I knew what I was saying." She considered for a moment, then tried something: "Rainbow?"

The calico cat continued rubbing Hanse's legs and arching to his hand, and yet surely the averting of its small head from Mignureal was no coincidence.

Mignureal said, "Shurina?" and the cat looked at her at once. Hanse swallowed hard and audibly. Mignureal was nodding.

"Yes. That is a woman named Shurina looking at me from those tilted green eyes, isn't it! You do understand! You understand that I have to know, Shurina. You know how important it is to you. So—show me that you understand. Please go over to Notable."

Instantly the cat swerved and without a normal feline swing of her hindquarters for a last rub against the leg she left, paced over to Notable. At the side of the big red cat, she turned to look at Mignureal.

"Damn," Hanse murmured. He stared at the floor. "It's sorcery, all right, but for the first time, I don't hate it. Who could hate Rainbow? Who could hate Shurina?" He looked at the cat. "Is it only Mignureal, Shurina, or can you understand me, too?"

Both cats gazed at him, tails moving lazily. Both looked attentive. Still, Hanse knew that such seeming alert attentiveness and motionlessness, except for moving tail, were typical feline behavior. A cat could do that for minute after minute, even until a human looked away. On the other hand the cat might well become interested in an insect or an itch, a supposed sound or a butterfly, and ignore the human completely.

"If you can understand me, too, Shurina, please walk to me and to Mignureal and back to Notable."

The glaring cat lashed her tail as if insulted. But then she paced rather stiffly to Hanse, only to veer off and approach Mignureal, and thence back to the other cat. Notable yawned, which was always one of the most hideous sights Hanse had to see. He always looked away when any cat yawned. He did not care to look at those ghastly fangs and that awful ability to distend the mouth so . . . accommodatingly. He did not care to think about the murderous ability of even a small cat, much less one such as Notable.

Now he did not even feel silly as he said, "I'm sorry, Shurina. I had to know. You want me to go after Corstic, that's clear." He paused while the calico hurried back to rub his legs.

"I guess I've done things just as dangerous, but here in Firaqa I don't know enough. I need your help, Shurina. You see—uh."

The cat had broken off rubbing to rear sinuously and set both forepaws on his knee. It stood there gazing into his eyes as if . . . as if awaiting instructions.

Hanse nodded and stroked the side of the animal's face. Shurina or no, the response was a cat's; she pressed her cheek to his fingers.

"Shurina is . . . *alive* in there," Mignureal said. "Nuris is . . . Notable. Notable is a cat."

"Going over the wall to Corstic's without knowing more would be stupid. Probably suicide," Hanse said, explaining to a small calico cat. "On the other hand, I also can't hope to explore that estate and learn what I need to learn. I can take you and Notable there on a horse, though, and avoid the whole problem of the wall by setting you on a tree-branch. You two can explore, observe, and meet me afterward. Somewhere; I wouldn't dare sit there on a horse close outside his wall. I'd be too noticeable, too obviously waiting for something. Will you do that? Can you do that? And can you, uh, sort of control Notable, Shurina? Communicate with him as a cat so he knows the danger and what he's supposed to be doing?"

"Hanse . . ." Mignureal began but broke off. With that sinuous slowness that bragged of feline musculature, the small cat dropped from Hanse's knee and began pacing from the room. She speeded to a trot.

Both humans exchanged a glance, and went to the doorway to look. The calico stood by the hall door, waiting to go out. When she made a small sound, Notable brushed between them in a beeline for the other cat.

Hanse put a hand on Mignureal's shoulder, and answered her. "What?"

"Nothing, I suppose." She sighed. "It's going to happen, I know that. You're going to do it. Except that by now it must be closer to dawn than midnight, darling, and this has got to wait. We have to rest."

"True," Hanse said. " 'Morrow night, then. Hmm . . . I mean much later, today!"

• • •

Two people rode up the main road of Town Hill, talking in the darkness, and neither noticed the big gray horse under the little roanberry grove over on their left. The black-clad man in the tree was not interested in berries, or in these two riders who were returning home from Firaqa at an unusually late hour. He watched their passage, and they never knew. He had no idea who they were; they had no idea he was there.

If cleared, the little grove would have provided a hemispherical widening of the road. Just beyond the roanberry trees was a steep drop-off, which was why no estate had grown here, and none would. Someone probably owned the land, but Shadowspawn didn't care about that. The owner would not be Corstic. The lower curve of his wall was a half league up the road, and on the other side. Shadowspawn waited. He had been waiting a long while. The bad part was not nervousness or apprehension, but the itching of his inner thigh. He would not scratch because the itch emanated from Notable's claw-wounds. The snugness of his leggings must have rubbed away that odd greenish stuff with which Mignureal had smeared his wounds. Just below, the Tejana gray cropped grass and occasionally sampled a few low-hanging leaves. Along with his master, the horse had been waiting here for over an hour. In the darkness, in the tree, Shadowspawn waited. And he pondered.

How was it that he had seen no pale new wounds on the trees inside Corstic's wall, where branches had been ripped away and hurled at him; hurled to impale Thuvarandis? Why, even upon dismounting and looking close, had he found no twigs, no sign of the leaves that should have been there, from branches he had heard dashing against the ground and against the road? He found nothing in the ditch across the road, either, or on the bank above it. Why in the name of all gods not to mention the Flame had Corstic gone to such trouble to have the area cleaned up? Suppose he had; how had he restored the branches to the trees? Was any mage capable of such sorcery as mending trees by *sticking their branches back on*?

Once again, waiting an hour later in the tree, Shadowspawn shook his head. Again the thought came: *What sorcerous glue did he use, damn him?* He found no answer. He had been waiting here for over an hour, and he could find no answer. Nor could he believe that even Firaqa's master mage was capable of such miracles.

He waited nearly another hour. By that time his mount stood motionless and silent just below his perch; the nameless horse was asleep.

As silent as Shadowspawn and perhaps more silent, the cats arrived without his knowledge until they were almost directly below. From the branch Notable was invisible in the darkness; Rainbow was a small patch of white. She uttered a perfectly normal "meow" in her small voice, and Shadowspawn swung down from the low branch. Instantly awake, the horse jerked its head around.

After squatting briefly to stroke the two cats, Hanse used the rope-loop he had slung from his saddle horn to get into the saddle. He patted the horse's neck and muttered to him for a moment, before looking down at the cats. He made a tiny sound with pursed lips. The calico made the spring first, landing without seeming impact on the blanket behind his saddle. Then Notable streaked up, to alight with a burbly sound on Hanse's thigh.

"Ouch! Damn," Shadowspawn muttered, and pulled the big red cat onto the saddle before him. He made the click sound in his cheek that he had learned persuaded the gray horse to move at a walk. He paced back down the hill to Firaqa, and Cochineal Street. Tip was snoozing in the stairwell, but was happy to be roused. He got to ride the fine big animal back to the stable behind the Green Goose!

Mignureal was waiting. She sat on the floor to draw Rainbow-Shurina into her lap. She stroked and stroked the little calico all the while that Shurina, through Mignureal, told them what she and Notable had learned.

To begin with, that odd patch of grass Hanse had noted was a safe place, not a dangerous one!

An incredulous Hanse bleated, "What?"

But Mignureal was speaking on, for Shurina. According to the intelligence the spell-wise woman in the body of the cat had gained while roaming the grounds, there was only one way into Corstic's manse. Hanse leaned forward eagerly, only to discover that he was being told what he must *not* do.

Seek to climb the wall and he would be killed. Aye, he had rather suspected that. Step to the top of the wall from the horse's back as he had considered, and he would die. There went that brilliant idea, he thought, and listened because that was all there was to do. He had sent the cats in for information. Surely what Mignureal was saying, as she sat stroking the calico, was from the woman who was the cat: from Shurina. She went on.

Should he try to stand in the saddle and pounce over the wall from the horse's back—as he had been practicing today, for hours—he would die horribly. Seek to gain entry by using one of the trees so temptingly close to the wall, she told him, and he would be taken just as Thuvarandis had been.

Blast, Hanse thought, *we're running out of options!*

True, and worse. He had no options. He had one and only one way to enter the mansion of Corstic the mage: enter the grounds by the front gate and gallop right up to the broad portico and run right up to the main entry, the front door, and walk in!

"What?!"

Aye. He was to take the handle in his gloved hand, and turn it, and walk in.

"But—but I'm a *thief*! How can I possibly go in the front way!"

She merely repeated: "Turn the handle with your gloved hand, and walk in."

Then her voice changed, and the cat in her lap turned its head to stare up at her. Obviously those pricked ears were hearing words that had not come from Shurina. This time it was the Seeing, the true S'danzo ability rather than the strange mental link with the cat, for Mignureal's eyes had gone blank and her voice had taken on that strange quality he had learned to recognize. Hanse smiled in happy anticipation, leaning forward. As she spoke she drew from around her neck the medallion that Strick had given her six weeks ago, in Maidenhead Wood.

"Hanse," she began, "*wear this amulet.*"

But then came the rest of it, and he listened in growing disbelief and disgust to injunctions that were less than inspiring. A few seconds later he sat glaring at her. His mouth was an open hole in his sagging jaw.

That was it, he thought desolately. *She's lost it. It's gone. If I do that, I'll be dead, dead, dead!*

Another day and part of a night had passed with nothing further from her. Hanse had questioned her about what he saw as lunacy, but she could not help him. As usual, she had no memory of what she had told him and indeed did not know she had said it. Now he and the cats had made their preparations and were preparing to go, and still Mignureal had nothing to add to Shurina's warnings or her own Seeing for him. Her nervousness and worry for him were obvious, but she Saw nothing new. No renewed Seeing came upon her. That only added to his sharing her nervousness about this night's venture.

They clutched each other at the door. He felt her fingernails through his blacks.

"By now Tip will be waiting downstairs, with the horse," he reminded her. "Because I've twice gone out through the northward gate and the first time all that . . . activity took place up at Corstic's, they could be suspicious. So I'm going out by the south gate, the way we came into Firaqa. I'll ride all the way around the city, and *then* up Town Hill."

"I know, darling," she murmured.

Aye, he knew that she knew. He had told her three times. The point was that he kept hoping that a renewed Seeing would come upon her, and he didn't want her chasing him down in the wrong direction! What she had told him was insanity. Surely her S'danzo talent was playing her false!

But now it was time, and she had nothing to offer. He squeezed her hard, stepped back, and looked at her for a moment. Then he whirled and headed for the steps. The cats were right with him. When he glanced back, Mignureal looked very tiny, standing there in the doorway. Shadowspawn went down, accompanied by the thump, thump-thump, of cats descending stairs. Both front feet, and pause, and then both back feet, and both front, and . . .

Tip was there with the horse, which was visibly excited even though this business of nocturnal uphill outings had become almost standard in its life. The boy went inside to wait in the building's entry corridor. He would not be bored. Nothing bored Tip; there wasn't enough brain in him. Cloak concealing his working clothes, Shadowspawn mounted. The cats joined him. When they were settled, he set off toward the south gate. He maintained a sedate pace by tensing his arm against the pull of old Iron-mouth. It wasn't just that this was the law; tonight he wanted to make sure that Mignureal had plenty of time to catch up.

He rode all the way to the gate expecting to hear her voice. He did not.

And then he was at the gate, glancing back, and a sleepy-looking sentry was waving a hand limply, bidding him be careful.

Oh sure, Shadowspawn thought. *Be careful. Just clutch the medallion—and walk in the front door with my eyes shut! Sure!*

He rode into the night. All the way around Firaqa's east side he expected her even while knowing in the inner keep of his mind that she was not coming. Having rounded most of Firaqa, the big gray horse started once again up Town Hill.

She has said it and that's that, Shadowspawn told himself. *So now do I cease heeding warnings and advice that have always been unbelievably to the mark, or do we behave sensibly instead?*

Hanse?

He did not know. He could not answer himself. Ole Iron-mouth was approaching Corstic's walls, and his rider dared not try to step onto the wall from the saddle, or onto a branch. Nor dared he stand in the saddle and attempt to leap that wall. What choice was left him? What option did he have?

And now here was Corstic's wall, with all those trees just on its other side.

I will experiment!

Reining close to the wall, he muttered words to the cats, sucked up a deep breath and steeled himself, and reached out with a black-gloved hand. He grasped a long branch.

On the instant he heard a loud cracking sound and flopped as far backward as the saddle and his backbone allowed. The broken bough drove across in front of him, at velocity. Leaves brushed his face and twigs scraped across his chest. Had he not lunged back out of the way, he'd have been impaled. He heard the bough slap leafily against the road. He looked at it, a large tree-branch lying half across the road. And he heard another leafy sound, and another loud *crack*.

At that moment Hanse heard in his mind her words of last night:

"Hanse. Wear this. When the branches begin to snap and fly, clutch the amulet and close your eyes until you hear them no more.

Hanse could only blurt and blither: "Close my eyes? But— *amulet*? But—"

He had thought: Madness! Was this all she had to offer? He was to clutch the piece of jewelry, the gold-edged triangle of varicolored bits of tortoise shell, closing his eyes the while so as to be sure to be killed? He could only splutter and stare at Mignureal as if she were mad. He could find no words. Coherence turned its back on him in the face of such lunacy. Surely this time her S'danzo talent had played her false.

Now his thoughts were different. Since she had known that branches would snap and fly, then . . .

It was far and far from easy, but Shadowspawn sucked up a deep breath and steeled himself. Still gazing at the branch in the roadway, he closed his eyes. At the same time he clasped the medallion slung around his neck to hang onto his chest.

How long should I keep my eyes closed, he wondered, and realized that he was hearing nothing save a few crickets and katydids. No cracking sounds. No whishy rushings through the air.

He opened his eyes. He had not moved his head. He was still gazing at the road. That was what it was, and all it was. No branch lay there. When he jerked his head to look, the branch he had touched, the bough that had broken off and driven at him, was still there. Or again there, right where and as it belonged: attached to the tree.

Damn, Hell, and Eyes of the All-Father! It was illusion! *Mignureal was right again!*

And so, likely, was the rest of the warning and injunction from her Sight. And now he knew why. *Because it is illusion! Illusion can kill me, too . . . but if I can't see it, it is nothing! I've got to charge the place—and walk in!*

Exultation soared in him so that he trembled. "Hang on, friends," he said to the cats, "because here we go in! *Haiya!*"

The knock at the door was an unpleasant surprise for Mignureal, since Hanse had not had time to accomplish the mission he had set for himself. Because of that she was apprehensive for him, rather than properly fearful for herself, at this hour. She hurried to the door and opened it to look questioningly at the man in the hall. His large eyes were intensely blue and looked right at her, almost as if into her.

Of average height and rising thirty-five or so, he was balding averagely around a center lock of gold-red hair that made him look high of forehead. That hair was a bit darker than his moustache, which was of the droop-tip variety, and well-trimmed. He was slim and small of bone but not thin, as if he had been thin but ate well and did not labor. That was borne out by the excellent fabric and superb color of his medium blue tunic. It was girt with a loose belt of soft white leather and worn over dove-gray leggings and tall black boots. They must be of everted leather or pigskin, since they looked soft and were without sheen. His very long cloak was as black as Hanse's working clothes, but again, fine; lined with deep red. She noted that he wore no weapons, not even a dagger. Only a thin staff or rod, white and about a foot and a half long, was tucked through his belt. That loop in the belt had been made there, she realized, for the round-tipped rod. It still did not resemble a weapon.

She had never seen him before, nor had she ever seen the two armed men who stood just behind and to either side of him.

"*You* are the source of the emanations?" he said, in a pleasant and well-modulated tenor. "One pretty girl?"

Suddenly Mignureal was intensely aware of the low, low "neck" of her gift-robe.

"But pardon that outburst, please," he said with a smile. "My name is Arcala."

The mane of the Tejana horse streamed in the wind of its own fleet passage. Shadowspawn's hair blew so that he squinted his eyes. The fur of the cats ruffled and the animals crouched behind the high cantle of the saddle to cut that wind. Up the road paralleled by the wall the big gray horse bucketed. When his rider nudged and tugged, he veered through the open gateway to gallop wildly onto Corstic's grounds. Eleven-foot monsters with foot-long fangs rose asnarl in yellow and black and vomitous chartreuse, talons clutching, and Shadowspawn shuddered as he muttered "Vaspa!" Yet even in his fear he dared use one hand to clutch the medallion while he closed his eyes and clung to the horse with all the strength of his legs.

Iron-mouth galloped on and his rider felt only the wind. Nothing touched him. The horrid guardians, too, were illusion.

Straight up a pretty lane to the looming porticoed mansion the gray galloped, and kept right on up the broad redstone steps while Shadowspawn leaned on the reins and shouted "Whoa! Mip, damn you, *mip!* WHOA!"

The iron-mouthed beast skidded to a stop on the porch, averting his big head at the last instant to avoid the tall and wide front door of Corstic's home. Shadowspawn swung off. Even as he dropped lightly to the porch he heard the high-pitched bee-sound followed by the thump. He glanced at the arrow that quivered in the door. It has missed him only because he had dismounted so swiftly. The arrow was no illusion.

His snarl sounded hardly human. He whirled with a missile cocked over his shoulder.

In an instant he saw the kneeling man twenty feet away, nocking another arrow to his bow, and without a thought Shadowspawn's arm swept forward. He bent far in a long follow-through. This was no ordinary roach job; this was a raid on a murderer on behalf of Notable and a horribly wronged woman named Shurina, and no time for his scruples against using weapons on a job. Besides, this bow-toting piece of cess was the employee of a monster. The steel star appeared in his forehead with three of its six needly points still showing, and he crumpled like a cut weed.

Excited, full of pumping adrenaline, Shadowspawn lowered the unneeded second star. He whirled, prepared to kick in the door of Corstic's manse and charge in. He was only just able to regain control and abort that act. Again he considered the rest of Mignureal's words, the second part of that Seeing which he had thought was lunacy:

"When you turn the handle to enter the house, close your eyes and keep them so until you are inside."

Sucking deep breaths, he glanced around. The cats stood poised, waiting. Shadowspawn seized the big brass handle with one hand, clasped Strick's amulet in the other, and closed his eyes. Then he turned the handle and shoved the door.

With his eyes closed, he never knew what horrors Corstic had conjured as illusion-guards of his lofty entry hall. Shadowspawn paced in, scalp and armpits prickling. The soft soles of his buskins brought only a whispery sound from the marble floor. He felt the brushing sensation against his leg and knew that a big red cat had just bolted past him. Heart pounding, he took two more steps before he heard the hideous shrieking sound, and knew it was no illusion. Shadowspawn opened his eyes.

He clutched the medallion hard, sharp edges biting even through the glove, and squeezed shut his eyes.

When he squinted one open, however, the thigh-thick serpent was still there, a dozen feet long and revoltingly, eye-searingly green and orange. It reared, head weaving, held at bay only by a large hissing cat with its back arched up to here and its tail straight up and ugly: every red hair stood straight out. Shadowspawn knew three facts at once: Mignureal's Sight had caught the illusory menaces here but somehow been blinded to the real one. That awful shriek he had heard had been Notable, saving his life once again; this overgrown snake was no illusion.

Shadowspawn forgot the amulet and reached for weapons.

Two blurred movements of a black-clad arm sent a knife into each of the reptile's eyes, despite the creature's violent lurch of pain after the first impact. Notable drove in at once, mouth wide and fangs gleaming, and Hanse was right with him. The Ilbarsi knife chopped and slashed. The improbable serpent became two, each half spewing its juices. One of those halves was being viciously shaken by the head housing the feline fangs that pierced it.

"Leave it, Notable. It'll flop around that way for an hour or longer maybe, but that big worm is dead, believe me. Let's go!"

The stairwell was three paces away and directly ahead. As

Hanse leaped lightly over one lashing half of the late snake, a calico cat blurred past him and hit the steps running. Notable let go his hold and followed, drooling serpent juice.

"Would you non-professionals wait just one moment? Some of us don't have our weapons built in!"

Shadowspawn retrieved his knives from the eyes of the dead but wildly flopping reptile, was struck by it, and grunted at the heaviness of the blow to his leg. He crouched to wipe the knives on a fine oval rug, multicolored. He was just returning the knives to their sheaths when the thick rug came up at him, seeking to envelop his face. Holding it down with one foot and a good deal of difficulty, Hanse grasped the amulet and closed his eyes. The predatory carpet subsided.

A chunk of dead snake bashed his leg again. That was too much. Angrily he grasped it, whirling, and hurled it out through the open front doorway. Since a cry followed, Shadowspawn dropped into a crouch while drawing Ilbarsi knife and steel star. He leaped past the doorway, looking that way as he flew by. A great shudder rushed through him, along with a flood of adrenaline.

He had just seen Shorty, blindly batting away half of a giant serpent while wearing a throwing star in his forehead.

"To the cold hell with the amulet!" Hanse snarled.

The steps and Corstic would wait a little longer. This could not be real because it could not be Shorty, but it could damned well be stopped. He pounced back and through the doorway and struck at a thigh as hard as he could. The Ilbarsi knife jarred on bone. Shadowspawn had to wiggle it to get it out while Shorty collapsed, without a sound. Hanse used both hands on the hilt and all his strength in another blow to the fallen man or Sending, and pain rushed up his arms as he chopped through the neck and the long blade slammed into Corstic's redstone porch. Sparks flashed and danced, bright in night's darkness. His horse whickered.

The head rolled away, no longer resembling Shorty at all, and Hanse lost interest in retrieving his thowing star just now.

He whirled back to the door only to face a drooling spider the size of a horse and the color of excrement. Such an arachnid parody could not be, but he nevertheless dived sidewise before he grasped the amulet and closed his eyes. When he peeped, the spider was gone.

The trouble is, a body doesn't know what's illusion and what's real. he thought, and was about to dive through the doorway when he remembered: first he grasped the amulet and closed his eyes. He pounced through the opening lightly, Shadowspawnly, and opened his eyes. It was actually pleasant to see only an empty stairwell and the twitching front half of a bisected snake.

He bounded up the marble stair two steps at a time until the eighth sprouted a man with a terribly long and silver-gleaming sword. That could not be, but Shadowspawn parried automatically before grasping the amulet and closing his eyes—briefly. When he opened them the man was gone and the step was only a step and he went on up, fast. Had he been slower, the six-foot steel shaft that hurtled down from the ceiling above the stairwell would have ended his heroism and his career. It was not an illusion.

Damn! This Corstic had more tricks than a silver-piece uptown whore!

"Notable! Shu—Rainbow! Dammit, wait for me!"

At least he had managed to revise the calico's name at the last moment. Shouting out the name of Corstic's supposedly dead wife seemed definitely the wrong thing to do. He bounded on up, ducking the lion's head that erupted from the wall and squeezing shut his eyes to send it into oblivion.

Then he saw the small calico cat awaiting him at the top of the stairs, and he smiled. At least he thought he did; what the cat saw was a dark-skinned human grimace akin to a feline snarl. Tail straight up, she whirled and trotted down a corridor dimly lit by no visible means.

Shadowspawn did what he knew he was supposed to do: he followed. When he saw her swerve wide to the left, so did he. He never knew what trap they avoided, illusory or otherwise. A noise behind him brought him spinning about to face a charging Marll. The blond bore a huge crescent-moon ax. In seconds he also wore a throwing star in the chest and a knife in the crotch—an accident—but kept on coming. Hanse tried the amulet-and-closed eyes ploy, and heard his blades drop to the floor. He opened his eyes to see weapons and no Marll.

Fleetingly, while he picked up the weapons, he wondered how these stickers could have stuck in an illusion through which they should have passed. But that was not as important as whirling again to hurry after the calico cat.

She fled, tail high, past a doorway from which a head emerged to look after her. It turned to look with wide eyes at a downrushing blade. That one must have been real; its thudding and bouncing on the floor was real enough. The calico glanced back.

"Right with you, Shurina! I don't know about you, but I'm running on pure adrenaline. *Never* have I been in such a place so full of horrors and death-dealers!"

The cat trotted on—and stopped, and turned. Side by side with the big red cat, she stood watching while their pet human caught up. He was actually panting a little. The animals waited with twitching tails before a tall, narrow, cream-colored door set flush with the cream-colored wall and only just visible.

"Mignue's told me that cats tolerate humans only because you can't open doors," he muttered, trying not to pant. "The trouble is, I don't see any way to open this one! Sure wish you could talk, Shurina."

The cat replied by hurling her tiny self against the door.

"Oh," Shadowspawn said, and with one hand grasping the amulet and the other poising a leaf-shaped throwing blade, he tried that.

The door flew inward and he was four running steps beyond before he could stop himself. That was the way he came into the presence of the man he thought he had never seen: the master spellmaker of Firaqa.

He saw Corstic just as the tall and very leggy fellow in the snowy tunic and tight beige leggings turned his head to stare. The flat knife shot from Hanse's hand without his thinking, on full automatic because he was a professional; had he paused long enough to register the face he recognized, he might have aborted the throw.

Not that it would have mattered: The master monster of Firaqa avoided it. Not with a majestic, magisterial and magicker's extending of arms and fluttering of fingers, but by undramatically and unsorcerously dropping into a squat. The slender leaf of steel whished over his head to thud into the wall beside a window. It was that same window through which Hanse had seen him, only two nights agone.

"That," Thuvarandis said, "is an exceedingly rude way to enter the presence of the most powerful man in Firaqa, not to mention your banker!"

The large chamber was wooden-floored, lit by at least a half-score lamps, six of which were wall-mounted. A broad long desk of oak was littered with the paraphernalia of reading and writing, along with a goblet, two mugs, a fancily wrapped wine pottle, and a platter bearing a bone and some scraps that must have been the mage's dinner. Two long tables against two different walls were obviously a sorcerer's work tables, cluttered with just about everything. Aye, Shadowspawn saw even some of those jars and closed pots all mages were supposed to have, likely containing things only Corstic wanted to see. Amid the clutter, in plain sight as he had been told by the plotters, rested a lustrous little figurine the color of pearl: a cat.

To the right of that table and a few feet out from that same wall, a curtain of emerald green hung from ceiling to floor. Hanse assumed that it concealed something; another table, perhaps; probably something that only Corstic wanted to see. Against another wall was a beautifully covered divan. He saw a tall wooden stool and a single chair, behind the desk. And he saw . . . Corstic?

Stupidly, Hanse said, "Thu . . . varandis? But . . ."

"You're not going to tell me it is impossible are you, young man? Obviously it is possible and true, since you see me. Since you come stomping in here with blood in your eye and in company with two darling pussycats I do believe I recognize, I must assume that you know their story. That little psychic whore you live with, no doubt. No no, don't strain yourself trying to draw and throw another sticker in anger, now; you cannot move your arms and will not until I wish it. Try to restrain your anger and I will try to restrain my language. She's doubtless a nice little girl, hmmm? It's just that this is a mages' city, and I and some others have had certain laws and regulations passed, concerning the S'danzo."

Smiling only a little, looking serene and confident, Thuvarandis pointed. *"Sit down."*

Shadowspawn's body immediately wished to sit. He tried to
fight the urge. It was irresistible. It wasn't that his mind had to
obey; his body did. Striving, he fell back against the wall and
slid down it into a sitting position on the floor—hard, since his
arms might as well have been loaded with chains for all the
good they were to him. This man controlled his very muscles,
and reflexes.

"Doubtless now you want an explanation. That's the way it
would be in a tale told by a storyteller, hmmm? Well, you can
whistle for that, thief! I've no time to waste on explaining
matters to such as you. I will show you something, however.
Doubtless it will prove enthralling to you, young man; even
instructive, if not overly enlightening!"

Thuvarandis drew aside the green curtain to reveal another
table. To it, Hanse could see even from his seated position on
the floor, was strapped an unclothed man. Shadowspawn could
see the shallow, shuddery rise and fall of his chest; a white-
haired man held supine by broad black straps. He was
unbelievably pale. The mage turned back to the intruder.

"Rise," he said, making a lifting gesture with both hands.
"Stand. Walk over here."

Horripilation took Hanse as he was *impelled* to his feet.
They moved; his legs moved. He had nothing to do with it. His
arms remained useless; totally moveless. The mage *impelled*
him to walk over to that newly revealed table, an armless
prisoner in his own body. He stared down at the victim strapped
there, and shuddered in a mingling of horror and outrage. A
closed fist could have gone into the gory hole in this pitiful
man's middle. Illusory or no, the tree-branch had done that,
and Hanse had seen it, for this was Thuvarandis. The
transpiercing branch could not, however, account for the fact
that the long-legged man had also been emasculated. And still
Thuvarandis breathed.

Hanse's lips moved, but no words emerged. He looked back
at the mage, and gasped. His stomach lurched. He was looking
into the face of Marll!

"No, I am not your kindly fellow-plotter. *That* is Thuvarandis, the treacherous swine. Illusion, remember? I thought

perhaps your amulet allowed you to see through my appearance, until you called me Thuvarandis and I knew that was what you saw. I can *appear* to be anyone, roach. No one has seen me in my real form for a number of years now. It amuses me. It is something to do. Wonder, young man: perhaps I am hideous and misshapen, hmm?''

"In the name of all gods, mage—*let that man die!*"

Marll smiled. "Oh, I shall. But not for a while. He hears us, he feels, he sees us, he feels his pain. As he should. The treacherous bastard put together a plot to gain something that is not his and that I worked very hard to obtain. He'd have sent in a common thief, wouldn't he, thief! A roach! I trapped him as I would have trapped a rat—or a harmless mouse!"

Again a shudder shook Hanse's voice: "Gods, man!"

"You'll find none of those around here, young man. Now as to dear Thuvarandis, here . . ."

Marll put forth a hand. His finger touched, only touched the raw lip of the awful wound. Shadowspawn shuddered. Striving with all his might and will to move his arms and obtaining not so much as the twitch of a thumb, he saw that Thuvarandis shuddered, too, from the pain of that mere touch.

"I really believe that I will keep him alive for a long, long time. You see, the genius Corstic tricked everyone; everyone." A hand laden with an ornate ring proudly touched the chest of Marll, who was Corstic. "All have been my tools! All of them. My treacherous, lustful wife and her lover who betrayed my trust and kindness, and all ten of those so-willing men you have heard about, young man, young roach!"

He despises them all, Shadowspawn realized, raging inside and fighting, fighting to regain use of his own arms. *He ensnared and entrapped them all. And he has been gloating and delighting in it ever since!*

"Aye, I think that I will keep him alive for a good while, yet. You see, the human essences within those two cats you so kindly returned to me . . . whether the animals live or die, those *ka*s will never know peace until all ten of Shurina's rapists are dead. Of late too many of them have expired. Aye, I think that I will keep Thuvarandis alive for a long, long time. I like cats, don't you, young roach?"

Hanse's brain staggered at this revelation of the limitless

treachery and cheerful cruelty of this man. But Corstic had a further shock for him:

"Of course! You must like cats—now wouldn't you just love to *be* one!"

Just then something caught Corstic's attention and he jerked his head violently to the side. His eyes went huge and staring at what he saw. His voice was almost a bellow. "Stop tha—*No!*"

Unable to turn, Hanse caught the blur of rushing movement only from the edge of his eye. Corstic had pronounced his intentions and given too much attention to Thuvarandis, and to Shadowspawn. Another person in that room heard and understood, though she was trapped in a small multicolored body. She had acted; was taking action. The calico cat pounced onto the table next to that of Thuvarandis's torment, and what she did there was certainly no accident. Even as Corstic jarred past Hanse in his desperate leap for Rainbow-Shurina, she succeeded in her mission. The calico cat knocked the pearly one from the table. It fell and shattered noisily. Bits of porcelain scattered across the floor.

A thief's hyper-observant eye saw that it had been only a little statue; nothing rolled or clattered forth.

Corstic's cry of rage was freighted with real horror. It told Hanse that the figurine had been inordinately valuable to the mage. Even his face and form flickered, as if all his attention was focused on his loss and on the offending Shurina, so that he could only just maintain the appearance of Marll. Hanse saw that he was a large man, with a large skull on which the forehead was growing loftier as his hair decamped.

Unfortunately Shurina, too, was focused: on her task. The enraged mage seized her little body with both hands, and an instant later had slammed her across the table and against the wall. Hanse heard the sharp cracking sound that accompanied the impact of her small head with the wall. He recognized it as more than the sound of impact. Seeing the blood that came from the cat's nostrils and mouth as she dropped back onto the table, he knew that she was mortally wounded. Rage boiled hot in him, so that it hurt, and suddenly sweat covered him in his attempt to free himself.

His fingers twitched.

I can mo—I can almost move . . .

• • •

It did not matter. The shrieking, hideous cry that accompanied Rainbow's falling back onto the table had not come from her. It was that sound called a caterwaul, and it was worse. Hanse was still effortfully turning his head when a streak of flame flashed through the air to hit the mage with a thud that staggered the big man. It was not flame, however; it was a large and enraged red cat. Claws thrust into clothing and skin and dug and worked; curved fangs slashed into the skin of Corstic's neck. Into the skin, and deeper, while Notable champed. When the mage bellowed his agony and tore the animal from him, human flesh ripped away as well, in claws and in needly teeth. The cat crashed onto the table amid a rattle of jars and bowls. Dust or some powder spilled and rose in a pale cloud. A few inches away, Rainbow twitched. Bleeding, the mage swept up his arms and the big cat, all red-mouthed, drove straight up and between them. This time, from the higher vantage of the table, Notable struck Corstic's face, which was Marll's face. And tore, and ripped, and fastened his fangs, and wagged his head violently as he strove, with all his strength, to pull.

The sound of the cat's snarling growl was enough to make Shadowspawn wish that he were deaf. That sound, and Corstic's moans.

Nearly falling as full control of his body rushed back into him, Shadowspawn saw only part of it because Corstic's back was to him while the man fought the demonic cat of his own creation. At the same time, Hanse saw the head and the shape of the apparent Marll change still more, and realized that the mage had lost all control of his spells. The master spellmaker was become only a man in agony. With both hands and all his attention he was striving to free himself of the cat. He gave himself more pain in the process, for teeth and talons were fast locked in face and chest. Locked, and working.

"Let—go—Notable—because—this—monster will be— *falling!*"

The mage whirled, tearing away the cat; literally tearing Notable from his face amid spurts of blood from ribboned flesh. Even as he turned, he was raising the cat high as a missile to dash at the man he had forgotten, the man whose weapons he had not bothered to take because of natural confidence in his own sorcerous talent. For a fleeting instant Hanse saw that Corstic had not concealed his features behind illusion because it was ugly or worse; the big man must have been handsome. No longer; not with bloody strips of his face dangling from the claws and fangs of the big red cat.

He did not throw Notable, for Shadowspawn moved too fast. Corstic's eyes went even wider when the blow low in his belly drove the six-inch sliver of steel into him. Almost simultaneously, Shadowspawn's right hand slammed a second knife into the monster's side. Corstic went rigid except for a spasmodic shivering throughout his body. Shadowspawn, his face twisted into an ugly snarl, jerked his arm to give the dagger a twist before yanking it forth. Even as Corstic began to sag and his hands relaxed on the cat, arms dropping, Notable dropped onto his head with all claws out. He resumed clawing and chewing.

Shadowspawn stepped back and out of the way, for the master spellmaker of Firaqa was crumpling. He fell, still twitching.

Hanse looked down at him. He saw no face; only erected red fur. "Notable. Notable!"

"Pro . . . fesh'n'l . . . ki'w mee . . ."

Shadowspawn jerked his head around to stare in renewed horror at the man strapped to the table. The horrible sounds, almost words, came from a tongueless mouth. Shadowspawn trembled, bit his lip, raised his dagger. He aborted that movement, looking with distaste at the blood-smeared blade. Whirling, he hurled it at the far wall. It was the knife that had slain the monster Corstic. He would not use it to end the misery of Thuvarandis, or for any other purpose.

He drew the long, long knife from the Ilbars hills. He changed his position and his stance. He sighted carefully. Tensed to strike, he bit his lip. Slowly he lowered the sword-like blade and returned it to its sheath. He could not do it. Not yet, anyhow. Besides, he told himself, Thuvarandis had been one of Shurina's rapists, and the injured cat needed attention.

"Notable," Hanse said again, for the big red animal was still at Corstic's face, still emitting those dreadful growls. Hanse left him alone; he bent over the table to stroke the calico cat. "You saved us, Shurina," he murmured. "Hold on now. You'll be all right."

No she won't, he thought. *Not with a cracked skull.* He was debating whether lifting her might be worse than leaving her when he heard the familiar voice:

"Hanse!"

He turned in astonishment to face Mignureal. Cloaked, she was in the doorway. She raced toward him. Beyond her he saw four others, men. One was a uniformed Red, and Hanse recognized Gaise. *Oh shit,* Shadowspawn thought, but held out his arms to embrace Mignureal just the same. She stopped short, for the first time seeing the body at his feet.

"Oh!" She stared down at the corpse, and a red-furred cat looked up at her. Darker red dripped from its whiskers and colored its nose. "Oh, Notable, what have you d—Hanse? Is this . . ."

"That's Corstic. That was Corstic."

"It appears that we arrived just a wee bit late," Gaise said, cheerfully.

He was approaching with one of the other three, a fellow of average height with thinning reddish hair and a pale moustache in which the red was only a whisper. He wore a fine, scarlet-lined cloak. The other two, armed but not uniformed, remained at the door.

"Maybe," Hanse said. "Too late for what?"

"Too late to help you, or to arrest Corstic either," the other man said. "Hanse, I have just met and talked with your brave Mignureal, and I am happy to meet a man of your bravery; a genuine adrenaline addict! My name is Arcala."

Swiftly Hanse learned that Arcala had "sensed emanations" from the Cochineal Street area, and traced them to the apartment. His mission was friendly. The two armed men were merely his bodyguards. Shadowspawn's apprehension on seeing Gaise was misplaced; Hanse was not in trouble with Council or FSA or the law. Corstic was. Or would have been, had he been alive. Mignureal had told Arcala the whole story of Corstic, and he knew enough to recognize it as truth. They had run into Gaise, on his way to investigate reports that a man

had fallen from a window to his death. He had rushed here with
them to try to prevent Hanse's certain death.

Since Corstic was unquestionably the most powerful mage
in Firaqa, Hanse realized that Arcala and Gaise and Mignureal
were braver than he. For now he understood more about
himself. He knew that what Arcala had said was true: Hanse
called Shadowspawn was addicted to adrenaline; to adventure
and the thrill of danger.

While Hanse learned these things, Notable stayed close to
him, peacefully licking his whiskers.

"Ah," Arcala said, looking down when his foot crunched
on pearly white shards, "the famous porcelain cat! Good,
good!"

Hanse was both pleased and surprised; he had assigned its
possession as Arcala's motive for coming here. He had
assumed that Corstic's rival would have coveted the figurine.

"There are other things to say," Arcala told him; "to talk
about."

Mignureal, cuddling the injured cat, looked up. "Not now!
Not in this place!"

"There is something else I must do, first," Shadowspawn
said. He drew the Ilbarsi blade. "Gaise, do not try to stop
me!"

Gaise shrugged. "I wouldn't dream of trying to stop you
from destroying any and all of this dreadful junk," he said.
"Lord Arcala might not appreciate it, though!"

"I have no intention of attacking Corstic's things. A man
must be put out of his pain."

He went to Thuvarandis then, and swiftly learned that the
tall man was already out of his pain.

"Corstic must have had a spell of un-life on him," Arcala
said. "The spell died with Corstic. So did Thuvarandis."

"But," Mignureal said, "but there's no change in the
cats . . ."

"That," Arcala said quietly, "is quite another matter. The
spell on Thuvarandis was a *holding* one. Corstic had not made
it permanent. I'd say many spells have ended tonight, in
Firaqa! The cats are not the result of any sort of spell, however;
they are cats. The only spell on Nuris and Shurina, apparently,
was one of awareness. In which case they *may* no longer be

aware of their humanity. But since that was a permanent spell wrought years ago, I'd say it remains. Nor can any mage remove the human awarenesses from the animals; both humans are dead."

Hanse sheathed his twenty-inch blade and hurried to retrieve the knife he had hurled from him. *"Spells!* Let us get out of this hole!"

As they descended the steps, Mignureal cradling Rainbow, Arcala said, "Do please come with me to my home. We need to do a bit of talking."

"Thank you, Lord Arcala," Gaise said. "As you can imagine, I have other duties."

Hanse said, "Do you have strong drink there?"

"Aye."

Hanse said, "Good. Oh, we will need to stop by the apartment, though. I want to check you-know-what, Mignue."

"We fetched along the coins," Arcala said over his shoulder, "and the tablet."

"Wonderful," Hanse said without enthusiasm, and he thought, *This sorcerer knows everything. Gods! O gods of my fathers, how I hate sorcery!*

Arcala lived down in the city, in Northgates. His large home on spacious grounds was located among trees at the very end of the tree-shaded street called Bitterwood. Interestingly then, he was a neighbor of Tethras the Changer. Hanse and Mignureal soon saw that the man favored floors of inlaid tile and mosaic, rather than carpets, and preferred divans and couches to chairs. A short and portly woman of considerable age advised Arcala that the children were fine, and asleep. That he had childen was somehow a surprise to his guests. She brought them wine and filled the strange request: she brought beer, and a bowl. Notable was soon assiduously lapping his reward.

Arcala, meanwhile, was alone with the calico cat. He had made it plain that he wanted privacy. Hanse was immediately suspicious, but Mignureal definitely was not and the wine was good.

When the mage returned to them, he stopped, gazing at that which lay on the low, mosaic-topped table before the couch draped in green and gold. Arcala knew their significance: a beeswax tablet of the folding kind, and two silver coins. The tablet was blank save for a single name.

"Someone named Elturas remains," the dark, sinuous young man said, "and one other."

He was talking to Mignureal, or to himself, but both looked up as their host rejoined them in his receiving room. Hanse was more than surprised to see that the man who was now master mage of Firaqa had removed his boots to pad about his home in stockinged feet.

"As you said, Hanse, her skull is cracked. I administered a bit of frankincense, which is good for cracked heads in some cases, and, probably more productive, I laid on a spell to take away her pain. Either it will repair itself or it will not. I am sorry to tell you that I doubt whether it will. So. Two coins remain. That tells us that two of Corstic's paid rapists still live, somewhere. Regrettably, I have never heard of an Elturas. There are, however, some things I want you two brave southerners to know."

Arcala poured himself wine, and took a seat to face them both.

"To begin with, you have done a great service for Firaqa and, at the risk of sounding dramatic: possibly for all humankind. For some years several of us have known that Corstic's were truly transcendent powers, and that not even a coalition of mages could match or hold him. We realized that he could take all power in Firaqa if he chose. We also knew that he would do it, and what such rule would be like. Among other things, Mignureal, he hated and despised the S'danzo. All S'danzo, irrationally. Five several laws in this city affect the S'danzo directly and were passed solely for—that is, against them. All were Corstic's laws. He was so definite, so impassioned in proposing and urging them, that no one dared long oppose him." He sipped from his flagon of ormolu decorated with a design in silver. "Those laws, I vow by the Flame Itself, will soon no longer exist!"

Hanse asked, "Why did he hate the S'danzo so much?"

"I know," Mignureal said quietly. "Shurina was—is S'danzo."

"You never told me!"

"I haven't known long, Hanse. It was a, a realization. That's why she and I have been able to communicate so well. That, along with the other abilities she learned while she was Corstic's wife."

"Corstic was a rational man in many ways, and irrational in others," Arcala said.

"He was a lunatic monster!" Hanse snapped.

Arcala shrugged. "Do just help yourself when your cup runs dry, Hanse."

Hanse did.

"Two years ago," Arcala said, "several of us were convinced that Corstic had decided to take Firaqa as dictator, and that he soon intended to make his move. By that time one of my associates had already ridden up to Baäbda and returned with the item we had secretly had made to use in our attempt to stop Corstic. With the utmost care, we saw to it that Corstic heard a *rumor:* I had come into possession of a certain talisman that afforded enormous occult powers. It was amusing, to realize from time to time that I was being so-o subtly pumped, so obliquely queried. I acted furtive even while I made denials, seeing to it that they were doubtworthy. That achieved our desire: Corstic and certain people allied with him were convinced that I did indeed possess such an object. This put enough doubt in his mind about the new extent of my powers that he decided he had best not make his grand attempt. At least not until he knew more about the supposed talisman, or . . . had it."

Arcala paused to smile. "We avoided having to submit to rule by Corstic alone, meaning that several of us averted being killed or at very least driven from Firaqa when he became dictator. This is what is called achieving a balance of power. We accomplished this by a rumor that was a lie. The supposed talisman was a small figurine: a perfectly ordinary statuette of a cat, in pearl-hued porcelain. I did imbue it with a webby, complicated aura of mystery; a smoke-screen of magic to diguise the fact that it was valueless. About a year later I was very glad that I had done, for it was stolen.

"That, I do not hesitate to admit, struck genuine fear into those of us who were plotting on Firaqa's behalf, for we were sure that the porcelain cat was in Corstic's hands. We were right. And yet, as it turned out, that too served our purpose.

For well over a year now, Corstic has put off his final stroke to seize all authority in Firaqa. Instead he has spent thousands of hours seeking to divine the secret of a 'talisman' that had no secrets save that it was only a pearl-colored cat made of porcelain! Meanwhile, my associates and I met, we talked, we tried to plan. We considered and even tried about everything—except employing a supernally brave man to storm boldly into Corstic's home in company with an attack-trained cat!''

They all glanced at Notable, who was quite asleep beside an empty bowl.

"I appreciate the cleverness of that plan, and that you doubtless saved your lives as well as Firaqa's," Hanse said, urged to more careful speech by Arcala's apparent devotion to it, and by the wine. "Yet why did Marll and Thuvarandis and the others plot to steal a worthless statue?"

Arcala shrugged. "None of those four was an intimate of mine, so I cannot say with any certitude. Malingasa I am unfamiliar with, and I actively disliked Marll. We had differing ideas about the employment of spells. We three can only guess. The rumor spread, you see, and others believed the tale of the cat-figure that was a great talisman. They may have wanted it out of Corstic's hands for the very reason Marll gave you: to save Firaqa from Corstic, and to destroy what they, too, thought was a talisman. More likely, they planned to use its *great magic* to gain control of the city, themselves."

Hanse sighed, shaking his head. "Every bit of it was a mistake, then. Corstic didn't need the statue, and neither did they. They never needed to approach me, and I never needed to go in at all! None of them needed to die so horribly."

He did not sip; he drank.

"Obviously all of it served a purpose, Hanse. Corstic is dead. Firaqa is saved. I assure you that I have no desire to be sole ruler. It would not help bring back my wife, and it would take me away from my children even more. I can do more for people by dealing in white magic. Yet I am in a position to see that no one else gains full power in my city, and I shall! Hanse . . . what were you to receive, for stealing the cat?"

"An early death, probably."

"Hanse," Mignureal said, "is a very suspicious individual, Lord Arcala."

"It pays," the mage said. "And I told you that my name is Arcala, not lord. What I meant, Hanse, is what did they promise you?"

Hanse took sudden interest in the wine pitcher. As he refilled his cup he told the truth: "Whatever I could carry out of there in addition to the figurine."

Arcala chuckled. "Please pardon me. I do not intend to laugh at you. It's just that you and that cat saved this city, and you come away from there with nothing at all for yourself!"

"That feels good," Hanse said. "And this wine is good." He shrugged, feeling an unaccustomed sensation: embarrassment. Too, he thought briefly on the ornate ring worn by the dead Corstic. It reposed snugly in Shadowspawn's concealed purse.

"You both have my admiration and friendship," Arcala said, looking at Mignureal. "And you would have the admiration and gratitude of many others, too, if we chose to reveal all that took place this night."

Very warm, Hanse looked up. "If?"

Arcala gestured with spread hands. "Do you want it known throughout the city what it is that you are very, very good at?" He paused, not quite smiling, gazing at Hanse from large and intensely blue eyes. "And that it was you personally who accomplished the impossible; destroyed the undestroyable?"

Hanse regarded him. "Uh . . . he had plenty of friends, cronies, didn't he. Mages and the like."

"Such men always do. Who knows what promises he had made to others, what they looked forward to, when he was dictator of Firaqa!"

"Or what threats he made," Mignureal said.

"That too," Arcala said, nodding. "As it is, we know of no one in Corstic's employ who saw you tonight, and lived. I and my two men and Gaise know, and you, Mignureal, and the cats. Gaise has promised to say nothing until he contacts me on the morrow. As it stands right now, Corstic has been found mysteriously dead in his home: murdered, along with two of his guards. Many people will rejoice at the news. Others will not."

Hanse bristled. "Murdered?"

"That is the way it looks, doesn't it."

"Oh."

"But Arcala," Mignureal said; "Gaise is a city employee, a sergeant of the Watch. Would he lie?"

Arcala rose and walked a few paces before facing them again. "No, but he could forget that he ever saw you there, Hanse. He and my men would know only that we went up there, just the four of us, and found Corstic dead." Seeing Hanse's openmouthed stare, he smiled. "Hanse, you are beyond expert at what you do. Give me credit: so am I! This would be no great exertion of my talent, and certainly the cause is worthy."

"It would . . . It would put me in your power."

"Sometimes, Hanse, sometimes a man can be *too* suspicious! I am offering you a favor, and that's all. Oh, I would ask one in return: as a favor, consider this house out of bounds should you decide to practice your . . . talent, again."

Hanse couldn't help it: he laughed.

Only when he awoke in the morning did he realize that he had slept at Arcala's. Furthermore, the thickness of his head and furry feeling of his tongue told him why. Lying still on the divan in Arcala's receiving room, Hanse once again vowed never to drink wine. *I like the damned stuff too much. Far better than it likes me.*

He sat up, muffling his groan, to discover Notable on the floor right beside his couch. He was stroking that cat's soft fur, thinking about last night, when Mignureal came into the room. She bore Rainbow in her arms as she might have borne an infant. Hanse gave her a sheepish smile.

"Oh don't look that way, Hanse. After all, you had a *very* active and dreadful night. And think what Arcala said: you and Notable saved Firaqa!"

"And you," he said, "*and* Shurina, *and*, I guess, Strick's amulet."

"Anyhow, Arcala and I have already breakfasted."

"Oh! You should have wakened me!"

"We didn't think so. What do you think you're going to do, Hanse?"

"About wha—oh, his suggestion, or offer. For once I'm going to welcome sorcery. Let him adjust the memories of

Gaise and his bodyguards. I believe I had rather be Firaqa's great unsung hero than the target of ten or twenty angry mages!''

She nodded. "That's exactly what Arcala and I thought. Good!"

His lower lip poked out a bit. "You and Arcala, hmm?"

"Yes."

Hanse sighed and decided he'd better not pursue that. Her serenely succinct response while looking directly into his eyes was unusual for her, unwontedly self-confident and almost challenging. He wanted no arguments today.

She squatted to lay the calico cat gently on the tabletop. The same table on which lay the two coins and the fold-over tablet, and Hanse gazed at them.

"It isn't over yet," he murmured. "What about the other two coins! Where are those men?"

"Oh, oh faint—oh my!" Mignureal was staring at Rainbow, as Hanse was.

Weakly that most unnatural of cats moved closer to the tablet. It was incredible and eerie to watch, as an extruded claw traced a shaky and misshappen S into the beeswax, and then an A, and an N; and then Shurina in Rainbow's form slumped, panting. Hanse put back a hand to the tingling hair on the back of his neck.

"Oh poor darling, you needn't try to do this," Mignureal said in a shaky voice, reaching for the cat.

"*Mignue.*"

With a little jerk, she froze to turn her head and large questioning eyes toward Hanse. She had heard that intense, warning tone before, but very, very seldom. She did not like it, but knew that she had better heed it.

He nodded to indicate the cat. "Leave her alone."

She looked back at Rainbow, who had summoned strength to go on with her message. C, she scratched, TU, and Hanse gasped, sure that he knew the rest of it. It took her another minute of rest and even more effort, but the cat completed the scratching of a single word into the tablet before she slumped again. He and Mignureal stared at it, her hand moving out automatically to his leg.

SANCTUARY

"Oh, shit."

"Oh, Hanse!"

"Same thing."

"No no," she said, sobbing; "it's Rainbow! She's stopped breathing!"

"Oh," he said, "no . . ."

Mignureal's voice was wistful, choking a little to hold back her weeping. "Remember when I ca-called her a S-S'danzo kitty . . ."

Notable moved to the table, reared up to place both front paws on it. A moment later he dropped to the floor and relieved himself of a long cry that rode the line between pitiful and horrible.

Rainbow was dead, and no matter how long Hanse watched, she did not turn into a woman, beautiful or otherwise, or anything else save a small dead S'danzo kitty.

At last he said, "Rainbow is dead. But Shurina will never know peace until all ten rapists are dead."

Her pale face was all tear-streaked as Mignureal swung to him. "What?"

He nodded. "That's what Corstic said. The monster meant it, too. He was gloating, and I believe him. The human *kas* in the cats will never know peace until all ten rapists are dead— whether the cats are alive or not."

"Oh," Mignureal sobbed, "oh, oh . . ." And she dropped head and arms onto the table, touching Rainbow, and wept.

Hanse touched her bowed head without looking at her. With stricken eyes he was staring at the tablet, and the word crudely scratched there. It was a word he had seen enough to recognize, even if Mignureal had not gasped it out just before Shurina completed the final letter.

"Sanctuary," he said. "Damn. *Sanctuary!* The coins say that two of the raping swine still live, and obviously Rainbow-I-mean-Shurina just told us where they are: in Sanctuary. I am a vengeful ass, Mignue, and I like these cats, and this is all vengeance and justice. Damn! I—I have to go back to Sanctuary, Mignue!"